THE VENTRILOQUIST'S TALE

SHAPE-SHIFTER

THE VENTRILOQUIST'S TALE

PAULINE MELVILLE

BLOOMSBURY

Published by Bloomsbury Publishing, New York and London.

A CIP catalogue record for this book
is available from the Library of Congress

ISBN 1-58234-009-9

First published in Great Britain 1997 by Bloomsbury Publishing Plc.

First U.S. Edition
10 9 8 7 6 5 4 3 2 1

Typeset by Hewer Text Ltd, Edinburgh, Scotland
Printed in the United States of America

Illustrations by Charlo Melville from traditional designs

CONTENTS

'There is a myth which is known throughout the whole of the Americas from southern Brazil to the Bering Strait via Amazonia and Guiana and which establishes a direct equivalence between eclipses and incest.'

Claude Lévi-Strauss

'There shall be no more novels about incest. No, not even ones in very bad taste.'

Julian Barnes

'Beyond the equator, everything is permitted.'

Fifteenth-century Portuguese proverb

PROLOGUE

Spite impels me to relate that my biographer, the noted Brazilian Senhor Mario Andrade, got it wrong when he consigned me to the skies in such a slapdash and cavalier manner. I suppose he thought I would lie for ever amongst the stars, gossiping – as we South American Indians usually do in our hammocks at night – and spitting over the side to make the early morning dew of star spittle. Well, excuse me while I shit from a great height. Excuse me while I laugh like a parrot . . . which reminds me. Did he tell you the whole story of the parrot or did he just leave it flapping its wings and heading for Lisbon? He didn't? I might have guessed. I'll tell you. Later.

But first, I lay claim to the position of narrator in this novel. Yes, me. Rumbustious, irrepressible, adorable me. I have black hair, bronze skin and I would look wonderful in a cream suit with a silk handkerchief. Cigars? Yes. Dark glasses? Yes – except that I do not wish to be mistaken for a gangster. But dark glasses are appropriate. My name translated means 'one who works in the dark'. You can call me Chico. It's my brother's name but so what. Where I come from it's not done to give your real name too easily. A black felt fedora hat worn tipped forward? Possibly. A fast-driving BMW when I am in London? A Porsche for New York? A Range Rover to drive or a helicopter when I am flying over the endless savannah and bush of my own region? Yes. Yes. Yes. Oh and I like to smell sweet. I like to rub myself in every orifice and crevice and nook and cranny with lotions, potions, balsams and creams.

Why am I not the hero, you ask. Because these days you all have forgotten how to make heroes. Your heroes and heroines are slaves to time. They don't excite wonder and amazement. They don't even attempt to astonish, enchant or amuse. They've forgotten how to be playful and have no appetite for adventure. Sub-zero heroes. A puny bunch, embedded in history, or worse, psychology – that wrinkle in the field of knowledge that hopefully will soon be ironed out, leaving us in our proper place between the monkey and the stars.

Believe in me. I am the one who can dig time's grave.

Besides, you choose your heroes too carelessly, without considering their antecedents. As for my ancestry, it is impeccable. I will have you know that I am descended from a group of stones in Ecuador. Where I come from people have long memories. Any one of us can recite our ancestry back for several hundred generations. I can listen to a speech for an hour and then repeat it for you verbatim or backwards without notes. Writing things down has made you forget everything.

My grandmother distrusts writing. She says all writing is fiction. Even writing that purports to be factual, that puts down the date of a man's birth and the date of his death, is some sort of fabrication. Do you think a man's life is slung between two dates like a hammock? Slung in the middle of history with no visible means of support? It takes more than one life to make a person.

PROLOGUE

Grandmother swears by the story of the stones in Ecuador although sometimes she might say Mexico or Venezuela for variety's sake – variety being so much more important than truth in her opinion. More reliable, she says. Truth changes. Variety remains constant. Of course, she will offer to tell you the truth if you give her enough honey, but she will never tell you how much honey is enough. We, in this part of the world, have a special veneration for the lie and all its consequences and ramifications. We treat the lie seriously, as a form of horticulture, to be tended and nurtured, all its little tendrils to be encouraged.

Where was I? Oh yes. My grandmother. She still refers with rage to a man called Charles Darwin who wandered through the region with the slow-motion frenzy of a sloth, measuring and collecting. No one round here likes measurers, collectors or enumerators. We cannot hoard in the tropics. Use it or some other creature will eat it. Sooner or later everything falls to the glorious spirit of rot with its fanfares of colour and nose-twisting stenches. The spirit of rot and its herald angel, smell, announce most events in my part of the world. Anyway, according to my grandmother, Charles Darwin without so much as a by-your-leave parked his behind on my ancestors and wrote the first line of *Origin of Species*, declaring that we were descended from monkeys. If his eyes had been in his arse he would have known better.

Every night before she goes to bed, Koko, as we call Grandmother, shaves a piece off the black tobacco roll hanging from the rafters and makes herself one sweet, strong, liquorice-tasting cigarette. Then she indulges in a little prophecy before conxing out in her hammock. She learned in her youth about the sacred ball-games that predict future events. That was how she got her reputation for releasing omens from bones and football matches. You know how grandmothers are. My grandmother is full of all that crap.

3

However, the wrinkles on her face follow almost exactly the contours of the rivers of the Amazonas. I used to trace them as she carried me around. That's how I got to know the geography of the region. I had to be carried. I refused to walk until I was six. I wouldn't talk either. Senhor Andrade got that right.

All I ever said was: 'Aw, what a fucking life!'

From the start I preferred coconut liqueurs to my mother's milk. My grandmother explained to my parents that my heart was outside my body, hidden in the form of a parrot somewhere in the bush. She said that I was indestructible for that reason. This depressed my parents so much that they set about producing several more siblings in the hope that they would knock the shit out of me. My mother had known there was something unusual about me because, when she was pregnant with me, I used to shout directions from the womb when she got lost.

One day, I was lying in my hammock, naked and chubby, with my sexual clobber pointing wistfully towards the palm-thatch roof, when one of the young girls came and peeked over the edge of the hammock.

'I spy a nice little pigeon sitting on two eggs,' she said and jumped in on top of me. I never stopped talking after that.

'He must have eaten parrot-bottom,' they used to say wearily, when they heard my non-stop chatter. The first sign that I was to be a narrator came when I lay in my hammock, peeing in a huge arc over the side on to my mother in the hammock below, because I was too lazy to get up, and composing a poem to my parents praising the cooking utensils I saw around me.

I never apologise. We have no word for sorry.

'Cockroach ate my conscience in the night,' I reply, whenever someone questions my behaviour. If you want to become a saint, live to please others, if you want to

4

become a god, live entirely to please yourself. That's my motto.

How did I discover that I was to play the role of narrator? Public acclaim, of course.

In my part of the world there are many lakes: navy-blue lakes, blood-red lakes, pewter-coloured lakes, black lakes. I went fishing in the lake of mud, a lake which is also a dump where people throw the remains of water coconut, fish bones, crab shells, defunct bicycles, all sorts of muck. Poking around there, I dredged up from the bottom of the muddy lake a word. Yes, you heard right, a word, heavy like a stone and covered in moss. It made a 'gluck' sound as I recovered it from the dark mud that tried to suck it back. But there was no returning. I cradled it to my chest with a mixture of fierce excitement and possessiveness. I hosed it down. Cleansed it. Scraped the moss of centuries from it.

Then I saw that on the word were carved other words, hieroglyphics, tiny rows of them, and they were in a language I could not understand. But I became aware of the noisy and voluble existence of words, an incessant chattering from the past, and as the babble grew louder, as the throng of words grew and approached along the forest trails, the savannah tracks, the lanes and by-ways and gullies, the words, some declaiming, some whispering, were joined, firstly by laughter and ribald whistles, then by rude farting sounds and finally by an unmistakable clattering that could only be the rattling dance of bones.

They came into sight. What a throng, a jostling, shoving, awesome throng of chattering, hobbling, jigging, ramshackle bones from as far back as the eye could see, along the road from the Brazilian border, streaming down the Pan-American highway. Some were scrambling into boats, clambering into skiffs, shoving their canoes off from the river bank; some strode along jabbering, their bony arms round each other. Some were remonstrating with those who lagged behind.

Child skeletons bounced rubber balls. Adults made lewd and suggestive wiggles with their pelvic bones, others began to picnic by the wayside, cooking in pots over hastily made fires. One began to drum with his own bones, taking one from his leg, twirling it in the air and setting up rhythms on an enormous upturned calabash. As the scurrying stampede approached down the trails and pathways, clickety-clacking like a stampede of whores on a pavement, as this huge and purposeful throng, so animated, so lively and so attractive, so noisy, what with the furious conversing, the screeches of laughter, the angry accusations and scurrilous suggestions, came towards me, I felt irresistibly drawn to such a joyous assembly.

And so, from where I had been peeping them through an ear-ring bush, I took a step forward, hesitating only for a second before plunging into the bobbing, undulating crowd which received me with whoops of joy and squeals of approval as they lifted me on to their skeleton shoulders, the excited babble mounting in volume until, with one massive voice that could be heard from Mahaica Creek to Quito City, the bony crew's chatter merged into one gigantic roar as they shouted: 'That's my boy.'

To which I replied, from the front of this glorious mob, punching my fist in the air, as delirious with ecstasy as if I had just scored for Brazil: 'Kiss my backside.'

That's how it was. I was there. I should know. I was chosen. That's it for the moment, folks. Gone a fish.

And how did I hone my skills as a narrator? For you to understand that, I shall have to tell you a little about the art of hunting because it was through hunting that I learned to excel as a ventriloquist.

6

In my language, hunting means making love with the animals. The hunt is a courtship, a sexual act. It is all a matter of disguise and smell. Make yourself attractive to your prey. Paint yourself in the colours that arouse them. We know which scents attract which creature. We know which fish like to be tickled where. We know that what flies does not like to be stroked. We know how to remove our own scent so that an animal will not get wind of us. We rub ourselves with whatever scents will allure the prey. We present ourselves as a sexual partner. It is always necessary to study which animal will risk his hide for what. You have to understand the desires of your prey. The jaguar, for instance, has a fierce appetite for hot and bitter peppers, sour, salty food and puppies.

We flirt with our prey like any serial killer. And here is where my sublime talent as a ventriloquist comes in. I can reproduce perfectly the mating call of every bird and beast in the Amazonas. Sometimes I do it unaided, sometimes with the help of certain leaves or grasses curled around my fingers. It seems magical, but then magic is always related to desire. The whole purpose of magic is the fulfilment and intensification of desire. Magic is private. It deals in secrecy and disguise. Religion, by comparison, is peanuts. A social affair. The world was ordered magically before it was ordered socially. Ah, secrecy, camouflage and treachery. What blessings to us all. Where I come from, disguise is the only truth and desire the only true measure of time.

Camouflage is the other required skill. I can efface myself easily like a chameleon – merge into the background. I scrunch up bitter-cassava leaves and rub them under my arms as a deodorant in case my smell gives me away. If you were to see me fishing, in the dim green light of the forest, you would never be able to tell my legs from the twisted tree branches at the side of the creek.

My gifts as a ventriloquist were spotted as soon as I began

to speak. I could reproduce the flickering hiss of the labaria snake and sing the Lilliburlero signature tune of the BBC's World Service within seconds of hearing them. Sometimes my grandmother used me as an early form of tape-recorder.

Once, I remember, she particularly wanted to hear a programme about the cosmic noise picked up by radio telescopes – that faint echo of the Big Bang that has spread through the universe over the aeons. We have always been crazy about astronomy. When she returned from fishing, she came to where I lay in my hammock and I repeated the whole programme about Einstein and Hawking, in the voice of Alvar Liddell, a famed BBC announcer.

'Which came first,' I wondered out loud, 'the equation or the story?'

'The story, of course,' she snapped, as she listened carefully to my perfect mimicking of those faint hissing sounds of the universe from the beginning of time, recorded by radio telescopes.

'What people are hearing,' she said, 'is the final wheeze of an enormous laugh.'

The programme continued to explain how the universe expands outwards over millions of years towards infinity and then contracts back over millions of years into a singularity.

'A very slow orgasm,' she said thoughtfully.

To cut an endless story short, I have a genius for ventriloquism. Any diva in the Scala Opera House, Milan would kill for my vocal range. I can do any voice: jaguar, London hoodlum, bell-bird, nineteenth-century novelist, ant-eater, epic poet, a chorus of howler monkeys, urban brutalist, a tapir. The list is infinite.

But out of the blue, things turned bad between Koko and myself. She flew into a rage when she heard I was going to write the stories down. She is a stickler for tradition. All novelty or innovation is a sign of death to her and history only to be trusted when it coincides with myth. She believes we Indians should keep ourselves to ourselves, retreating from the modern world like the contracting stars. We fought. She rubbed pepper in my eyes. I knocked her out – temporarily – with a war club.

So why am I telling this story, out of so many?

All stories are told for revenge or tribute. Take your pick.

Sad though it is, in order to tell these tales of love and disaster, I must put away everything fantastical that my nature and the South American continent prescribe and become a realist. No more men with members the size of zeppelins and women flapping off into the skies – a frequent occurrence on the other side of the continent. Why realism, you ask. Because hard-nosed, tough-minded realism is what is required these days. Facts are King. Fancy is in the dog-house. Perhaps it has something to do with protestants or puritans and the tedious desire to bear witness that makes people prefer testimony these days. Now, alas, fiction has to disguise itself as fact and I must bow to the trend and become a realist.

Ah well, as they say, monkey cut 'e tail to be in fashion.

I invite you to my homeland, the parched savannahs that belong to the Indians on either side of the Kanaku Mountains north of the Amazon, the plains where, it is said, people have so little that a poor man's dog has to lean against the wall and brace itself in order to muster the strength to bark.

That's all for now, folks. The narrator must appear to vanish. I gone.

PART ONE

THE BANANA-FISH BOY

The boy who brought the banana fish brought the news. The gate had long fallen down and he stood where the two gate-posts framed the empty red savannah. A hot wind blew. Stuffed in the bottom of his pocket was a catastrophe in the form of a note. The boy did not know or care much what it said. The fish was his overriding concern. He wiped the dust from it and waited. The sun scorched down. Heat bounced off the red earth. For a long time he stood with the great fish in his arms, frightened to come nearer because of the dogs. The place seemed deserted.

Eventually, an old lady with silver hair down to her shoulders came to the open door. She pushed her way past a tangle of derelict bicycles and an old rocking chair and shaded her eyes in order to see who was there. The boy knew the woman slightly. No one around those parts could guess how old Auntie Wifreda was.

When anyone asked her, she just shrugged amiably and said: 'I don't know. If I was a horse, they'd shoot me.'

She disappeared back inside and a stocky, well-proportioned, black-haired man with pale skin came out, cleaning a hunting knife on the side of his jeans. Chofy McKinnon brought the dogs under control and then beckoned the boy into the house and walked off in the direction of the creek.

He had just quarrelled with his wife and wanted to stay out of the house until he regained control of himself.

The argument, originally about their son's future, spiralled inevitably into the row about whether they should move nearer to Marietta's parents. Her parents looked after their few cattle on the south side of the Kanaku Mountains. She had always resented the fact that when they married he had not moved with her to be near her parents, as was the custom amongst savannah Indians. Instead, she had moved in with him and his Auntie Wifreda. It still felt wrong-sided to her. Besides, the north savannahs were Macusi territory. They were Wapisiana from the south. That made her uneasy too.

Marietta insisted that her parents were too old and tired to tend cattle any longer. He did not like her mother and refused to move nearer them in order to help. The fight had ended with her flustered and him in one of his cold furies.

Chofy stood by the creek. He disliked confrontation. In arguments, he became icily polite and blank. Given the choice, he preferred to melt into the background whenever there was contention.

Since he'd reached forty, he had understood that this was his life. It was not going to change or improve. Mostly, he accepted it. He belonged in the savannahs. His existence was tied into the landscape and the seasons, rainy or dry. Like many others, he resented the increasing number of alien coastlanders and Brazilians who were invading the region to settle there. But recently he had felt a small worm of dissatisfaction with his own life. It gnawed away just under his rib-cage. It made him want to get away. Usually, when he had that sort of feeling, he took off into the bush for a while. But this time the restlessness made him feel like striking out for somewhere new, even though it was accompanied by a warning reminder, somewhere at the bottom of his stomach, that any change was the beginning of disintegration.

However, the ceaseless effort required to scratch a living from the place exhausted him.

He slashed half-heartedly at a snake-whip bush with his knife and then was forced to walk further downstream because he had accidentally disturbed a nest of marabunta hornets on the trunk of a neighbouring tree. He ducked through the tangle of foliage at the creek's edge to avoid the few hornets that buzzed angrily after him and grinned wryly to himself in acknowledgement of the fact that, in this place, even the smallest moves were made only as a response to disaster. Bad luck – usually wished on you by some enemy – was the most common trigger for change.

Somewhere further upstream, a waam beetle whirr-whirred with increasing intensity and volume, sounding like a minia-ture chain-saw. That meant the rains were coming. He looked to see if the level of the creek was rising. The rains would begin with drizzle and showers, winds and isolated storms. Then the frogs would start to sing and rising headwaters fill the tributaries and streams. At the height of the rainy season, the creek could rise thirty feet in a night.

Inside the house was dark and cool. The boy came right into the part that was used as a kitchen. Marietta was splashing water from the rinsing bucket over the plastic plates, her face still flushed from the argument. The only light came from the wide opening in the wall which looked on to the land at the back. The boy laid the fish down on the table.

As Marietta washed the wares, she scraped any leftovers out of this opening in the wall and the fowls flapped and screeched and rushed to get them. Outside, the light dazzled and struck at the metal post which supported the washing-line. Marietta turned round, wiping her hands on her skirt, and came over to examine the great creature that the boy had laid on the table. Its flesh gleamed yellow with black stripey markings and it had an orange tail.

'Do you want to drink water?' She spoke to the boy in Wapisiana. He nodded and went to the big earthenware jar, lifted the dipper and gulped down some cool water. As he glanced to one side he saw the figure of Auntie Wifreda in another room, lying sideways in her hammock, her silver hair spread over one shoulder. Three jaguar skulls rested on a beam over her head, alongside other knick-knacks and a hanging sifter decorated with feathers. She was surrounded by dust-layered shelves crammed with cartons, old tins, tissue boxes, jars, one or two old Marmite bottles and general, useful junk.

He peeked around. Behind Auntie Wifreda, the back door was open. Clothes were mostly washed in the creek but sometimes they were scrubbed outside and chickweed had run wild in places where the water had spilled. Auntie Wifreda's garden consisted of two rusted kerosene drums with a plank balanced on them. The plants grew in a row of old tins, bowls and chipped ceramic pots. There were plants to clean out the stomach, plants to stop girls getting pregnant, plants to keep angry people away from the house, plants to make a man hard, plants to make a man soft.

Through a door to the left, he could see three empty hammocks, their nets twined round them, and a single bed with no mattress, only its springs showing. Rolls of stiffened deer- and cow-hides leaned against the wall giving the place its musty, animal smell.

There were no ceilings. The inside walls were plank-wood and reached halfway to the roof leaving the whole top of the house open. Beams and poles of bloodwood and silverballi reached all the way up to the eaves of the dry and dusty palm thatch.

Behind every door was a set of bow and arrows to repel invaders. By the front door stood Chofy McKinnon's shotgun, next to the cylindrical palm container which held his hunting knives. Nibi hats hung on nails on the wall and some old photos, curling at the edges, were stuck up there.

From somewhere outside in a mango tree, one of the family's pet parrots was calling plaintively in Portuguese: 'Louro. Louro.'

While the boy drank, Marietta inspected the fish. It weighed about twelve pounds – too big to have been caught in a creek. It must have been caught in the Rupununi or the Takatu. The fish was still firm and fresh even though the boy had walked for miles with it. Marietta measured off a portion, nearly a third, including the head, and cut it off. She collected up several bags of sorrel and gave it to him in exchange for the fish.

The boy went outside to rest under the guava tree where some half-eaten fruit lay on the ground. He looked up. Parakeets clustered in the branches overhead. Out of habit, he picked up a stone and threw it into the tree to keep the birds off the fruit.

Inside the house, Marietta put the portions of fish in a bucket of water with a cloth over it to keep off the flies and returned to throwing lukewarm water over the plates with a wooden dipper.

Marietta was a vibrant, vigorous woman who never stopped working. Two buckets of water stood in front of her, one for washing and one for rinsing. As she busied herself with the dishes, her stocky, robust figure bent from one to the other. Two of her bottom front teeth were missing which never prevented her from smiling. Her complexion was a dark ruddy brown. She wore her black hair in a loose plait. Quite often she sang around the house, but now she was hardly aware of what she was doing. She was upset by the argument. They had been rowing like this for months.

Even before this last quarrel, Chofy had been going through a patch of moodiness that worried her. She did not know what to do about it. For a while he had stopped shaving. He stared out of the window for hours. He fingered his chin and smiled to himself. Once, he hurriedly shut a drawer when she came into the room, as if he were hiding something from her. She had gone and looked in the drawer later when he was scraping hides down by the creek. What she found puzzled her. It was a clipping from an old *Time* magazine that someone must have lent him. The photo showed millionaire Claus von Bülow and his wife attending a movie première in New York. Mrs von Bülow wore a low-cut, clinging, shimmering, white evening dress. Marietta slipped the old clipping back in the drawer.

After dark, by the light of the kerosene lamp, Chofy occupied himself by carving, obsessively and meticulously, the precise pattern of a turtle-shell on to the flat stones he had picked up from the savannahs. Or he would whittle perfect orbs from wood, in the way his father had taught him. One night he went hunting and shot two deer. He was happier then, for a couple of days.

Despite the customary distrust of in-laws, Marietta finally came round to consulting Auntie Wifreda about the problem. In the mornings, after she had bathed in the creek, she would stand in Auntie Wifreda's room, hair still wet, towel wrapped round her sturdy body, and recount her dreams.

'I dreamed there was this brash, new, white Land Rover with bright lights on top. It was coming this way. At the side of the road there were little stalls, snackettes. A lady with a baby came up to me and said her husband wanted to talk with me. I get frighten. I get the feeling that the men in the Land Rover want to steal me away. I said: "I don't want to go. I married to Chofy." And then a plane arrive on the airstrip with a dead person in it.'

Auntie Wifreda noticed that many of these dreams had someone dead or sick in them.

'There were some steps near the river and I was selling something next to them. Chofy was nearby. I saw him sit down and then suddenly lie flat on the ground. "I will get a pillow," I said and ran home. There were some white people picking ripe yellow mangoes alongside some negroes and East Indians.'

And then another time.

'There were more steps, steep and narrow. I climbed them and halfway up I became frighten because I saw him drunk at the top. I went to fetch water. He disappeared. Then I saw him lying by a small fence. A woman stood by and I said: "I will chop you like a tree," and the woman turned into wood and I chopped her into tiny pieces.'

Auntie Wifreda frowned and hoped that Chofy was not going to turn out like her brother Danny and succumb to bouts of bush fever. Rupununi fever, they called it.

When Chofy's Uncle Danny was alive, he was notorious for being an isolate, despite his various marriages and children. There would be times when Danny drank heavily before disappearing to live in the bush on his own for long periods of time. The most vivid memory she had of Danny was of him on his death-bed, his bronze face and black eyes impassive as he deliberately lied to the priest with his last words and his last breath. The shock of it remained with her. Auntie Wifreda could see his face in front of her when she came to with a start and realised that Marietta was still speaking.

'I will just have to wait till Chofy catch himself back,' said Marietta, her face full of frank misery.

Meanwhile, Marietta moved out of their bedroom and

slung her hammock in the other room that was dusty and smelled of old deer-hides. They had not slept together for months.

A movement behind the monkey-cup tree on the other side of the creek caught Chofy's eye.

'Why you aren't at school?' shouted Chofy.

Eight-year-old Bla-Bla emerged reluctantly from behind the bush holding his arrows and bow. His short black hair stood up like iron filings under a magnet. His face was stricken with horror and his mouth already filling with lies to tell his father.

'School finish. No teacher,' said Bla-Bla, running sure-footed towards his father, balancing easily along the tacouba that bridged the creek.

'Come here, Manicole-Leaf Head.' Chofy grabbed him and tried to quell an unruly spike of hair. Bla-Bla twisted away.

'Get the barrow and fetch firewood,' yelled Chofy after his son who was skirting the house and running towards the barracong. 'I am going to check on that school, you know. This keeps happening.'

Bla-Bla, red in the face from manhandling the barrow over the rough ground, finished collecting firewood and dumped the load by the outside stove. He whistled to the banana-fish boy and in single file they walked to the creek and scrambled down the steep red scree to stand by the water. They decided to look for awara nuts to make tops.

On each bank, tall grey stems of moco-moco plants, with green, heart-shaped leaves, formed a sort of wattle fence. The trail led down to the clearing at the edge of the creek where people bathed and washed clothes. The creek was murky, too murky to see fish. The water had muddied where someone had been earlier and thrown in a heap of rotten cassava that stunk out the place.

'A little girl did drown here,' said Bla-Bla, pointing out the spot with a stick.

'Was it a numb-fish got her?'

'No. She did get caught in tree roots. They carry her up to the house and put her on the shelf in Koko Wifreda's room.'

The other boy imagined the body of the little girl on the dusty shelf with the Marmite jars and decided not to go back in that room.

They collected two suitable nuts from a nearby awara tree, scooped out the centre with a knife and sat by the creek to whittle them. Bla-Bla whittled his in the shape of a fish and the other boy chose the shape of a leaf. They worked in comradely silence, heads bent, making four openings in each top so that it would make that strange humming noise with a dying fall. Then they went back to the house and tied a piece of cloth over one of Marietta's huge pots, leaving a dip in the middle to prevent the tops spinning out. They carried the pot outside and set about competing ferociously to knock each other's top out of the ring.

When the banana-fish boy thought it was time to leave, he went to pick up his sorrel and tell Marietta he was going, averting his eyes from Auntie Wifreda's room in case he saw any sign of the dead girl. Just before he left, he delved into the pocket of his torn pants and handed over the note that he had brought from Marietta's parents.

Marietta frowned as she tried to decipher the barely legible scrawl on the letter. It was from her father. It said that the cattle had been attacked by a plague of vampire bats.

That same night, Marietta heard the squeak of a bullock cart and a faint 'He-hey' from outside.

She lit a speak-easy lamp. Her father stood in front of them, his eyes troubled, his black hair shining in the lamplight and his face creased with worry. He had travelled thirty miles. There was nothing they could do. The cattle had been bitten all over. The evening sky had suddenly turned dark as the horde of bats wheeled out of the Kanaku Mountains. The creatures attached themselves like small, black, inside-out umbrellas on to the cattle. Nine calves were killed, drained of blood. He and some other men had stayed awake for two nights, trying to fight off the bats and stop them attacking more cattle and horses. Many of the surviving cows were now showing signs of rabies. Two days after the bats had come, a whole set of owls had arrived and feasted on the bats.

Marietta provided her father with a glass of lemonade and a piece of cassava bread. He would leave and go back at first light. She managed to resist saying 'What did I tell you?' to Chofy, for several hours. And then, just before she went to bed, she said it.

For the rest of the night, even after the light had gone out, Chofy sat at the kitchen table, his head in his hands and his mind in turmoil. Although they had a small cassava garden three miles away, and he was good at both hunting and fishing, they relied on the cattle when they needed cash. When he was a young boy growing up, money had rarely been used. Everything was done by exchange of gifts. But these days cash was increasingly necessary.

The next morning he rode back to Potarinau with his father-in-law to inspect the damage. Together, they manoeuvred the bullock cart over the Sawariwau crossing. As they approached the corral from the top of the hill, Chofy's heart sank. It was a disaster. He could see from there that the corral was half empty under the blue sky. They had owned thirty head of cattle. Only a handful of the white cows was left, some staggering, stiff-legged, and more than one foaming at the mouth. A horse swayed on the road ahead of them. Already weak, its barrel-chested ribs showing like basket-work, the creature dropped on to its knees. Vultures wheeled overhead. Chofy felt sick at the sight.

He walked silently behind his father-in-law to the house. Chofy ducked into the entrance. The tiny room opened out into another, equally small. Chofy stepped over the wooden bar in the doorway that separated the two rooms. The bar was to keep out floods during the rainy season. There were no objects in the house except an empty table and a bench. Everything inside was ash-grey from woodsmoke. The only colour in the small dwelling came from the richly gleaming brown and black feathers of a powis bird hanging from a nail on a housepost. The interior smelled of woodsmoke. Marietta's mother sat at the table.

'We're waiting for someone to come with DDT and spray. They told us a man would come.' She gestured around the house to explain why their few possessions were stacked outside. 'There was nothing we could do about the cattle.' Chofy sensed an element of smugness in the apologetic tone.

He felt, bitterly as usual, that Marietta's elderly mother took some obscure pleasure in his failure.

The morning after he returned, Marietta and Chofy sat at the table and discussed the situation, their most recent quarrel lost in the wake of events. Chofy lapsed into silent thought as he spooned down the lumpy cassava porridge and weighed up various courses of action. Auntie Wifreda pottered about looking for a line and hook to go fishing.

'Tamukang playing his flute,' said Auntie Wifreda, at the sound of the wind.

'Who's Tamukang?' enquired Bla-Bla as he scrabbled for his school notebook.

'He plays for Brazil,' Marietta joked. 'No. No. Not really. He's the Master of Fish. He's in the stars. I'll show you one night.'

It was April and the house was wrapped in wind. The winds had loosened and shaken themselves out, moaning over the plains. Now they blustered around the savannah with easy strength, testing the resistance of the houses with small, teasing sallies. Because of the openness of the structure, the breeze blew inside the house as well as outside. The wind rummaged playfully in and out of the rooms. It fanned Chofy's cheeks and parted his hair with impudent familiarity.

The gusting air unsettled him, as if they might all float away on it. He cursed as it lifted one of the pieces of cassava bread from the table. The airy draughts felt to him like the undoing of everything, the unfastening of ties, a harbinger of chaos. Marietta snatched at the wafer of bread.

Chofy looked dour and spoke firmly, as if by sounding decisive, he might be capable of anchoring the family to the earth.

'I'll go to Georgetown and try to dig up a job somewhere. Mining maybe. Or logging. Perhaps I'll have to find something in Georgetown itself. I'll send money back and we'll build up the herd again. Can you manage the farm?'

They lived on the outskirts of Moco-moco village, some distance from any other houses. Moco-moco was one of the last villages before the foothills on the northern side of the Kanaku Mountains. Many of the houses were scattered up to several hours' walk from one another. There were no immediate neighbours to help. Their cassava farm or garden was planted on a bush-island three miles' walk away beside the river.

Despite his recent feelings of dissatisfaction, now that he was being forced to leave, Chofy felt unhappy. The idea of town filled him with dread. The wind in the house seemed to be an airy omen of disarray. It seemed to be laughing at him, even playing with him. As he spoke, his words sounded hollow, no defence against winds that could scatter human plans in any direction.

He pushed his plate away abruptly and went to collect up his hunting knives. Through the window he caught sight of five small figures, headed by Bla-Bla, running pell-mell across the savannah towards a clump of mango trees in the opposite direction from the school.

'There goes the Mango Truancy Squad,' he said grimly.

The tension in his shoulders signalled to Marietta that he was subsiding into one of his sulks.

'You must beat him,' she said. 'When I was young, if we were lazy, they used to slap mucru squares on our back, especially woven so that the head of the ant came out one end and the sting the other. They'd slap the stinging end on us and hold it there. Or put pepper in our eyes. He'd soon learn.'

Chofy ignored her and stalked outside. Grudgingly, he unpinned one of the deer-hides that was drying on the side of the house, as if he resented paying it attention. Then he went the two hundred yards down to the creek where he had left the other hides to soak. Two men who had come to help sat on the bank waiting for him. One deerskin was already softened, treated with white lime to remove some of the hair. The hides that had been scraped clean were in the barracong, soaking in a tub of water with mari-mari bark until they turned brown.

He flung the softened deerskin over the trunk of a tree in the water and handed the other men a knife each. Then they waded in to scrape the rest of the hair off with the hunting knives.

By the afternoon, the combination of standing up to his waist in water, the heat, the smell of the hide, the other men's jokes and the arm-breaking physical work had made him temporarily forget his uneasiness about the future.

The men were still down at the creek when Marietta noticed that the air inside the house suddenly smelt damp. Then everything went dark. As the storm broke overhead, she ran about the house collecting pails, pans, buckets, calabashes, gourds, anything that could be placed on the earth floor at the points where the rains came through the thatch. The first bolt of lightning struck an old defunct electricity post near the house, relic of some long-forgotten scheme to bring electricity to the area. It brought down the wires in a smoking tangle.

Auntie Wifreda, clutching a cloth to her head, pushed her way through the pelting rain towards her row of plants at the back of the house. Bla-Bla was running home from the direction of the school. Lightning skittered down to the ground just in front of him.

'Lightning juk me in the foot. I saw blood,' gasped Bla-Bla to Marietta who was flying past him to get in the washing from the line. He tried to examine his foot, water pouring from his head on to his shoulders.

'You must cover you head,' shouted Auntie Wifreda who was waddling over to rescue her plants from the onslaught of the rain. 'Lightning don' like we hair. There's too much iron about the place. Lightning gettin' vex. 'E don' like wires and all this.' She snatched up two pots that contained seedlings and took them inside.

Under the dishwater sky, Chofy and the other men struggled to carry the sodden skins up from the creek. They dumped them outside and came in the house. Chofy immediately, without a word, went out again and climbed up on to the roof to make sure the falling electricity post had not damaged the thatch.

In the distance he saw lightning zigzagging along the

Kanaku Mountains from the peak of Darukaban to the peak of Shiriri.

Marietta took the fish out of the pan, put a cloth over her head and went to clear leaves from the trench round the house. Brown water gurgled and gushed past the back door.

'Bla-Bla. Tomorrow you must help clear the trench and dig another one round the barracong,' she said as she came back inside, drenched, holding her soaking dress away from her breasts.

She called to Chofy: 'Chofy. Come, let us drink tea.'

Chofy came in, wiping his head and his hands on a rag. The four of them sat with the other two workers at the table. Thunder crashed outside. Spindles of rain twisted through the holes in the thatch and spattered on the floor.

'This is not a roof,' said Marietta ruefully, looking up at the thatch. 'This is a strainer we livin' under.'

The fact that the rainy season was beginning hastened the decision. It was agreed that Chofy should stay for the planting which had to be done before the rains set in properly. Then he would leave for Georgetown straight away in case flooding made the journey impossible.

He would take Auntie Wifreda with him for the long-overdue cataract operation on her eyes. Although he grumbled about taking her, secretly he was grateful to have company. Every time he thought of leaving, he experienced a sinking feeling in the pit of his stomach. The priest at Lethem had told them there was a Catholic home for the elderly where she could stay for nothing while she attended the hospital. He would have to find lodgings for himself.

The night before he left, Marietta had just gone to lie in her hammock when she heard his voice calling from the other room.

'Where is my darling?'

'I am here, Chofy, and I love you,' she called back in the night. Then she made her way, rather shyly, through the palpable darkness to join him on the bed which consisted of an old mattress resting on some boxes and crates, and they made love for the first time for months, feeling rusty and out of practice, a little embarrassed and happy.

A CITY BUILT OF SPACE

The city of Georgetown darkened Chofy's spirits like a black crow overhead. The room that he rented in the district of Albouystown was cramped and cheap. His new East Indian landlord, Rohit Persaud, however, appeared anxious to please.

'Tell me whatever is missing here that you might need,' he said, waving a triumphant hand around the dilapidated room, 'and I will tell you how to do without it.'

On his third Saturday, Chofy was woken by the bar of blazing sunlight that fell across his eyes from the window and by the sound of bitter fighting from the next room.

Every morning was the same. The house got off to a noisy start with the sound of Rohit Persaud arguing with his wife. Rohit's wife would not sleep with him because she suspected him of having an affair. Rohit's almighty battle to get some sex was heard by everybody. Walls were thin. The whole house knew about it.

'What happen, Mistress Arctic-Front? Legs closed? You shut up shop or what?'

'If I find you bin seein' that dog-bone, I goin' take your balls and push them down your throat.'

'What dog-bone?'

'You know who I mean. Grater-face. Broomstick-leg. Dhal and rice. That Guava Jelly Queen of Sixth Street you so keen on.'

'An' if you ain' game, what I supposed to do? Hold my prick between my legs and bite my tongue?'

Then came the sound of the wife levering herself out of bed and moving around on the other side of the wall, smacking pots and pans down on the stove. After a while the smell of dhal being heated wafted over the partition.

They make so much noise, these people, thought Chofy as he fetched water and bathed. He dressed neatly in cotton trousers, a well-ironed blue shirt and the brown boots he always wore in the bush. He still found looking in a mirror to comb his hair an odd experience. The mirror reflected back with vicious clarity a stranger – some other man with black hair, similar to his, that came to a widow's peak at the front, giving a heart-shaped appearance to his round face. His eyes stared back at him reminding him of an otter.

He hung a towel over the mirror.

On his way out, Chofy bumped into Rohit coming up the stairs with a bucket of water from the stand-pipe, his face swimming in sweat and his chest gleaming a bilious yellow under his vest.

'Me na know is warung wid dat woman,' he said, shaking his head in exasperation. 'She swell up and vex about de least little ting. Can't take de rockings.'

Mrs Persaud stared at her husband from the open window with disdain, her head settled back on her fat neck like a pigeon on its nest.

'Look at you, greaseball,' she sneered. 'No wonder people does call you the Sardine of Surinam.' She pursed her lips in disgust.

'You could do with some greasing yourself, Madam Dry-dock.'

A half-eaten portion of dhal flew out of the window just missing Rohit's head.

Relieved to escape from the house, Chofy headed for Stabroek market to make a connection with a Macusi man whose wife had a stall there on Saturdays and who was travelling by truck to the Rupununi. He had agreed to carry money home for Marietta. Chofy's new job did not require him to be there until ten o'clock on a Saturday and he finished at twelve. After that, he would visit Auntie Wifreda and check to see how she was settling in at the St Francis of Assisi home.

He let himself through the broken gate on to the street, emerging into the raucous noise and the ramshackle, grey, sun-bleached, wooden slums of the neighbourhood. He picked his way over stinking trenches, piles of trash and junked tyres, holding his breath as much as possible against a variety of stomach-churning smells. The tingalinga tingalinga sound of a steel band fought to gain ascendancy over the tireless thump of reggae, tata toom, tata toom, bombarding his ears as people pushed past him and shouted to each other across the street. He longed for the peace of the Rupununi savannahs.

A sharp-faced boy, black as ebony, played with his friends on the twisted metal frame of a derelict car. As Chofy passed, he yelled out, 'Hey, buck man,' after him and then, 'Look at de moon-face buck man.' One of the others threw a chewed mango seed at him. 'Get back to the bush, buck man.' Chofy ignored them, seething inwardly. He put on a blank expression and continued walking.

With the help of a letter from the priest in the Rupununi, Chofy had found himself a temporary job in the main library, shifting and re-stacking books while the library was being refurbished. For the first few days he suffered from continuous headaches.

It was the first time he had ever been employed by anyone else. Working indoors made him feel imprisoned and breathless. He deliberately put on what he called his 'buck-man face', polite but expressionless, revealing nothing of what he really felt, even though he suspected that it made people think he was stupid. As each day passed, he felt diminished, like a deflating balloon with the air slowly fizzling out.

Working to a rigid time-table irked him but the most difficult adaptation of all was to the idea of leisure, of work being one thing and leisure another. In the Rupununi, he never made the distinction. There was always some task to be done and usually someone to do it alongside. You stopped to eat, or you zopped in your hammock. Otherwise, there were always fishing nets to be made, arrow-heads to be whittled, guns cleaned, planting or weeding to be done, roofs to be mended, skins to be scraped. Work was continuous and varied.

Confining work to certain hours and then having nothing to do appalled him. For the first week, when he had finished at the library, he would go home, get into bed, although it was not yet dark, and turn his face to the plank wall, pulling the sheet over his head to keep out the daylight. Sometimes he hugged his pillow, to avoid confronting the endless acres of waste-time.

As Chofy walked with light, rather hesitant step over the rough concourse towards Stabroek market, he was aware of numerous pairs of eyes watching him. He made his way tentatively inside the vast iron structure of the old Dutch slave market and through the maze of stalls, looking for the man who would deliver the money to Marietta.

At first, the cavernous gloom of the huge market over-whelmed him. It seemed to him to be a market of lethargy. There were few people shopping that early. A tubby man sprawled on the counter asleep next to the beef he was selling. A slow-moving woman sold rolls of cloth by candlelight. Another thin-faced woman with liquid, treacherous eyes lounged next to a stall which displayed some shallots, bunches of fine-leaf thyme and a few bottles of Cutex nail varnish.

Chofy found the Macusi man he was looking for sitting by his wife's stall and he handed over the money for Marietta. The man had been about to accompany Chofy outside, when his wife developed a violent headache and he decided to stay with her. Chofy said his goodbyes and began to look for a way out of the labyrinth.

He came to a crossroads of passages. Suddenly, there seemed to be a whirlwind of draughts, a tornado of breeze. His knees began to give and he found himself leaning slowly backwards. Then it felt as if little flies were settling all over him. Little hands. His body moved as if it were being manipulated. He felt the pickpockets' light touch like flies on a carcass. Realising what was happening, he pivoted slightly on his heel and took a low swing, punching out behind him. His fist scrunched into a face at the height of his hip. Figures pressed in on him, Chofy skipped sideways and ran through the alleyways towards the light.

Outside, he half ran and half walked away from the place, looking at people with suspicion, his heart pounding. In his agitation, the notion struck him that everyone around him was controlled by the Master of Pickpockets. The Master of Pickpockets must have organised the whole thing: the woman's sudden headache, the confluence of winds, the pickpockets themselves.

He shook his head and tried to regain control of himself.

33

His hand felt to see that his few dollars were still in his pocket. At least he had delivered Marietta's money safely before they pounced. The blow he had landed on someone's face worried him. He dreaded becoming involved with the police or the courts in any way. He hurried blindly through the streets, instinctively walking close to the wall or fence like a cat, protected at least on one side.

Within ten minutes, he was lost.

Eventually, he slowed down somewhere near Camp Street and Brickdam. The broad, spacious street was nearly empty. Few people had ventured out into the morning's hazy heat. Making sure he had not been followed, Chofy walked along Brickdam, uncertain of his direction, looking at the great, detached, white, wooden colonial mansions, like huge birds with folded wings that had come to rest some way back from the street.

He slowed to a halt outside one house that had 'Mynheer Nicklaus' written in wrought-iron lettering on the gates and sat down on the short stone post that supported the gate, gradually recovering his composure. As his breathing slowed down, he became more aware of his surroundings.

There is a strange emptiness in some cities.

Chofy had not visited Georgetown often. From his first visit as a young boy, the city had made him uneasy. It was not just the geometrical grid of the Georgetown streets, the parallels, squares and rectangles which disorientated him after the meandering Indian trails of his own region, but as he walked over the dry brown clumps of grass along the verges, he experienced the unaccountable sense of loss that hung in the spaces between buildings renowned for their symmetry and Dutch orderliness.

From early on in its history, there had been something pale about the city of Stabroek, as Georgetown was known in the eighteenth century. It was as if the architects and builders had attempted to subdue that part of the coast with a geometry to which it was not suited and which hid something else. The labours of men had thrown up a city made of Euclidean shapes, obtuse-angled red roofs, square-framed houses on evenly spaced stilts, delicately angled Demerara shutters, all constructed around transparency, emptiness and light.

From the start, the city's population was not great enough to cause bustle. Even the width of the streets produced melancholy amongst the European colonists, used to the narrow cobbled alleys and uproarious slums of their own capital cities.

Water Street, in those early days, was one of the few areas where the movement and stir of business was perceptible. Merchants' shops, retail premises, watch-makers, cigar-makers, saddlers and apothecaries buzzed with activity. The Africans, clad mainly in blue trousers and coarse shirts, retained some spirit of gaiety, despite their circumstances. The white men, lounging under their umbrellas, dressed in nankeen pantaloons and fine calico shirts, were the ones who succumbed frequently to mental instability through languor and apathy.

Other parts of Stabroek were more silent. Heat made people walk slowly as if they walked through water. The streets were wide and divided along their length by canals. A European woman out for a stroll in those early days would wave to an acquaintance across the width of the street rather than cross to greet her in the heat of the day. This lethargy yielded up into isolation. The space surrounding each person was too great. It fostered a particular kind of madness amongst those early colonists, a loss of grip on reality. Visitors or outsiders mistook this lethargy for serenity, rather than the incipient madness it foretold.

Many of the colonists were gripped by a fear of the existence

35

of something they could not see. Slave conspiracies. Illnesses that could kill within hours. What they also failed to perceive was that the continent was tilting and sinking towards the sea in a manner which even the Dutch, with their gift for managing water and planting grasses to prevent the erosion of river banks, did not suspect. There was a whole plane that they failed to take into account, a dimension which they did not fully understand. The non-Euclidean waters which in some rivers ran backwards were as incomprehensible to them as the fish discovered in the south of the country which, apparently, walked on land.

The region would not submit easily to measurement. The intentions of those who designed the canals and kokers – which looked like guillotines – and who attempted to measure the tidal gradation of rivers were insidiously confounded and the capital city seemed to have been stretched out beyond its ideal size to keep at bay the citizens' terror of the land mass at its back. And so it smiled out to sea, believing that its future lay beyond the horizon, and ignored the lands behind it and the peoples who lived there.

One planter, Mynheer Nicklaus, who, in harmony with the streets of the city, possessed blue eyes set so wide apart that it seemed possible that the fields of his vision did not overlap – that there was a gap in the middle where he saw nothing, yet where something existed – tried to fasten his lids back at night in order not to sleep because he was so frightened of this 'something'.

At night, in his enormous house, built from the profits of the slave trade, he had glass cones placed over the spermaceti candles so that they would not flicker in the breeze as he lay staring up through his mosquito net, struggling to focus on whatever he might be missing at the centre of his vision.

He developed the habit of moving his head from side to side like a scanner. But still, the feeling that he never managed to see everything that was there drove him into a frenzy. When he was sure he could see everything at the centre, he became convinced that there was something on the outer edges of his range of vision that remained just beyond his sight.

Hearing how the savannah Indians believed that everyday life was just an illusion behind which could be divined another reality, he ordered that one should be captured and brought to his house in order to prise from him the secrets of his philosophy. A Wapisiana Indian was seized and carried to Mynheer Nicklaus's plantation house.

The captured Wapisiana man became so distressed that he stood on a stool, neither eating, nor drinking, nor speaking, until it became clear that he would die and the Dutchman was forced to release him without discovering what he wanted to know. The man then returned to the Rupununi with stories of the amazing round wooden doorknobs he had seen and the perfectly spherical wooden orbs that could be found at the bottom of banisters.

When the Dutchman, an expert in accountancy, lay dying, he tried never to blink because he was fearful of whatever might reveal itself when his lids were closed for a fraction of a second. In his last fever, he sustained such an enormous erection that his devout wife was obliged to avert her eyes from the death-bed and, when he did finally die, no one was able to shut his eyes at all. His wife returned to Holland, swearing that the Europeans could not ever see what was really going on in the place.

Feeling calmer, Chofy stood up and decided to find his bearings from the most familiar landmark of all in Georgetown, the great Anglican Cathedral of St George. The library where he worked was virtually next door to it.

He walked to the corner and caught sight of the topmost point of the building. Not that he could always find his bearings in relation to the cathedral either. It had tricked him on several occasions. The giant wooden structure, painted all over in dazzling white, never seemed to be in the same place twice. When he was walking around town, it would suddenly loom into sight close by when he was not expecting it. Then it showed itself a distance away when he had thought it would be nearer. The building seemed to be on elastic. Sometimes it vanished altogether.

This time, however, he located it and headed for the library. He knocked on the door of his new boss's stuffy office and went in.

Carmella de Pereira was on the telephone. Carmella was a large, operatic woman of African and Portuguese descent. A bun of jet-black hair sat primly on the top of her head. Despite her weighty thighs, she walked with tiny steps which gave her the premature appearance of middle age. She stood with the telephone in her hand, as if about to launch into an aria, continuing the conversation on the phone while beckoning to Chofy who stood in the doorway. She put a hand to her full bosom and laughed a tinkling laugh.

'Yes. Certainly. I will tell him to go to that address. He could come now. No problem. Yes. He is a McKinnon from the Rupununi.' She nodded to Chofy as if he should know what it was about. 'Not at all. Delighted to be of assistance. Please come and consult us at the library if it would help your research. Good morning.'

She turned to Chofy and gave him the piece of paper she had been scribbling on.

'Greetings. Please zoom straightaway to this house in Brickdam. You can leave stacking the books for today. An English woman there would like to meet you – Rosa Mendelson or some such body. She is doing research into Evelyn Waugh and wants to meet some McKinnons.'

A quarter of an hour later, to his surprise, Chofy found

himself once more outside the Mynheer Nicklaus Lodge where he had been sitting earlier. He now realised that the large house was run as a semi-hotel. The night watchman, still on duty, let him in through the wrought-iron gates.

Tables were laid out under one area of the bottom-house. At one of these tables sat a European woman in a kingfisher-blue T-shirt, eating breakfast in the open. He came and stood in front of the table. Unaware of his presence, she was leaning forward, reading a book balanced against a coffee pot and eating freshly cooked bakes.

Something his Uncle Danny had once told him during a drinking spree came unexpectedly into his head: 'Always watch a woman eat because that's how she fucks.'

He lowered his eyes for a moment in case she looked up suddenly and was somehow able to read his thoughts.

The bottom-house where she sat was divided by wooden partitions of various heights, all latticed and painted white. They stood at different angles like open-work screens. Some had a slanting diamond trellis, some had a finer grid of squares. The criss-crossing intersections created an intricate background like a mathematical puzzle. Behind this lattice fencing, ginger-lilies, hibiscus and heliconia burgeoned and tried to push their way through.

Chofy waited politely for her to look up. He noted her breasts under the T-shirt, framing the coffee pot. She ate slowly and delicately but with relish.

'Excuse me. Good morning. I'm sorry to interrupt your meal. My name is Chofy McKinnon. I believe you want to see me.'

When she lifted her eyes, Chofy did not know whether he was dazzled by the apparent movement of the criss-crossing lattices creating some kind of optical illusion, or by the way she smiled at him. The smile was brimming with delight.

'Oh how wonderful,' she said.

It was love before first sight. The smile struck him with such familiarity that he felt he had always known it. Her hair stood out round her head in a bush of coarse black curls. Later, he found out that her father was a Russian Jew which accounted for the broad cheekbones and the wide mouth. Her blue eyes slanted and were large, dreamy and a little bulbous. The whites showed under the irises when she looked up, like a cartoon animal when it blinks.

Besides the smell of coffee and bakes, which made him hungry, he could smell something else sweet and unfamiliar that intoxicated him.

He apologised again: 'I'm sorry to interrupt your meal. Is this a bad time to call on you?'

She rose to her feet and choked on a crumb, putting her hand to her throat, coughing and laughing at the same time. She was tall, wearing jeans.

'I'm sorry. I've made you choke.'

'There's no need to keep apologising.' She recovered herself.

'I was partly raised by a priest,' Chofy said defensively. 'He taught us to say sorry as if it was the most important thing in the world. I was taught to say please, sorry and thank you.'

'All words that make you feel inferior,' she replied quickly. 'My name is Rosa Mendelson.'

They shook hands. The sun pushed its way through the lattices. Chofy felt light-headed.

'You can always tell the children of Jewish communists of a certain period.' She made a jokey grimace. 'We are all called after people like Rosa Luxemburg or Leon Trotsky.'

Chofy laughed. Secretly, he was a little shocked. He had heard that communists were dangerous.

'I'm doing some research on Evelyn Waugh and his journey here in the thirties.' She sat down again. 'I'm trying to find out if there is anyone still alive here who might have met him. Apparently, he spent some time with the McKinnon family.'

'Oh, I don't know about that. But I know the name Evelyn Waugh – except that I didn't know how to pronounce it. On Saturdays, when I was a youngster, I had to brush the priest's books. There were books on the shelf by Evelyn Waugh and T.S. Eliot, I remember. You're lucky. Good timing. My Auntie Wifreda is in Georgetown for an operation. She would more likely remember.'

Rosa had the habit of rolling her eyes when she laughed.

'Oh great. Could I meet her?'

'Of course.' Chofy hesitated for a moment, wondering how he could overcome Auntie Wifreda's detestation of strangers. 'She's not well at the moment. Perhaps in a week or so.'

There was silence. It was then that Chofy McKinnon did something completely unexpected in the early morning sunshine, with the maids chattering in the kitchen like birds in the trees and the yellow hibiscus blooms lolling and letting their lustful tongues drool out behind the fence. Chofy leaned forward with his hands on the table, looked down at the milk jug, the bakes and the slices of paw-paw and took an enormous gamble.

He said in a voice lower than his own: 'I love you. I've fallen in love with you.'

His tone was so matter-of-fact that Rosa Mendelson was not sure that she had heard him correctly. And he too was not sure what he had said. And so they both ignored the words that seemed to have come from nowhere.

Chofy thought fast.

'Have you managed to visit the interior at all?' he asked after another silence.

'No. I've only stayed in Georgetown and travelled out to the university.'

'Well, if you would like the chance, my cousin Tenga has

married a girl in Pakuri village about three hours' drive into the interior. I could take you there if you want to see something of the bush.'

'I'd love to. Thank you.'

He arranged to pick her up the next Saturday and promised to ask Auntie Wifreda if she would mind talking to Rosa. Then he left, trembling slightly as he tried to control his excitement, and went to organise some transportation to Pakuri for next week.

I CUT
EVELYN WAUGH'S HAIR

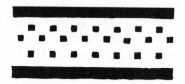

Rosa Mendelson preferred a degree of orderliness and rationality in her life. Soon after her arrival in Guyana she was warned by one of the other guests to prepare for life without either.

One morning she had been attracted downstairs by the sound of classical guitar music floating up from one of the rooms below. The door of his room open, Arthur Singh sat on his bed and introduced himself without ceasing to play. He was a languid, balding Guyanese musician, based in Trinidad, who returned to Georgetown once a year to teach classical guitar at Queen's College.

'I always stay here when I come back to Guyana. I act as informal major-domo around the house. It is a feature of this place that rooms are prepared for people who do not arrive and people arrive for whom there are no rooms. Sometimes I feel that it is because we Guyanese live in houses on stilts that we do not quite have our feet on the ground as a nation.'

And it was he who had told her: 'You must know that this is a country where you will have to surrender to the unexpected. The ferry will break down but another boat will go. As your car sticks in a rut, a donkey-cart will miraculously appear out of the blue. You are at the mercy of the random. Don't look for a pattern and don't try to impose one. Wait until something happens and then go with it. In my opinion, the virus is king on this planet. We should take our cue from him. People only exist to be host to this master of the quantum jump which adapts so miraculously to what it had not anticipated.'

For all his homage to the unexpected, Rosa noticed that Arthur Singh hoarded tea-bags and powdered milk like a miser and occasionally arranged to invite himself upstairs for a cup of tea with her.

She had rented the whole of the attic space in Mynheer Nicklaus Lodge, because it had its own bathroom and a kitchenette where she could make herself coffee while she worked. Her research was on Evelyn Waugh's attitude towards the colonies.

On the morning that Chofy McKinnon was supposed to take her to Pakuri, she settled down to put her work in some sort of order. She laid her papers and documents out in neat piles on the crabwood desk, on the bed, and piled some books on the rosewood dressing-table with its oval mirror.

She worked slowly and thoughtfully, compiling a list of what she had achieved so far.

The first item on the list said 'Georgetown Club'. She crossed it off as completed. The day after her arrival, she had telephoned the elegant colonial club with its rows of white Demerara shutters all opening bottom-out at the same discreet angle, where Evelyn Waugh had stayed for a while during his visit to Georgetown. She discovered that one of the club's old retainers did, indeed, remember Evelyn Waugh and she arranged to meet him there.

As she stood in the entrance of the club, the unmistakable atmosphere of the country's colonial past rose up and enveloped her. The confidently unpretentious, almost

44

shabby interior, with its faded photographs and cabinets of stuffed animals, its aura of an old boys' club, the sound of rum swizzles chinking with ice in glasses both attracted and repelled her.

She waited in the large bar room for the man to arrive. A group of businessmen drank and talked noisily at a table nearby. It was impossible for her not to remember her father in these circumstances, a stunted little man, beaming and earnest, a die-hard communist who had stood as Communist candidate for the wealthy London suburb of Dulwich. She had been ten years old at the time. An embarrassingly small group of them had marched through the leafy streets of Dulwich Village with a poster displaying her father's face, shouting 'Vote for Mendelson'. Mortified at the idea of being seen by any of her schoolfriends, she had mooched along sulkily at her mother's side. Her father had mounted a bench in Dulwich Park and made a passionate speech about Paul Robeson and colonialism to which nobody listened.

And now, her parents were dead and this colonial club still flourished smugly as if cocking a snook at her father's memory. Rosa was glad that both her parents had died before the collapse of the Soviet bloc. They would have been bewildered. All their adult lives had been spent working in the hope of a socialist world.

A hearty guffaw of laughter from the next table made her look at her watch. Her interviewee was late. She wondered what her parents would have thought of the world turning into one enormous capitalist market.

Just before she left England, she had attended a dinner given by the Arts Council in honour of a noted East German actor, an old friend of her mother and father. He had finally defected to the West in the mid-eighties. As the coffee was being passed around, another guest had approached the distinguished white-haired actor, grasped his shoulder and congratulated him energetically on the defeat of communism in his country. The actor had pressed his linen napkin to the corners of his mouth and then risen to his feet to face the man.

'You will never know,' he said graciously, 'how hard we tried to make it work. I did not wish to leave East Germany. In the end, I had no choice but to go. But many of us desperately wanted it to succeed. We preferred the idea of social justice even to our own freedom. What you are talking about so enthusiastically is the death of a great dream for us.'

And with that, he had nodded courteously and with dignity excused himself from the table, his small, shiny-haired wife accompanying him with frequent worried glances up at his face.

Rosa raised her head to see a spry, sallow, elderly man standing in the doorway, looking inquisitively around the bar where she sat. It turned out that the old retainer, a nervously camp, Brylcreemed chatter-box, could recall little about Evelyn Waugh except that he liked to have the ends of his cigars clipped to a certain length before he smoked them. He had then asked Rosa if she would assist in buying him a ticket to England as he longed to see the Queen.

In the attic where Rosa worked, the windows were open letting in the warm air of morning. Outside, the voice of Bob Marley singing: 'Every little thing's gonna be all right,' drifted up from a house at the back. Something flew across her vision. A tiny green frog, not more than an inch long, landed on the window frame, its throat delicately pulsing. She forced herself to concentrate on the notes she had made about the Georgetown Club.

The next item on the list just said 'Find the McKinnons'.

Rosa Mendelson had come to hear of the McKinnons through

a Miss Nancy Freeman, a Guyanese woman living in London. A friend had put them in touch.

'Oh yes, I cut Evelyn Waugh's hair when he was in the colony,' she said proudly, on the telephone.

Rosa had tramped through the endless terraced streets of red houses in Acton, identical as rows of paper cut-outs, until she came to where Miss Freeman lived.

The tall, slim, athletic woman who bounded to open the door must have been in her seventies although she looked younger. Her crinkly grey hair was tied loosely at the back. She had light-skinned African features and an attractive snub nose. Rosa felt a sort of excitement at seeing the three-dimensional version of a woman she had read about in Evelyn Waugh's diaries.

'I gather you want to hear about my time in the savannahs,' she said, after introductions.

'I really wanted to know what you remember of Evelyn Waugh.' Rosa took out her notebook.

They sat in a front room full of plants and knick-knacks. While she spoke, Nancy Freeman stitched away, embroidering a linen chair-back.

'Not much really. I had gone to work on the Brazilian border. Oh I spent the happiest days of my life there. Riding. Outdoors. There's nothing so sweet as the savannah breeze.'

Rosa settled down to what she realised might be a circuitous route to any information about Waugh.

'I worked for one of the McKinnon family – Wifreda. The McKinnons were a big Amerindian family. Well, Amerindian and some European. But they were mainly thought of as "buck" people. I met Wifreda when she came on her annual trip to Georgetown for supplies. She was looking for someone to come and teach her children. There were no schools or anything like that there. And some of the McKinnons had become quite prosperous through ranching – although they never really stopped living Indian-style.

'Well, I was young and adventurous and so I volunteered. I went up the cattle trail. Wifreda McKinnon was still young then, although she had six children. She was a typical Indian. She din explain anything to me. Watch and copy is the Indian way. They don' ask questions. You're expected to find out for yourself. All she said to me was: "Don' carry much. Wear boots because of the tics."

'Well, half the bloody horses died on the journey. We had to light fires at night because of the tigers. At one point we saw the creek water still shaking where a tiger had crossed just ahead of us. We had saltfish and cocoa in the morning and then nothing till rice and saltfish at night. The longest day's walk was twenty-one and a half miles through the bush. You have to keep up. Nobody waits for anybody. Sometimes we walked through mud from ankle to knee. When we came to the savannahs, I rushed to soak in one of the creeks. I was so dry, there was no saliva in my mouth.

'Wifreda McKinnon barely spoke all the way. Later, I learned it was shyness. She was all right with other Indians but with strangers she went quiet. I found her a shut up, silent sort of character. And her eyes were bad. Sometimes she would stumble and the other Indians would laugh. They have a cruel side to them, you know.'

Rosa tried to turn the conversation back to Evelyn Waugh.

'Oh yes.' Nancy bit off the green embroidery thread with her teeth. 'Well, one day this Englishman turned up out of the blue on horseback. He said he was a writer and looking for material. Later we heard that he had come that far because he had trouble with a woman. I remember he arrived on an Ash Wednesday.'

Rosa fiddled with her pen.

48

'What else do you remember about him?'

'Not a great deal. We felt sorry for him. Poor man. He was so out of place. He sat out in the open that first day and that was when I gave him a haircut. Nobody really knew what the hell he was doing there. Danny McKinnon, Wifreda's brother, was obliged to sit and listen to him reading out loud for hours – Dickens, I think.'

Rosa noted that down.

'For all that he was looking for material, he missed one story that was under his nose.'

'What was that?'

A tone crept into Nancy Freeman's voice which Rosa recognised as the reluctance of someone giving in to her better judgement and forgoing the pleasure of muck-raking.

'We . . . ell. I'm not sure that I should say too much about that. You say you are going there?' She said cautiously.

'Yes. I'm going to see if there is anyone left who remembers him. I'm going next month.'

'If you find any of the McKinnons they will be able to tell you about Mr Waugh. The other business had to do with Danny McKinnon and one of his sisters. Her name was Beatrice. Wifreda confided in me. Perhaps you shouldn't enquire about it. It might cause trouble. I don't know why Mr Waugh didn't write about that. He certainly knew about it.'

'Perhaps it was not Evelyn Waugh's sort of story.'

'Perhaps not. But it interested me. I only met Beatrice McKinnon once, many years later. You see, when I first arrived in the Rupununi she had already left and gone to Canada – because of this . . . matter. People even said that she might be liable for criminal prosecution. But the Rupununi was so remote, the law didn't really reach there. She only came back to the country once, as far as I know, and even then she did not return to the Rupununi.

'I met her on that one occasion. I had already left the savannahs by then and gone to live in Berbice. Word came upriver that a Mr and Mrs Horatio Sands were returning to the country and would be staying with the Superintendent of Public Works.

'Well, I knew that Mrs Horatio Sands was Beatrice McKinnon. I was very curious about her because of what Wifreda had told me and because I had taught Beatrice's son. I made sure that I was invited to tea. We were introduced. She looked like any Canadian matron but with an Indian build. Short and thickset. You often see that with Indians, the slimmest of girls turning into stout women. Her hair was still jet black and scraped back into a knot. Her husband was Canadian, a gangly, mild-mannered sort of man.

'Late in the afternoon, she and I went walking out on a little patch of savannah. I told her I knew her family in the Rupununi, that I had lived with Wifreda for a while.

' "Oh, is that so?" she said and she stood still on the dry earth for a moment. Everything seemed to go quiet. I even thought the keskidee birds stopped singing. The sun was prickling the back of my neck. Then she continued to stroll, stooping every now and then to take up one of those small white savannah flowers – the ones that look like moonshine. Burial-ground flowers, I think they call them. I waited for her to enquire about her family – Danny or her son, or Wifreda or anyone. But she never said another word and after a quarter of an hour or so, we returned to the house.'

The interview was clearly at an end. Rosa had imagined she would uncover a wealth of information about Evelyn Waugh and there was not much at all.

Nancy Freeman saw her to the door.

'I can't remember any more. Oh, his feet were bad. He walked with a snake-wood stick. You must find the McKinnons.

If Wifreda is still alive she would remember. I've lost touch with them all now.'

Rosa lost her concentration and put the notebook away. She glanced through the window. Down below, Mr Aristotle Crane, the elderly carpenter who worked at the Lodge, was seated at his leisure, contemplating the world from a stack of lumber.

She dashed off two postcards, one to her daughter who was a student in Manchester and one to her ex-husband in Holland. To pass time, she looked at a map and tried to find the Rupununi. Her eyes wandered from the mapped interior to the coast. Villages and plantations had names which reminded her of *The Pilgrim's Progress*: Whim, Adventure, Perseverance, Makeshift. Then she put the map away and consulted her watch. Chofy McKinnon had said he would come to pick her up around now.

A few seconds later, she looked down and saw him waiting at the gate in his brightly coloured shirt.

WHERE THE FROGS
MEET TO MATE

The visit to Pakuri was nearly a disaster.

All through the week, Chofy had alternated between euphoria and the desperate conviction that he had imagined everything, that Rosa could never find him attractive. All the same, he fantasised about the trip to Pakuri in great detail: how he would cut water-coconuts for her to drink; show her the kingfishers flying alongside the creek; bathe together with her by the landing. The daydreams always got stuck at a certain point and he had to go back to the beginning and start again. Imagination brings on the event, his grandmother used to say.

The bush village of Pakuri nestled in forest some sixty miles from the coast. The truck was full of Lokono Arawaks returning home for the weekend. As soon as they had left the open savannah and the green tunnel of forest closed over them, Chofy worried because he thought he saw Rosa flinch with a sort of claustrophobia.

'What does Pakuri mean?' she asked.

'Where the frogs meet to mate,' replied a short man with protruding teeth.

After a three-hour drive, the truck rumbled into a silent

village with troolie-palm-roofed houses built on stilts in white sandy soil. As they climbed down from the vehicle, Chofy got cold feet. Instead of strolling across to the creek with her and going for a bathe as he had planned, in his nervousness he dumped Rosa unceremoniously with some women and disappeared to find his cousin and fortify himself with liquor.

His cousin Tenga's house was at the far edge of a second clearing. Tenga knelt outside plaiting rows of troolie-palm leaves for the roof of a neighbour's house. Tenga was short, his face creased by the sun. His hands stank with the glutinous smell of the leaves. He stood up, wiped his hands on his jeans, winked at Chofy and nodded over to a tumbledown hut where they could buy rum.

'Let's go to Jonestown.'

'Why do you call it Jonestown?' asked Chofy, bemused.

'Because people go in there and disappear,' laughed Tenga.

They began to toss back the sweet liquor.

'How are things?' enquired Chofy, relaxing as the rum cut a warm trail down to his stomach.

'OK. I want to go back to the Rupununi. I miss my farine and my shibi. But my wife's family are all here and she don't want to leave.' He sighed.

'I've brought a woman here.' Chofy could not resist introducing the subject casually but with elation. 'She's paying. That's the only way I could afford to come.'

'What kind of woman? A tourist?'

'No. She's come to do some work. Research.'

Tenga grunted.

'They're the worst. It's like a zoo here. People come and stare at this village because it's the nearest to Georgetown. We smile and give them gifts, little pieces of craft and so. We who don't have shit, find ourselves giving things to these people. We don't show them what grows fastest here – the children's part of the burial ground.'

The two of them began to get drunk. Tenga became more resentful.

'We Amerindian people are fools, you know. We've been colonised twice. First by the Europeans and then by the coastlanders. I don't know which is worse. Big companies come to mine gold or cut timber. Scholars come and worm their way into our communities, studying us and grabbing our knowledge for their own benefit. Aid agencies come and interfere with us. Tourists stare at us. Politicians crawl round us at election times.'

Tenga spat on the ground. Chofy tried to change the subject.

'Do you remember when Granny used to spit on the ground like that and say, "If you not back by the time this dry you in trouble"?'

But Tenga refused to be deflected.

'Amerindians have no chance in this country.'

'I don't agree,' said Chofy earnestly, his eyes glazed with the rum. 'I think we have to mix. Otherwise we have no future. We must get educated.'

Tenga poured out more liquor.

'Let them get educated our way.'

Chofy raised his glass to his lips.

'We can't go backwards. Guyana has to develop.'

Tenga was staring at Chofy with suspicion.

'I'm not Guyanese. I'm Wapisiana. How's Marietta?' he asked suddenly.

'She's doing fine. And Bla-Bla too. He's out all day. Comes back at night like a bird.'

Chofy did not look him in the eye. He prayed that Tenga would not mention Marietta when he met Rosa. It would spoil everything.

'You say we should mix,' said Tenga bitterly. 'What to do? We're destroyed if we mix. And we're destroyed if we don't.'

Chofy shook his head in disagreement and swallowed down more rum.

'But sometimes they try to help, these outsiders.

The two men had lapsed into speaking Wapisiana.

'Even when an outsider tries to help, he messes us up,' said Tenga, baring his teeth in a drunken grimace. 'But he will never leave us alone. That he will never do. He sits on our back. He is full of sympathy for our suffering, at the burden we have to carry. He offers to help. He will do anything he can – except get off our back.'

Tenga gestured round the little shop where they sat.

'Look at this shop. Before it opened, people used to fish and share everything with the other families here. Now they take the fish to sell in Georgetown for money to buy things in the shop. And did you see the well outside? Some people came and asked us what we wanted. We didn't know. We just said a well. They built it for us. But people missed going down to the creek to fetch water and talking to each other. It destroyed the social life of the village. And the well water tastes different – horrible – like iron. Then somebody shat in the well or children threw rubbish in it and half the village got poisoned.

Chofy noticed the sun was setting and felt anxious about Rosa.

'I better go chase down this woman and see if she's all right.'

'The worst thing is when they come and marry us,' Tenga said maliciously as Chofy went through the door.

Abandoned by Chofy and feeling awkward, Rosa remained sitting shyly on a bench sandwiched between several other women who spoke in Arawak. After a couple of hours, weariness overcame politeness and her head began to nod. A fat woman nudged her and asked her if she would like to go inside and lie down in a hammock. There was no sign of Chofy. Rosa crawled into a hammock and slept.

When she awoke it was dark. She came out and crossed the clearing to join the other women who had by now drifted to sit outside on the steps of neighbouring houses. The sand made walking difficult and slow.

The schoolteacher had brought out his guitar. Somebody kept beat on a hand-drum while he plucked the chords of 'Knock-knock-knocking on Heaven's Door' slowly and mournfully under the stars with people joining in a melancholy chorus. Two or three shadowy couples danced together on the white sands which shimmered between the houses. A sense of desolation hung over the village.

After a while, came the sound of an engine revving and somebody shouting. Chofy, now drunk, came weaving across the sands from the other side of the village. He helped Rosa climb into the vehicle.

Men, women and children crammed into the truck. Most people smelled of liquor. A man with a broken nose took the wheel and drove. Chofy sat on the back flap of the jeep with some other men, casting frequent glances at Rosa.

The vehicle hurtled along the rough track out of the village. Scrubby bushes slashed at them as they passed. Everyone held on to the side of the truck. After about an hour, they left the forest behind and emerged into a patch of savannah. The moon was high in the sky. The night air was warm.

Stars reeled overhead. Bumping along, Rosa saw Orion sprawled out sideways along the horizon as if he too were drunk, a constellation hanging between his legs.

'Mabukili,' said the man next to her when he saw where she was looking. 'The one-legged man.'

Everyone swayed as the truck sped through the night.

Chofy's eyes had shrunk in his head. He sang out loudly in a sort of chant: 'I've got an erection. Where shall I put it?' He kept an eye on Rosa. People were laughing.

'Not in me. Not in me,' intoned the man next to him solemnly. He was a squat man with a Charlie Chaplin moustache, sitting with his arm round his wife.

Rosa tried to doze. Chofy reached over and grabbed her hair, jerking her head up. She pulled away.

'I've got an erection. Who shall I stick it in?' A general hilarity overtook the passengers.

'Put it down. Put it down,' chanted the other man in a deep voice, imitating Paul Robeson.

A ribald chorus started up. The men sitting in the back yelled in unison: 'Don't put no condoms on me. Don't put no condoms on me.'

The truck pulled up under the night sky so that anyone who needed to could take a piss. People jumped off and went a little way away into the bush. The journey resumed.

The man drove wildly, heedless of safety. The rattling of the truck and its reckless advance frightened Rosa. It was as if everybody else somehow relished this headlong plunge towards oblivion, as if the journey somehow represented their path to extinction.

By now they were going at breakneck speed.

'We're going to die. We're going to die,' chorused the truckload of Indians to the stars above. It felt to Rosa as if they had surrendered all hope and were embracing destruction with a carefree abandon, exhilarated by the danger and inevitability of annihilation.

Suddenly the truck came to the point where the track joined the main highway. The smoothness and quiet of the road after the rough track immediately had the effect of bringing everybody back to a different reality and the wildness went out of the journey. Still travelling fast, they burst through the toll gate without stopping and the gate-keeper's oaths were snatched away behind them as they sped on. But the sense of playing with destiny had passed. They drove on to Georgetown in silence.

The driver circled town, dropping people off at various destinations. He stopped outside the great white house where Rosa was staying. She climbed down. Chofy had already jumped down on the other side. The night was quiet except for the chirping of crickets and frogs. The two remaining occupants of the truck looked on with sleepy curiosity. The driver, dog-tired, drooped over the wheel, a dark bloom of sweat on his grey T-shirt between the shoulder blades.

Chofy stood beside the vehicle. Rosa was aware of his brightly patterned shirt and his black hair and the heat of the night.

'Can I stay?'

The sound of the engine ticking over.

'Are you drunk?'

'I'm stone cold sober.' He swayed slightly, tried to pull himself erect but still stood askew.

Rosa remembered the man saying: 'Wait until something happens and then go with it.'

'Yes. You can stay,' she said.

Chofy's heart uplifted and began to beat fast.

The dogs set up a ferocious barking. Abdul the night watchman came out to open the gates.

'Are you coming out again?' he asked Chofy.

'No. I'm staying.'

Abdul stepped back with a look of theatrical disgust on his face.

They climbed three flights of wooden stairs. The attic stretched the length of the house. Although the Demerara shutters were wide open, framing the black night, the attic still held all the warmth of the day. Chofy lowered himself stiffly on to the hard-backed sofa. He sat upright and shut his eyes, half overcome by alcohol and the jolting ride. He remained motionless.

Rosa waited and when she thought he was asleep, tiptoed through the eaved space, which was separated by half-partitions on each side so that it was possible to walk the full length without opening any doors. Her bed was at the far end where the roof was lower. The windows had been closed there and it felt more violently stuffy.

She went to the bathroom, brushed her teeth and undressed, feeling as if she had got away with something. Then she lay down under the sheet and was on the point of drifting into sleep when she became aware of his figure standing hesitantly in the shadows of the adjoining space. He was waiting, one hand tentatively on the eaves, foot half raised, toe on the ground. She shut her eyes and did nothing. She never heard him come to the bedside or undress.

UNDER THE EAVES

These were the words spoken that night, under the low eaves where all the hot air from the day seemed to have gathered. It doesn't matter who said what or in what order:

May I lie down with you?
Yes.
May I suck your breasts?
Yes.
You're like a bird. Your body is like a dancer's.
You're so warm. You're so warm.
You're strong.
You're a baby.
Suck me a little.
I want to make love to you.
You're hot, girl.
I've been lusting after you since I first saw you.
When I do that your nipples stand upright.
Give me your tongue.
My spirit is flying away from my body.

You're naive. You're shaking.

You're paying more attention to that mosquito than you are to me.

You're beautiful.

Do you want me to go slower?

Put your legs against the eaves.

I want to keep making love to you. I want to hurt you.

Let me kiss you.

Oh I can feel that.

It's not fair. It's not fair.

We shouldn't be doing this.

You don't give a shit, do you?

I love it. Coming's not important.

And then laughter and deep, gurgling giggles.

Are you married?

I'm on my own.

How many women have you got?

You'd like to be the only one, wouldn't you?

Don't hit me there.

Come, let me pull you further down in the bed.

Better shut the door. Anyone could come up.

I don't know which door to shut.

The one at the top of the stairs. I'll do it.

Soft footsteps treading across the warm floor.

Come back into bed.

No. I want some sleep.

I want to ravish you. I want part of your spirit.

What is that scar on your arm?

Someone tried to rob me of my watch.

You're a wonderful lover.

I'm a homosexual.

You can be what you want.

You're not listening. You're not listening.

I want some affection.

You're beautiful.

Keep doing that.

Hold me. Hold on to me.

You're a superb lover.

Don't patronise me.

I want to fuck you.

What do you think you are doing?

Making love to you.

Slower. Go slower.

No.

Your legs are like silk.

I can feel you contracting. It feels like you're holding me.

Can you tell lies?

When necessary.

You're shy. You're vulgar.

Come on top of me.

I'm lazy. I told you I was lazy.

You come on top of me.

You smell so sweet.

You taste salty.

That's sweat.

Let me kiss you.

There's a cockroach. Quick. Quick. It's gone under the mattress.

Do you want me to kill it?

Yes.

Give me your sandal.

Let's sleep.

Let me put my leg over your thigh. I once saw my father like that with my mother.

The house in whose attic the two lovers slept was like an enormous sea-going vessel. It was constructed entirely of wood and painted white. Like a ship, it creaked and groaned. On all four storeys, the Demerara shutters stretched out like unfurled wooden wings. And as if in reminder of a seafaring past, the windowsills of the upper floors were lined with bottles that had been salvaged from the muddy waters of the Demerara estuary: bottles with tall necks, ginger-coloured bottles, stout black bottles, green glass flagons, bottles tinged with sea green that were used on the prison ships from Africa and bottles that, despite being tiny, weighed heavily in the hand.

Like a ship too, the house contained galleries and passage-ways, verandahs, decks and stairways. There were so many different levels and rooms that visitors lost their way. A guest had once opened a door and come across a whole family, whom he had never seen before but who lived there, sitting at breakfast.

It was a galleon that had come to ground, beached in a city amongst a host of other craft – Georgetown being a city built almost entirely of wood – the houses were like large schooners, sailing ships, brigs, tiny skiffs, ramshackle craft, junks and sloops. It was as if all the houses in Georgetown, from the most palatial to the tiniest of shacks, had once, in the process of evolution, been a flotilla of sea-vessels which the sea had tossed on shore. It was an armada turned city, a wooden fleet on land.

While the two of them drifted in and out of sleep, turning under the single, damp sheet, sometimes at the same time and sometimes separately, the morning sun began to brighten the attic and the household staff gradually assembled for the day's work.

From below, the strident sound of Anita the cook singing 'How Sweet the Name of Jesus Sounds' floated up to the attic windows. She sang in a high, reedy voice that always remained pitched within soaring distance of hysteria and her tone of voice held a sullen threat, as if defying God to treat her badly.

In the kitchen, she wiped the steam from her shining black face and took the aluminium pan of boiled milk for the dogs off the stove. She wiped the surface of the table and laid out the cow-heel, pork, salt beef, cloves, spices and thyme. Then she went to fetch the casreep and the red maiwiri peppers.

Through the window, she spotted Cuthbert ambling through the gate. Cuthbert was a mechanic who had jumped ship and come to work in the timber yard of the Lodge with Mr Crane.

'When you goin' back to sea?' she called out.

'This place like fly-paper. People stick to it,' he called back.

Anita let out a long, high-pitched laugh.

'Yes. This is a story-house,' and she continued singing: '"In a believer's ear."'

Mr Aristotle Crane, the chief carpenter, strolled in, as he did every morning of his life, even on Sundays. At seventy-five, he had slackened his pace a little and spent a considerable amount of time sitting on a stack of lumber, his long legs stretched out in front of him.

No one could remember a time when Mr Crane was not working on the house and work on the house was never finished. He was a lean man with one protruding tooth, who understood everything about wood: the stresses and strains each variety of wood could bear; which woods were best able to withstand the salt carried by the sea-winds;

which conditions helped wood to breathe and stretch; which methods of seasoning strengthened the timber. Even his face was grainy and the colour of mahogany.

As a young man he had attended night classes at Queen's and technical school. One good teacher taught him the rudiments. His father and grandfather had taught him the rest. He could make half-doors, sash windows, Demerara shutters and jalousies. He could move the kitchen from the top of the house to the bottom and back again. He understood how to design lattices, windows and partitions that would catch the slightest breeze or gust of the Trade Winds and so the house always remained cool.

Mr Crane had only one fear – that one day he would come to work and the house would no longer be there. When he became ill and his doctor advised him to go for treatment and possibly retire in the United States, he solemnly recited this hymn in response:

> Our fathers' sepulchres are here
> And here our kindred dwell
> Our children too
> How can we love another land so well

Together with the other workmen, Cuthbert, Boops, Henri and Boso, Mr Crane formed what was known as the Parliament of the Lodge. At around four o'clock in the afternoon, they met in the shed at the back of the yard where Mr Crane stored his lumber. Here, Henri the cabinet-maker who claimed French, Amerindian, Bajan and Spanish blood, worked assiduously to fashion handsome guitars and small boxes inlaid with precious woods. As Henri worked, Mr Crane assisted everybody by pouring out the rum as he polished a table or cupboard he was making. Boops was usually dispatched to fetch ice and fresh limes. They were joined by Cuthbert and Boso and sometimes by the occasional passer-by who knew, by some secret means, that Parliament was in session.

And then, in the dying heat of the afternoon, leisurely and considered debates took place, slow as molasses going up a hill, punctuated by thoughtful pauses that could last as long as ten minutes, during which Leonard the parrot would sometimes offer his contribution from deep in the branches of the mango tree which shaded the hut. In slow time, mellowed by rum, the shed redolent with the aroma of cedar and greenheart wood, up to their ankles in wood-shavings, this prestigious and dignified assembly of parliamentarians discussed the entire range of life's topics, from the ridiculous antics of government, to the efficacy of Pif-paf insect repellent and even to the nature of the supernatural, several of whose ambassadors had lately taken to calling on Mr Crane.

It was that most venerable of institutions, a parliament uncorrupted by power.

At roughly the same time that Parliament was in session in the afternoon, the judiciary kicked their shoes off and held court upstairs in the cool of the drawing-room. The judiciary consisted of Anita the cook; Indira her assistant; Mrs Hassett the manageress, whose mind was like a bird's nest hedged in with such tiny economies that it barely saw the light of day, and who attended only when she could be tempted from the scraps of paper on which she scribbled her tangled sums. The last two members of the judiciary were Eileen who came to clean and Clara the petite black girl who washed and ironed clothes.

In the customary manner of any court, they sat to pass judgement. They passed judgement on everybody from film stars to politicians, on the sporadic guests who turned up, on other members of the workforce and on each other's husbands and boyfriends. And when any one member of the judiciary happened herself to be absent, naturally the others passed judgement on her too. Once judgement was passed, there was little chance of appeal.

Holding the office of Lord Chamberlain and keeper of the keys to the Lodge was Mr Roy. Two years earlier he had had a stroke which caused one side of his face to sing a different song from the other. That, combined with advanced age, meant that his progress through the house was slow. Forgetfulness made him repeat many of the journeys through the Lodge because he had left some object or other behind. You could hear his slow tread come to a halt and after a pause you could hear him retracing his steps.

His years as one of the clerks in the ornate, blue-turreted city hall had left their imprint. There was no tea-bag or spoonful of powdered milk that could not be accounted for by Mr Roy. The kitchen was kept locked after the staff had gone home. But his work was cut out to control the contents of the fridge and the cupboards. Stocks disappeared mysteriously in the night. It was as though phantoms passed through and inhaled the food. It vanished. Sometimes, he came into the kitchen during the day to find strange children, sitting spooning bowlfuls of rice into their stomachs. The half-eaten remains of a cucumber and avocado salad that he had checked in the late afternoon had gone by evening. A jug full of plum juice in the fridge was three-quarters empty by the time he descended the stairs to check again. His endless tours of the house always revealed objects either missing or misplaced.

'The coffee has migrated,' he could be heard muttering as he made his rounds of inspection. However many cupboards he locked, ghostly hands seemed able to remove the contents.

On the morning that Chofy and Rosa lay sleeping at the top of the house, Mr Roy slowly made his rounds, taking especial care to check the stores because some American guests from Hawk Oil company were flying in from the States that day.

It was mid-morning. Trying to avoid being seen by any of the staff, Chofy McKinnon made his way down from the top of the house as though he were walking on air.

Dizzy with happiness, he left the Lodge and picked his way over stagnant drainage trenches and patches of dry grass, stepping carefully between the piles of dust-covered stones being used to repair pot-holes in the road. Then, the recollection of what had just happened overwhelmed him to such an extent that he stood still for a moment on the roadside.

He had decided he must visit Auntie Wifreda. She would be wondering what had happened to him. But first, he could not resist going to sit for a while in the Botanic Gardens to run over again and again in his mind what had been happening in his life since the beginning of the week.

He found a bench in the gardens near to where the abandoned statue of Queen Victoria stood in undergrowth that had run wild. He watched the egrets perch on Queen Victoria's white marble shoulders, then he shut his eyes and settled into a blissful daydream repeating continually the events of the last few days. He felt that his whole life had been transformed. Endless possibilities opened up before him. He would go to live in Europe. Or perhaps Rosa would come to live with him here. He would build a house for her. Marietta would understand. Bla-Bla could come and visit.

Half an hour later, a screech of brakes made him open his eyes. Rohit Persaud, his landlord, pulled up to a halt beside him on his bicycle. He stood tipsily, one foot on the pedal, his sweaty chest shining in the opening of his black shirt.

Chofy greeted him.

'How things, man?'

Rohit shook his head in disappointment and frustration.

'Still the same. Red flag up. Rain. No play. She threw me out. She does dress in flimsy-flimsy nightie to get me excited and then it's no go. She jealous bad. I goin' kill myself.'

Chofy grinned.

'What you goin' do? Shoot yourself?'

'No. When it rainin', I goin' put my head in one of the pot-holes in D'Urban Street and drown myself.'

Rohit raised his arms and started to sing calypso in a maudlin voice:

'Oh my commanding wife,
She want to control my life.

I goin' get sweet-up, boy. Come lewwe drink nuh?'

Chofy excused himself as he got up.

'I have to go find my aunt. She's sick.'

Rohit levered himself back on to his bike and wobbled off in the direction of one of the rum shops in Robb Street.

The St Francis of Assisi home, where Auntie Wifreda lay, occupied a patch of ground in Thomas Street. It was a city within a city, a city of the old, known as the City of Crones, consisting of a collection of one-room shacks run as a charity by the Catholic Church.

As he came through the gate, not even the sight of the dismal shacks could dispel Chofy's happiness. From the window of the first hut, the Matron turned her head lethargically and nodded at him as he pushed open the gates. Still in her nightgown, her puffy face saffron yellow, she fanned herself slowly and explained that she was sick with an enlarged heart.

There were two rows of these single wooden rooms standing opposite each other. As the place had grown, other ramshackle wooden dwellings had sprung up here and there, all looking topsy-turvy and intoxicated, tacked together with criss-cross planks and with tiny, footworn rabbit paths between them. Each shack rested on stilts with four or five steps leading up to the door. Outside every one stood a little shed for cooking, covered by a single sheet of zinc. Where the ground was marshy, planks had been laid over the maze of stinking alleyways that separated the houses.

Women came to their windows to see who was passing. One or two asked for money. Some busied themselves washing or sweeping dust from the sun-bleached shacks out through the doors into mid-air. Some stood and stared. To his right, one ancient shrivelled woman lifted up her orange skirt and evacuated her bowels in a ditch at the side of her home.

Auntie Wifreda's room was at the far end of the row. From the top of the cooking shed outside, her green parrot hopped noisily along the tin roof and gave a bronchitic chuckle as Chofy approached.

Chofy ran up the steps and opened the door.

Auntie Wifreda lay sprawled in a blue nightdress on the bed, a patch over her right eye, which had already undergone surgery. On the left side of the room stood a yellow plastic bucket and several pans.

She opened her good eye.

'You bring me tobacco, Chofy?'

'No, Auntie.'

'My head is paining me. Please to fetch me some black tobacco.'

Chofy cursed himself for forgetting. He would have to walk all the way home. Black Rupununi tobacco was almost impossible to find in Georgetown.

'I'll go and get some. How are you feeling?'

'Sore.'

'Auntie Wifreda.' Chofy could not wait to ask. 'Do you remember someone called Evelyn Waugh coming to the Rupununi a long time ago?'

'What?'

'I want to bring a friend of mine to meet you. She wants to know if you remember a Mr Evelyn Waugh coming to the savannahs.'

Auntie Wifreda groaned.

'I don' want to meet anyone. Tell them to go away. Yes, I remember him. A pushed-up face and little pebble eyes. He said mass with us outdoors.'

'You don't have to feel shy. She just wants to ask you some questions.'

Auntie Wifreda moaned, turned on her side and pretended to be too ill to respond.

'Well, perhaps I could bring her in a few days when you are feeling better,' Chofy persisted. 'I'll come back later with the tobacco.'

He let himself out through the door.

Not even the long journey back to his lodgings, the sun beating down on his back, through Le Repentir cemetery with its tombstones like broken teeth stuck at angles in the ground, could extinguish his feelings of elation. He turned into the part of town where he lived. The familiar smell of stale oil from the street vendors in Albouystown no longer sickened him.

Just as he approached his lodgings, he heard the voice of Rohit's wife, yelling at another woman from the window.

'Everybody knows how yuh behind too hot to sit in church these days. Ain' that so, Miss Lady?'

A figure slunk behind the door jamb of the house opposite.

'Look how she hidin' sheself. See how she don' dare come out. And when she does, I go buss she fuckin' head.'

Rohit edged into view, drunk, pushing his bike.

'That's it,' he yelled. 'Drop your pants and skin your arse up at dem, Madam War-Zone. But I goin' jump you tonight, like it or not, Mistress Hostility Head.'

Chofy let himself in quietly. His small bare room closed itself affectionately round him. Everything in the room looked full of promise, even the black plastic chair with the stuffing poking out. He fixed the gas canister on to the stove and rummaged in his bag for some tobacco. Then he took the towel off the mirror and looked at his reflection. Immediately, he panicked at the thought that he was getting too fat. It wouldn't do to get fat. He sank into the chair.

For a few minutes he frowned guiltily and bit his lip. It was the time of day when Marietta would be watering the fruit trees. He pictured her broad back and shoulders as she tipped water from the bucket. He pictured Bla-Bla wrestling with the wheelbarrow full of firewood.

'But life is such a struggle and I deserve some happiness,' he pleaded to himself.

Some time after Chofy had left, Auntie Wifreda sat up on the bed in her blue nightie and put her feet on the floor. The room was hot and airless.

Ever since the mention of Evelyn Waugh, she had been fretting. It brought the whole business back to her. Wifreda still carried a burden of guilt. Not many people were left who knew what had happened. She pulled the patch off her eye, but the lid and surrounding flesh were still so swollen that she could not open it properly and test her sight. All her adult life, she had feared that she would go blind simply because of her kinship with her brother Danny and sister Beatrice. Kinship with them was itself enough to warrant some sort of supernatural reprisal.

She ran her hands over her forehead where the headache

sat behind her eyes, the thoughts clawing at her brain like crabs in a barrel. Don't say the whole matter was going to re-surface now. She would say as little about Mr Evelyn Waugh as possible – not that he had anything directly to do with it. But she herself had told him the truth of the story and for all she knew, he was still alive. Beatrice, her sister, might still be liable to criminal prosecution over the business with the priest. Wifreda knew that she was alive, in an old people's home somewhere in Canada.

Yes indeed, she remembered Mr Waugh. She remembered him standing in plus fours by the long trestle-tables under the mango tree where the family sometimes ate. He had been curious to see the McKinnons sitting down to eat in European clothes, but talking in Wapisiana and with their feet bare under the table and bows and arrows slung over the backs of the chairs.

And she remembered Mr Waugh's encounter with her nephew Sonny. Sonny was her sister Beatrice's child. When Beatrice left for Canada, she had asked Wifreda to raise him.

It was odd how memories from so far back were more vivid in her mind than what happened yesterday.

She could clearly see Mr Waugh, stick in hand, coming out of the house and walking towards the river. Sonny was about fourteen. He was seated on his own at the trestle-tables under the huge, spreading mango tree, eyes open but with that small smile on his lips which meant he was asleep. The family's pet monkey was gibbering in its cage and a red macaw looked down in silence from the mango tree above. He was a beautiful-looking boy with black hair and wide, black eyes punched slantwise into a heart-shaped face. Mr Waugh was not to know that Sonny slept with his eyes open.

Sonny sat upright. Diamond-shaped leaf shadows flickered over his face and the top half of his body. He held himself erect, with his hands placed on the table in front of him. The moving pattern made him look like a harlequin. Sometimes the leaf shadows clustered together like the black, rosetted hide of a jaguar. A night wizard, sitting at a sunlit table.

There were two rules with Sonny. Do not startle him, was one. Do not speak too fast, was the other. Mr Waugh went up to him and broke both at once.

'Good afternoon,' he said, in a high, jovial voice that sounded as if he were trying to be companionable. 'I thought everyone had gone off fishing in . . .'

He had not finished his sentence before Sonny exploded into a windmill of agitated, ungainly movement, his passionately guarded enclosure shattered. He rose clumsily, knocking a calabash from the table, and headed for the house. After a minute or two, the shadow of his hammock could be seen swinging to and fro inside his room.

Mr Waugh, vexed, stared after him for a bit and then sat down at the table to read *Dombey and Son* until the kaboura flies drove him inside.

It was to compensate for that encounter that Wifreda, in a rare fit of openness, had confided in Mr Waugh and explained Sonny's history, not that the writer seemed particularly interested, in fact, she detected a certain distaste as he listened. The next day she had sneaked a look at his diary and discovered a cryptic reference to the affair and to her 'dotty bastard nephew'.

Auntie Wifreda shut her eyes. Even now after all these years, she regretted what had happened and missed her sister Beatrice more than she could express. An iron ache weighed on her stomach as she recalled the separation. Beatrice had been the elder sister who looked after them all. Everybody loved her. If anybody belonged in the savannahs, it was Beatrice. She had known every creature, every rock-stone and river, gully, bush and plant for miles around.

Auntie Wifreda clenched her fists and grimaced as she remembered how she had been indirectly responsible for Beatrice's final departure.

She lay down and tossed restlessly on the bed in the stifling room.

The picture of Beatrice finally leaving Waronawa pushed itself into her mind, clear in every detail.

The whole family had risen before dawn. Danny, their eldest brother, went to and fro in the dark from the house to the bullock cart outside, stacking her bags and baskets. Beatrice had seemed perfectly calm. She sat at the table, sipping tapioca porridge. Most of her nine brothers and sisters sat or stood round in the kitchen with the two mamais, Maba and Zuna. Some of the vaqueiros were there too, up early because one of the horses was foaling. Very little was said.

Wifreda had ridden over from Pirara to say goodbye and to collect Sonny. She was holding Sonny in her arms. Danny had wanted to leave before sunrise, but the sky was already streaked pink and duck-egg green and the sun had caught the top of the Kanaku Mountains by the time they were ready to set off. The mountains themselves seemed suddenly to have crept nearer to Beatrice as the sun touched them.

When Beatrice climbed into the cart, Wifreda lifted Sonny towards her to say goodbye. The boy smiled at something over his mother's shoulder, but not noticeably at his mother. He averted his head and pulled away a little as Beatrice ran her hand over and through his hair. Then Danny twitched the reins and the cart rumbled off.

The last Wifreda had ever seen of Beatrice was the back of that straight, defiant figure, her dark hair down to her shoulders, holding on to the side of the cart and looking ahead towards the sky-foot where the Kanaku Mountains ended and the savannah began.

HUMMING-BIRD
SUCKING HONEY

The night's love-making had left Rosa feeling calm, elated and oddly weightless as if she were floating. Most of all she was surprised. She folded her arms behind her head and pushed her toes up under the sheet. What was to be the outcome of all this? She could not imagine. Her actions were normally those of a slow, thoughtful woman whose progress through life was methodical and thorough. She exercised caution in her dealings with the world. What had happened? On the other hand, she had been warned that this was a country of the random. It occurred to her that she might never see Chofy again. Or possibly end up with him as a lifelong partner. There was no telling. The used sheet coiled itself round her legs as she turned to doze off once more, the events of the night staying with her like a good dream.

It was late in the morning when Rosa finally got up, bathed and dressed in a fresh cotton print dress. Eyes half shut, she looked in the black-spotted mirror and pulled a comb through the tangled corona of black hair. A sort of dreaminess had hold of her which prevented her from doing any work so she went downstairs to find breakfast. She sat at the table outside, feeling self-conscious, as if the sexual activity of the night before was written all over her like the luminous entry stamp of a London disco.

As if to confirm her fears, another guest was peering curiously across at her from his table through spectacles, rimless at the top and steel-rimmed at the bottom. Straggling wisps of hair wandered sideways over the top of his balding pink scalp. After a few minutes, he got up and made his awkward way over to her, his jacket flapping about him.

'May I introduce myself. My name is Michael Wormoal. I am an anthropologist from the University of Berne. Did I see you yesterday going off somewhere with a group of Amerindians?'

'Yes, you did,' said Rosa cautiously.

'I am a Czech. My research field is comparative mythology amongst South American Indians. When I saw you yesterday I wondered if you were ... well ... doing something in my area.'

Rosa detected a competitive challenge in his enquiry.

'I'm here to do research but in literature,' she replied politely.

He laughed.

'Ah well, many of us anthropologists are just writing bad fiction these days. It seems to be the fashion. Analysis by metaphor. A sort of laziness really.'

Rosa smiled with him.

'I am here to do research into the English writer, Evelyn Waugh, who came here in the thirties.'

He seemed relieved.

'Your friend who left a while ago ... what sort of Indian is he?'

'Wapisiana.'

'Oh really? Part of my fieldwork was amongst the Wapisiana people. I think I probably know more about the Amerindian peoples than they know about themselves. What is his name?'

'His name is Chofoye McKinnon. Chofy for short. Apparently it's a Wai-Wai name. It means "explosion of rapids or fast-flowing waters".'

'That's interesting.' Wormoal jotted it down in his notebook. 'I would very much like to meet with him.'

An inexplicable rush of possessiveness made Rosa prevaricate.

'I'm not sure when he'll be back.'

Wormoal asked with a gesture whether he could sit down at her table. She nodded.

'It is a shame,' Wormoal said as he sat down, 'how rapidly Indian culture is disintegrating these days – contaminated mainly by contact with other races.'

Rosa took his words personally and flushed.

'Well, I'm an internationalist, I suppose. I believe in a mixture of the races,' she said hesitantly.

Within minutes, a steely argument developed under the pleasantries.

'You are going against the modern grain then,' he continued. His glasses glinted in the midday sun. 'People want to be with their own kind. Everyone nowadays is retreating into their own homogeneous group. Black with black. Serb with Serb. Muslim with Muslim. Look at me. I'm a Czech. First of all we got rid of the Soviet Union and then we parted from the Slovaks. Now we're happy.'

One of the kitchen staff arrived to put a plate of red water-melon slices on the table. Rosa found herself standing up defensively for the old Czechoslovakia.

'I used to go on holiday to Czechoslovakia with my parents. We always had a wonderful time.'

Wormoal gave Rosa a slightly patronising smile.

'Real existing socialism was different if you lived it. I have gone in the other direction now. I believe in the purity of the nation.'

Rosa was taken aback.

'People have suffered a great deal from those sort of ideas,' she retorted. 'That sort of purity casts a dark shadow.'

'Yes, but you must admit it has its attractions.' His tone was teasing. 'And you Jews also choose to stick together now in Israel.'

'As a matter of fact, I am not a Zionist,' she replied sharply. 'I support the Palestinians on most issues.'

Rosa could not believe the argument had escalated on to such dangerous ground so quickly. She tried to neutralise the conversation.

'You do your research entirely into Amerindian mythology?'

'Yes. I'm going to present a paper at the university here on the scientific approach to mythology. I have a copy on me if you'd like to read it.' Perspiration darkened a strand of fair hair that fell over his pink forehead as he fished in his briefcase and handed it over to her.

'But surely, you yourself are contaminating the Indians when you stay with them,' she could not resist saying, as she glanced through the paper.

A rueful expression crossed Wormoal's face. Plates could be heard clattering in the kitchen.

'I'm afraid you are right. We try just to observe but our very presence alters things. Mine are the wasted talents of a secret agent. I have the entire map of this country in my head. I know about the history and movements of the indigenous peoples here, their kinship structures, occupations, philosophies, cosmologies, labour pattern, languages. We Europeans have access to all the books and documentation that they lack. And what do I do with it? I become a professor and enrich European and American culture with it.'

Rosa looked at him curiously.

'You make knowledge sound like a new form of colonial power.'

Wormoal startled her by suddenly leaning forward with an intense expression on his face.

'But of course. Information is the new gold. You, as a scholar, must know that. My knowledge of the Indians is a way of owning them – I admit it. We fight over the intellectual territory. But it's better than stealing their land, isn't it?'

Confused, Rosa shrank from being bracketed with him. Wishing to extricate herself from his presence, she rose to leave the table.

'Thank you for your paper. I'll read it as soon as possible. I must go upstairs and sort out my work.'

'I'll let you know when I'm speaking at the university. You might like to come.'

'Thank you very much.'

As she stood up to go, a sparkling new Land Rover, with the words 'Hawk Oil' on the side, swung into the yard. Five burly, weather-beaten white men, all wearing baseball caps, got out. Two wore light suits. Three wore T-shirts and jeans.

'Dey's come. De Americans.' Anita the cook stood in the yard and yelled upstairs excitedly. Mrs Hassett, the manageress, bustled out to greet them. The new arrivals gazed round with a proprietorial stare.

As Rosa went up to the attic, she passed Anita and Indira on the stairs.

'Perhaps they can get us a visa.' Anita was giggling. 'Or perhaps one of them will marry me. Or perhaps they will carry us out to America in their pockets or hide us in their suitcases.'

The attic felt warm and peaceful, a safe retreat. The conversation with Wormoal had disturbed Rosa. She flopped on to the bed frowning and began to study the academic paper he had given her. His views had unsettled her. Racial integration had always been the bedrock of her outlook. But he had made her feel self-conscious about her relationship with Chofy, as if slipping a poisoned wedge between them. She started to read:

The Structural Elements of Myth by M. J. Wormoal

It is my intention today to talk to you about the science of mythology. I think we must all agree that science is the winning strategy of the modern world. Science and reason are now invoked in every field, including areas which have previously evaded them such as mythology.

There is nothing that cannot be tackled by reason. As Stephen Hawking has said: 'We live in a universe governed by rational laws.'

Everything finally is written in mathematical language. It has only to be decoded and the world surrenders. It used to be thought that by obeying nature we commanded it. This was the basis of much ancient Amerindian culture. Now, however, it is generally understood that man has become the master and possessor of nature. The need to obey has disappeared.

After many years of research, we have discovered that the most effective and fertile methods of analysing myths are those regulated by algebra. With algebra, we can constitute a set of elements of units by which myths can be compared and by which we can analyse their internal logic. It is to science that we must now look for explanations of mythology. Even such a rambling and misshapen body of artistic entities as mythology can be proven to have a scientific basis.

I shall take several myths indigenous to the Americas and divide them structurally into a set of elements with ordering relations.

The myths I have taken are from the Bering Straits, the Wapisiana people of the Rupununi savannahs and the Tupinamba of Brazil. Amerindian cosmology is at the root of these studies.

Throughout the Americas from as far north as the Bering Straits to the southernmost part of Brazil, one of the most widespread, indigenous myths concerns the eclipse, which represents brother-and-sister incest in the form of a copulating sun and moon. The myths all vary in detail with some overlaps.

What I intend to do is to relate the myths briefly and work out what are constants and what are variables. We can then take certain elements of units and find them repeated in a variety of combinations to which we can apply a mathematical formula.

The first myth is from the Eskimo of the Bering Straits. It concerns a brother who falls in love with his sister and pursues her relentlessly. She takes refuge in the sky and becomes the moon. He continues pursuit in the form of the sun. When he catches up with her they embrace and there is an eclipse.

The Wapisiana myth I am using also concerns the eclipse. They believed that man was at one with nature – incest I should add is the symbol of nature as opposed to society – until an eclipse separated humankind from the animals and plants. They believed that a brother came secretly to his sister at nights. She enjoyed this but, not knowing who he was, blackened his face with the magical genipap plant to identify him. In his shame he rose to the sky and became the moon. That is why the moon has dark patches on its face.

The Tupinamba myth is similar except that the sister deliberately seduces her intoxicated brother at a child-naming feast. She paints his face with genipap to make him beautiful. When he realises what he has done, he rushes out of the house with a bundle of arrows and runs to a clearing in the bush. There, he shoots an arrow into the sky and another one into that and so on until they form a ladder of arrows. He climbs into the sky and becomes the moon. She takes off her skirt and follows him, naked, into the sky and becomes the evening star. Below there remains a child who is never named.

Now, in all these stories there are certain similarities and overlaps. The eclipse. Incest. Metamorphosis into sun, moon or evening star. The split of man from nature. The founding of a magical order. I must also introduce one other element, the tapir, which is the animal symbol for incest amongst many of the South American tribes and which guards the tree of life. There is a savannah creation myth in which two brothers cut down this tree – Mount Roraima, in fact – and a flood gushes from the trunk.

Therefore we have one set of connecting links between:
The eclipse. Incest. The deluge.
And another set of links between:
The tapir. The deluge. Chaos.
If we call each myth by a number, for instance M1, M2, et cetera and let S=sun and M=moon and so on, we can complete a full algebraic set of equivalences.

'What are you reading?'
Rosa looked up. Chofy had approached silently and stood by the bed smiling at her.
'There was this man downstairs who gave me his work to read.'
'What man?'

'Another guest.'

'I want to make love to you.'

'Again?' Rosa was laughing. 'When can I get some work done?'

Chofy flung himself down on the bed next to her.

'I want to dive into that honey-pot and smear myself with honey.' He held her and kissed her on the neck. She ducked out of it. He sat on the bed gazing at her.

'I'm overwhelmed by you. I want to jump you now, this minute. I'm intoxicated by you.'

Rosa attempted to deflect him.

'The man was talking about Wapisiana mythology. You must know something about that. He wants to meet you.'

'I don't know any mythology. Who is this man?'

'His name is Michael Wormoal.'

'Did you talk to him for long?'

Chofy lay across Rosa's bed, his face blank with jealousy.

'I told him about you and what your name means.' She tried to appease him.

'You shouldn't have done that.'

'Why not?'

'We're not supposed to tell people about our names. It's a belief. I only told you because I trusted you.'

'I'm sorry. I didn't know that.'

'I would have come back earlier but I had to fetch this tobacco for my aunt.' He took the packet of tobacco from his pocket and threw it down on the bed.

'Couldn't we go and see your Auntie Wifreda and come back here later?' suggested Rosa.

'I told you, she's sick. I don't know if she can see anyone,' said Chofy coldly.

'Well, I'd like to post some letters. Would you walk to the post office with me?'

'Certainly,' said Chofy with a deliberate display of politeness.

On the way back from the post office, they went upstairs to the Demico Café and sat at one of the white wrought-iron tables ordering a beer each. Rosa paid.

'I'm sorry,' said Chofy. 'I shouldn't have behaved like that. I hardly know you but I feel so jealous about you.'

She smiled at him. Creepers and vines twisted through the lattice behind her head. Her skirt was hitched up by one of the spokes on the chair's arm. Chofy's eyes slid down the length of her pale legs. He watched her drink. As he drank, his face became swollen with lust and he kept staring at her.

'Let's go to the house. I want to screw you. Do you mind me using the word screw?'

'No.'

'I'd just like to put you up against a wall and screw you.'

'Let me finish my beer. And what about your Auntie Wifreda's tobacco?' She laughed.

'Well, we can deliver that first.' He grinned and excused himself to go to the toilet. Beneath the café at the back was a lorry depot. The heat and smell of the grey exhaust fumes and the melting tarmac hung in the hot air. Rosa relaxed. The industrial smell reminded her of London.

'Would you like to come to England? Come and stay with me there?' she asked when he returned.

'Of course.'

They finished another beer each and got up to leave.

Auntie Wifreda had left her sick-bed and was reclining in a chair by the door, the patch still over her eye. After sleeping in a hammock, the bed felt hard.

Chofy introduced Rosa. Auntie Wifreda rolled herself a cigarette, holding it up in front of her good eye. The green parrot perched on the back of her chair, its head on one side, quizzically. Rosa leaned forward and spoke rather loudly, as if Auntie Wifreda might be deaf.

'I met someone called Nancy Freeman in England. She told me that you would remember Evelyn Waugh's visit. I am trying to collect all the information I can about him.'

Auntie Wifreda shifted uncomfortably in her chair and gave an embarrassed laugh.

'That was a long time ago. I can't recall too much.'

Her face showed nothing. It was impossible to tell whether or not she was affected by the visit.

'Can you remember anything, Auntie, that Evelyn Waugh might have done or said?' Chofy intervened eagerly on Rosa's behalf.

'No. Not really.'

'I am hoping to travel to the Rupununi in case I can meet anyone there who might remember him,' Rosa said, trying to jog the old woman's memory.

After thinking for a moment, the old lady replied: 'They all dead now and the rains have started. You wouldn't be able to travel. If my brother Danny was alive, he could have taken you. In his canoe, Danny could find his way like a fish. But he's dead too.'

There it was again, the picture of Danny on his death-bed. Auntie Wifreda began to sweat. The priest was asking Danny exactly what happened to Father Napier and Danny, his bronze skin glowing even more yellow with liver failure, was telling lies with his last breath and saying: 'An epidemic killed him. Nothing else. Just a local epidemic.' Minutes later Danny died. Within hours his body stank so much they had to take it out of the house and the funeral was conducted with his body on a table outside by the river.

Rosa was saying something.

'What?' Auntie Wifreda wiped her brow with the sleeve of her nightdress.

'I was just saying that there was someone else who might like to speak to you. A Mr Wormoal. He's done some research into Wapisiana beliefs about the eclipse. I was just reading about it.'

Suddenly, Auntie Wifreda felt violently ill and hot. She could hear a booming sound in her ears as if someone had struck a heavy bell that vibrated on a long single note. Rosa's face began to melt at the edges and metamorphose into the face of her sister Beatrice. The whole room began to waver. The floor and the walls billowed slowly.

'Leave me. Go away.' She spoke to Chofy in Wapisiana. Chofy anxiously helped her put out her cigarette and climb back into bed. He signalled to Rosa to wait for him outside.

'Do you think she will be all right?' said Rosa anxiously.

'I hope so,' said Chofy.

They walked back towards the Lodge slowly and in silence through the hot afternoon.

'What are you thinking about?' she asked, wondering if he was worrying about his aunt.

'Humming-bird sucking honey,' he replied.

After they had gone, Wifreda lay in bed and understood without doubt that she was losing her sight. Everything rippled like the wake of a boat on the Essequibo. But a blackness was spreading out from the centre. Nausea had loosened her bowels. Even with her one good eye open, all she could see was Beatrice's face whichever way she turned her head. The face moved and distorted like a reflection in creek water when a canoe passes. Wifreda shut her good eye. When she opened it again, everything was entirely black. Beatrice's face still floated in front of her but she knew it was in her mind only. In reality she could see nothing. The long-awaited blindness had finally struck. She heard Beatrice's voice from long ago, screaming with fury.

'I will make you blind, like a termite.'

It had come true. She took off the eye patch and opened and closed her eyes several more times. Everything was black as a parrot's tongue. She heard Beatrice laughing as clearly as if she had just walked into the room. The laughter became jumbled up with the sound of the parrot's chesty giggle behind her. Then Beatrice was sitting at her side, talking to her, prattling on cheerfully about their childhood in the savannahs.

'Yes,' Beatrice was saying. 'The thing I remember best, my first and most vivid memory, is laughing with Danny at Waronawa. I couldn't have been more than three and Danny must have been about five, although who knows, births were never registered in those days. I shall remember the bliss of laughing like that till the day I die.'

PART TWO

WARONAWA

The two of them were naked at the back of the house. A line of washing flapped between the fruit trees and the adobe wall. Three rounds of cassava bread sat drying on the thatch roof and a dirty, white half moon hung in the blue sky. Danny was playing with a wheeler, a pole with two small wooden wheels at the bottom, pushing it backwards and forwards. Beatrice squatted in the red earth, poking at some leaves with a stick. Her face was blotched with dirt.

It was the same red dirt that sat in the fine wire gauze mesh of the windows, the same red dirt that blew through all the savannah Indian dwellings and settled on shelves and beams and rafters; the same fine red dust that coated the drinking water in the huge pottery jar they called the potch. It filled the creases of clothing, clogged the feathers of the bows and arrows, blocked up the barrels of guns, covered the saddles and harnesses hanging on the walls, choked the plants and made everyone's skin thirsty, like a red plague.

'You look like someone paint you with annatto for a party,' said her mother in Wapisiana, smiling at her daughter's smudged face.

Mamai Maba stood by the stove. She wore only a cotton

skirt and her breasts shivered as she worked, feet planted firmly apart, cleaning and gutting a pile of small round silver patwa fish. She threw the intestines on the ground and let the hens dive for them.

Most of the cooking took place outside under a palm-thatch shelter. A long trestle had been rigged up of forked poles with a metal sheet on top. Resting on this, the stove consisted of loosely stacked clay bricks with a gap in the middle; a blackened sheet of metal with a hole in it lay on the bricks and underneath this burned a log, the flames clawing at the air through the hole in the metal.

Every time Mamai Maba threw a handful of fish in the large pan, they jumped. Now and then she flicked her long black hair back over her bare shoulder and wiped her eyes with her forearm because of the stinging woodsmoke.

Beatrice looked up from playing and watched the fish leaping in silver arcs as if to get away from the fire. She had the same beautiful slanting eyes as her mother, black and set so wide apart they seemed ready to fly out of the side of her head. Her complexion was paler and creamier than her mother's. At home they nicknamed her Tapioca-face.

As the smell of frying fish wafted over to him, Danny began to feel hungry. He flung aside the wheeler and came running towards them. Beatrice laughed at the way his penis wiggle-woggled as he ran. Catching her mood, he began to strut and show off in front of his sister, thrusting his little pelvis forward. Beatrice laughed with all the more excitement because she realised that his penis danced like one of the fish cavorting in the pan. It was the first time that she had understood that one thing can be like another. The discovery exhilarated her.

'Do it again. Do it again. Do it some more.'

The more he did it, the more she laughed and he laughed too.

Then he threw himself on top of her and began to tickle her until she went into paroxysms. She squealed and giggled and squirmed in the warm dust. She laughed so much that she nearly choked. She could not tell whether the laughter was inside her or outside her. It was as if she had become a balloon of laughter. She screamed and laughed so much that she thought she would rise into the blue sky with pleasure.

The day was scorching hot. Hearing the children shout, Zuna, Mamai Maba's sister, came lazily to the door of the thatched benab to see if something was the matter. She was pregnant. Both sisters were married to the same white man. They had been jealous of each other at first. Sometimes the jealousy still flared up. But as time went on and especially after Maba had given birth to Danny and Beatrice, they both appreciated that there was too much work for one woman.

'I'll give you a hand with the farine.' Zuna yawned, stretched and waddled over to them. Maba took the pan of fish off the fire and set it aside to cool. The sun filtered through the ite-palm leaves of the roof so that shadows slashed at their faces and turned them to red-gold as they hauled the heavy metal trough over to the flames and struggled to hoist it on to the fire. They filled it with farine and started the back-breaking work of parching it, turning the farine with great paddles, raking it back and forth until it turned golden yellow and fluffy.

Heat from the fire blasted into their faces as they worked. Their eyes turned red with smoke. Zuna began to sweat heavily.

'Go to the lake,' said Maba, looking at her sister's dripping forehead. 'I'll get on with the farine.'

Zuna put down her paddle and rubbed her aching back. Her hair was long like Maba's but her brow was lower which somehow made her look more anxious than her sister. Maba's placid round face rarely looked troubled. Although Maba wore a skirt, Zuna had gone back to wearing her seed apron because clothes felt too hot and restricting now that the baby was nearly due. The little rectangular apron sat beneath her huge belly. It was made entirely of tiny, flat, dun-coloured seeds threaded together, with a fringe of cotton and three yellow macaw feathers fastened to each side.

The small lake at the back drained into the river. It was dry season. Water in both the river and the lake was low. The place stood on a slight rise by the east bank of the Rupununi River. It was called Waronawa – hills of the parrot – but the slope on which they lived was known as the hill of the spirit macaw, because a great scarlet macaw was supposed to live in the lake and to drag unwary passers-by down under the waters.

It was for this reason that Zuna stood stock still when she heard a rustling behind her just as she was bending down at the edge of the lake to throw water on her face and arms. Her heart banged. She turned around. Facing her head-on was the long, brown, pointed snout of a bushy-tailed ant-eater. It stood there, the weight on its great forelegs, and turned a small malevolent eye to look at her. She yelled and the creature grunted and started to amble off through the tufts of dried grass.

Stricken with the thought that the animal had been sent to harm her unborn baby, Zuna just stood where she was and shrieked. Maba threw down her paddle and came running down the trail. When she heard about the ant-eater, she laughed.

'You stupid bad. It's just an ant-eater. Come quick. The farine will spoil.'

That night Zuna gave birth to a daughter. She knelt on the ground and held the hammock in both hands, forcing it down against her belly to help push the baby out. Beatrice and Danny slept through it all in the hammock above. Maba and some of the other women from the settlement helped with the birth by the light of a flickering kerosene lamp and then they all walked down to the river to bathe the new baby. Zuna was relieved that it was over. She was longing to eat beef again and mangoes both of which were forbidden during pregnancy.

They decided to wait until McKinnon returned from Brazil to name the child. When the little girl turned out to have bad eyesight, Zuna blamed it on the way the ant-eater had looked at her. Years later, other people in the settlement said that the child's eyes were already trying to go blind in order not to see what she was eventually to see.

BLUE EYES
MEAN IGNORANCE

A few weeks later, McKinnon returned in high spirits on horseback from a visit to Boa Vista in Brazil where he had heard that someone was able to grow apples. He named the new baby Wifreda after the wife of a friend he had stayed with there.

Alexander McKinnon was a lean, energetic Scotsman in his thirties who prided himself on being a free-thinker. He had arrived in the colony via Jamaica where his father was an archdeacon and where he had been raised. Rejecting the Church and determined to get as far away from civilisation as possible, he struck off into the interior of Guiana with a group of nomadic Atorad Indians who had come to Georgetown to trade. After travelling for several weeks through the wild rain forest which, they told him, was neither darkness nor light but a gigantic memory, he did not know exactly how far up the Essequibo River he had come. Having eaten nothing but cassava bread and saltfish, he fell ill. When he could no longer keep up with them, the Indians abandoned him to lie in his hammock by the river. It was not their custom either to ask for or to give help in such circumstances.

During the daytime, he was tormented by kaboura flies

and mosquitoes and at night he felt the chill river mist reaching into his bones. Thinking he was going to die, he deliberately swallowed all the laudanum in his possession in order to be unconscious at the time of his death. How long he lay in that state he never knew, but eventually, he came round and started to vomit up black stuff like coffee grounds. Having no idea where he was, he crawled along the river bank and after half a day, came to the Wapisiana village of Katiwau in the savannahs.

'When we first saw him,' Maba told the children as she spread clothes on to the prickly bushes to dry in the sun, 'he was creeping along the ground like a dung-beetle, so we couldn't tell what sort of man he was or even if he was a man at all. Usually, you judge a man by how he does walk. If he walk brisk or slapdash or to show himself off, or day-dreamy or idle – the walk will betray him.

'At first I didn't like him. He was thin as a blade of savannah grass and when we were little we were told about a man who pulled a brother out of one eye and a sister out of the other, leaving his own eyes blue and empty like the sky, with no thoughts. Blue eyes meant ignorance. So I kept far from him.

'Then Daddy made me nurse him and I helped him to learn to speak Wapisiana. In the end we got on well. He wanted to stay. We all lived in one huge house then. Everyone in the village discussed it and Daddy gave him permission to hang his hammock next to mine in the big house, which meant that we were married.

'Another man in the village wanted to marry Zuna but our father said that McKinnon must have first choice because it was the tradition amongst Wapisiana people that if a man marries one sister he has first choice of the next one. Your father accepted both of us, so here we are.'

By the time Maba was expecting Danny, McKinnon decided to move away from Katiwau. He travelled as far as possible along the Rupununi River and built a ranch-house. The place was Waronawa. Three miles to the north there was an isolated tree and beyond that, the Kanaku Mountains rose a thousand feet from the savannah floor. He bought cattle from a Dutchman, the only other white man for hundreds of miles, who was selling up and leaving.

Soon most members of Maba and Zuna's family joined them, including their father and mother and brother Shibi-din. Other villagers came and before long a whole Wapisiana settlement grew up there.

The new arrivals helped McKinnon plant fruit trees. They cut cassava farms for themselves and carried on hunting and fishing as usual. They thought McKinnon odd because he liked to experiment. He kept guinea fowl and erected boxes on tarred legs to keep away the cushi ants from the tomatoes he tried to grow in manured earth. He accumulated a flock of sheep. At first, he planned to take parrots and monkeys to sell in Georgetown but the long journey made it impracticable. He tried to send down samples of dried beef, but people ate the samples and didn't put in any orders. He tried Brazil nuts. That failed too. His herd of cattle grew, more by default than anything.

Gradually, he gave up the ideas he had once had of creating a flourishing business of one sort or another. The land seemed set against it. The harsh surroundings defeated one project after another and little by little, he settled into the traditions of the Wapisiana people. He spoke nothing but Wapisiana because nobody around him knew any English. After a while, he picked up enough Portuguese to manage when he went over the river to Brazil. On his rare visits to Georgetown, he always returned with books for his library and with photographic equipment because photography was his great passion.

He was aware that Maba and Zuna and the others on the settlement tolerated with good humour his efforts to be innovative because he often saw them catching each other's eyes and giggling when he suggested a new scheme. He wondered why they were never surprised or disappointed when each fresh idea of his failed and gradually he came to realise that they laughed at the idea of progress, despised novelty and treated it with suspicion. Novelty, in fact, was dangerous. It meant that something was wrong with the order of things. Maba, particularly, treated his enthusiasm for innovation with squeaks of lighthearted derision.

It was confusing for McKinnon. He settled in to the life well at one level, but every now and then he caught a glimpse of a world he did not understand at all. He tried to discuss things with his father-in-law who was something of a philosopher and who explained to McKinnon that there was no point in trying to do anything about everyday life. It was an illusion behind which lay the unchanging reality of dream and myth.

'We look for the mask behind the face,' he said, shaking his finger and laughing. McKinnon decided he would be better off just concentrating on the practicalities of life.

All the same, he could not help being disappointed at the apathy which greeted his experiments. When he first developed photographs of the Kanaku Mountains and showed them to people, he thought they would be astounded. But no one took much notice. He asked Maba why there was so little interest in the photographs. She laughed in an embarrassed way, sensing that her own people had disappointed him.

'It is because they are not required,' she tried to explain about the photographs.

Similarly, he once found her running in panic down the trail to the house. When he asked her what was the matter, she took him and showed him a white fungus growing on the path.

'What's the matter? Is it poisonous?' he asked.

'No. It is not poisonous. But it doesn't need to be there.'

On the other hand, people welcomed anything he brought back from town that proved useful: knives, fish-hooks, axe-heads, gunpowder and bolts of cloth for making cotton trousers and skirts. Nobody could understand what drove him to keep trying out new things or why he continually pottered about when he could have been lying in his hammock. But he was tolerated with equanimity. People could see that it pleased him to have these plans.

'These plans – they help him to avoid seeing what life is really like,' said Maba's father, who knew that the books McKinnon brought back would soon be attacked by wood-ants, blotched by cockroaches, perforated by bookworms or eaten by scale-moths.

In Georgetown, the gossip was that McKinnon was now more Indian than European. The upper classes of the colony despised him when he arrived from the bush in a leather vaqueiro hat. They reserved for him that particular hatred which colonists have for one who they feel has betrayed his race and class. They said he was useless at animal husbandry and that his cattle roamed uncontrollably without supervision. Because he worked in the Indian manner alongside family and friends, tending livestock without the usual division between employer and employee, they feared what such an example might do to the colony. Fortunately, he was in such a remote part of the hinterland, he could more or less be forgotten. One man who travelled back with him as far as the Potaro River returned and reported how McKinnon would light fires like an Indian to signal his approach and avoid confrontation with other Indians who might be hostile.

'He gone buck,' they sneered behind his back.

McKinnon must have brought the measles back with him when he returned from Brazil. Both Beatrice and the new baby caught it.

Maba took Beatrice into the bedroom. It was the only room that contained a bed. McKinnon preferred to make love in a bed rather than a hammock or down by the river. It had taken him eight weeks to transport the iron bedstead and mattress from Georgetown. He had also introduced tables and the idea of using plates instead of eating from leaves. His two wives grumbled at the extra work.

Maba put the child on the bed. Zuna stood by cradling the baby. Maba knew that the illness stretched like a web over her daughter but was not sure whether it extended up the walls and over part of the floor as well. Because she was not sure of the boundaries of the illness, she kept everybody else out of the room until she could call the piaiwoman. Beatrice lay still, her face swollen and spotted, her black hair plastered down with perspiration. Maba bathed her incessantly to keep down the fever.

Koko Lupi arrived in the afternoon. She was well known for her sulky temper and her talent for quarrelling and drinking as well as her ability to fly. Children stared at the goitre on her neck, her black teeth, and her claw-like hands as she examined Beatrice who lay stewing in fever. Immediately, she pointed out that the clustered rosettes over Beatrice's body were like the imprints on a jaguar's hide. She instructed that the room be kept pitch dark. Every crack or crevice where light could enter was covered. Zuna had laid the baby down next to Beatrice. People crowded into the room and settled down in the dark. The room was stifling. Koko Lupi lifted Beatrice first and blew on her with tobacco smoke, first on her head, then on her breast, belly, hands and feet. Then she did the same with the baby, chanting a healing tareng all the while.

The airless room began to stink of smoke. Koko Lupi took a swig of parakari from a calabash, gargled with some tobacco juice and spat on the floor. Then she set about calling down certain spirits to heal the children. There was the sound of leaves rustling and branches creaking. Making noises from her throat like a drum roll, the piaiwoman called down a liana vine spirit for the other spirits to climb down. The baby whimpered.

A few moments later there was the clear sound of a great otter wailing and then the chatter of a macaw. Neither of these seemed to be what Koko Lupi wanted because she yelled at them to go away. After a long wait, there came the unmistakable sound of a jaguar's throaty snuffle and a phenomenally deep roar rumbled round the room. These noises alternated with the piaiwoman's voice clearly pleading with the beast, scolding it and flattering it and remonstrating with it, telling it to go away and stop troubling the children. The crowded room was silent. Everyone could hear the jaguar pad up to the bed, snort, roar and pad away again.

The session lasted several hours. After it was over and everyone emerged dazed into the daylight, Beatrice was allowed to stay in the bed for a few days until the jaguar prints faded. McKinnon was relieved to see both children recover. He had been leaning back against the wall during the healing ceremony. Privately, he thought that the ceremony was just as likely to produce results as praying to a Christian god.

Beatrice remained weak for a long time afterwards. Her mother noticed that she was more serious and played on her own at the back of the house. The illness left her with a slight cast in her right eye which looked outward more than it should have done. Maba was not unhappy about this. Secretly she had worried that her daughter was too beautiful. Some of the other women had been jealous and she had seen one poking at Beatrice with a stick. She preferred Beatrice to have a slight flaw. As Beatrice grew up, the cast which pulled her right eye slightly to one side made her look, when she talked to people, as if she constantly desired to escape elsewhere.

After a few months, Beatrice was back to being her happy-go-lucky self and Wifreda had also recovered completely. Beatrice and Wifreda developed different temperaments as they grew. Beatrice was outgoing and congenial. Wifreda had a closed-in face and clung to her own mother.

Maba and Zuna had overlapping pregnancies. Alice arrived next, then Joachim and Laurie and eventually four others. By that time, nobody could remember very well who belonged to which mother. Besides, in the Wapisiana language the word 'mamai' for mother and aunt was the same. There was no distinction. The family structure was entirely different from anything McKinnon had known.

McKinnon constructed more buildings and outhouses to accommodate the extra infants. He also built a little store house where people came from miles around to barter goods.

Danny and Beatrice ran wild. All the children grew in a way that reminded McKinnon of the game of grandmother's footsteps that he used to play when he was young. Every time he looked round they seemed to have secretly grown taller. Danny particularly grew headstrong and wicked with a radiant, malignant wildness both playful and deadly.

'I want to burn it. I want to burn it,' he would say, eagerly holding a moth in the flame of a lamp.

Maba and Zuna tried to restrain him in various ways.

'I goin' to spit on the ground. If you're not back by the time it dry, you're in trouble,' Maba would tell him and then chop at his legs with a cutlass if he disobeyed. One day, he came in inconsolable after a fight and flung himself in a hammock and refused to eat for two days.

Nobody could get out of him what was wrong. Then one of the other children told Maba. Danny's cousin had been taunting him that McKinnon was a white man and not a Wapisiana. Danny refused to look his father in the face. He took his hammock and went over to his grandmother's benab.

'I'm a Macusi. They don't like me either,' grumbled his ancient grandmother sourly. She was sitting on the ground in the doorway spinning cotton. The flesh hung from her upper arm in minute concertina folds and swung to and fro as she worked the spindle. Danny remained sulking in the dark, watching. She embarked on a story designed to make him feel better but also to foster in him a dislike of his father whom she had always distrusted.

'Long time ago, the sun was a person like us. He spent all day clearing and burning a field to plant. His face shone with work. One day when he went to the stream to bathe, he saw a mysterious whirlpool gurgling in the centre of the stream. When he looked close he saw a small woman with long hair playing, smacking the water with her hair, splashing about and bathing.

'He grabbed her by the hair.

'"Let me go and I'll send you a wife," she yelled.

'He let her go. The next day he saw a white woman approaching across the field. She did various jobs for him and then he told her to go to the stream and fetch water. She went with her gourd but as she bent down to fill it, her fingers softened and lost their shape, then her arms and then her whole body. She collapsed into a little heap of clay. The woman had been made of white earth.

'When the sun went to look for her, he only found some murky water and had to go further upstream to drink.

'"Useless," he said.

'The next day, a black woman appeared. He sent her to fetch water. She brought water back and they ate together. When the meal was finished, he returned to work. She went to light a fire, but as she blew on it, her face melted, then her arms then her whole body. She had been made of wax.

'The sun was livid. He went and threatened to dry up all the water in the stream. The water spirit hid and called to him she would send someone else.

'As he stooped over his work the next day, a reddish, rock-coloured woman appeared. She lit the fire and didn't melt. She fetched water and didn't melt. She went away that night and came back in the morning to prepare food for him. He found that she didn't dissolve or melt or break apart. She became attractive to him. When they bathed together he found that she was a reddy-bronze colour, like the bits of firestone found in river beds.

'He wanted her to come to his house. She said she would have to ask Tuenkaron, the water spirit. That night she came back to sleep with the sun. They had several children. These were the Macunaima. The two eldest brothers, Macunaima and Chico, are our heroes.

'Now,' said Danny's grandmother, 'come into the doorway and look at your arm in the sunlight.' Danny came grudgingly. 'You're a reddish brown. You talk Wapisiana. You belong in the savannahs with us.' Danny continued to wind thread around the butt of an arrow while studying his arm.

'I hope my father melts,' he said. 'Melts away altogether.'

A BLAST OF HEAT

In 1905, when Beatrice and Danny were still playing in the dirt, a man arrived in the colony who was to have as far-reaching an effect on their destiny as they were to have on his. Father Napier, a Jesuit with a fine tenor voice, stood on deck, leaning with one elbow on the rail as the ship waited outside the Demerara bar to dock. He was a thin, nervous man whose top teeth protruded a little as if he had sucked his thumb too much as a child. He held back his fine, sandy hair with his hand to stop it blowing in his eyes as he surveyed the scene.

The first sight of the place depressed him beyond belief. The coast ahead of him was flat and uninspiring, fringed with low, green bush and divided by numerous inlets. He gripped the rail, feeling a little nauseous at the slight swell, and looked down. Sea waters the colour of pea soup slapped lethargically at the side of the boat. The smell of mud, fish and salt gave him a forlorn feeling and the blowing of a steady warm wind filled him with melancholy. The sun already seemed to have struck at his bowels.

With a forced smile on his face, as if to encourage the other passengers alongside him at the deck-rail – lest they too felt disheartened at the prospects ahead of them – he braced himself to defy whatever hardships were to face him, arguing to himself that the greater the hardships, the greater the glory to God in overcoming them. He was here to serve the Master.

Ignoring his presentiments and the oblique warning given to him by the Wild Coast, he made up his mind to pit himself against whatever befell him. It was his ambition to strike into the interior of the country as soon as possible, to evangelise the most remote regions of the empire. Whatever was of the utmost difficulty he would embrace.

Before the ship even docked, he had mistaken an omen for a challenge.

As the tide turned and the ship came in to dock on the current, Father Napier was overcome by the sickly, sweet smell of brown sugar from the wharves and downcast by the sight of several dismal harbour buildings clustered together. Large clouds of insects buzzed around the tin-roofed customs sheds.

He returned to the cramped cabin below deck to collect his two small bags and lie down for a minute or two while the other passengers crowded off the gangplank. He prayed for the success of his mission. The prayer deteriorated into fantasies of his own heroism in the eyes of God. Thoughts of martyrdom and possibly even sainthood crossed his mind as he lay on his bunk. Hastily, he tried to suppress them. He prayed for humility. But the thoughts kept creeping back, leaving him with a warm glow inside.

The next day, Father Napier, desperately eager to start on his mission, stood on the sloping, wooden top floor of the presbytery, which was the Bishop's office. The rattle of passing dray-carts drifted in from the street through the open window.

The Bishop was a heavy-set, Germanic-looking man with

steel-rimmed glasses, whose enormous ego grazed quietly every day on tit-bits of flattery. He was half asleep.

Father Napier wanted permission to go straight away into the interior. The Bishop, a man whose serenity was, in fact, a discreet camouflage for sloth, tried to dissuade him from going, fearing that he himself would be obliged to undertake an unpleasant journey into the interior to supervise the founding of such a mission.

'Spend a little time here in Georgetown.' He spoke slowly, his mouth struggling against a yawn. 'Get to know the place gradually.' Father Napier was obliged to concede to his wishes.

By dint of burning fervour, Father Napier overcame some of the habitual apathy and lassitude he encountered in Georgetown society. Apart from his regular duties, taking mass, marrying and baptising, he set about organising a cathedral choir with Portuguese, black, East Indian and coloured choristers whom he trained personally. Music was one of his passions. He would tap on the chair back with his baton, delighted at the opportunity of demonstrating some cadence or other in his own melodic tenor voice.

He mounted concerts too in the Assembly Rooms for which extra chairs had to be brought in, so eager were the upper classes of the colony to hear excerpts from *Peer Gynt*, the Grand March from *Tannhäuser* and, of course, the solos performed by the Governor's daughter. This last creature was a tall, gangly girl with long fair hair, who leaned backwards when she walked and raised her knees like a giraffe. But she had a passable voice and Father Napier included her in his programmes, hoping to use his influence to convert her from the Protestant heresy.

There was no giving up, however, on his overriding ambition to evangelise the interior and after five years in Georgetown, the Bishop's will was eventually eroded by

Father Napier's persistent requests and he gave permission for the evangelisation of the savannahs. Father Napier had explained to the Bishop that, if they both undertook a tour of the south-west borders of the country, he could be sure that the Brazilians on the other side would give a mammoth, triumphal greeting to a man of his stature. Vanity overcame sloth and the Bishop agreed.

In November, 1909, the apprehensive Bishop and an enthusiastic Father Napier arranged for a boat to be stacked with provisions. They hired a crew and set off up the Essequibo River, to journey through the forest until they reached their final destination in the savannahs.

As he stepped out of the forest and into the savannahs, the heat struck Father Napier like a blast from an oven door.

After the long journey through the forest, the Bishop and Father Napier reacted entirely differently when they finally emerged into the savannahs. The Bishop heaved a sigh of relief, mopped his face with a handkerchief and blessed God that he was in the open once more. He found the forest oppressive.

Father Napier took one look out over the red plains and his heart sank. It was midday. No clouds in the sky. Dry season made the parched earth and rocks act as reflectors for the sun's rays. There were no roads or bridges, just Indian trails in all directions. The trails were all narrow and appeared to meander. Father Napier bent down and picked up a handful of soil. It was light and sandy. Nowhere was there any shade.

It had been arranged that the two churchmen would meet McKinnon at Zariwa, a spot high on bare ground near the bank of the Takatu River. McKinnon wanted to photograph the Bishop under the triumphal arch which the Brazilians had indeed erected for the occasion. A band with hoarse, seductive trumpets and a horde of Indian children accompanied the Bishop wherever he went. The Bishop looked around him in horror at the aridity of the place. There were a few thatched shacks. The band had come together from various scattered Brazilian ranches in the area. He raised his crook in acknowledgement of the curious populace, most of whom had come in from Bom Success. The sweat gathered in the creases of his fat neck and beads appeared in the indentation above his top lip.

The sun had started to sink when McKinnon shook hands with Father Napier. The two men took an almost instant dislike to each other.

A strong evening breeze stroked flat the dun-coloured grasses where they stood on a slight slope near the river, with the blue mountains silhouetted in the background.

'You'd better understand straightaway that I do not belong to any religion. I am a free-thinker,' McKinnon announced mischievously as he introduced himself. It was a pleasure to be speaking English again after so many months, even to a priest.

Father Napier ran his fingers through his sandy hair, barely able to suppress his disgust. His future success in founding missions could depend on McKinnon who had lived amongst the south savannah Indians for years and so he did not say what was on his mind. But when he discovered that McKinnon lived with two sisters as his wives, he could not restrain himself.

'I myself think that is an intolerable arrangement,' he said sharply.

'Nevertheless, that is the case. It is an Indian tradition.' McKinnon enjoyed the priest's discomfort and continued: 'Two of my daughters are over there.' And he pointed to Beatrice and Wifreda who were amongst a group of mainly naked children, listening to the musicians. 'They're staying with the Marinheiro family to learn Portuguese.'

The cacophonous band started up again in the background. The Bishop was making a speech in halting Portuguese that was not understood by most of the Macusi Indians who had gathered round.

'I think I should found a mission right here,' said Father Napier.

'It is not a good place,' said McKinnon, spurred by a resentment of the priest. 'Nothing grows here and there is no good fishing and no game. The Indians would not like it here.'

Immediately, Father Napier suspected that McKinnon was trying to subvert his evangelical purpose.

'Well. I shall give it a try anyway,' he said defiantly.

Within weeks, Father Napier had set up a mission and changed the name of Zariwa to St Ignatius.

It was some months later, after he had firmly established himself in the north savannahs, that Father Napier made his first, tentative journey beyond the Kanaku Mountains to the Wapisiana territory of the south. He travelled to Waronawa by bullock cart. Progress was slow. Gradually, the Kanakus grew closer and with his guide, he made his way round the most westerly point of the range and across the Sawariwau creek.

In the dry season, the palm-thatch roofs of the small Indian settlements look ash-grey from a distance and glint silver in the sun. This was the sight that greeted Father Napier as he approached Waronawa.

Despite his reservations about the new priest, McKinnon would never have dreamed of refusing him hospitality. With no roads, hotels, lodging houses or shops, the savannahs could prove a harsh environment for strangers. Droughts and floods alternately scoured the arid landscape. For months at a time, the sky was a stretched blue canvas bleached almost white by the heat. Then, during the rainy season, grey blubbery clouds filled the sky and tempestuous rains and winds whipped lake, rivers and ponds into a frenzy.

As he approached the settlement, a Wapisiana man of about forty came running up from the direction of the Rupununi River. It was Uncle Shibi-din. His brown back gleamed. His arrows were grasped in one hand and his bow was slung over one shoulder. Several large houri fish swung to and fro, skewered on one of his arrows. Father Napier was struck by the man's face, full of life and vigour. He nodded and smiled a greeting. Shibi-din ran straight on and ignored him.

Maba watched cautiously from the door as the sandy-haired priest in his black robe climbed over the side of the cart and jumped to the ground. She noted immediately that his springy gait was not suited to the savannahs. It wasted energy. You have to walk at the right pace in the savannahs. Walk too fast and the savannah will slow you down. Walk too slow and it will leave you behind and you will die. This man was nervous and jerky like a fowl-cock.

Maba dissolved back into the shadows as he came up the slope, leaving the greetings to McKinnon who came to the door in jovial and expansive mood and showed Father Napier to a hammock where he could rest after his bone-shaking ride.

Later the priest got up and explored his surroundings.

Beatrice and Danny were now the oldest of ten children and the family had spread through two other adobe and thatch buildings. Inside the first of these, Father Napier found that it was darker but with more space than he had imagined. Rooms had been made with wooden partition walls that did not reach all the way up to the eaves so that air could circulate easily. The place was full of pets. Close to the wall, a baby ant-eater slunk past him. Green parrots perched on top of the partitions. Puppies survived as best they could. Baby tortoises dithered underfoot. A brown monkey gibbered in a cage that hung by the back door and a tapir made free use of all the facilities.

Some of the rooms had beds but in most of them, hammocks had been slung. One room seemed to have been put aside for leather work and was full of deer- and cow-hides. Another was used by McKinnon as a dark room for his photography. Outside were two open outhouses for storing tackle and harnesses and mending gear for the ranch cowboys.

While Father Napier poked around downstairs, McKinnon sat upstairs reading. Unusually, the main house had a second storey, another of McKinnon's innovations. To his delight, Father Napier had brought with him several old and yellowing copies of *The Times*. The sun poured in as he read.

Apart from the treat of having newspapers to read, McKinnon was relishing the perverse pleasure of having told both the Anglican priest from Yupokari and Father Napier, the Catholic, that whichever one of them reached Waronawa first could baptise his children. He reckoned himself to be a liberal and not fanatical enough to ban religion from his house altogether just because he himself had rejected it.

The two priests had been involved in an undignified race across eighty miles of savannah in order to be the first to rescue the lost souls of the McKinnon family. Father Napier had won.

'You can use my dark room for mass,' said McKinnon casually.

All the children were gathered together except Danny, who had been baptised an Anglican on a previous visit to Yupokari, and Beatrice and Wifreda who had already been baptised by the Bishop when they were in Brazil.

When Father Napier enquired about Maba and Zuna, McKinnon replied provocatively: 'Oh it's too late for them to change. They believe in a wonderful tree, you know, that has all the fruits of the earth on it. It was chopped down by two brothers, Tuminkar and Duid – the Macusi call them Macunaima and Chico. Anyway, a huge flood sprang out of the stump. I think I rather prefer that story to the story of Noah.'

Father Napier bristled but refused to become involved in an argument although he sensed the mockery in McKinnon's tone. He understood that Waronawa was a key settlement in the south savannahs. Wapisiana came from miles around to squat on the ground, exchange news, discuss problems and barter goods at the small wooden store. McKinnon seemed to be accepted as an unofficial touchau or chief of the Wapisiana. The priest could not afford to antagonise him. However, time was on his side. I will convert the Macusi first, he thought. I have already made a beginning there.

The women took their morning bathe together naked in the lake under a blank sky. One fat, smooth-browed woman trod water, keeping afloat by paddling her arms.

'I don't like that priest. He walk funny,' she said.

'Just wait. He'll go away. They all go away if you wait long enough.' Her neighbour was washing her hair and ducking underwater to rinse it. 'My husband met some Macusi who said he's causing problems there. Apparently he built himself a church-house and a couple went and spent the night making love in it. He came shouting round the village in a big, loud voice and said he'd have to build it all over again.'

'I don't trust Macusis,' said the first woman. 'You can't believe a word they say. They might be getting something nice from him that they don't want us to have.'

'He likes a man to have one wife and so do I,' said Auntie Bobo, floating face up like an overturned turtle. 'If I thought my husband had someone else, I would chop him.'

'Maba and Zuna seem to get on all right now,' said another woman, out of the blue.

'Yes. Better than they used to. They were jealous bad. They never knew whose hammock he was going to rock. It drove Maba mad. She cut Zuna's head open with a stone once.'

THE GIANT
GRASSHOPPER

That evening, most of the Wapisiana from the settlement crowded silently round McKinnon's table and helped themselves to the food. People had come out of curiosity to see the new priest. Some of the villagers settled down to eat sitting on the floor with their backs to the plank walls.

On the table stood a huge cauldron filled to the brim with pepper-pot. The children climbed on the benches to dip their cassava bread into the pot. A side of roast deer had been carried in from the outside kitchen and sat next to a clay dish of farine stuffing. Piles of cassava bread stood alongside dishes of rice, bowls of shibi and gourds of coconut water.

Two of the vaqueiros started to discusss in Wapisiana whether or not to go after the jaguar which had caught a calf and bitten it on the head. Father Napier could not understand a word of what was being said. He made a mental note that he must learn the language if he was to make any headway at all with converting these people. McKinnon was listening seriously to the discussion. It was not even the rainy season yet, the time when jaguars and pumas usually come after the pigs and cattle. Occasionally, McKinnon remembered to translate for his guest.

Auntie Bobo, who had stout legs and a man's laugh, sat with her back to the wall and wriggled her toes.

'I wouldn't like to get him down by the river,' she said, looking over at Father Napier. 'He's so thin he looks like he'd snap in two in my arms like a twig.' She roared with laughter.

Beatrice and Wifreda came running over to join the fun.

'There was this girl,' continued Auntie Bobo, warming to her audience, 'who was told not to go down by the river when her husband was away. Well, she did of course. And a huge hairy monster came and had sex with her. His penis was so big and he fucked so hard that the penis came right out through the top of her head. And the girl turned into – oh what's the bird's name – the one with a bald patch on its head that waddles like it's sore?'

'A coot,' giggled Beatrice.

All the women were smiling and Auntie Bobo laughed so hard she had to wipe her eyes with the corner of her skirt. Maba was frowning as she looked at Wifreda.

'We must do something about Wifreda's eyes. She can hardly see the small grass seeds when she's threading necklaces.'

'Get Koko Lupi to ask the ducks for help. That's what she did for my daughter's eyes. Ducks make a good, clear path through the muck on top of a pond. She'll get them to make Wifreda's eyes shiny and clear the same way,' said a neighbour.

Father Napier was explaining earnestly to McKinnon that he would confirm the children when they were old enough to received proper instruction.

'They must be able to understand the idea of eternal life after death through Christ and the resurrection,' he said earnestly. McKinnon grinned cynically.

Maba was taking in what her neighbour had said about the ducks.

'Yes, ducks,' she said thoughtfully, 'and maybe parrots too. They cut a clean path through woodsmoke. She needs help from any of those creatures that would make her eyes clear.'

Something had set Auntie Bobo off again. She rocked with laughter and pointed at Shibi-din who was drunk on parakari and staggering towards a bench.

Just then, Danny came flying through the door, his black hair sticking up on top like two crossed fingers, his face glowing.

'Mamai. I kill a rat. I mash it on the head, then I cut it, then I lick it in the belly and all the guts spill out. It was a young one.'

'Where was the rat?' asked Maba.

'Under my hammock.'

'Take one of the dogs in there with you tonight.'

McKinnon called Danny over and introduced Father Napier to his eldest son who grimaced with shyness as he mumbled hello in English.

'Well, young man. Soon it will be Easter and you will be on holiday. What do you do then?'

Danny was confused.

'I walk about and I sleep,' he answered.

And for the first time it occurred to McKinnon that his son could barely speak English and that he had had no schooling.

'The children are going to school in Georgetown soon,' he mumbled gruffly.

Which was the first anyone had heard of it.

Shadows jigged on the high thatched eaves. The women and children cleared everything away, throwing bones and scraps outside for the dogs and chickens.

And then Father Napier did an astonishing thing that was remembered and talked about for months afterwards. In the gloomy, flickering light, he got up from the table, went over to his bags, took a violin out from its case and began to tune it.

He then proceeded to play the last movement of Mozart Sonata K.304 in E minor.

Auntie Bobo's body stiffened and jerked as she clamped her hand over her mouth to prevent the laughter bursting out. Everybody watched as the priest paced the floor, his body bending backwards and forwards, his right arm holding the bow, sawing at the instrument with gusto.

Someone remarked that he looked and sounded like a great grasshopper rubbing its legs together and the room fell silent as everybody absorbed this information with some concern.

Moved by the idea that he was introducing these people to the classics for the first time and convinced, even as he played, that the awed silence proved how entranced they were by the music, Father Napier felt his eyes fill with tears.

Everyone else in the room, except McKinnon who was just amused, watched with a sort of horror as, before their eyes, the priest turned into a giant, buzzing, savannah grasshopper.

That night as Beatrice lay in her hammock, the light of the moon punched a hole the size of a fist in the thatch and seemed to spread down the rope until she was suspended in a hammock of light. The foot of the hammock looked like the prow of a canoe. She glanced over to where her sisters slept. Their hammocks too floated like shadow canoes suspended in dark space. Through the door, she could see Danny sitting on a stool pretending to read by the light from a flaming wick in a bowl of beef fat. The flame was unsteady but she could see Danny staring with great intensity at a book, his hair still sticking up. The moon bathed her part of the room in the light of a strong ghost.

As she dozed off, she wondered why he was doing that – pretending to read when he couldn't.

DEER HUNT

It was night and the deer was hiding somewhere in the tall grasses. Danny lay on the side of the sloping hill. The rough grass under him felt like the pelt of an animal. He almost imagined he could feel it breathing. In the moonlight, he could just see the outline of Uncle Shibi-din's back. Then Shibi-din signalled him silently to move down-wind of the deer and they set off as quietly as possible in the moonlight, avoiding any twigs that might crack or rustle underfoot. His uncle had rubbed them both down with the scent gland of a deer, and painted the outline of deer bones vertically on their cheeks.

Shibi-din had seen the deer's eyes glint green for a second in the light of the moon. Danny had already learned that at night the deer's eyes shine green, the tiger's orange and the alligator's red.

As they closed in on where he had seen the animal, Shibi-din fired off an arrow. The wounded deer bolted further into the undergrowth. Shibi-din pretended he was too tired to follow it.

'You go and get it,' he said.

Danny felt sick with nerves. He knew he was being sent

for his first deer and the adrenalin rushed through him. His uncle had trained him how to smell blood. Danny approached the grasses which were taller than he was and let his nostrils open until he scented the slightly metallic smell of blood on the leaves. Then he moved forward in the dark, following the scent, feeling for broken bushes and looking for where the grass was trampled down. His heart was banging. Even wounded, the animal could give a vicious kick. Suddenly, the stench of blood and hair was overwhelming and the deer was panting on the ground in front of him under a bush. He hesitated for a moment because of the way the animal looked at him and then finished it off with another arrow through the eye.

Danny was exuberant as they dragged it to where they had tethered the horse.

'I felt sad when it looked at me, though,' Danny said, watching Shibi-din, strong as an ox, sling the dead animal over the horse's back.

'I know. I shot a monkey in a tree once. It wasn't a good shot and the monkey was just wounded in the thigh. But I saw him gather bunches of leaves to staunch the wound. I've never liked to shoot a monkey since. It was too human. Animals are people in disguise, they say. I can believe that. Some people say we are just the prophetic dreams of animals. Their nightmares. I could believe that too.'

They began to walk back under the bright stars. Shibi-din went on talking seriously.

'You know, a long time ago we could all speak the language of plants and animals. Animals was people like we. No difference between us. Then one day this man cut a bow and arrow and shot a deer for meat. He dragged it through the bushes and roasted it. Where the blood fell, all the plants shrank back and accused him of murder.

'"You killed a deer. You killed a creature," they screamed.

"Keep away from us." He cut more plants and they screamed. That day, a bite seemed to be taken from the sun. Everything went dark and the whole savannah turned the colour of rust-coloured blood. When the eclipse was over and the sun became itself again, we Wapisiana people had lost our immortality and we could no longer speak to the plants and animals. Everywhere there was a dreadful stink. That's why they say the loss of immortality has to do with a bad smell.'

Danny's calf muscles were aching so much he could hardly walk another step. He kept getting a stitch in his side and slowing down. All he wanted to do was ride home on horseback. Shibi-din kept pushing him on.

'The horse needs to save its strength,' he said.

It took them five hours to cover the fourteen miles home.

The next morning, Danny was darting around, elated and boasting, while Maba and Zuna skinned the deer and stretched and pinned the hide out on the wall to dry in the sun.

All the rest of that dry season, Danny hung around after Shibi-din, going everywhere with him.

Gradually, Shibi-din unravelled for him the complex tangle of stars in the sky until Danny thoroughly understood which stars indicated which season.

'Everything has its master in the stars,' explained Shibi-din. 'Everything that moves, that is. You don't find plants and trees in the sky because they have roots and can't move.'

He pointed out a certain constellation.

'That's the Master of Fish. That constellation signals the rains and tells you when it's fish-breeding time. The little group of stars at the top we call the Tapir – the tapir is also connected to the rainy season. You've heard people say: "Shoot a tapir and rain soon come." They're numerous around the time of the rains.'

He pointed out the topmost star of the Southern Cross.

'When that top star reaches its highest point in the sky you'll hear the powis bird cry – that grunting cough. It cries at a different time every night – but always when that star is at its height.'

A few minutes later they heard the bird call.

Danny soaked up all the knowledge. He learned that each constellation was a being who used to live on earth and had gone up to the sky to avoid persecution and to be in charge of a particular creature. Soon he could tell by the stars when labba or bush-hog would be plentiful; when the high grasses of the thunder maize were likely to seed; when the frogs would start to sing and the fish spawn. He could distinguish the scorpion rainfall from the crab rainfall and predict when the black swallows would come twittering from the caves and rivers, darkening the sky as they dived after the swarms of insects.

Sometimes Shibi-din frightened him. Everyone knew to avoid Shibi-din when he was drinking. Once he had shaken the beams and pulled his own roof down leaving his wife and children looking at the stars.

The only time the children saw Maba angry enough to raise her voice was when she miscarried and lost twins – for which she was profoundly grateful, twins being a bad sign. One of the men in the village, a skinny, hollow-cheeked trouble-maker, started up the rumour that she had been having sex with a river dolphin and that she had given birth early to two little pink dolphins.

He said that he had been watching from the other side of the bank when she put them back in the river and had seen them wriggle away downstream.

'They had nice firm flesh like silver balata,' he said.

It was rainy season. Maba, furious, waded through the flooded tracts of land and went from house to house tracking down the source of the rumour. Finally, she confronted the man inside his benab.

'We all know how you like to dig in your wife's bottom and spread it round everywhere,' she shouted from the doorway. 'Well, get your wife to sew her bottom up so you can't find any more shit.'

The wife threw a log at her but she ducked and walked firmly back through the sheeting rain which plastered her hair all round her head and broad shoulders as she splashed her way back to the house.

She too had had a fright at the sight of the two foetuses in the sac when she miscarried in a patch of bush near the river. To her the tiny embryos looked as if they had horse's heads and lizard's feet.

Maba was not sure why she did not entirely trust her eldest daughter. Most people praised Beatrice for being a hard-working, happy-natured girl but Maba had her private reservations. She sensed something secretive about Beatrice and Maba did not approve of mystery.

Although she never mentioned it to anyone, not even Zuna, it had occurred to her that Beatrice might be one of the water people, who live on earth during the day and underwater at night, but who are otherwise indistinguishable from ordinary people. She did not know for the life of her why she felt that way about Beatrice but she did. Maba was practical and this aspect of her daughter offended her in some way. She noticed that Beatrice never paired up with any of the boys although most girls of her age were doing so. She seemed to keep herself apart.

When Beatrice herself was older and looked back to try

and understand what had happened, she remembered that her first sexual experiences had not come about through human agency.

It was at the blazing height of the dry season. She was about eleven and was leaning against the doorpost of the house, one foot raised and resting against it, watching some of the other children. Two of them were having a wrestling match in the dust. Some others were kicking a balata ball around on the hard ground where the tawny earth had been baked by the sun and tamped down by years of footsteps and horses' hooves.

Beatrice's chest was still flat but her nipples had begun to swell and they pushed against her skimpy dress like two baby turtle heads. Her hair was tied at the neck. The doorpost was hot against her back. Boom. Bang. The ball smacked against the yellow adobe wall beside her head. The heat was making her newly sprouted breasts tingle and the hotter the sun became, the more she became aware of an incandescent darkness at the bottom of her belly, between her legs, in a mysterious place that she had hardly been aware of before.

She vaguely heard the others shouting as they played but they seemed to be calling from a distance, some faraway place. The sun burned even more fiercely and as the sun grew in intensity, so the darkness inside her turned into a delicious fizzing feeling that just teetered on the edge of an explosion and then died away again. She just stood there. The other children had stopped playing and were collecting their arrows and bows to go fishing.

They called for her to join them but she turned away and went into the house and swung in her hammock.

After that, Beatrice often tried to make the feeling come back again. Sometimes she could just be sitting astride the rough poles of a fence and it would start. The heat could trigger it too, when she was standing in the sun leaning against one of the houseposts. Occasionally, she could almost make it happen if she hoisted herself up between two tree branches, clenched her thigh muscles and just wriggled. Her body knew that if she could only keep that feeling going for long enough something wonderful would happen, but her arms always grew tired first and she would drop to the ground. The puzzling thing was that it was unpredictable. Sometimes it happened and sometimes not. Sometimes it just happened when she was walking down to the creek. She preferred it when the sun got into her belly and started it all up.

By now, the other children were regularly playing sex games which Beatrice did not enjoy. They would all go down to the river and couples would lie down on top of one another in the shelter of the bushes. Beatrice went through it mechanically. She did it because everybody was doing it, this clambering over each other's bodies. She never associated what they were doing with that nice fizzing feeling she had recently discovered.

Experimenting more, she found that, if she was patient and lay in her hammock and rubbed herself for long enough, there would first of all come that sensation of warmth spreading through the bottom half of her body and then an increase of intensity that built up to a burst of pleasure followed by deep, pulsing pulls that only gradually subsided. She learned how to control the bursts of pleasure. They reminded her of the spinning, golden catherine-wheel fireworks she had seen when she was staying with the Marinheiro family who had taken her to a fête in Boa Vista. The only worry she had was connected to the fact that her father had recently brought back a torch from Brazil that worked by batteries. Beatrice worried that this newly discovered pleasure might also work on some sort of internal battery and she did not know how many more goes she could have before the batteries ran out. For a while she rationed herself.

A short while later, something similar happened, this time in the forest where hardly any sun at all penetrated the gigantic trees. Beatrice, Danny and Wifreda had all gone with Shibi-din and some of their cousins to collect mari-mari bark. Shibi-din used the bark to tan his deer- and cowskins. He said that the bark from deep in the forest was better.

There, Beatrice discovered that the intense colours of certain flowers had the same effect on her as the sun. Branching off on her own to look for bark, taking all the usual precautions to mark her trail, she came across some scarlet flowers under a ceiba tree. The shade from the huge trees prevented much plant life on the ground. But these flowers seemed to burn the air around them. She stared, fascinated. The flowers blazed like sores. She could not take her eyes off them. First came the familiar tingling in her nipples and then the other feeling started up in the bottom of her belly. She lay down on her back under the huge tree and began to play with herself, her hand diving between her legs like a duck's head.

Her older cousin Gina followed her trail and came back to look for her, a warishi full of bark slung on her back. She saw Beatrice gasping and panting under the tree and thought for a moment she had been poisoned.

'What are you doing?' she asked and then said, matter-of-factly: 'Oh I see. You're making love with ghosts.' And she left Beatrice to find her own way back to the others along the marked trails.

Later, Beatrice discovered that the vivid, electric blue of jacaranda petals started her nipples tingling in the same way. Certain blossoms with a particular vibrating wavelength of colour affected her sexually like that.

At home, the tapir had the habit of climbing on to one of the beds and rolling around. Once Beatrice had crept up to the creature and lain down beside it, rubbing her pelvis against its thick skin and breathing in its near-human smell. The creature shook itself and got off the bed as if in protest.

Her mother was standing in the doorway, a slight frown on her round face.

'Come on, Tapioca-face, I need you to help carry the farine pan.'

Maba saw the muddied flanks of the tapir as it stood in the middle of the room with its look of blind innocence, sniffing with its prehensile nose.

'You mustn't let that animal on the bed. It spends all its time in the river. Look. It's left mud on the mattress.' Then sensing that there was something odd about the way Beatrice looked, she added: 'You shouldn't keep a pet too long, you know. They become able to read your thoughts and they become enemies.'

Wifreda found Beatrice shocking in a lot of ways although she admired her daring. When they had stayed with the Marinheiros in Brazil, Beatrice had stolen some of the communion wine and shared it out amongst the children. When Wifreda said she did not want to join in Beatrice just lay on the bed and stared at her and giggled.

She did not only break the rules of the Church. She broke all the rules. When they were back home, Wifreda saw Beatrice bathing in the part of the river where the men usually bathed because she was too lazy to walk further downstream. And Beatrice lied about when she had her period and was not supposed to fish or bathe in the river. She just seemed to follow her own impulses. If Wifreda threatened to tell anybody, Beatrice said she would just leave and go away somewhere else.

Wifreda thought that life without Beatrice would be unbearable so she kept quiet.

THE LONG WAIT

It had been decided that Danny, Beatrice, Wifreda and Alice were all to go to school next year in Georgetown. Beatrice was the only one who was excited. Danny shrugged his shoulders. Wifreda and Alice tried not to think about it. But to Beatrice, that year's cycle seemed endless.

First it was time for the round-up. The horses were fed on corn for weeks to give them strength. Because of the poor-quality grazing on the savannahs, Waronawa's cattle spread far and wide across the savannahs looking for decent grass. It took months to round them up. The vaqueiros, their bronze, wrinkled faces becoming ever redder in the sun, chased the lowing beasts for miles in a thundering flurry of white dust. The savannahs echoed with drumming hooves and bellowing cattle. Everyone at Waronawa, even the youngest children, could ride. The vaqueiros were all skilled horsemen, mostly bareback and barefoot.

Danny and Lallo, one of his younger brothers, perched on the corral fence in their shorts and listened for the bellowing of the herds as the cattle were driven towards the river. Danny held on to Lallo by the arm. The previous year Lallo had fallen off and suffered a greenstick fracture. When the men returned with the cattle, the children ran back and forth filling buckets with water for the men to drink somewhere in the shade before they set about branding and castrating the animals.

That night Shibi-din, his hands badly blistered from the reins, drank heavily. He knocked his wife unconscious after he found no meat in the pepper-pot and in a fit of rage, set fire to his own family house. The unusual, flaring light and screams woke the McKinnon girls. Beatrice, Wifreda and Alice climbed out of their hammocks and stumbled sleepily outside to see what was going on.

People were running frantically to and from the lake to fetch water. Maba and Zuna were already standing with a crowd, the heat fanning their anxious faces. Everyone had gathered round to try and help but the flames were too fierce and thrust them back. The whole scene was bathed in a strange, pink light. Burning orange flakes of thatch, bordered with black, floated up into the night sky. A keskidee, thinking it was dawn, started to sing.

Aro, Shibi-din's wife, had recovered and escaped. She moaned as Zuna gripped on to her arm to prevent her running back inside for her children. When Shibi-din appeared out of the darkness from nowhere, still befuddled, people had to keep them apart.

The burning house sagged and slowly subsided into a pile of blazing timbers. It was clear that none of the three children inside could have survived. Eventually, Maba and Zuna took Shibi-din's wife into their house and the last of the villagers went to bed.

In the soft, clear light of early morning, where the house had stood, the mass of hot white ashes and charred timbers still smoked. Some of the men were trying to keep the dogs at bay with sticks. The dogs were padding excitedly around the embers, trying to snatch the sticky, tarry log which lay there. It was all that remained of the six-month-old baby.

The settlement awoke to find that Shibi-din had taken a horse and left for Brazil. If ever it was unclear who was to blame in such a case, Koko Lupi would come and rub bitter-cassava leaf on the corpse and the culprit was supposed to run out of the village within two hours. But this time everyone knew who had done it.

Maba and Zuna stayed up with Aro all that night of the fire. They told her she could stay with them as long as she wanted. She stared silently ahead, her eyes enlarged and straining from their sockets like those of a young deer. But Maba and Zuna were Shibi-din's sisters and she began to distrust them because all in-laws, finally, are not to be trusted.

Maba got hold of Beatrice and told her to stay with Aro all the time and not leave her for a minute. Beatrice was the only person she could tolerate. Beatrice sat beside her and said nothing until Aro was ready to leave.

Two days later Aro set off south to walk to Baidanau where she had relatives. She took a little bag of tasso and farine with her. Beatrice went with her to keep her company for the first part of the journey. They walked in single file over the barren land, along the trails, Aro humming a sad chant as they wove their way through the sentinel termite nests, in silence until midday. Then it was time for Beatrice to turn back if she was to reach Waronawa again before dark. They said goodbye and Beatrice watched Aro's plump figure depart in the distance before she herself turned for home. It pleased her to know that her presence had been a comfort to Aro.

Danny was distraught at the loss of his Uncle Shibi-din. He wanted to follow him over to Brazil. He picked out some bows and arrows, slung his hammock over his shoulder and prepared to follow him. He said he could fend for himself until he found Shibi-din. Eventually, he was dissuaded from going and moped around the house for months.

Then it was time to collect up the cashew nuts. Most people on the settlement went to camp on the bush-islands. There everyone drank themselves into oblivion on the fermented cashew liquor in one endless party. Dancing. Singing. Mass vomiting sessions. Fights and quarrels broke out. Someone always pulled a knife. No one was ever killed. After two weeks of camping, everyone packed up and went home.

To Beatrice, the dry season seemed to go on for ever. Whole groups of families set off, for the fish-poisoning. When they reached the side of the creek, Maba, Zuna and the rest of the women pounded the poison plant. They mixed some grated bitter cassava and mixed it with kunami leaves. Then they rolled it into pellets. Soon after it was sprinkled on the creek, the fish started rising to the surface and leaping out of the water. The men and boys just scooped them up in whatever containers they had to hand. They were cooked right there on the fire.

McKinnon got stung by a sting-ray. In agony, he pulled himself out of the water and went over to the fire where Zuna held his foot as near the flames as possible, using the one pain to distract him from the other.

A German man appeared from nowhere on horseback, shimmering like a mirage in the hot air. He was exhausted. His legs from ankle to knee were swollen and covered in sores. Burst saddle blisters meant that his trousers stuck to him with pus and blood. He lay in the house craving oranges. The children picked hundreds of oranges and grapefruits for him. He ate nothing else. After about six weeks, he got on to his horse and rode off again.

At Waronawa, the men and women always bathed separately but the children bathed together. In the days before she went to the convent in Georgetown, Beatrice stood beside the waters while the other children shrieked with fun as they bathed in the lake. The lake was sheltered on the far side by reeds and bamboo. White clouds scudded across the sky over their heads. The children played dog and labba, diving and chasing each other in the water.

Beatrice began to feel detached. She experienced a sort of loneliness. The other children seemed to be avoiding her.

'Why won't anyone speak to me?' she asked her cousin Gina.

'You're going away to become a coastlander,' said Gina, slyly. 'And we don't like them.'

Danny did not appear to suffer the same doubts about going to Georgetown. His ferocity sometimes alarmed Beatrice. He had lassoed two of his younger brothers and tied them to a tree till nightfall despite their shrieks of fright. He never seemed to give a thought to the fact that he would soon be leaving.

Now he was preoccupied with new company. Some Wai-Wai were passing through on their way to trade on the Rio Negro. He spent most of his time with one of the boys, Wario. They disappeared off fishing together.

They walked for miles until they reached the foothills of the Kanakus where someone had reported seeing a harpy eagle. Wario's hair was long. He still wore a lap and feathers. The bow he used was so large that Danny did not have the strength to draw back the string. He was impressed to see Wario manage it effortlessly and send arrows skimming over the top of a huge ite-palm tree as he aimed at a sloth. They made their way uphill through tangled forest to the top of a small waterfall where they built a hide in the trees and waited for the white eagle.

They waited for three days but saw no sign of it. Then they returned to Waronawa.

McKinnon was clearing out rusty tackle from one of the outhouses. The oldest of the Wai-Wai men, who wore two scarlet macaw feathers that pierced his nose and hung down like a mandarin's moustache, accosted him and pointed to two rolls of cloth, one plain and one patterned, that had been brought from Georgetown and were stored there.

'It's the same spirit that makes both of these?' he asked McKinnon, in halting Wapisiana, pointing at the rolls of cloth.

'Yes,' said McKinnon, who went on lifting the heavy tackle down from the walls. The place smelt of musty old leather. He could not be bothered to explain about the manufacturing of cloth.

'We've heard there is a man in the savannahs who knows about this spirit.'

'You mean Father Napier. He is in the north savannahs at the moment. I'll tell him to come south and see you when you've come back from the Rio Negro.'

McKinnon was happy to divert Father Napier away from Wapisiana territory for as long as possible.

The next day, the Wai-Wai set off in two long canoes, anxious to reach the Rio Negro and trade before the rains set in.

The first warnings of thunder cracked over the Kanaku Mountains. Families went out to clear and burn fields in the forest. After the first rains, everyone planted their cassava, corn, tobacco, hill rice and beans.

Then the storms came. Lightning ran along the iron-ore

deposits between Darukuban and Shiriri Mountains. One afternoon, Zuna saw the lightning roll over the ground in a luminous crackling ball and settle in a sandpaper tree.

A woman came gasping to the ranch-house. She claimed to have seen the little man of the savannahs who blows tunes on a stone pipe and kills your children. Maba, Zuna and Auntie Bobo quietened her down and she quickly went off again to check on her own family.

The rains and then nothing.

That year, the wet season seemed interminable to Beatrice. The rains came and stole the land away completely. The settlement was cut off and isolated. The house looked on to one vast lake. Beatrice saw an enormous jabiru bird wading through the water at the back of the house. Egrets and cranes huddled in the trees for protection against the violent winds and storms. Nobody visited. The road to the north savannahs was impassable. The younger children got on her nerves. Jaguars and pumas crept nearer. One of the horses got mauled. Cattle sores became infested with worms. And the kaboura flies were everywhere, biting at their fiercest. Danny was always off fishing somewhere, but for the first time in her life Beatrice had grown tired of fishing expeditions.

Finally, September came. The sun became stronger and they were able to travel.

CONVENT DAYS

Two ancient nuns, arm in arm, heads leaning towards each other, twittered like birds as they came through the cloisters to welcome the three McKinnon sisters into the cool world behind the convent gate.

The girls had travelled with their father for six weeks by bullock cart, on horseback and by river. Danny had been dropped off at a house in Queenstown to lodge with a family there. His sisters were not to see him again for three years.

Only at the last minute did Danny seem to realise what was happening and that he would no longer be able to go fishing.

'But what will happen to all the fish?' he asked his father, in distress at the thought of leaving the creeks and rivers full of fish.

'They'll still be there when you get back,' laughed McKinnon.

For the first few weeks, all three girls felt sick in the pit of their stomachs. What depressed Beatrice most was wearing shoes. Her feet weighed so heavily, dragging her to the ground. The school uniform felt as restraining as one of the harnesses that hung in the outhouse at Waronawa.

The convent smelled strangely of polish and disinfectant. Beatrice peeped into the large rooms which reminded her of empty, unused caves. Although afflicted by shyness at first, she managed to speak English more confidently after a while. Wifreda remained reticent – 'as closed as the Japanese art of paper-folding' was how one of the nuns described her, 'a real buck girl'. Alice the youngest had to struggle to prevent herself bursting into tears whenever she caught sight of one of her sisters and begged to go home.

Beatrice soon found a way of surviving and consoling her sisters. She convinced herself and them that they were Wapisiana spies. One morning after prayers, she grabbed both of them to explain in Wapisiana that they were all on a special mission and had been sent to learn the secrets of an enemy camp. Their task was to learn about the coastlanders and report back to the Rupununi. They would have to be brave and careful because they were in hostile territory.

'Go to your classrooms, please, girls,' said Sister Fidelia, shooing them along.

In some way, they all felt comforted by this idea. Beatrice instructed them that they were like warriors who had been sent there in order to infiltrate and learn how to pretend to live like the enemy. They must merge in with their surroundings, copy the coastlanders while somehow keeping themselves intact. She told them that any creature, be it a bird or spider or even a flea, might be bringing a message from the Rupununi. Whenever they could the girls met, out of sight of the teachers, and spoke in Wapisiana, taking pleasure in the fact that nobody else could understand them. The nuns watched bemused as the three sisters walked, always in single file, through the grounds, a habit from following the narrow trails of the savannahs.

'This life here will be like a shell,' said Beatrice, 'that will hide us but that we can take off when we leave.'

They called themselves the three turtles – keepers of the secret.

The convent catered for seventy young girls. It was well furnished and considered to be amongst the best of the schools available. The Venezuelan Ambassador sent his daughter there as did many of the coloured upper classes. There were three classrooms with backrests for the pupils, a gymnasium, four dormitories and a sanatorium. Water tanks provided drinking water. Tuition included English, Portuguese, Italian, French, music and drawing. Every so often, the girls would give a concert and the tinkle of the piano, the thump of feet and the spatter of parental applause could be heard issuing from the open windows of the gymnasium into the warm air of the cloistered garden with its ginger-lilies and hibiscus.

Gradually, Beatrice was introduced to the complicated colour-coding that afflicted Georgetown society. Behind the natural friendships that sprang up at school lay the poisoned knowledge of who was 'high-yellow', 'high-brown', 'red' or 'black'.

Beatrice caused confusion. She was not black and she was not white. People circled her warily, not certain where to place her, proffering friendship and then arbitrarily withdrawing it. One of the most forthright girls in the class took the opportunity to consult with her parents on the matter. She came back triumphantly and stood on a table in the classroom to make the announcement: 'The McKinnons are bucks.' She said this firmly, as if that put an end to the matter. It then became permissible to taunt them. But despite the occasional sniggers behind her back, Beatrice was the most popular of the three sisters.

There were bewildering new excitements. She met a girl who had been to New York where people's noses and ears froze in winter and could be snapped off. She learned to draw. A girl in her dormitory brought back a kaleidoscope from England. Beatrice loved to look through it and see the endless, breathtaking transformations of patterns.

The nuns discussed the new arrivals in the staff-room. They found Beatrice the most intelligent and outgoing. She was also the prettiest, they agreed, with her heart-shaped face and wide black eyes, even though one of the eyes wandered a little. True, she giggled rather a lot, partly through spasms of shyness, but it was not, the nuns agreed, enough to be a nuisance.

In singing class, Beatrice stood next to Maria de Freitas, a tone-deaf Portuguese girl whose sallow face was covered in butter-boils. The two girls shared a worn song book which had 'Boosey and Hawkes' printed on the cover. The nun struck up the first chords on the piano.

'"It was a lover and his lass."'

The class sang heartily about a spring-time which they would never experience. The shutters stood wide open and the hall was filled with airy breezes. The nun playing the piano broke off when she heard the tuneless barking of Maria de Freitas. She looked round the class until she identified her.

'Please to keep quiet and mime the songs, chile. Just mouth the words. You are throwing the whole choir off.'

The nun started up again but they got no further than '"Hey ding a ding a ding, Sweet lovers love the spring,"' with Maria de Freitas obediently miming, when another deep bass voice joined them from the street:

> Monkey want snuff, O,
> Monkey want rum, O,
> Monkey very dry, O,
> Monkey want coffee, O,

> Monkey very tired, O,
> Five o'clock, Monkey, O!

The music mistress was unable to halt the stampede of pupils to the window. A gang of labourers, laying the foundations for an extension on to one of the colonial houses opposite, was responsible for the chorus.

Micklemas Crane, the foreman and an experienced carpenter, led the work chant. The men's black skin shone with sweat and dust in the heat as they hammered the greenheart logs into the clay, slamming the fifteen-inch-square 'monkey' on to the logs to fix them in place. After a few minutes, the men set up the chant again and the girls leaned, giggling and waving, through the window. One of the men looked up and took the handkerchief off his head to wave back. The others ignored the schoolgirls.

Exasperated, the nun banged down the lid of the piano.

The dazzle from the metal hammers pierced Beatrice through the eye and she stepped back.

'Ow. Get off my foot, dirty buck girl . . .'

Beatrice turned to stare at the haughty brown face and frizzy hair of Nella Hawkins who, in return, screwed up her face into a hostile leer.

Beatrice's heart thumped with fright. At the same time she felt humiliated.

'What is going on?' enquired the music teacher as the rest of the class drifted back to their places, leaving the two girls staring at each other. Nella Hawkins rushed in with her story.

'Beatrice McKinnon trod on my foot really hard.' She began to limp back to where she had been standing in the choir.

'Well. I'm sure it was an accident, wasn't it, Beatrice?' said the nun kindly.

Beatrice remained silent and motionless. Some of the other girls began to snigger.

'Usually we apologise when we do something like that, Beatrice. Say you're sorry.'

No words came. Beatrice could not get her tongue round the unfamiliar word that was required. She found herself unable to speak and walked silently back to her place.

'Well, you must wait behind after the class and speak to me, Beatrice.' The teacher turned back to the piano and the chorus struck up again.

Beatrice's mouth was already dry and her heart beating fast. She bent her head over her song book. When she looked up from the book, she saw that the left half of the nun's face had disappeared and was swallowed up in blackness. The Ursuline habit consisted of a black gown with a white bib, white crown, black head-dress and a white bandeau.

Beatrice blinked her eyes in case she was confusing these bands of black and white. But wherever she looked, the left half of her field of vision was blacked out. A cold sweat broke out over her body. She looked down at her book, hoping everything would return to normal. Only half the book appeared in front of her. She began to tremble. Then a brilliant, zigzag, star-shaped line appeared dancing inside her left eye, whether she kept the eye open or shut. The jagged line was like the lightning that ran along the ground from the peak of Darukuban to Shiriri Mountain heralding storms. She thought she was going blind. There was a mounting wave of nausea and then Beatrice McKinnon fainted on the parquet floor of the gymnasium.

The sanatorium had recently been painted and smelled of linseed oil. Beatrice rested there for three days until the sick headache wore off. On the third night when she felt completely well again, she sat up in bed and listened as

Sister Fidelia, who originated from Ireland but who had spent most of her life in the colony, made her nightly round of the dormitories.

Sister Fidelia alarmed the younger girls because she had a face as long as a horse and a large birthmark, like a dried purple cow-pat, covering her right cheek. She suffered from melancholia and was frowned on by the other nuns who deplored her tendency to lapse into Creolese. Now, she swept along the corridor, past the gymnasium, rapping on the doors for them to put out the lights and calling: 'Out de light now, girls, please. Out de light,' as she began to ascend the wide, sweeping wooden staircase to the sanatorium on the top floor.

In the street outside, a rum-soaked man sat on the grass verge. He heard the nun's voice and mimicked it.

'Yes, out de light. Out de light. But who goin' out de moon?' He cackled. And, indeed, the convent and the surrounding streets were flooded with moonlight, a light that soaked all colour from the saman trees and the tall, emaciated royal palms of the capital city. The man staggered to his feet and tottered towards the convent. He stopped to pee in a ditch.

'Who goin' out de moon?' He mumbled before crumpling into a heap on the roadside where he lay amongst the white stones till morning.

The moon stared down with its carnal, dirty face.

Sister Fidelia peeked in at Beatrice, whom she adored, and went back downstairs. When she had gone, Beatrice got up and looked through the shuttered windows at the moonlit scene below. A huge toad sat panting and puffing on the path beneath the window, the markings on its back clearly visible. Beatrice felt that it had come to cheer her up. After a while it turned and hopped away into a ditch.

The ragged man who lay like a collapsed puppet beneath

the window reminded her of Shibi-din after he had been on a drinking binge.

Beatrice climbed back into bed and wondered what was happening at Waronawa. When they left, the roof was being re-thatched. That meant that the men had to be up before sunrise while the dew was still on the leaves. Once the sun had dried them out, it was impossible to weave them. The leaves had to be cut on a night when there was no moon because the insects that lay their eggs in the leaves do so by moonlight. If the leaves are cut then, the eggs will hatch later and destroy the roof.

She remembered being told once that Koko Lupi could fly long distances and find out what people were doing and bring back news. But here she was utterly cut off from home. The thought made her feel as though she were choking on sand.

That night she dreamed she was on the Rupununi River, leaning over the side of a canoe. Someone behind her was paddling. The black, glass waters swelled beneath the boat and she broke the solid, curved chunks of water by trailing her fingers over the side. Seeds floated on top of the river, slowly near the bank and faster mid-stream. She could feel the deep eddies pulling and tugging beneath the boat. Whoever was paddling leaned forward and whispered something in her ear from behind her left shoulder. The voice was familiar. The breath of the speaker warmed her neck.

Trees closed in overhead and the colour of the water changed to burnt sienna. Reflections in this mahogany water were brown and orange. Everything, down to the tiniest insect, was uncannily reproduced. The images remained perfectly still even though the river moved through them like time.

Beatrice wondered how water that moved could throw back such a clear image. The foliage was mirrored so exactly that it seemed impossible to know which was the real world.

Suddenly, she was lying on her back at the bottom of the river, blissfully happy. Above, she could see the canoe which now looked like a parrot flying through the sky. Then ripples from the boat started to shake the images to the core. Everything disintegrated and she woke up to the brilliant light of morning.

The school vibrated with the scandal. Sister Fidelia was being moved to another establishment in Mexico. A mountain of empty rum bottles had been found under the mournful nun's bed. She had been secretly consuming huge quantities of spirits.

A whole class had been present, on their way back from the gymnasium, when Sister Fidelia slid down the banisters from the top of the great circular staircase to the bottom, her habit hoiked up round her waist. Two other nuns rushed to help as she collapsed at the bottom.

Catching sight of Beatrice in the group of astonished pupils, she burbled: 'Ah. There's Beatrice McKinnon . . . now she has it . . . she understands the secret magnificence of death.' Then she started to sing: ' "Oh Danny Boy, the pipes, the pipes are calling," ' before passing out cold while one of the nuns ushered the girls away.

Very little disturbed the smooth routine of convent life, but about a year later, there was more news of Sister Fidelia.

Mother Superior, a tiny, wizened woman in her seventies, assembled the whole school in the gymnasium and stood on the dais in front of them.

'Good morning, girls. Today we have need of your prayers. Most of you will remember Sister Fidelia who left us to serve God in Mexico. Today I have received a letter from her asking for our help. I shall read some of the letter to you:

Dear Mother Superior and all at St Joseph's,

Well, the Lord help us but an awful tragedy has occurred here and we need your prayers.

A month ago, I mentioned to my class that there was to be an eclipse which would be visible in our part of the world and if any of the children wanted to watch it, I would take them to the park to see it. I warned them that they must not look directly at the sun as it would not be good for their eyes.

Two volunteered. Miguel and his sister wanted to see the eclipse. I picked them up from their home – one of those pretty, white-painted houses with bougainvillaea that makes me wish I could paint – and we set off for the local park in the suburbs of Mexico City.

Having been warned not to watch the eclipse directly, the children obediently – and I must say they were as good as gold about this – watched the eclipse in the pond where they normally sailed their toy boats. I stood and waited with them. We checked the time. The eclipse was due to start in four minutes.

The pond waters were still and dark, lapping against the stone surround. Reflections were clear and I reckoned we would get a good sighting. Miguel took his sister's hand, God bless him, and they both gazed at the water.

At 11.15 a.m., just as I had told them it would, the dark edge of the moon began to bite into the sun. The children watched, fascinated by the double-edged disc floating in the pond. Naturally enough, in the time it took for the eclipse to be completed, it became dusk and then dark. Everything was quiet. Another child on the other side of the pond launched his sailboat to catch the chill breeze that sprang up. It caused ripples. Miguel and his sister continued to watch, enthralled. I kept an eye on them to make sure they didn't look up. The phenomenon was nearly over. The morning became bright and hot again. I took the children home.

Within an hour, both children were blind.

The parents became hysterical. I feel so responsible. Since then it has been one long round of clinics, specialists, hospital waiting rooms and the eventual placement of the children in a school for the blind.

Here, Mother Superior stopped and asked the school to pray for the two blind children and Sister Fidelia.

Maria de Freitas, standing next to Beatrice, made her giggle by pulling her eye into a horrendous squint. Beatrice whispered in her ear that she thought there ought to be another saint in the Catholic canon – St Giggles.

In the staff-room afterwards, the nuns gathered round to read that part of the letter which had been kept from the pupils:

You can imagine how I feel. The newspapers have blown it all up and sensationalised it. I have been attacked in the press. Historians have raked up the story of the last solar eclipse in this region on July 16th, AD 789 when Quetzalcoatl, one of their pagan gods, headed east on a raft of serpents and had to leave Mexico because he made love to his sister. He is supposed to have risen up in the sky to become the evening star or some such nonsense. Now I feel ashamed that I should be the cause of their digging up all this rubbish.

I feel like a cat in a swing-swong. And I had been settling in here so well too. Please remember the poor children in your prayers and me as well.

Yours in Christ,
Sister Fidelia.

Some while afterwards, the nuns at the Ursuline convent in Georgetown heard of an incident at their sister convent in Mexico when the bells had boomed out for no reason in the middle of the night, with a slow, funereal tolling, disturbing the whole neighbourhood. Sister Fidelia had been found blind drunk tugging at the bell-rope and had been moved to a convent in Peru.

THE EVANGELIST

During those years when the older McKinnon children were away at school, Father Napier's black soutane became a familiar sight on the savannahs, like a black crow on the landscape. Sometimes he travelled on horseback, more often on foot. Walking, he said, was good for prayer.

In his first months there, Father Napier had set up his base at Zariwa, which he had given the Christian name of St Ignatius. He brought three boys from the nearest villages to live with him. They helped him with the chores and he trained them in the ways of God. They also helped him to build the first Catholic church in the Rupununi, a simple construction of adobe, wattle-and-daub and palm thatch.

Father Napier developed an intense crush on one of these boys, whom he called Little Ignatius. Little Ignatius was slow, serious and shy. When Father Napier praised him, he lowered his eyes and flushed, not knowing how to respond. The priest saw this as a charming sign of humility in the boy and saw him as a symbol of the advent of real Christianity to the savannahs, rather than the Protestant heresy that had already been established at Yupokari.

He experienced a mixture of pain and pleasure as the boy

dutifully dug jiggers out of his feet with a pin. The Jesuit felt that there was a special communication between them. The boy was intelligent and trusting. Whenever Father Napier looked at him, he was flooded with a fierce joy that he attributed to an overflow of Christ's love through him and into the boy. There was a particular thrill in bringing Little Ignatius to Jesus.

And it was through Little Ignatius that he found a way to destroy Indian beliefs. The boy explained to him that all animals had a master or owner who protected them on earth as well as in the sky. This master might appear as an animal himself. He is also the master of the hunt and protects magical herbs that bring luck to the hunter and decides how many animals the hunter is allowed to kill, depending on whether there is a glut or a scarcity. You can find out when he is present because he smells strongly of the juice of these herbs.

With that information, Father Napier, subtly, like a cancer virus mimicking the workings of a cell it has entered, gradually introduced to the Indians the idea of his own all-powerful master.

At St Ignatius, the priest lived in a simple hut with a dirt floor. Men would come there, sit on the floor and say nothing, quite at ease. Sometimes they would eat, dipping into his pot. Once he discovered that they had looked through all his possessions although nothing had been taken. He remonstrated with them, raising his voice. Immediately, they all left. He came to understand that they did not like harsh voices. If he ever reprimanded any of them, they just disappeared.

'They do not like people who shout and they have no memory for dates!!' he wrote in his diary.

From the start of his ministry, he undertook a series of arduous journeys, concentrating first on the Macusi in the north savannahs, building churches, converting whole villages at a time and founding new missions. He would start with the children, getting them to play games and sing hymns. Then he would progress to the adults. At one point, he calculated with pride that Little Ignatius had built a new altar every day for a month.

Often he had to sleep under a tarpaulin, shivering with cold at night and roasted by the sun in the day. And, on more than one occasion, all his clothes and belongings became soaking wet when the floor of some half-built church, where he had spent the night, turned to mud. Nothing deterred him. As soon as one mission was complete and the Indians had received basic instruction and could chant and pray, he started out on the next, criss-crossing the savannahs. If the rivers could not be forded, he would get men to make a woodskin. If there were no trees to make a woodskin, he would get them to make a raft. When he could not find the right materials, he improvised.

The Macusi people found him tolerable, but puzzling, especially on the occasion when he insisted on reconsecrating the church after a young couple had spent the night there. They were confounded by his energy because it was the custom in the savannahs to do nothing that seemed unnecessary. But he always invented something else to do. They gathered around him, all the same, associating all sorts of material advantages with the adoption of this new god.

One of the triumphs recorded in his diary was the conducting of an improvised Easter Sunday mass at Nappi. He constructed the paschal candle with the help of a tobacco tin. The candles were made of black beeswax. The tabernacle consisted of a kerosene tin lined with muslin. Every part of the service which should have been sung, he sung himself in his high tenor voice.

Then disaster struck.

'Come, Ignatius,' he announced to his young follower. 'We are going to have a special celebration in Christ's name.

He had decided to climb Mount Roraima and celebrate mass at the top. It was a three-week walk to the mountain in the blazing heat. Little Ignatius hesitated as he approached the black sides of the sacred, flat-topped mountain. It reared up ahead of him. They came closer to the base. Every time he lifted his head to see the top of Roraima, the mountain seemed to raise itself up further as if to outdo him, as if threatening to crush him if he came closer. The mountain felt alive.

Father Napier pushed the boy hard. He made him carry on his back all the equipment for mass, as well as his own camera, a prospecting bag and kitchen utensils.

On the lower slopes around the base stood the bleached skeletons of hundreds of trees. The cliffsides of the mountain were sheer and black with numerous waterfalls plunging down from the summit. They climbed up crevices and ravines, clinging on to tufts of grass and holding on by their fingertips to slippery fissures of rock. In some places, moss and streamers of greenery blanketed the damp tree trunks. Ferns grew at the base of these trees with fronds of jelly-like substance instead of leaves. Tiny black frogs plopped into pools in fright as they passed.

'Come on. You can do it,' said Father Napier with a surge of his old school-prefect cruelty as they neared the flat top of the mountain.

They celebrated mass in eerie silence on top of the great plateau. When it was over, Little Ignatius guided the priest down through the wooded gullies on the south side of the mountain, despite being freezing cold and exhausted. Three days later, he died.

The two men faced each other in the dark hut where the child's body lay. The boy's grief-stricken father tried to explain that the mountain was a special place and Father Napier should never have taken his son there. The boy's mother and sisters, none of whom had any teeth despite being young, stood silently by the child's stiff corpse.

'The mountain was once a great tree,' the father tried to explain through his tears. 'On this tree grew every sort of fruit. The only creature who know its whereabout was the tapir.'

Father Napier hid his exasperation. He too felt anguish at the loss of Little Ignatius, his favourite boy. The last thing he wanted to hear was this man prattling on about a tree and a tapir. He bitterly regretted being too late to administer the last rites. The priest frowned and bared his teeth with the effort of trying to understand the man who was speaking Macusi.

The distraught man was pacing up and down in front of the priest. Three steps brought him to his son's body, another three brought him back.

'Two brothers, Macunaima and Chico, found a tic that had hitched a ride on the tapir. The tic wept bitterly because he had fallen off and was lost. He told the brothers that the tapir knew where the tree was and they followed it. When they saw all the fruits, they cut the tree down. A huge river burst out of the trunk and flooded the savannahs. The mountain was covered by a sea full of dolphins . . .'

Here, the boy's father broke down into uncontrollable sobs while the rest of the family stood by in embarrassment.

Father Napier interrupted.

'Little Ignatius is safely in the arms of Christ now.'

The man looked frankly disbelieving.

Father Napier felt a sudden claustrophobia in the dark hut and went outside for a walk. A few stunted coimbe trees and cashew trees stood between the house and the creek. He walked amongst them, picking his way over the dry soil and through sparse, prickly bushes.

When he looked back, he saw that the family had taken their few belongings out of the hut and set fire to it with the child's body inside. The thatch blazed up in seconds and as he watched, the family walked away from him down a trail leading towards the Pakaraima Mountains, with everything they owned packed in warishis on their backs.

By dint of a few weeks' hyperactive evangelising, he managed to push responsibility for the affair to the back of his mind.

No one ever saw Father Napier without his priest's habit. Dressed in his black robe, he carried with him everywhere the tin trunk which contained his bible, the baptismal records of the newly converted and his own diaries.

The Wapisiana people in the south savannahs discussed the priest's ideas which they had heard about from the Macusis.

One woman said that she had seen the priest trying to climb Bottle Mountain in the Kanakus, a tall, bottle-shaped peak that shone like crystal. It was the mountain where one of their legendary heroes was supposed to have imprisoned his son in a rock. She said the winds came and blew the priest back down again. The surface was slippery with agate, jasper and some green stone. She said too that she had seen a dazzling figure close by at a point where many trails crossed. When questioned closely as to whether it could have been the new Christ, she shook her head emphatically and said that the dazzling figure had been an Amerindian man. But some people began to say afterwards that perhaps it was Christ who was imprisoned in the rock.

Trips to the south savannahs on the other side of the Kanaku Mountains were less frequent. Father Napier felt increasingly that McKinnon was an obstacle to his progress. He thought McKinnon deliberately tried to obstruct his communications with the Wapisiana people.

Certainly, McKinnon did not like the priest's influence. He believed that the Wapisiana did not need a missioner. Once he even wrote to the Bishop in Georgetown suggesting that Father Napier was overdoing it and needed a holiday. But the priest returned with the persistence of a mosquito. Soon he was constructing churches in the south savannahs. Eventually, McKinnon accepted the situation with good grace and always offered hospitality to the priest when he was in the area.

'The Wai-Wai have been asking to see you for some time now,' McKinnon reminded him.

'I shall get round to them as soon as I can.' Father Napier studied his diary and decided to go in January. He would have to leave enough time to get there and back before the rains set in. It would be a long trip south, deep into the forest in an area he had never visited before.

People noticed that Father Napier's eyes, when he spoke to them, seemed to be increasingly fixed on something distant, an imaginary citadel.

AN AFFAIR

The time came for Beatrice, Alice and Wifreda to leave the convent for good. They stood outside the tall metal gate with their bags packed, waiting for the horse and cart which was to take them to where they would catch a boat upriver. The girls had said goodbye to the Mother Superior who had given them each a rosary. Alice was finishing her schooling early because she could not bear to be left behind on her own. It had been arranged that Danny would stay for another few weeks to do a course in basic mechanics. He would travel back on his own later.

As soon as they reached Annai and saw the sprawling, golden landscape of the savannahs, Beatrice's heart lifted. They set off for home by bullock cart as the sun was rising over the Makarapang Mountains in the east. In the distant south, the sun's rays caught the top of the Kanaku Mountains. Even the butterflies seemed drunk on the streaming sunshine.

They were all overjoyed to be back. Beatrice leaned over the side of the cart to feel the breeze on her face.

Maba did not stop pounding the clothes on the flat rocks by the river as Beatrice came running down towards her.

She looked up and her round features cracked open into a big smile. It was not the custom to embrace. But she stood up half frowning and half smiling to inspect her daughter. Beatrice felt a mixture of shyness and embarrassment when she greeted both Maba and Zuna, as if she had changed. She noticed for the first time how weather-beaten the faces of the two mamais were in contrast to the cool, untouched flesh of the convent nuns.

As soon as she had discarded her shoes and put on a cotton dress, Beatrice ran over to see her cousin Gina.

Everything was as she remembered it. Gina looked the same only a little fatter. She was in the benab grating cassava and squeezing the mushy pulp through the matapee with her mother and sisters. Sunlight filtered on to their faces from the thatch roof as they worked. The shadows and the faces blended. The whole scene struck Beatrice as one of relaxation and ease, of melting into the background. Gina's mother leaned against the shed posts chewing on a mango seed, grinning at her. The warm ochre light, the untreated beams covered with palm leaves, the soft laughter, the familiar, mild, yeasty tang of cassava, Beatrice soaked it all in, relishing the contrast with the harsh lines and edges of the convent building she had just left, with its smells of disinfectant, and the cantankerous noise of mechanical implements, school bells and harsh piano playing. She sat on a bench and wriggled her toes in the warm dirt.

Gina smiled at her and continued pulling at the matapee which hung from the roof, her fingers sticky with the pulp. A young man Beatrice recognised from the settlement ducked under the low thatch and helped himself to a bowl of shibi.

'I'm married now,' said Gina, nodding over at the boy. 'He lives with us now. His hammock is next to mine at home.'

Hammock, the symbol of marriage. Beatrice felt both

jealous and dislocated as if she had been left behind in the march of things, as if convent life had retarded her in some way. No one asked her what the convent was like. No one was interested.

Instead of staying to help with the work, Beatrice talked for a little while about what had been happening at Waronawa in her absence and then returned to the house.

'I told you what would happen if she went away,' said Gina.

Beatrice had forgotten how to work. Initially, she found it difficult to settle back into the rhythm of it. She and Wifreda had to fetch water and then water the fruit trees, inspect the backs of tobacco plants for caterpillars, weed cassava plots, skin and chop up deer or labba or agouti, gut fish that the men brought in, wash clothes, spin cotton, help with hammock weaving, prepare farine, cut strips of beef to dry in the sun for tasso and deal with the younger children's ailments.

Danny arrived back. He said nothing and just nodded at his sisters but his eyes shone with the pleasure of being home. Maba noticed that he was taller than most of the other young men of his age in the settlement. That must be the European in him, she thought critically. His shining black hair no longer stood up in a tuft but had grown and fell forward over his eyes.

Somehow, Danny had managed to slide through his schooling without being touched too much by it. His teachers considered him to be agreeable enough – if rather on the silent side. He never hurried. He had his mother's sloe-black eyes and copper complexion. His gift was for making and mending and his hands were always busy with something, whittling arrow-heads mainly.

Beatrice listened to his voice one night through the

partition and wondered when it had become so deep. It was dark brown and slow, like molasses.

'Don' trouble me,' he was warning his younger brothers as they jumped all over him, teasing him, 'or I'll dash you down from the bullock cart one day when we're riding.'

But they were laughing and squealing.

'Do it again, Danny,' they said at whatever he was doing there in the dark.

Beatrice wondered if Danny too felt odd at being back. But if he did, he never showed it. He seemed to settle in as if he had never been away, fishing and hunting with increased confidence, handling his father's guns as well as his own arrows and bow.

McKinnon had asked a group of black coastlanders to come and help him cut lumber. They made an enormous difference to the settlement. They brought jazz.

At nights after work, these young men would clown around, dancing and singing and playing the buffoon upstairs in the McKinnon household. They formed an orchestra. The tallest of them, whose name was Raymond, made a bassoon from brown paper, and a double bass was made from a kerosene tin with a bow of Indian rubber and a triangle from a piece of bent metal. People from the settlement came to dance and the lumber-cutters, carefree and full of laughter, called the way the Indians danced 'the Rupununi shuffle' and in contrast to it, demonstrated their own snake-hip dance style with great good humour.

Several of the older men from the settlement grumbled privately and said that these intruders were too noisy around the place and frightened the fish. They did not like their loud voices and how they waved their arms around when they talked. But they gave no outward sign of this discontent and were always friendly to their faces. The piaiwoman,

Koko Lupi, however, made no secret of her hatred for the newcomers. When she came in from the outskirts of Waronawa, she told everyone that she had poisons to make them impotent if necessary. Impotent for ever, she stressed.

Raymond took a shine to Beatrice. He asked her to dance in the evenings whenever he was not playing one of the instruments and he looked at her with longing from his warm brown eyes with their short, curly lashes. He raised his eyebrows and winked at her as he twanged away at his kerosene-tin double bass.

One night, Beatrice was trying to imitate Raymond's jitterbugging footwork. Danny watched them idly. He was seated on a rough old shaman's stool with a jaguar head hewn at one end and an alligator head at the other. The musicians had cracked open a bottle of rum. Danny swirled some around in a cup and tossed it back. He had already been drinking parakari. Now he alternately swigged parakari and rum. He was trying to whittle a perfectly round ball out of wallaba wood as his uncle had once shown him. But his fingers and thumbs were uncoordinated because of the liquor. In the end he let the knife and the ball drop to the floor.

Beatrice was swirling around in front of him. Her hair flew out behind her. Whenever she mistimed a step, she stopped for a minute, put her hand in front of her mouth and giggled.

For some reason he could not understand, the sight of Beatrice twirling round with this black boy made Danny feel sick and miserable. He wanted to drag her away. The whole business made him dizzy. He tried to snatch at her skirt as she whirled past him, but missed. He got up and tried to dance like the black boys but his body did not move in the same way. Embarrassed and feeling foolish, he sat down again. He drank more of the sour parakari from a calabash and it dribbled down his chin. Someone passed him some fermented cashew liquor. He gulped it down.

After a while, Danny's eyes narrowed into two obsidian slits in his brown face. He looked glazed. He threw up in a dark corner of the room and staggered out into the fresh night air, half stumbling down the stairs. After a while Beatrice came out on to the top of the stairs.

'I'm shamed of you,' he said in Wapisiana.

'Too bad, isn't it?' she replied in English, which infuriated him. She saw his face looking up at her, closed and impenetrable as she had often seen it when he was a child. For a minute she wanted to comfort him. Then Raymond came out to look for her. He gave a gentlemanly bow, took her gracefully by the hand and led her back inside.

Danny swayed along the trail, under the stars, to the lake, burning with envy and some unidentifiable misery. He wanted to kill something. Demolish or destroy something. A night-hawk flew past and he threw a rock at it, wildly off target. When he reached the edge of the lake, he squatted there, listening to the quiet movement of the water in the rushes and wondering if he could cut his hair short all over and look like the negro boys.

Raymond felt himself melting whenever he looked at Beatrice. She, in turn, leaned against the wall by the door and giggled at whatever he said, more than his words warranted. On one side, a strand of her long black hair had become unfastened and stuck damply to her neck. She looked up at him flirtatiously from her wide eyes. The dancing had made her breathless.

Then Maba called her. She needed help to wash the wares. Both Wifreda and Alice had gone to stay with friends on the other side of the village and she was on her own. Beatrice turned with a flourish of her skirt and said a mischievous good-night to Raymond. Then she went to help rinse the wooden plates which clacked as she put them away.

When they had finished the work and before they went to bed, Maba and Beatrice made their way to the latrine fifty yards away, carrying a kerosene lamp and stepping carefully along the short trail.

They took it in turns to use the latrine, one waiting outside while the other took the lamp inside. From where Raymond lay in his room, he could hear their soft voices in the night.

'No moon,' said Beatrice's mother as they made their way back. 'A good night for fishing.'

Beatrice climbed into her hammock. The night was hot. Without moonlight, everything was inky black. It was well into the night and she was already more than half asleep when she heard the door creak. She opened her eyes, but it was so dark that it made no difference whether her eyes were open or shut. She could see nothing. Alert, she waited. After a few seconds of dead silence, she heard soft steps in the room. Someone lifted up the mosquito net that fell to the ground round her hammock.

A warm hand began to move gently over her left breast, cupping and kneading it while the thumb stroked her nipple. After a while, the hand moved to the other breast and explored that in the same way, as if making a careful map of her body. She could hear somebody's slow and regular breathing.

Then she felt a mouth on hers, lips pressing down firmly and methodically as if they had a job to do, printing something all over her face. The hand moved down her body, seeking the underground entrance, and played with her there for a while. The hammock swayed a little.

Darkness and anonymity relieved her of any shyness. The

AN AFFAIR

beam to which the hammock was tied creaked and the hammock swung violently as he climbed in on top of her. She clung tightly to the sides of the cotton hammock as she felt him shift and lose balance, almost throwing them both out.

The back which she held on to with both arms was as smooth as Aishalton rock. She felt him nuzzling into her neck. Something about the head brushing against her ear puzzled her for a moment but she concentrated on twisting herself sideways, letting one leg hang over the edge of the hammock so that he could come inside her more easily. The weight of both of them wriggling to lie slantwise rocked the hammock making her feel as though she were flying through the night. She clung on tightly; the top half of her body arced backwards over the side. Her hair brushed the floor. As he fucked she felt a dark, aching pain mingled with the far-off intimations of that familiar pleasure, but she was too alert and too curious to lose herself in the sensation and it faded away.

She liked the fact that Raymond had not said a word. After he was spent, he lay breathing hard on her chest. The hammock came to a standstill. Two minutes later, she felt a kiss on her neck. Then the hammock rocked violently as he swung himself out, slid under the net like a larva leaving its cocoon and a minute later was gone.

Beatrice levered herself up and looked towards the door but she could still see nothing. She put her hand over her mouth and raised her eyebrows, pleased and wanting to laugh. She thought she could have dreamed it but the hammock was still swinging. She felt contented. It was as though she had finally completed a long overdue chore. Now she was like Gina. She thought about Raymond and imagined being his wife and living in Georgetown. What especially satisfied her was that it had all happened without the awkwardness of speech. It made Raymond feel to her more like an Indian. Tomorrow she would pretend in public that nothing had occurred. It would be their secret.

In the morning, she got up early and scrubbed the stain from the hammock with soap. The lumber-cutters had left at first light for the forest. Beatrice helped Maba and Zuna sieve mapir berries. At the table, she poured the purple-brown juice which tasted like cocoa over her tapioca porridge, spilling some down the front of her dress in a state of bleary-eyed dreaminess.

The lumber-cutters returned in the afternoon by bullock cart bringing the felled trees.

Beatrice finished picking lemons and, a little nervously, walked over to where McKinnon was instructing Raymond how to chop cedar wood to make shingles. He had decided to experiment with a shingle roof instead of ite palm. The sweet smell of the freshly cut wood made her nostrils curl. The two men were in the shade of the great spreading mango tree. McKinnon was explaining the exact size he wanted and how to cut it.

She strolled over to Raymond, trying to look confident but unsure how to greet him. Raymond looked up from his workbench and grinned shyly at her as if appealing for her to come and speak to him. Immediately, she knew that something was not right. It was the look of a young man who was still hoping. He smiled and his brow wrinkled questioningly. She looked at his hairline and her stomach tightened as if someone had kicked her viciously in the belly.

The hair was wrong.

The head that had brushed against hers the night before had hair as smooth and straight as a bird's feather, not the springy, tight, frizzy hair that sat on Raymond's scalp like a moss cap.

It had been one of the other boys. Feeling suddenly furious and tricked and as if Raymond was somehow to blame, she swung round and stomped off, her heart thumping with outrage. Raymond seemed green and stupid. She stalked back to the house.

ROCK-STONE

'Danny says you must come and plant corn.'

Wifreda sounded miserable. She was peering through the doorway, her eyes watering with pain from a sore throat, and her voice was hoarse. Beatrice had been lying about and sulking in her hammock for days. No one knew what was the matter. Both mamais accused her of laziness. She swung herself crossly out of her hammock and went outside to see what Danny wanted.

The first showers of the rainy season had begun. Between showers, the sun blazed down more fiercely than ever. On the savannahs, people were busy planting their corn, cassava, plantain and pumpkin.

The field Danny had chosen to plant was the site of a disused corral some way from the settlement. Old horse-dung had made the land more fertile. For the last week he had been clearing the land, hacking at the dried, prickly undergrowth with a cutlass.

The two of them walked the three miles there in silence.

They set about planting the corn under a clear, blue afternoon sky. Danny went ahead with the hoe, smashing it down on the solid clods of earth and trying to make a furrow in the hard ground. Beatrice followed behind, patches of sweat darkening the underarms of her blue dress, the gritty soil scratching at her toes. She threw the seeds and pushed them in with a turn of her heel. By the time they had planted half the field, her face was streaked with light-brown dust where she repeatedly pushed her damp hair behind her ears with her hand.

Halfway through the afternoon, they both stopped, out of breath. Danny leaned on his hoe. A lizard dashed for safety over the rutted ground. Danny was parched. Beatrice could see the flecks of dried spittle at the side of his mouth.

'Let's swim,' he said.

They went down to the river, far from the spot where most people bathed. She walked behind him. The brown grass was long, dry and sparse. A few waist-high sucubera bushes marked the faint trail. She wondered if it would trouble Danny to break the custom of men and women bathing separately unless they were married. Watching his smooth brown back ahead of her, she felt a curious sense of familiarity. Then suddenly, Beatrice understood. She stopped in her tracks.

'It was you, wasn't it?' she said.

Danny continued walking.

'So what if it was,' he replied, grinning over his shoulder at her with a look half defiant and half proud.

Beatrice remained silent as she absorbed the news with a mixture of fury and mysterious pleasure.

They sat far apart, without speaking, under some trees near to where the river had eaten into the bank. Full of resentment, Beatrice hugged her knees and stared out at the glinting amber waters. She was resentful because, reluctantly, and although unwilling to show it, she knew she had already forgiven him.

After a while she stood up. When she looked round,

Danny was approaching her through the trees, moving so smoothly he appeared to be gliding on ball-bearings. As he came nearer, his eyes, which had grown dark and deliquescent, exerted a lodestone attraction over her which brought about an unexpected loss of will.

He took her by the hand and led her towards the river. She winced as the sharp stones in the sludge underfoot dug into her feet. They hung their clothes on a monkey-cup bush and waded naked into the water. Screwing up her eyes against the light, she looked to where Danny stood mid-river, the sun behind him, ripples slapping against his brown waist. The water was a deep tan with shifting patches of orange gel. He waited for her to join him.

First they swam breast-stroke downriver to where the trees met overhead and the bare tree roots reared out of the water into great twisted arches above them. Kingfishers swooped and dived along the banks beside them.

Then they turned around and Beatrice hooked her arms over his shoulders and let him pull her back upriver against the current. Danny swam rhythmically, enjoying the feel of her breasts pressing against his back in the warm, silky waters.

All the rest of the afternoon they spent lazing in the river. They looked at each other steadily, eyeball to eyeball. As the sun lost its intense heat they continued to bathe. The waters turned the colour of blood. A little water-snake, delicate with blue and silver markings, wriggled sideways past them towards the bank. They both dipped and rose from the water, slicking back their black polls of hair.

'Dog and labba,' said Danny and jumped on her, holding her arms and forcing her underwater. She exploded back up out of the river, bursting with laughter.

Afterwards, without speaking, they found a spot under the trees, set back from the swampy tangle of the river's edge, where there was a spongy carpet made from undisturbed layers of orange and brown leaves. The overpowering, glutinous smell of the bush filled the air.

Danny spread her slim legs open like a wishbone on the ground. Slowly, he lowered the whole of his weight on to her so that she felt deliciously trapped. He sucked each breast in turn. Tiny currents of electricity ran down to a dark centre, the same dark centre that the sun had first penetrated all those years ago, a centre which seemed to be both inside her and outside her, a centre indistinguishable from the circumference. He pushed himself inside her and moved his hips in a slow, circular motion. She could feel him like a baffled root in the darkness seeking moisture, striking out and always trying to go deeper.

The pleasure started at the outside of the circle transcribed by this blind seeker. It felt to her as if a potter was running his thumb around the top edge of a spinning, wavering, moist clay pot, like one she had seen at the convent, so that the rim grew sometimes bigger and sometimes smaller. For a long time, she waited, and then she squeezed and the pleasure came unstoppably from the outer rim to the dark base and burst outwards from there.

Danny could feel her contracting round him. He felt as if he were being swallowed. As if she were drinking him down. And he ejaculated into the black pit.

When they got back to Waronawa, everything was in a furor. Wifreda's sore throat had developed into a huge abscess in her throat. She lay motionless in her hammock, her head turned towards the wall, her throat spiked with pain. The back of her tongue was covered in what looked like a white fungus with spots. She was beginning to have difficulty in breathing. Maba looked down her throat and remembered the strange white fungus she had seen on the path years ago. Immediately, she thought that some enemy had turned into this fungus on purpose to harm Wifreda. Koko Lupi was out of reach, further south in Aishalton. Zuna sent a vaqueiro to ride over and fetch Father Napier, in case he had medicine, but they thought he was too far away to come in time. In the end, Danny took a knife and lanced the abscess and after a few days of spitting blood, Wifreda recovered.

There is a certain sort of black rock-stone to be found on the banks of savannah creeks. The rocks lie scattered all around. If you take one in your left hand and one in your right and circle them round each other, they become magnetised and it is impossible to prise them apart.

Danny and Beatrice became as inseparable as the savannah rocks.

No one suspected what was happening because nothing is less suspicious, nothing is more innocent than a brother and sister carrying out certain tasks together. It was a secret perfectly camouflaged by the surroundings.

Just like the brown and black patterns in the artwork on the woven baskets and sifters and matapees, where it is not always possible to tell foreground from background and the animal symbols are disguised by being embedded in a geometrical whole, Beatrice and Danny were miraculously concealed by their home setting.

For Beatrice, the affair became an addiction. They made love whenever they could, wherever they could. It was not as often as either of them would have liked. Danny had a horror of being discovered. And to Beatrice's irritation, the younger children popped up everywhere and she was expected to carry them with her. Whenever she and Danny tried to sneak down to the river, it seemed that some vaqueiro would be watering his horse or someone would be bathing or a couple would be paddling their canoe nearby.

Sporadic showers had already turned the savannahs a fresh green. It will be worse when the rains set in properly and the land floods over, she thought. There will be nowhere to go then.

During one week, they managed to slip out to one of the tanning sheds and make love there. Beatrice stood with her back against the supporting beam near the plank wall by a trough full of soaking hides. It was dark inside and the air was bitter with the smell of mari-mari bark. There was the constant sound of dripping as water leaked from the trough into a bucket. Above that was the sound of the beam creaking and their breath coming in gasps.

Beatrice watched Danny carefully, sideways from the corners of her eyes, when he was in the house. She liked the way he leaned against the door jamb, one brown shoulder raised higher than the other, one hip jutting out, his bottom lip pulled over the top one as he worked to string a bow or to make one of the blunt arrow-heads he used for stunning birds.

She was happy to watch him doing anything. To Beatrice the other youths at Waronawa seemed callow and dumb compared with Danny.

'You lookin' at me too much,' snarled Danny when they were on their own. And Beatrice knew it was true. It even alarmed her, the way she seemed to have lost her own will. Sometimes she felt numb, like one of the walking dead the girls at the convent had told her about. Numb but exhilarated. The attraction was both inexplicable and irresistible. And growing stronger.

Both Maba and Zuna were pleased to see Beatrice settling back into savannah life. McKinnon was always busy with cattle or fencing or mending buildings. He barely paid any attention to his children. Often he was away in Brazil. Occasionally he went gold prospecting in the Acarai Mountains, more for the adventure than the gold.

Beatrice and Danny stood on the flat rocks at Orinduik where Danny had come to try and trade for balata. The rocks shone with pink jasper. They had been bathing in the stepped, cascading falls that form part of the Ireng River.

'No in-laws to trouble we,' grinned Danny after they had made love in the gap between the waterfall and the rockface. Beatrice was brushing off the bits of grit and stone that clung to her back.

'Ow. Kaboura flies.' She slapped at her arms and legs as she sat on the rocks.

Beatrice sat in the running water. When they made love, her insides felt as if they changed pattern like a kaleidoscope or the expanding and contracting geometrical pattern of a snake's skin. She was about to tell him this. Then she looked over to where he stood in the spray of the waterfall and knew that it would be of no interest to him, so she kept it to herself.

'Yes,' repeated Danny, almost to himself. 'No in-laws to trouble we. We'd be fools not to.' He flung a rock in the water. It suited him to be able to ignore Beatrice when they were at home and treat her just like anyone else in the family.

Six months after they had arrived, the coastlanders who had come to cut lumber were packing up to go home. One or two of them had considered staying behind to bleed balata but then changed their minds. The initial excitement they had felt at being in the interior had worn off. Life was not comfortable. They sometimes felt awkward in the community, as if they did not quite belong, and they began to miss Georgetown, the Saturday afternoon rum sessions, the noise and the races.

Raymond no longer mooned after Beatrice. At first he had been puzzled at the way the flirtation suddenly fizzled out. She looked at him with complete indifference now and he wondered if he had imagined that there had ever been a spark between them.

On the night the lumber-jacks left, the McKinnon house felt particularly quiet. Wifreda, hot and unable to sleep, got up in the night and for some reason went to sleep on a chest under the window, in the tiny room adjoining the outhouse which the lumber-cutters had used for their bedroom.

From the other side of the partition, she heard voices.

'Come on top of me.'

'Just a minute. Let me throw off this cover.'

Wifreda crouched on the chest, then raised herself to peep over the dividing wall. It was too dark to see clearly but she could distinguish moving shapes and she heard the squeaking of the iron bedstead and the voices of Beatrice and Danny.

'Your hands smell of guava leaves.'

'I been feedin' the turtle.'

'What will happen to us?'

'We'll be all right.'

'I want to be with you always.'

'We can manage that. We could go to the Wai-Wai. I know people there. I could build a house for us.'

'Yes?'

'Let me play with you like this a little.'

When everything had gone quiet, Wifreda, too frightened of being discovered to get off the chest in case it creaked, fell uncomfortably asleep where she was and dreamed that she had been mysteriously impregnated by a ball of feathers while sweeping the kitchen.

Two days later, Beatrice and Wifreda were at the back of the house making soap. The sky was overcast. Beatrice took a kerosene tin, mixed caustic soda with hot water from a pot on the embers and then poured the mixture on to the pig suet. It required concentration because the temperature in the two cans had to be the same for the soap to set. It was Wifreda's job to test the temperature with her finger as the contents were poured from one tin to the other.

'I know something about you,' said Wifreda.

'What?' asked Beatrice as she examined the frothy liquid.

'I hear you and Danny in bed together.'

Beatrice went pale. She picked up the tin of hot liquid and flung it over Wifreda. Wifreda shrieked.

'You see how your eyes is bad? If you tell anybody I goin' make you blind,' screamed Beatrice. 'Blind like a termite.'

When Beatrice told Danny, his palms sweated and sharp pins and needles ran up and down his arms. He watched Beatrice walk back to the house, looking at the ground as she went, her long black plait snaking to her waist.

Danny could not understand what had happened to him. It was not as if he wanted to leave Waronawa and disrupt his life. But he knew he would, almost against his will. It exasperated him, this feeling that something was pulling him to act in a way that common sense warned him was foolish. He decided to stop his secret meetings with Beatrice. But even as he decided with one part of his brain, he knew in another that the affair would continue.

That evening, when everybody had eaten, Danny heard himself saying casually that he was going to Wai-Wai country to look for a good hunting dog.

The next morning, the sun scorched down as usual.

There was no sign of either Danny or Beatrice and the old corial that was used for ferrying goods to and fro across the river had gone.

THE MASTER OF FISH

During the month of May, the slow dive of a certain constellation takes place in the night sky, headfirst and arching steadily backwards over the western horizon. It signals the advent of the rains and in the Rupununi district of the Guianas, in the red, parched savannahs, the fish-runs begin.

The constellation is called Tamukang, the Master of Fish, because he orchestrates the silver battalions that come leaping along the rivers at this time. To Europeans, that same configuration of stars is known as the Pleiades, the Hyades and part of Orion. But the constellation of Tamukang does, indeed, look like the skeleton of a fish, head and backbone rolling through the singing blackness in a descent towards oblivion. The moaning winds, they say, are Tamukang blowing his flute. He remains out of sight until his resurrection over the eastern horizon in the months of August and September.

It was one particular cluster of stars in the constellation, the one that the Europeans called the Hyades, that was thought to control the tapirs which were so plentiful during the rainy season.

The evening visit to the latrine was the only time Maba had to herself to think. One night, soon after Danny and

Beatrice had disappeared, she came out of the latrine and walked up on to the rising ground away from the house. She stood on top of the slope and looked up at the infinitely slow, whirling lasso of stars in the night sky.

She sought out the constellation of Tamukang. But Maba's mind was not on fish as she scanned the skies. It was the small cluster of stars that represented the tapir which she strained her eyes to see. That morning she had heard one of the vaqueiros talking to another near the corral fence. She thought he was speaking deliberately loudly for her to hear.

'His mouth calls her "sister" but his bottom half calls her "wife".' And he had laughed unpleasantly and slanted his eyes towards her. She shivered in the slight breeze. She had her own suspicions about Beatrice and Danny. Not that it was unheard of for a brother and sister to live 'close' as it was known. She would just have preferred it not to be her own children.

What made her uneasy was that the patch of tapir stars seemed to be getting brighter as she watched. Everybody knew that the sniffly-snouted, short-sighted, night-trotting tapir was too lazy to mate outside its own family. The stars seemed to be confirming what she suspected.

She turned and walked back to the house, planting her feet sturdily on the rough, sloping ground, avoiding the tufts of springy goat's beard along the way. At home she mentioned her concerns to nobody, not even Zuna. Other men in the village had noticed the brightness of the 'tapir' stars and organised a tapir hunt.

When McKinnon returned from a long trip away and discovered that Beatrice and Danny had gone to Wai-Wai country he thought nothing of it. There was another distraction. Everyone at Waronawa had been pleased to welcome the arrival of a stranger who seemed to fit in easily. His name was Sam Deershanks and he was part Sioux Indian from Texas. He was tall, with high cheekbones and a stoop.

'What brings him to these parts?' asked someone.

'He came because of the railways,' was the reply.

'But there are no railways.'

'That's the funny part about it.'

McKinnon enjoyed having another English speaker on the ranch. And it turned out that, although Sam Deershanks spoke little, he had a gift for handling cattle. He settled in well and soon it became clear that he had eyes for no one else but Wifreda.

Wifreda buttoned up her face more tightly than ever and ignored him completely. The more people teased her about it, the angrier she became.

All the time that he had been away in Brazil, McKinnon had been longing to read the bundle of torn newspapers that he knew awaited him at home. Every six months or so, the out-of-date newspapers arrived from Georgetown, sometimes in unreadable condition, and generated enormous excitement in McKinnon. He would banish the children from the room upstairs and settle down to become engrossed in his only link with the world at large.

It was now over twenty years since he had settled in the savannahs. His hair was already beginning to grow white. Maba laughed at him and said a fog was getting into his hair. Sometimes she or Zuna would cradle his head in their lap and try to pull out the white hairs. But they were becoming too numerous.

He went upstairs, pulled the shutters to keep out the worst of the blinding sun and sank into a Berbice chair, resting his legs on the long arm. He cut the string round the newspapers and checked the dates. The earliest was a yellowing copy of *The Times*, dated November 12th, 1917. He started with that.

First of all, he devoured avidly the detailed accounts of the Great War in Europe. He studied all the facts about the storming of Passchendaele; the bravery of the Canadian troops; the losses; the number of casualties.

As he scoured the paper for the rest of the war news, another item caught his attention. It was a long article by the science correspondent of *The Times* with the intriguing title 'The Weighing of Light'.

He began to read slowly, savouring every morsel of information:

It was my pleasure last Tuesday, in my capacity as science correspondent of this newspaper, to attend a meeting in the august and learned setting of the Royal Society.

The meeting was called by Sir Frank Dyson, the Astronomer Royal, on behalf of the Joint Permanent Eclipse Committee. We were to be addressed by the distinguished mathematician and physicist, Sir Arthur Stanley Eddington.

As we in the audience sat in our leather chairs, wreathed in cigar smoke, one eminent scientist pointed out that we were being overlooked by the disapproving portrait of Sir Isaac Newton. And well he might have disapproved, for Sir Frank Dyson told us, in his opening speech, that there seemed, at last, to be a unique opportunity to verify a certain prediction made by Einstein's Theory of Relativity.

The prediction of the theory is that a ray of light from a distant star would be deflected when it was close to the gravitational field of the sun. Final proof from physical experiments is needed to test and clinch the theory beyond doubt.

Sir Arthur Eddington is to be excused from joining his fellow Quakers peeling potatoes in camps in northern England on the following condition. Should the Great

War be finished by May, 1919, he must undertake to organise an expedition for the purposes of verifying Einstein's prediction.

The tall figure of Eddington himself then rose to address the excited audience.

'Good afternoon, gentlemen. Let me proceed directly with the matter in hand.

'The bending of light affects stars near the sun and accordingly the only chance of making the observation is during a total eclipse of the sun, when the moon cuts off the dazzling light. Even then, there is a great deal of light from the sun's corona which stretches far above the disc. It is thus necessary to have rather bright stars near the sun, which will not be lost in the glare of the corona. Further, the displacement of these stars can only be measured relatively to other stars, preferably more distant from the sun and less displaced. We need, therefore, a reasonable number of outer bright stars to serve as reference points.

'Any astronomer today, consulting the stars, would announce the most favourable day for weighing light as May 29th, 1919. The reason is that the sun in its annual journey around the ecliptic goes through fields of stars of varying richness, but on May 29th, it is in the midst of a quite exceptional patch of bright stars – part of the Hyades – by far the best starlit field encountered.

'Now if this problem had been put forward at some other period of history, it might have been necessary to wait some thousands of years for a total eclipse of the sun to happen on that lucky date. But by strange good fortune, such an eclipse is forecast to take place on May 29th, 1919.

'This eclipse will not be visible in Europe. The total eclipse will only be visible over a narrow band of the earth's surface some hundred miles wide, a tiny proportion of the earth's surface area. The track of the eclipse will fall across the southern Guiana highlands and the north-east of Brazil as well as the island of Principe off the African coast.

'We hope to send expeditions to Brazil and Africa to photograph the eclipse and thus to obtain the final verification of Einstein's theory.'

McKinnon gave a whoop and put down the paper. He went over to a drawer where he kept a calendar. The trouble was he had no idea what the date was. Blast it, he thought, Father Napier has already left to convert the Wai-Wai. Father Napier was the only person who would have any notion of the precise date. McKinnon knew it was 1919. And he knew it was May, but no more.

It was an opportunity that no amateur photographer could miss. Even if the total eclipse was not entirely visible from Waronawa – to be a hundred per cent sure of seeing it he should be a little further south – he would be able to take some fine photographs of a partial eclipse.

He sent one of the children to find Maba and Zuna. They came and stood on the stairs while he told them excitedly about the expected solar eclipse.

'You must alert me at the first sight of it so that I can take photographs.'

Maba fell stonily silent at the news. Her spirits sank. An eclipse too, she remembered, was a brother and sister coming together and eloping. It seemed there was no way to avoid what was happening.

'What's the matter?' asked McKinnon, surprised by the silence of the two sisters.

Zuna explained.

'We wouldn't too much like an eclipse,' she said, as if McKinnon could arrange to have it cancelled. 'An eclipse is a disgrace. It brings chaos. Monsters come out of the bush and attack people. The big anacondas that float in the rivers, when an eclipse comes, they lift their great heads up to the sky. Even the dead rise up to see what is happening. And everything can change into something else. Animals into people. People into animals. The dead and the living all mix up.'

Maba had hurried back downstairs.

McKinnon went back eagerly to sit down and read more about the preparations being made for the expeditions.

The scientists would be laden with clocks, coelostats and the object glasses of astrographic telescopes. The carpenter employed by the Observatory had not yet been released from military service and so a civil engineer at the Royal Naval College had undertaken the construction of frame huts covered with canvas that were easily put together. A joiner had been loaned as well to deal with the woodwork of the instruments. The small mirrors had been silvered at the Observatory, but it was necessary to send the large ones away to be silvered. Photographic plates would be suitably packed in hermetically sealed tin boxes. All the instruments were to be packed in cases inside hampers.

It dawned on McKinnon that he did not know whether or not the Great War was over. If the war was still going on and the expeditions could not take place, he might be the only person to photograph the eclipse. Then he realised that his equipment was not good enough to take pictures that would prove Einstein's theory. However, he cheered himself with the thought that there was no harm in trying. He hurried downstairs to make sure that he had enough supplies of film and developing fluid.

The eclipse. A loss. A forsaking.

Maba developed a blinding headache. She poked a piece of razor grass into her nose to make it bleed, but the pain in both sides of her head persisted until she went to sleep alone in her hammock. Zuna slept in the hammock next to her. McKinnon slept in the bed, also alone. The night was too hot and sticky to tolerate anyone's embrace.

And so it came about that, at the same time, although for very different reasons, one constellation, the Hyades, also known as part of Tamukang, came under the simultaneous gaze of a group of European scientists and a few Amerindians in the south savannahs and the southern bush of Guiana.

Which came first, the equation or the story?

The story, of course.

THE DIRTY FACE
OF THE MOON

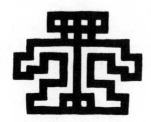

Father Napier was in high spirits as he packed up to leave St Ignatius and set off on his mission to convert the Wai-Wai. Although he was several months later than he had intended, at last he was ready. Happily, his chafed neck, caused by the rubbing of his priest's collar, had been cured just in time by a woman who gave him a concoction of aloes to rub on it.

He planned to cross Wapisiana country, go through Taruma territory, although there were few Taruma left now, and from there strike into the deep forest of the far south, if necessary into Brazil, to bring news of Christ to the Wai-Wai. He hoped to be back by the end of May.

On the journey, he was taking with him Titus, a lugubrious Macusi with a dry sense of humour, and Titus's two young sons, both of whom had the brown, slanting eyes of young agouti. He was also bringing three rather silent Taruma Indian brothers to translate the Wai-Wai language for him and a cheerfully energetic Wapisiana man called Siriko who wanted to make the journey to acquire some of the famed Wai-Wai graters.

The party set off. From Aishalton, they walked quickly through the last part of the savannahs. The two youngsters went running on ahead, always able to find the trail even though they had never been there before. When the trail forked, they would split up and each would take one of the forks until one or the other was certain he had hit the right track and would then call out to his brother.

The two boys walked in single file, chattering, always able to distinguish horse tracks from cattle or deer tracks and to tell how old the tracks were. The older boy was telling the younger one why the sun is supposed to be so pale at that time of year.

'He goes a long way away on a trading journey to a place where some rivers meet. He's looking to buy milk and salt. He gets drunk and weak and he's vomiting and spitting.' The boy, who was leading the way, jumped and staggered around imitating the drunken sun and the younger one grinned. 'Then he's captured and put in an upturned pot. His sons, Macunaima and Chico, are searching everywhere for him when Chico sees the light just glinting out from under the rim of the pot. He takes a gun and shatters the pot – "pow" – to set his father free. The sun goes up to the sky again but he's still pale and it takes a while for him to get his strength back.'

As they plunged into the gloom of the forest, Father Napier noticed that the Taruma men seemed to cheer up. It turned out that they did not entirely trust the Wapisiana through whose territory they were travelling.

Now the men went ahead of the boys and told them to stop chattering. Every stream had dried up and the only way to find water was to dig in a dried bed. That night, the Taruma men, annoyed at being unable to find water for cooking, travelled on ahead while the rest of the party set up camp. Father Napier could not imagine how the Tarumas found their way through such dense forest in the dark.

The next morning, the rest of the party made their way

out of the forest into a small area of savannah. The sight of the sky after walking in the gloom sent the boys sky-larking around. The breeze blew fresh and sweet. One of the boys found a shiny black scorpion, six inches long, and killed it with a rock.

The Tarumas were already squatting on the ground, eating. They called everyone over to share the food. Next to them on the ground was a crocodile with a huge, square piece cut out of its underbelly. Father Napier said grace and then chewed on the meat which tasted like fish but had the texture of leather.

After they had eaten, Father Napier insisted that they say thank you to God. He explained as best as he could in his halting Macusi what was required. Titus, the Macusi, looked confused and spoke in Wapisiana to Siriko who in turn spoke to the Tarumas. Only then did Father Napier remember being advised that none of the languages had a word for thank you. In the end, when they had all finished eating, Titus, trying to oblige, held the palm of his hand to the sky and said bluntly: 'That's enough, god.'

They moved on. The Kudiuwini River had dried up further down and so they had to make their way overland through another stretch of forest to the Kassikaitiu River. When they camped at night, the Indians lay in their hammocks and tried to learn each other's languages. Father Napier listened, astounded by their talent for mimicry and ventriloquism. Each man took it in turns to imitate a wild animal or bird and then name it in his own language.

Father Napier frowned as he lay in his hammock. He had been preoccupied with the difficulty of teaching the gospel in these languages. The Portuguese Jesuits in Brazil had warned him of the problem.

'These people think entirely in the concrete. You will have difficulty preaching the Christian gospel in languages that have no word for sin, virtue, mercy, kindness, truth, joy, please, thank you or sorry. The Wapisiana do not even have a word for friend.'

Father Napier had tried to learn a little Wapisiana from Danny when he was first at Waronawa, some years earlier.

'What is the word for sorry in Wapisiana?' he had asked.

Danny had looked blank. The priest put it another way.

'What would you say to me if you accidentally trod on my foot?'

'I would say what a stupid place to leave a foot,' replied Danny.

They reached the Kassikaitiu and to Father Napier's relief, Titus found an old corial which meant they could paddle downriver to the Taruma village of Barakako.

Just before they reached the village, Siriko the Wapisiana gave a shout for the boat to be brought into land. He had spotted some tracks. They got out and groped their way up the low bank. At the top of the bank stood two rackety sheds with a few old dried palm leaves covering the roofs.

'You know Danny McKinnon from Waronawa?' asked Siriko after inspecting the ground close to the sheds.

'I most certainly do,' replied the priest. 'I know the whole family well.'

'He was staying here with his sister until a few days ago.' Siriko pointed out their prints.

'What are they doing all the way down here?' asked Father Napier. He had skirted round Waronawa on his way south and knew nothing of their disappearance.

Siriko shrugged.

'They are living close,' he said, betraying nothing from his expression.

'Oh you mean they are somewhere nearby?' Father Napier's blue eyes sparkled with pleasure. The McKinnons would be good company if they were travelling in his direction.

'No. They are living close,' Siriko repeated, leaving Father Napier puzzled as to exactly what he meant. There was a double row of shelves in one of the sheds. 'They waited here until the shelves were filled with baskets of farine before they continued their journey. They are some way ahead of us.'

Father Napier hoped that he would catch up with them.

Next to the sheds were the charred remains of another Indian house. The occupants had clearly set fire to it and left.

They paddled the short distance to the village of Barakako. The village was out of their way but it was the only place where they could stock up with supplies. Father Napier used the time they were obliged to wait for supplies of cassava and farine to hold mass and instruction in the shed by the waterside.

It was eight days before they approached the first Wai-Wai village along a tributary of the Essequibo. Kabaikidiu, their final goal, was still some distance away across several mountains, some of which would take three hours to climb and another three to descend on the other side.

The fine weather had broken. A mist of rain drifted across the waters as they paddled along against the current. The trees nearly met overhead, forming a lofty fretwork of grey sky. On either side, dense banks of foliage, dripping with water, sloped down to the river. Giant green water lilies, their ridged sides turned up like pastry flans, nearly sank under the weight of the water. Father Napier felt chilled and damp. The seats in the boat were wet and uncomfortable. He suffered cramp in his buttocks. Something flapped over the surface of the river. The priest could not even recognise what species of creature it was. It could have been some sort of duck, a bird, a frog or a huge butterfly.

Then Father Napier caught his first glimpse of some Wai-Wai people in a canoe. The canoe shot out unexpectedly from the concealed entrance of a stream. Standing at the bow of the canoe was a boy whose appearance made Father Napier draw his breath in admiration.

The boy's hair was long, flowing and jet black. To the priest's eye he seemed so handsome that he thought immediately that the boy should be a model for a portrait of Christ. That night he wrote in his diary: 'I have never seen a boy or girl so exquisitely beautiful.'

The canoe hovered near them for a few moments while the occupants of the two boats studied each other, then the Wai-Wai turned and disappeared back into the sidewaters. Most of them had been wearing ornate feather ornaments.

'Like apparitions from a story-book,' Father Napier wrote in his diary.

It rained heavily. The bush was sodden and dripping when they eventually reached the part of the forest where Kabaikidiu was situated. They had walked through the trees for several hours. As they approached the village, the rain cleared and the bell-bird began to announce sunshine with its twanging, metallic call like a zither. From deeper inside the forest, Father Napier heard what sounded to him like a piccolo. Through his interpreter, he asked the children who had run to meet him whether someone was playing the flute.

'Kuparuko.' That, they told him, was a bird. But then they explained that Wai-Wai men do also play the flute when they are entering or leaving the village.

It was humid and sticky after the rain. As usual when it rained, the hem of Father Napier's soutane was soaked and heavy as they entered the clearing where the village was built.

The villagers were awaiting his arrival. All the men of the village wore their hair long, loose if they were young, plaited if they were older. The plaits ended in a foot-long tube decked with feathers. Some wore small bunches of blue and yellow macaw feathers and humming-bird feathers as ear-rings. Some wore scarlet macaw feathers stuck through their top lip. Others had stiff, long, black powis feathers dangling from armlets. A few had the white down of the harpy eagle stuck in their hair over their foreheads.

Nobody took much notice of the visitors, except the children. The Taruma immediately engaged in a long conversation with the touchau of the village, outlining every detail of what had happened on the journey.

That afternoon, Father Napier wasted no time before starting to indoctrinate the children by his usual method. He gathered them together and taught them an 'action' song. Soon all the children were joining in with him clapping and shouting 'Bang-bang' as he showed them what to do. Then he sat them in a circle and taught them the tune of 'How Sweet the Name of Jesus Sounds' amidst much laughing and giggling.

At nightfall, Father Napier found himself preparing to sling his hammock in the enormous cone-shaped building about eighty foot high and eighty foot across, which housed some forty men and women. As he prepared to sleep, he was almost overwhelmed by the dank, pungent smell of damp thatch mixed with the reek of woodsmoke. The proximity of so many people made him feel uncomfortable.

People's hammocks were slung close to the wall and near to each other. Eight or ten fires blazed on the floor, lighting up the underbellies of the hammocks and throwing moving shadows on the walls.

The hunting dogs, for which the Wai-Wai were renowned,

slept on shelves built into the circular walls. Every now and then, someone who was responsible for a dog's training would run with the animal into the forest for it to do its toilet. One of the Wai-Wai was explaining to Titus, through the Taruma interpreter, the precise circumstances of every single animal his dog had ever tracked down.

Through his interpreter, Father Napier asked if Danny and Beatrice were there and was disappointed to find that they had already pushed further south to where the rest of the Wai-Wai lived in Brazil. They had exchanged large amounts of cassava bread for a hunting dog.

People wandered about completing their last chores before getting into their hammocks and chatting.

Father Napier's enquiries about Danny and Beatrice produced an unexpected result. The young man he had found so breath-takingly beautiful jumped down from his hammock and appeared to be asking permission to do something from one of the older men who nodded his head in assent. The boy was the same boy that Danny had taken hunting and fishing when some of the Wai-Wai passed through Waronawa. His name was Wario.

Immediately, he took a stick and poked the embers of the central fire until the subdued glow broke into flames which flickered over the disintegrating logs and white wood ash like snake-tongues. Men and women lolled in their hammocks watching him.

He had dispensed with his feather ornaments and wore nothing but a loin cloth made of thick material from which hung one tassel of feathers. Father Napier gazed at him entranced. Wario prodded the embers again and began to whisper in a hoarse voice which everyone could hear, but in a language which Father Napier could not understand.

The priest watched as the androgynous boy began not only to narrate, but to act out the parts of each character.

'A long time ago, Nuni made love to his sister. Yes, he made love to his own sister.'

Wario hugged his chest while he spoke, as if the dying fire did not keep him warm enough, and then he made a long, low sucking noise as he drew in his breath through his lips.

The darkness of the congealed night felt almost palpably dense to Father Napier as he stared at the boy's fine limbs and flat stomach. There was the sort of silence throughout the house that meant everyone was listening.

'He came into his sister's arms right after playing the flute. His spirit remained playing the flute but his body came and lay down beside her.

'"Hello, darling, I want to lie in your arms."

'"Is that so? All right. Jump up into my hammock."

'"All right."

'"Who are you?"

'"I'm from another village far away. I've come to lie with you."

'"All right. Get up in the hammock then."

'And he climbed into the hammock and made love to her.

'"I'm going back home now."

'"All right. Why did you come?"

'"I just came. That's all."

'The flute was still playing, the sound of it running along the breeze.

'The next night he came again. He left his spirit to play the flute and let his body come to her. He came over and over again.'

Wario stopped speaking and crouched to throw some aromatic hiawa gum in the embers. The resin cracked and popped. Soon the air filled with a sharp, pungent smell like eucalyptus. He continued, now acting the girl's part, an expression of fear on his face.

'"Why does he keep coming?" she asked herself.

'"You must live close by. If your home is so far away, how is it you come so often?"

'"To tell you the truth, I used to be terribly lazy. I've had to overcome all my laziness in order to visit you this often. I tell you, I come from far."

'Maybe it's my own brother who's coming, she thought.'

Wario placed his hand over his heart and shrank back in a gesture of wariness.

'That night, to catch him out, she painted him with genipap all over his face. His face got very black.

'"Hey. What did she put on me?"'

There was a look of disgust on Wario's face as he wiped his cheek and examined his palm.

'It would not come off. He didn't come back until after sunset. He had only caught one labba because he spent all the time trying to get the black marks off his face. It would not come off. It was there to stay.'

The fire next to Wario blazed up a little just as the other fires were dying down. Father Napier continued to gaze in admiration at the boy's crow-black hair and the attractive forward thrust of his wide mouth.

A lizard, overcome by the heat, fell out of the thatch to the ground. Most people were awake and listening or just drowsing off. If a child cried, the mother would take it into her hammock. Father Napier was captivated by the youth's movements and gestures although he did not understand one word of the story.

Wario walked a few paces up and down, shaking and shuddering.

'The brother went away for ages. He was too ashamed to face his sister. But when eventually he returned, she took his arm and swung him round.'

Once more acting the part of the girl, the same look of distrust as before leapt into Wario's face.

'"It was you who made love to me."

'She saw him in the daylight. He had been too tired to leave in the dark as he usually did. He had his face covered with his hands.

'"Oh my eyes are hurting. Oh my eyes are killing me."

'"What's the matter with you?" she asked.

'"My eyes are stinging."

'She pulled his hands away and saw the black patterns on his face.

'"You're lying. You fucked me as if I was from another family."'

Wario looked round at his audience in the dim light, about to bring his story to a close.

'The brother changed after that. He was sad because he knew that he could not have his sister for his wife here on earth, so he rushed out of his hut with his bow and arrows. He came to a clearing and shot an arrow into the sky. It stuck there. He shot another into the butt of the first and so on until he made a ladder of arrows from the ground to the sky. He climbed up until he reached the sky. His sister came after him naked, having thrown away her skirt.'

Wario mimed climbing into the sky, arm over arm.

'In those days there was no moon. So, after he reached the sky, he became the moon. That's why the moon's got a dirty face. She became the evening star. They were able to live together in the sky.'

Father Napier tried to exert an iron will over his erection as he gazed at the young story-teller. He tried to quench it. He prayed. He imagined his whole body cased in metal. He imagined Christ's image blazing in the heavens and as he turned his head away, he ejaculated uncontrollably and lay staring at the damp thatch, filled with misery, shame and pleasure.

At that point, a short tubby man with a flat nose and

shiny hair that swung as he walked climbed out of his hammock and in full view of everyone started to mimic the walk of a tapir. Even Father Napier, when he looked round, recognised the animal, the man was so accurate and comical in his impersonation. His behind wobbled obscenely. He stopped and sniffed the air, peering short-sightedly into the gloom. He whistled like a tapir and lifted up his loin cloth to examine his genitals and blow on them. People began to chuckle.

'We have a different version,' said one of the Taruma from where his hammock hung in the gloom.

'We say that the brother became the sun and she became the moon. He is still chasing her round the sky. Whenever he catches her and makes love to her there is an eclipse. Demons come from the forest and rivers to attack people. Those massive camoodies in the rivers raise their heads from the water to see why the sky has gone dark.'

'They say the moon is the nocturnal sun,' chipped in somebody else.

A sleepy argument followed about how, if that were the case, you can sometimes see both the sun and the moon in the sky together.

Little by little, conversation stopped and people slept. Father Napier tried to focus his mind on his plans for the next day, ignoring the stickiness between his legs.

Occasionally, during the night, there was a cough or a moan. Once or twice, people who were cold got up to revive one of the dying fires and talk quietly beside it for a while.

THE RIVER OF THE DEAD

In unremitting heat, like a steam bath, Beatrice and Danny paddled down the olive-green waters of the River Kassikaitiu.

Danny wore nothing but a pair of white shorts. Beatrice had hitched her blue skirt into the waistband and wore one of Danny's vests. In the back of the boat lay the brown and white hunting dog that Danny had been given by the Wai-Wai. Roots and dead lianas protruded in a stiff tangle from the high sandy banks on either side.

As they passed, a flock of scarlet macaws that had been resting at different angles on these branches took off. Their bright-blue tail feathers flashed in the sun as the stubby bodies and long tails wheeled and they flew screaming into the sky and settled, almost out of sight, in the top of the tallest trees.

'The Taruma call this the River of the Dead,' said Danny.

The Taruma had so named the Kassikaitiu because in times of severe drought, when the waters were low, there were ancient petroglyph writings on the rocks at the base of the river. These writings were rarely visible. They were reckoned to be older than the great flood which once submerged the region. The Taruma said that it was by means of those marks, halfway between writing and drawing, that the dead were still able to speak to the living.

Beatrice, unaware of the ancient signs beneath her, thought that she had never seen surroundings that were more alive. The river was about thirty feet across. The trees on either side shimmered, tingled and exploded with exuberant bird noise. The surface of the water teemed with ducks and otters. Over by the far bank an alligator lazed, his goggle-eyes just above the water.

'See him,' giggled Beatrice. 'Mamai Zuna used to say he was hiding because he stole the sun's fish.'

Danny himself seemed to come alive in the bush. He was more alert, vigilant and inventive than at home. He discovered how to extract oil from paku fish so that they could cook. He invented a way of making cartridges for the gun, although these were often unreliable. And instead of farine, they grated Brazil nuts on their grater and roasted them.

After several weeks hunting and fishing, neither of them missed cultivated food. The supplies they had collected at Barakako, they bartered when they reached the Wai-Wai and Danny got himself a hunting dog. For Danny, meeting up with his friend Wario again should have been a pleasure, but Beatrice's presence put a damper on it for him. He felt embarrassed so they only stayed a day or two before moving on.

There was an abundance of food. They lived well on fish, nuts, fruit and game. Once Danny shot a monkey. Beatrice singed the hair over a fire she had made on the rocks and scraped it before taking out the intestines and moulding the kidney fat into a sausage. Then they cut the rest and threw it in the pot. After they had eaten, they lazed on the smooth grey rocks in the sweltering heat. Soon they were bitten all over by insects.

Beatrice relished having Danny entirely to herself.

'Why do you keep staring at me?' He complained.

She scratched the insect bites on her legs and arms. It puzzled Beatrice too that she still felt this yearning for Danny even though she had him constantly by her side. She turned from him and looked deliberately away towards where the water spouted in a tiny fall at the bottom of the rocks. It has something to do with the passing of time, she thought. I wish I could stop the passage of time.

Danny took off his shorts which were spattered with monkey fat. He balanced himself in the boat and Beatrice pushed it off. She watched him float downstream, a bronze statue, bow drawn, the tree shadows occasionally striping him like a tiger fish. Suddenly, the back of the arapaima he'd spotted earlier became visible to him under the water. He let fly the arrow well below the fish to allow for the refraction of light and then scrambled, all arms and legs, to grab at the shaft which wobbled as the fish struggled.

He brought the boat and the fish back and Beatrice got in the front, trailing her fingers in the water as he paddled. He leaned forward to whisper something in her ear and as he did so, Beatrice experienced a powerful feeling of recognition. All this had already happened. Everything around her seemed startlingly familiar as if she had done it all before, as if she could anticipate everything that was about to take place. She saw every leaf, twig and branch on the bank, every insect on the surface of the sienna water outlined with astonishing clarity. An eternity lasted a few seconds and passed. She recognised the warning.

'I'm going to have a migraine attack,' she said.

After the attack was over and she was fully recovered, they slung a hammock in the trees near the bank. Danny fondled her and played with her as a preliminary to long, slow, vegetable acts of love. Later in the night, both of them bitten to pieces by mosquitoes, sandflies and kaboura, they made love more violently as if rubbing against each other frantically would relieve the itching. Smeared with each other's blood from the bites, they finally fell asleep, arms, thighs and legs entangled like roots.

Broiling hot in his soutane, Father Napier prepared to leave the Wai-Wai. He carried his tin trunk down to the river and supervised the packing of the boat at the landing. His first mission had been a triumphant success.

Several of the Wai-Wai had gathered to say goodbye. Father Napier cast a furtive eye round to see if Wario had come. His brief infatuation with the young man had given an extra vibrant zeal to his teachings. The last two weeks had seen a flurry of baptisms, all of which he had duly recorded in his baptismal book. He was a little disappointed to hear, when he enquired, that Wario had gone off fishing. There had been no sign of Danny and Beatrice returning since they passed through that way.

Siriko beamed as he loaded up a pile of graters to take home. Titus and his boys climbed on board. As the boat pushed off from the landing, Father Napier promised through his interpreter to return in a year or so to carry out confirmations. The priest waved farewell. For a while, they raced with one of the Wai-Wai boats but the Wai-Wai soon streaked ahead and disappeared into one of the creeks.

Six weeks later, he reached St Ignatius in the north savannahs, exhausted but happy. As soon as he had unpacked and bathed his feet, he got two of the boys to boil up some coffee which he drank, revelling in the luxury of condensed milk which he had not tasted for months.

Danny and Beatrice headed even further south. They set off

on foot, with the dog, across the Acarai Mountains. In the hills the breezes were cooler and they made their way along trails that led round great black boulders and old burial caves. They camped for two nights in a cave under an overhanging boulder before Danny discovered some old, whitened jaguar shit in a corner and they decided it might not be safe. Soon they entered another stretch of lightly wooded forest.

The dog made hunting easier. Danny would listen for its bark. If the sound moved, he knew the dog was chasing quarry. If the sound came from one place, he knew the dog had either caught the creature, or it had gone to ground or it was a turtle. He regularly cleansed the dog's nostrils with pepper so that its sense of smell would be keener. He shot parakeets and roasted them as a treat for the dog.

The fourth day after they had left the cave, they were threading their way through the forest when the dog began to growl. Beatrice looked down on the ground to see what was troubling it. Danny laughed.

'Look up,' he said.

Hanging down, almost in Beatrice's face, was the tail of a jaguar. She followed the line of the body sprawled along the large branch and was dazzled by two phosphorescent eyes that hung, three feet above her, in a moving pattern of spots, leaf shadow and amber sunlight. As the pattern shifted, the animal appeared to be juggling with its own eyes. She stared, mesmerised, so close that she could see the pale yellow-green eyes in segments like a halved grapefruit.

'It's all right,' said Danny. 'She's just eaten. You din see the hog carcass back there?'

They continued, single file, along the trail.

The proximity of the jaguar excited Danny and he became talkative.

'Never underestimate a tiger. They have fantastic imagination. Uncle Shibi-din saw one get in a boat once and float downriver. Another time he saw one rearranging a cow it had killed so that the cow looked as if it was asleep. That way he fooled the vultures and could come back for meat the next day. And once he was lured into the forest by the sound of someone chopping wood. When he got close, he found it was a tiger lashing the trunk of a tree with its tail. They can swim, climb trees and run fast. Uncle Shibi-din said they were the sun on earth. They're ventriloquists too. They can make their voice sound as if it's coming from somewhere else.'

'Yes,' Beatrice joined in. 'And Daddy saw one trying to drag a cow up a steep bank but the horns kept catching. The tiger broke the horns against a rock until it could pull the cow up easily.'

Beatrice could have bitten her lip. The mention of their father threw a pall over the conversation. Danny became silent. Beatrice followed behind him.

When they came right up close to the next Wai-Wai settlement in Brazil, Danny suddenly lost his nerve and refused to go on. He felt as though there was an invisible barrier round the village, a magnetic field keeping him out.

They began to quarrel. Beatrice's voice became high and querulous as he consistently objected to approaching the village. She tried begging and cajoling but he insisted on building a shelter a mile or so away from the settlement.

'The kaboura flies are biting me to pieces,' she sulked. 'We could hang our hammocks in their big house. It would be much better.'

'I'm not going,' said Danny fiercely. 'People are saying things about us.' His face flushed the way she remembered it doing when he was upset as a child.

Beatrice had no qualms about visiting other villages because, at heart, she did not believe that they were doing anything wrong. Any partnership that felt so natural could not, in her eyes, be bad. She knew that, for some reason, what they were doing was not totally acceptable to people but, in her own mind, her conscience was clear. And she believed that everybody would agree with her secretly, in their own heart of hearts.

Later, Danny cheered up a bit. They discovered an abandoned canoe in the river. Danny took it and paddled along on his own until he found a suitable creek. He was relieved to be away from Beatrice for a while. She did not seem to be overcome with shame the way he was when they were in company. He wondered if he was a coward.

He set about making a fish-trap. Focusing on the mechanics of constructing the trap relieved him of his unease. By the time he had finished weaving the rushes into a conical trap and set it, building a dam further downstream, he was himself again. He moved up and down the bank setting a couple more spring-traps.

Instead of returning straightaway to Beatrice, he sat on some sand at the edge of the creek and stared at the water.

The sun steamed down. The waters were stained reddish brown from vegetable matter. A ripple the shape of a lifted eyelid in the water rolled towards him. The sweet, sickly smell of grasses, wild eddoes and mangrove bushes hung in the humid air. A film of sweat covered Danny's body and soaked the roots of his hair as he sat there.

When the insects became too troublesome, he decided to go back and find Beatrice. He could check the traps in the morning. Paddling along the creek, he ducked to avoid low branches and finally emerged into the wide main river. After about fifty yards, the black waters began to slap the side of the boat with an ominous 'thunk' and to churn unexpectedly all round the canoe.

At this point the river was some forty feet wide. Trees

leaned out from both banks, their exposed twisted roots holding precariously on to the sandy soil. Danny checked to see what was causing the turbulence.

Small bush-hogs go around in groups of five or six. Adult ones herd together in groups of thirty or forty. Wild hogs are fierce. They can kill a tiger. Danny found himself surrounded by one of these large herds as they tried to swim across the river. The boat started to buck and twist as the animals smacked against it.

Suddenly as though by a signal, they attacked *en masse*. Danny stood up unsteadily in the boat and tried fending them off with his paddle. The boat rocked violently. He was beset by seething mounds of bristling black and grey hog backs. They smashed at the boat in a fury, trying to break it with their yellow teeth and tusks.

His foot skidded as he reached down into the canoe for the axe and the boat nearly overturned. Danny somehow regained his balance and hacked at the hogs, at their writhing backs, their black lips and snapping jaws with desperate, flailing swings of his axe. The water boiled with blood and spray. He was covered in blood. He killed three before the others took heed.

As suddenly as the attack began, it was over. The herd swam leisurely to the other side.

Danny's chest heaved as he struggled for breath. He watched the carcasses float downriver without even trying to keep one for food. He managed to get the boat to the side of the river and hold on to some branches, retching and waiting for the nausea to pass.

He thought the herd had been acting as if they were under a spell. The whole episode felt like a bad sign.

As soon as Beatrice saw Danny coming towards her, she could see that something was wrong. His shorts were streaked with blood. His gait was stiff and slow. He stared straight ahead without looking to see where he put his feet and he was carrying no fish.

He told her what had happened, then slung his hammock between two giant mora trees and curled up in it, hanging there between the trees like a leaf. She took his shorts down to the river to wash the blood from them, using the lather from black sage leaves for soap. When she came back he was shivering and refused to eat, although the pot was on the fire. She tried to bring back some semblance of normality by chatting in a wifely way.

'We should get ourselves two Wai-Wai hammocks. They're smaller and easier to carry. They make theirs with fibre. Our Wapisiana ones are cotton. Ours dry well in the savannah but in the forest they stay wet.'

Danny remained silent.

She climbed into the hammock with him and put her leg over his thigh, trying to comfort him. After a while, he began to make love half-heartedly.

Neither Beatrice nor Danny were aware that an eclipse had begun.

Not much sun penetrated the forest and neither of them noticed that it was growing gradually as dark as night and that the chatter and piercing calls of the birds had stopped altogether. It was pitch black. During the eclipse, the forest became as quiet as death. Then bats began to squeak. A night-hawk, that usually remains immobile on a branch all day, took off and flapped overhead. Somewhere in the far distance, they heard the distressed grunting of a jaguar.

Danny twisted in the hammock to face Beatrice.

'I'm cold,' he said.

She thought that it was just the coolness of the creek

water which he had dashed over himself to get the blood off. But then something happened to Danny. He was seized with a terrible icy coldness all through his gut, a coldness indistinguishable from sadness. He gave an almighty shudder that rocked the hammock. She held on to him but he could not control the shivering. She rubbed his back vigorously. The shudders rocked him four or five times more, leaving him helpless. She tried to warm him and soothe him by rubbing and stroking him and holding him tightly in her arms.

'I'm so cold,' he kept mumbling. He tried to hold on to her in the grip of this chilling nausea and those icy shivers but his arms felt like lead and he was unable to absorb her warmth. He felt as if he would never be warm again. They lay there wrapped in each other's arms without moving, neglecting to check on the boat or cover the food in the pot which the dog nosed around, waiting for it to cool.

The convulsions left Danny feeling as though all the bones in his body had been taken out and rearranged.

'I'll paint you with genipap,' said Beatrice anxiously, shocked at his condition. She thought he might feel protected by it.

A dismal grey-green light began to filter through the trees once more. And for the next few hours, with the utmost concentration, Beatrice drew patterns all over his face and body with the black dye that she had collected from the Wai-Wai; she painted him with concentric squares like the rotating ones she had once seen when she fainted; she marked him with long stripes and geometric shapes down his bronze back until he looked like a beautifully patterned insect.

He took no interest in the proceedings but lay still while she worked, feeling too sick and exhausted to move. She covered every inch of his face and body with mathematical precision as if the construction of these austere, symmetrical patterns might somehow shore him up and hold him together.

SAVANNAH ECLIPSE

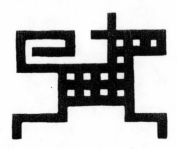

On the savannahs, the eclipse made it grow dark quickly like someone's heart sinking. Birds stopped singing. Cattle started to wend their way home. The tamarind tree at the back of Waronawa, which normally at that time of year was one gigantic, flowering buzz, became silent as the bees flew in black swarms through the darkening air for their hives. The first bats started to flit through the sky.

As soon as the moon began to encroach on the sun in the middle of the morning, everybody came out of their thatch houses at Waronawa and began to bang pots and utensils together and started shouting to frighten the two celestial bodies apart. Auntie Bobo's husband fired two shots into the air with his gun. Some of the men fired off arrows towards the eclipse.

Mamai Maba stood outside the house shouting: 'No. No. No,' in a loud voice, as if she was deeply offended by something. Too terrified to look up at the sky, she kept her head averted from the sun while continuing to bang two metal pots together with her powerful arms. Zuna, her hollow black eyes full of anxiety, made a great racket by clashing a metal ladle and a metal bucket together.

As soon as he realised what was going on, McKinnon rushed to the rising ground behind the house and set up his tripod. As the sun was gradually quenched and the savannahs grew dark around him, he snapped at regular intervals in an attempt to catch each phase of the phenomenon. In the distance he could hear people screaming.

When the eclipse was over, he wound up the film and headed for his dark room to develop it as quickly as possible.

When he got there, his precious dark room was in disarray. Maba was tipping everything upside down. The door was wide open letting in all the light and ruining some film he had already taken. The trough of liquid which he used to develop film had been up-ended and the fluid spilt all over the floor. Angrily, he went through the house to discover that every container, bowl, dish, gourd, pot, monkey-cup and bucket had been emptied of its contents and turned upside down.

'What's going on here?' he asked, furious. Maba and Zuna were struggling to overturn a barrel of rainwater outside.

'It's the slime from the eclipse,' panted Mamai Maba. 'It will get into everything and poison us.'

McKinnon shook his head in exasperation. Maba had a look in her eyes that he had never seen before, an expression of contempt and malicious defiance. He went upstairs and sat swinging on a hammock to calm himself down. Disappointed and bemused, he looked at the one photograph he had managed to salvage. It belonged to Father Napier and had come out quite well. It showed some thirty or forty alligators sprawled out on the rocks one misty day on the banks of the Ireng River.

By midday when it was quite clear that the monstrous episode was over and the sun had fully recovered, the community at Waronawa came to, rather shamefaced as if they had all been on a temporary drinking spree, and prepared to leave for a manorin at Achimeriwau. People took hoes and cutlasses. They were going to help a young couple clear the land and plant before the rains set in properly. The couple had left it perilously late. Luckily, the rains were delayed that year. There had been a false start with showers and squalls and then the sun had continued grilling the earth as fiercely as ever.

Maba stayed behind. The eclipse had both disturbed her and settled something in her mind. It made her feel better about Danny and Beatrice. What they were doing was more understandable in relation to an eclipse. She went and shaved a piece off the roll of black Rupununi shag tobacco hanging on the wall and made herself a long cigarette. She sucked on it, exhaling the smoke in slow, thoughtful gusts as she looked out of the window.

Everything was dry. It was as if the rains would never come. The road beyond the house was cracked like a turtle back. The sun blazed down, scorching the cashew and sandpaper trees. The dry leaves made a scratching sound as the wind shook them.

She decided then and there to consult her father about the whole business. McKinnon seemed to be completely unaware of what was happening.

Her father had died two years earlier. His bones hung in a gaily beaded and feathered basket from one of the rafters. She took them down. His spirit, she reckoned, must be almost gone from them by now. Still, she took them out carefully and threw them on the dried-earth floor to study the pattern.

Several things happened almost simultaneously. A cloud crossed the sun, throwing the room into darkness and making the bones invisible. The house filled with the oily, bitter-sweet smell of citrus trees and Mamai Maba heard a sort of groan rolling around the room. She grabbed a brush and tried to sweep it out. But the noise grew and got inside her ears. She shook her head and decided it was time to discuss the whole matter with McKinnon.

At first, he did not understand what was being said. Mamai Maba told him so casually and in such a matter-of-fact way that he thought she was just worried because Danny and Beatrice had been away in the bush for so long.

They stood in the upstairs room. The sun came through the windows and buttered the room in slabs with stripes of shadow. Maba looked sad and soft. She was fatalistic about the affair and no longer distraught. Now it was a matter of providence.

'Looks like the sun and moon repeat their crime,' she said and shrugged her shoulders as she spoke, her eyebrows lifting up and making the wrinkles stream down on either side of her forehead.

Too startled to reply, McKinnon stared at the woman whose life, with that of her sister, he had shared for so many years. Her hair was still black and tied back in a knot as it had been when he first knew her, but she looked rounder and smoother, like a boulder worn down by the river.

He had felt a wave of nausea at the news. In part it was because he felt foolish for not having guessed. But part of the shock also came in realising that he did not know his own boundaries. He thought he was an open-minded man, a free-thinker, not restricted by conventional morality, but the news shocked and revolted him.

He stood there without moving a muscle. One of the shutters squeaked as it blew back and forth. Mamai Maba, having delivered the news, collected up some clothes to wash and went downstairs.

As soon as she had left, McKinnon felt as if he were

suffocating. Driven by an urge to go outside and walk on the savannahs, he left the house.

The sun flashed off the pond behind the house. The air burned all round him. He took one of the trails leading in the direction of the Kanaku Mountains. Here and there rose dead trees stripped of bark. The countryside all round was pure desert, dotted with termite nests. As he walked he could see no living thing, not even a blade of grass, just the charred remains of lifeless trees and withered twigs. Every hundred yards or so he had to stop because a blackness seemed to be gathering inside his head and he could hear the explosive banging of his heart. He stood still on the savannahs.

After a few minutes, he turned to face the house. The ranch and settlement of houses round it lay in the bright sunlight. The Rupununi River glinted behind them. One of the dogs stood halfway along the trail wondering whether to follow him or not. The dog moved off on its own.

And then, quite out of the blue, McKinnon knew that he would leave the savannahs, that he did not belong, however much of his life had been spent there. He was not sure exactly when he would go. There was no rush, but eventually he would leave. He was astounded to think he had been there so long. The whole of the last twenty-five years felt like a dream.

After an hour or so, the palpitations and dizziness both lessened and he began to walk slowly back to the ranch-house. As soon as he was inside, he wrote a note to Father Napier at St Ignatius asking him to come to Waronawa as a matter of urgency.

Although it was getting late, he sent one of the vaqueiros with it. The man set off. Maba and Zuna watched him gallop away in the direction of the Kanakus. The moon on the horizon was bloated and the colour of blood.

THE GREAT FALL

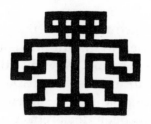

It was June, 1919. Father Napier responded immediately to the summons. The rains had finally started, making his journey to Waronawa a wet and uncomfortable one. Water sloshed around in the bottom of the boat and his boots were soaking wet and heavy. He felt irritable. In the steady drizzle, he scrambled out at the Waronawa landing and started tugging his trunk out of the boat. The lean figure of McKinnon splashed over the muddy ground to meet him.

'I really have news for you,' said McKinnon. 'The war is at an end.'

Despite the damp, McKinnon looked dry and desiccated as if the savannahs had squeezed all the juices out of him. Father Napier noticed that he suddenly seemed to have aged.

News that the First World War had ended finally reached the Rupununi savannahs more than six months after the armistice of November, 1918. When McKinnon had ploughed his way through to the end of his pile of old newspapers he had come across the announcement.

Father Napier hoisted his slippery tin trunk on to his hip and the two men walked up the slope to the house.

'That's not why you summoned me here so urgently, surely?' The priest looked at him sideways with the sly curiosity of a bird. 'You could have just sent a note.'

'You don't seem very pleased at the news,' said McKinnon, prevaricating, unwilling to divulge immediately the reason for his summons.

'It depends on the conditions of the peace.'

A flock of cranes flew by. McKinnon could hardly keep his mind on what he was saying. Now that the priest was here, he resented having to tell him about Danny and Beatrice.

'Apparently the Germans have surrendered unconditionally. An armistice has been declared. A peace conference is being held at Versailles.'

'In that case I am very dissatisfied,' Father Napier replied, bristling with patriotism under the grey sky. 'We should have entered Berlin with flags flying and bands playing. I hate half measures. The Germans will be laughing at us up their sleeves.'

The two men entered the cool darkness of the house. McKinnon sent one of the children to bring a glass of lemonade for the visitor.

Upstairs, McKinnon stood by the window looking out towards the ford where four vaqueiros on horseback were taking a small group of cattle across the river in the grey mist.

'What was the urgent message about?' enquired the priest.

'I need to see my son Danny.'

The water swirled where the cattle had crossed.

'Ah. I saw signs of them on my visit to the Wai-Wai. But I kept missing them. They've been away for some time. What are they doing down there?'

McKinnon's face was half hidden by the wooden shutter but something about the rigidity of the upturned profile made Father Napier stop speaking.

McKinnon prided himself on his rationalism. He looked upon himself as a man of the world. He thought he could discuss any subject with equanimity. But now he hesitated. He found the thought of having to seek help from a priest demeaning. He looked greenish and sick as he spoke.

'Could you go and find him for me?' His tone was almost pleading. 'I'm thinking of selling some cattle. I need his help.'

Father Napier stood stock still in astonishment.

'What! It has just taken me six weeks to get back from there. Besides, they could be anywhere. It's impossible. It would be like finding a needle in a haystack.'

McKinnon said nothing. He licked his dry lips with little motions like a lizard. Outside they could hear shouts from the children and the thwacks of a lasso as they practised harnessing a wet post.

'Look,' protested Father Napier, 'I have only just got back. The whole journey took me four months. Apart from the fact that I'm extremely tired, as far as my mission work is concerned, I have a great deal to do here in the savannahs. I don't plan to return to that area for a year or more when it will be time for confirmations. I'm sorry but it's out of the question.'

The priest found himself enjoying that particular exercise of petty power which comes with being righteously justified in refusing a request.

'I believe they have left Wai-Wai country now,' continued McKinnon as if Father Napier had just agreed to go and look for them. 'There have been sightings and reports that they are headed for the Great Fall on the Essequibo.'

Father Napier tried, unsuccessfully, to stifle his annoyance.

'For goodness sake. I'm not a messenger,' he burst out irritably. 'Send one of the vaqueiros or some men from the settlement. I have the Lord's work to attend to.'

McKinnon turned to look at the priest who had swung round away from him in exasperation and stood, one hand on his hip, fidgeting with his straggly beard. Something in the other man's manner infuriated him. His self-assured cockiness. McKinnon wanted to dent that assurance. He did not take his eyes off the priest as he spoke.

'I think as a Christian minister it is your duty to go. They have run away together.' He spoke slowly and deliberately, emphasising the last sentence.

Father Napier still failed to understand fully what he was being told.

'Well, they're old enough to do what they want. You can't hang on to your children for ever. They'll come back eventually, I'm sure.'

McKinnon hammered it home.

'Father Napier. They are full-blooded brother and sister. In your terms, I believe they are committing what you would call a mortal sin.'

His own distress abated somewhat in his pleasure at the priest's shock.

'Are you sure about that?'

'Yes.'

'Then I will go straightaway. Can you find men and provisions for me?'

'Yes.'

Father Napier caught the relief in McKinnon's face.

'I hope that, in return, you will consider letting me build a church here for the people of Waronawa.'

'Most certainly,' replied McKinnon, concealing his dislike of the man. He knew that the church would never be built. He had already decided to sell his cattle and get out of Waronawa.

Later that evening after McKinnon had told Maba that Father Napier was going to look for the couple, Maba said shrewdly to Zuna: 'It's because they are part white that he is going. If they were full Indians he would never make all this fuss. And we would never ask him. We should look after our own affairs. Besides, I know it's not good, what Danny and Beatrice are doing, but it's not the worst thing in the world. It's happened before. It's just fate. He shouldn't interfere.'

McKinnon provided the priest with what he could for the journey. He sent four of the vaqueiros with him. There was a cassava shortage so he could only offer some rice and Bovril. Father Napier and the men would have to subsist on what they could catch.

The party set off on June 21st, 1919. The rainy season had now begun in earnest.

Where previously, the sun burned down on the clear outline of trails and village settlements, now everything on the savannahs seemed to be dissolving in the teeming rains. This dissolution of contours, the blotting out of differences, the melting of edges made Father Napier feel that the distinction between everything was being blurred. He thrust his chin up in defiance against the rain as they made their slow way to the Kudiuwini River by bullock cart. The water ran down his face. Every so often, they had to stop and push the cart out of a rain-filled rut. Sometimes the track disappeared altogether in a flooded part of the terrain.

He kept looking towards the horizon to try and find his bearings but the rains obliterated the rim of the earth and stirred the land into the sky. He had no idea where he was and relied entirely on his Indian escorts. Roads turned into rivers and plains into lakes. The Indians told him that the rains heralded invisibility and change.

It took them fifteen days to reach the Kudiuwini River which was running high and allowed Father Napier to travel straight down to Barakako without having to go via the Kassikaitiu as he had done previously. When they reached Barakako, the weather broke and a pale sun gleamed through the clouds. The ground had dried out and the villagers were sitting in a circle outside the touchau's hut.

Father Napier pulled at his beard impatiently. It was the same in every village they passed through. One of his escorts would spend two hours reciting to the chief every single event, however trivial, that had occurred on the journey.

He looked round. The women stood in a line outside the house. All of them were dressed in seed aprons and bead ornaments except one who stood proudly in front. She wore what Father Napier recognised immediately as Beatrice McKinnon's blue skirt. Several of the men too were decked out in what must have been some of Danny's clothing. One had on a vest, another a cotton jacket and someone else a battered grey felt hat.

Father Napier enquired if anyone had seen Danny and Beatrice lately.

'Yes. They are asleep in one of the houses at the back,' replied a beaming old man, trying to be helpful.

It had started to rain again and they were standing in the open on sodden ground. Father Napier asked to be taken there immediately.

'They will soon wake up. Wait a little,' said the man.

After a few hours, Father Napier realised that Beatrice and Danny were not there at all. The old man had been indulging in the customary Indian habit of trying to please him by telling him what he would like to hear. He had been taken in by it over and over again in his years as a missionary and had never become used to it.

But he discovered that Beatrice and Danny had passed through there recently. The evidence was in the bartered clothes. They had been given a canoe in exchange. The delay meant that the search party had to stay the night at Barakako. The next day, Father Napier's party continued along the Essequibo, over some small rapids, heading towards the Great Fall.

Danny was dabbling his fingers in some tepid waters, trying to give the fish the impression that other fish were eating there. A few scrawny bushes leant into the water which was translucent, the colour of tea without milk.

A malaise, halfway between boredom and depression, had wrapped itself around Danny ever since the incident with the wild hogs. Beatrice tried to tease him out of it by saying that he must have swapped spirits with a sloth and left his own spirit hanging in a tree somewhere. When they were small and had bad diarrhoea, Koko Lupi used to blow on them and call on the sloth to make their shit hard like its own pellets. Danny smiled wanly.

'That's all stupidness,' he said.

Part of his melancholy came from the death of his dog. The dog had been running ahead of him, following the scent of an agouti, when a labaria snake leapt ten feet and struck it. Danny watched, powerless, as the snake struck over and over again until its venom was exhausted. The dog whimpered, screeched, convulsed and was dead within minutes. To Danny, it seemed that this was just another one of the endless signs that things were going wrong.

He lay face down, moving his fingers gently in the water, next to the stream that flowed into an inlet of the Essequibo where they had left their boat. The painted marks of the genipap were fading but still visible over his face and body. His legs were dotted with the black dots from kaboura-fly bites.

Beatrice was a few hundred yards inside the forest, following an old deserted trail amongst the towering mora and green-heart trees. She was looking for any fruit trees, particularly the yellow ishura fruit that Danny preferred or the tiny kum fruit that was not much more than purple skin and stone but made a welcome change to their diet.

As always in the forest, Beatrice had the feeling she was being watched. When she heard a long, low, choral moan, she assumed for a minute that it must be a band of howler monkeys swinging through the forest. But almost immediately, it was followed by a rustling and she realised that it was the wind sighing in the upper branches of the trees.

It was a storm. Lightning lit up the topmost arches of the trees and a massive crash of thunder burst overhead. A distant clattering in the canopy of leaves hundreds of feet above signalled rain. After a few minutes, dead leaves and twigs began to float and drop to the forest floor. Beatrice stood still, alerted by movement in a nearby bush. Movement usually meant an animal. But all at once, everything started moving. Bushes swayed. Leaves upturned and shivered, showing their pale sides. Everything shook. Little rivulets and streams began to run down the tree trunks. Soon pools occupied every hollow.

Unnerved as the thunder crashed again, Beatrice sheltered between the giant roots of a silk cotton tree. The huge triangular buttress was large enough for a hut to be built between the fin-shaped roots. She wore only a lap, having left behind the last of her clothes in Barakako. After a while the grey rain began to penetrate that far down. Some dainty white flowers at her feet gave off a nauseating stench. Beatrice decided to make a run for it, the half-full basket of fruits bumping against her shoulder.

Danny was securing the boat. Heavy spears of rain lacerated the surface of the water. She helped him wedge the canoe in the undergrowth and tie it to a bush and then they both ran towards the shelter which Danny had erected on the bank of the inlet, where they had been staying for the last few days.

Within minutes, the downpour turned the bank into a slippery shelf of mud. The pair of them clambered up the slope, slithering back every few steps. Ropes of water twisted around them, transparent lassos ensnaring their arms, legs and necks, tugging them back towards the river.

They made it to the top. Beatrice stood in the shed panting, wiping water from her lashes and wringing out her hair. Danny took off his shorts and wrung them out. Still breathless, she pointed to one of the struts in the roof of the hut. A large toucan perched there, its brilliantly coloured, top-heavy head glistening with raindrops. It looked sideways at them from its painted eye with that pale blue rim that is said to come from too much weeping. Beatrice and Danny laughed simultaneously.

'Those birds are stupid bad,' said Danny. 'You can chase them across the savannah and they'll fall down before they reach the next tree. The head is too heavy for them to keep airborne for long.'

He crouched on the ground but it was impossible to light a fire. The damp wood refused to catch. There was nothing else to do but lie curled up together in the miserably cold and damp hammock and listen to the roaring of the nearby river until the storm passed.

Father Napier leaned back in the boat, tired and disappointed. The day was dull and the sight of the vast Essequibo River with its sullen indifference to human affairs somehow depressed him. Thousands of inlets and tiny tributaries and creeks notched the banks of the river. It was a hopeless task to search for anybody in this giant wilderness.

They had arrived at the Great Fall on the Essequibo and

could see no trace of the missing couple. Initially, he had set off feeling that he was undertaking yet another heroic mission – the salvation of two souls. Now, it seemed, his mission would fail. No one they had spoken to for the last few days had any news of Danny and Beatrice.

A storm sent them scurrying for the tarpaulins in the back of the boat. They pulled the boat into a swamp of enmeshed roots at the river's edge and crouched under the tarpaulins as the rain drummed down over their heads. Cold rain ran down Father Napier's neck. Two men held on to the branches against the pull of the great river.

The men were already disgruntled and discussing how they could get back. Someone suggested a route down the Kubanawau from the mouth of the Sidawau to the Rupununi. Heavy rains meant that cataracts and rapids were gushing at full strength. So far they had managed to shoot the rapids, remaining in the boat, or streak them, attaching a rope and guiding the craft, stern first, between rocks and ledges. They were all exhausted.

As soon as they saw the Great Fall, they knew that Danny and Beatrice could not have taken their boat over by themselves. It was roaring and thundering in full spate. They decided to turn back. The captain thought they would be able to reach the shed above the next falls where they had left two baskets of cassava bread.

Father Napier nodded his glum approval. When the storm abated, they turned round. Progress against the current was slow. Although the rain had become no more than a drizzle, mists hampered visibility. The sun was going down. Continuing was too risky. They decided to camp out and get into their hammocks without eating that night. At first light they would make for the shed where they had left their food.

'Let's go in there.' Father Napier pointed to one of

the numerous channels leading from the river, a small opening between the trees. Two of the crew got out and went ahead.

'A canoe,' one called out.

'Danny's canoe,' called out the other as he spotted the bows, arrows and the gun.

I have found the needle in the haystack, thought Father Napier. Praise be to God.

Shouting penetrated the gloom. Beatrice opened her eyes. It was a man's voice calling.

'Danny. Danny. Danny.'

The voice sounded like a bird of ill omen flapping and screeching round her ears. Half asleep, they scrambled out of the hammock. It was not quite dark. Both of them recognised the voice. Danny, panic-stricken, fumbled around for his wet shorts. He turned to Beatrice aghast.

'It is Father Napier,' he said, trembling. 'God has sent him here.'

Within minutes, the priest had found them. Before she could see him clearly, Beatrice could smell him. The soaking-wet cloth of his black soutane exuded a damp, gaseous aura like the smell of rotting cassava or a secreted compost heap. To Beatrice the stench was overwhelming.

For hours Beatrice stayed in the darkness listening to them speaking just outside the shelter. Alert and straining every sinew to catch what they were saying, over the noise of the river, she knew by his tone of voice that Danny was agreeing to return to Waronawa. She heard them laugh briefly over a shared joke and then she heard Father Napier's voice turn serious. She slid out of the hammock in order to eavesdrop more easily. The ground underfoot was wet and cold. The rains had stopped. Father

Napier and Danny stood a few yards away, faceless in the black night.

Danny was promising to build a church for Father Napier at Wanawanatuk. That will never work, thought Beatrice scornfully, remembering the mosquitoes there. Danny's voice sounded weak and insincere. Beatrice listened for a while longer, then the night mists made her shiver with cold. She climbed back into the damp hammock, sick with misery.

Danny did not return to their hammock that night. He stayed with the other men in an adjoining shelter they had erected. Beatrice lay awake all night long. The rains started again. The thatch leaked. Splodges of cold rain fell on her, scurrying down her neck, and water trickled down her hammock rope. She made no attempt to avoid any of it. She wished that the rain would fall until the waters rose and drowned them all in a muddy burial. She lay in the darkness, dreading the dawn.

The next morning, in grey opal light under an overcast sky, Father Napier tried to light a fire. Everything was still sodden and he gave up. Apart from a 'Good morning' which barely concealed his disapproval, he had not spoken to Beatrice. The sight of her in a seeded apron disgusted him.

'I would have thought you had learned better than that at St Joseph's,' he remarked tartly.

Beatrice felt herself burn. She could not tell whether it was with shame or fury. With Danny, however, Father Napier was different, full of anxious bonhomie and conciliation, almost sycophantic.

It was decided that the priest's party would start off straightaway because Danny had to do some work on his canoe, caulking it with resin against the flood waters. He and Beatrice would follow on behind.

Beatrice and Danny watched the black-robed figure climbing into his boat from where they stood on the bank. Mists and drizzle hung in a cloud over the water. Jubilant at his success, Father Napier started to sing. He turned to wave and shouted something but the roar of the river drowned him out.

On the journey back, Father Napier was overjoyed. He thought it could only have been the hand of God which guided him to that one inlet of the thousands of criss-crossing waterways leading into the Essequibo.

As soon as they reached Wanawanatuk, he marked out roughly the spot where Danny should build the church. One clearing, he thought, was particularly suitable. They decided to overnight there.

That night, a monstrous battalion of mosquitoes stung Father Napier through his hammock, pyjamas and blanket. He tried wrapping himself in a tarpaulin but they crawled in there too. The place was less than two degrees from the Equator. The heat was appalling. He got out of his hammock and fought his way through what felt like a wall of mosquitoes. He breathed them in. He did not dare open his mouth. Finally, he took his hammock into the forest and slept under a tree.

In the morning, he was woken by piercing whistles. He dressed quickly, picked up his gun and went to see what was happening.

'Bush-cow. Tapir,' said one of the men, gesturing for the priest to stay still.

A whistle came from the other side of the creek. One of the men imitated it. The tapir whistled again in response. Every time the man whistled, the tapir became increasingly excited. Father Napier could see movements behind the bushes across the strip of water. Unable to move closer, he aimed at where he guessed the tapir's shoulder might be and fired. The men waded over the creek and gave chase but despite the trail of blood, they never caught it.

Three weeks later, Father Napier arrived triumphantly back in the savannahs.

SILENCE

Neither Danny nor Beatrice spoke while Danny worked methodically and silently on their canoe. Beatrice felt her heart beating in a stone body. From the way he consistently avoided her eyes when she looked at him, she knew there was no point in trying to persuade him not to go back. Rather than risk a real rupture, she said nothing.

The next morning, they moved between the boat and the shed, packing bows, arrows, warishis, the axe, gun and hammocks. Danny's tension showed in his abrupt jerky movements. He gashed his shoulder open on a jagged branch as he slithered down the bank with the cooking pot and a cutlass.

The day after Father Napier's return, Beatrice and Danny's canoe beached further along from the landing at Waronawa.

The land surrounding Waronawa turned into a vast lake, deep enough for the children to swim at the back. Beatrice and Danny were absorbed back into the household. Nothing was said about their long absence. The silence was like the flood waters. It seeped everywhere through the settlement.

It covered the landscape. Sometimes Beatrice felt herself floundering in this ocean of silence. But, despite everything, she held on to the conviction that her relationship with Danny was indestructible.

McKinnon spent as much time as he could away from Waronawa. As soon as he returned from a fishing trip or a visit to Brazil, he would invent another excuse to leave. Maba and Zuna went about their business, seeing to the children and household affairs. Once, when they went to bathe, they discussed Danny and Beatrice as they bobbed up and down in the water.

'I don't know why he would want to look in his own family and not outside in the village like everyone else,' said Mamai Maba, standing on the ground near the lake and towelling her hair with rough, spasmodic rubs. Zuna came out of the water.

'These things happen. No one could stop it,' Zuna sympathised. Nevertheless, the muscles at the bottom of Zuna's stomach clenched with the obscure pleasure of knowing that both Beatrice and Danny were Maba's children and not her own.

Danny was unable, for long, to endure the snide comments from the other young men of the settlement.

'Hello, oily face,' said one of them. 'Do you know how the moon got his dirty face? I'll tell you one of these days.'

Sometimes, they disappeared fishing without him.

'Have they gone already?' he asked a small boy who stared at him without blinking.

'Yes. They does 'smart you,' replied the boy with a sly smile.

Danny packed up and left. He went over to Brazil to work as a balata agent. His employers, two Brazilian traders, thought themselves lucky that they had found someone who could speak Wapisiana and Macusi and could handle himself so well in the bush.

Sam Deershanks had fallen in love with and courted Wifreda despite her bad eyesight and crotchety, keep-to-herself manner. She, for her part, remained as steadfastly indifferent to him as she had since he came to live there. He worked hard, joined the fishing expeditions and proved to be an expert deer-hunter, always finding the good bush-islands where the deer had been cut off by the floods.

Wifreda still suffered from guilt at being the one who had discovered Beatrice and Danny together. When the couple returned, she became flustered and did not know what to say to her sister, although Beatrice coolly resumed her chores as if nothing had happened. Just before Danny went away, Wifreda, having shown not the least sign of interest in Sam Deershanks, suddenly went off to live with him in the north savannahs. They set up house at a place called Pirara. McKinnon gave them a few head of cattle to start them off. No one knew why she went because initially she did not appear to like him one bit. And they made an odd couple, with him so tall and her short and peering around with her poor eyesight.

For the first few months that they were together, Wifreda regularly tore up the few pieces of mail that got through to him from America before he could read them. Often she would not speak to him for days. But Sam Deershanks persevered and suddenly, she relented and fell in love with him and they remained devoted from then on.

Waronawa settled back into its old routine dictated by the seasons and the stars.

One baking-hot afternoon, five months into the dry season, Beatrice gave birth to a son. The birth was not difficult and

Beatrice felt like an anaconda whose elasticated jaws dislocate to swallow prey – except that this process was happening in reverse and she was disgorging something. Maba helped her and took the placenta and buried it in a termite's nest. The only thing wrong with the child was that his navel string would not dry up. It remained soggy. Eventually, Mamai Maba showed Beatrice how to burn some charcoal, heat her thumb and finger with it and pinch the spot. Within an hour the navel string dried up.

The child had the same heart-shaped face and sloe eyes as his parents. They never gave him a name. Everyone called him Son or Sonny. Beatrice was enchanted by him. She swung in her hammock, feeding the baby and smiling.

She was not even excessively troubled when, a few months later, Danny returned with a handsome, young, square-faced Brazilian woman called Sylvana, who smoked a pipe and made lace. He built a house at Wichabai and she lived with him there.

Beatrice was so taken up with her baby son that, when Danny rode over and brought Sylvana to see her and the child, she did not really mind. She did not even ask whether Danny had told Sylvana that the baby was his son. It did not seem to matter. It had vaguely occurred to her before that both she and Danny might have to wed other people, for the look of things, but that, in reality, they would be married to each other for ever. Sylvana did not appear to be an obstacle.

Mamai Maba watched Beatrice anxiously but she seemed perfectly contented. Then, three weeks after Danny's return, Beatrice went into a sudden depression. The household woke up one morning at cock-crow to find that she and the baby had gone missing.

Beatrice left in the middle of the night carrying the baby in a sling. A couple in a bullock cart gave her a ride all the way to Annai. She had suddenly felt agitated and restless and decided to go to Georgetown. She waited at Annai until she could organise a boat going downriver.

Usually, when any of the McKinnons had reason to visit Georgetown, they would get out of the boat at the dangerous parts of the journey and walk along the side of the bank past the falls and the rapids until the boat could be manoeuvred to a suitable pick-up point.

This time Beatrice decided not to leave the boat. The bowman looked questioningly at the attractive young woman as she climbed into the craft with her baby. The journey was hazardous. She smiled and told him that if they overturned he must save the baby and not worry with her.

The great leaden river stretched out on either side of her. Overhead spread a vast chaos of clouds with patches of silver curdled sky. Beatrice felt the wooden seat of the boat dig into the small of her back. She took a deep breath. The river could decide whether she should live or die. It gave her an enormous feeling of liberation, this decision not to decide. It made her feel completely calm. She would toss everything into the lap of the river.

As they progressed, she felt increasingly exhilarated. Each time they approached one of the thundering falls or rapids, she ducked her head against the spray and sheltered the baby's head with her hand. But she felt poised on top of her life as though she were riding it. The boat bucked and dived and smacked down on the waves. It shot between and over rocks and gushing waters. The baby lay across her lap, utterly relaxed. They journeyed like that for days in a state of benign indifference.

The boat reached Bartica without mishap. It was something of an anti-climax. Beatrice wandered around the tiny town with its few rum shops and hotels and semi-derelict shacks.

Then she decided she would not bother to continue to Georgetown and she returned to the Rupununi.

It was after she got back that Beatrice noticed that the baby sometimes slept with his eyes open. Other than that he grew. He was very quiet, hardly ever making a sound. When he started to crawl, they had to stop him licking limewash from the walls and eating sand.

THE WEDDING

Danny and Sylvana were to be married. Father Napier had arranged it. He would come to the south savannahs and conduct the ceremony himself at the house at Waronawa. Then he intended to continue his journey to Wai-Wai country where he would confirm those he had baptised three years earlier.

For days, food was prepared. Piles of cassava bread were cooked. The men brought back deer, labba, powis and bush-hog from hunting trips. The meat was smoked. Three of the tame guinea fowl were killed and four suckling pigs.

The day before the wedding, Beatrice, hot, dusty and sweating, lugged four rice sacks filled with sorrel up the stairs. Her black hair had been cut to shoulder-length and she wore it loose although it meant she had to keep tucking it behind her ears. She was plump. Her figure had filled out and become heavier so that her plain white blouse and pink skirt were a tight fit. Her wide eyes flashed as she laughed at something one of the vaqueiros had said.

The sun shouldered its way into the room behind her and spread itself across the floor. The whole room was filled with the smell of guava jelly which had been boiling on the stove before being ladled into jars and brought upstairs.

'How much more sorrel do we need?' she asked Wifreda, who had ridden over from Pirara with Sam for the wedding, leaving her two small sons behind.

'Two more sacks,' replied Wifreda, studying her sister's face to see if she could detect anything from the expression. There was not the least sign of discomposure.

Beatrice's bare feet thudded across the floor as she went to fetch more sorrel from the racks outside where it was drying in the sun.

Even in the face of Danny's marriage to Sylvana, Beatrice was able to behave in an open and cheerful manner because she believed that she and Danny were an indivisible couple. She nursed the secret knowledge to herself that nothing could sever their relationship. Not absence. Not even the fact that they both might marry other people. They were brother and sister. The relationship was by nature indissoluble.

She scooped the piles of sorrel that looked like faded rose petals into the sacks, convinced that if she were ever to say to Danny: 'Leave everything and come with me now,' he would do so. He too was keeping up a pretence to the outside world. This marriage was an act. An imitation of the real world. A decoy.

The wedding was not a stumbling block. Even if she were never to see him again they would still belong together. As long as she and Danny were joined in their private union, then either of them could go anywhere and do anything – marry, beget children – it would all be a kind of masquerade, a joke on the rest of the world. It would be their way of fooling the enemy. Their public behaviour was merely an act. Their real union was magical and indestructible. They had a child as a result of it.

In this way, Beatrice kept herself calm over Danny's

forthcoming marriage. She even joined happily in the preparations for it. But she decided to speak to him all the same. She thought that they should make a pact. She made up her mind that there should be another wedding in which they married each other before Father Napier conducted the Catholic one. They should have their own wedding in which they made their vows in Wapisiana. The real wedding.

The bridal couple rode over from Wichabai in the morning. Heat bounced off the red-earth tracks. Gnarled, stumpy, sandpaper trees clawed at a barren sky. They had to shade their eyes where the sun blazed off the lake which had dried out at the edges. The bamboo scratched and rasped in the quiet morning as they rode past the pond towards the house.

Sylvana wore a cerise dress which she had made herself from a pattern given to her by a dressmaker in Boa Vista. She sat on the veranda drinking sorrel, her rocking-chair creaking on the wooden boards. For the occasion, she had braided her crinkly hair with coloured ribbons. Everyone noted with satisfaction how happy she looked. She had the air of a sensible, strong young woman, outward-looking and practical. A good match for Danny, they thought, as she sat with her thick ankles crossed, smiling round at everybody.

Beatrice was flushed. She stood on the veranda, in a fresh yellow blouse with short, fluttering sleeves and a plain black skirt, talking vivaciously to Sylvana in Portuguese. She could feel herself talking too much. It was impossible for Beatrice to tell from Sylvana's demeanour whether she knew what had happened between herself and Danny. Sylvana seemed perfectly relaxed. She smiled and pointed up at a scarlet macaw sitting in the guava tree.

'Stare too long a red macaw and you go bald or mad,'

said Beatrice with a slight giggle, immediately feeling that she had said the wrong thing.

Sylvana, who was descended in a direct line from Portuguese shopkeepers, looked puzzled.

'It's just an Indian superstition,' said Beatrice dismissively. 'You want more sorrel?'

Sylvana shook her head in refusal. And then Beatrice could not resist a moment of proprietorial knowledge.

'I expect Danny is off drinking 'kari somewhere,' she said with the air of a sister who will always know her brother better than anybody.

In the distance, the sun caught the top of the Kanaku Mountains as they rose from the savannah floor.

Everyone was waiting for Father Napier to arrive. Mamai Maba and Mamai Zuna, both wearing bead and feather necklaces over their cotton dresses, came out and joined McKinnon on the verandah. The children, their hair combed with butter-nut oil, ran around in items of European dress instead of naked. Five musicians had arrived from Brazil, stiff and exhausted from the eight-hour ride, and strolled around the compound in waistcoats and gaiters, preparing themselves for yet another drunken spree.

Beatrice urged Sylvana to have more drink.

'It have plenty. It have plenty.' She gestured cheerily towards the inside kitchen. Sylvana gave in, laughing, and said yes. Beatrice went off to fetch more sorrel.

Danny came into the kitchen. It was dark in there and his clean white shirt gleamed although his face was barely visible. Beatrice could just see the birthmark on his temple that always reddened when he had been drinking parakari.

'I'm glad I ain' going to be married to you,' she teased him in Wapisiana.

'Why?'

'Because you too own-way and sometimish.' She giggled and went over to kiss him. She hugged him tightly. He pulled away.

'Watch my clean shirt,' he said.

'That girl have you stupid or what?' She held on to his hands, unsettled by the way he was looking at her, with his eyes screwed up as if he were trying to see her at a distance. 'Is you goin' suffer for it.'

'Suffer for what?'

'Is we should be marry. We should marry in secret this minute here and now. A pledge for life. In Wapisiana. The real wedding. It would only take a minute. Let us do it now.'

Danny gave that evasive chuckle she had known from childhood, a high, almost girlish laugh that meant he was embarrassed.

Just then, Alice burst in through the door chasing Freddie, their youngest brother. She was scolding him in Wapisiana.

'Freddie did business in the bedroom,' she explained breathlessly, trying to grab hold of him. 'An' he din even wipe himself.'

'I din see no stick round there,' pouted the little boy defiantly. He ran out with Alice behind him.

'I been talking to Father Napier,' said Danny. 'This business between us must done now.' And then he added with that ancient cruelty that exists between brother and sister, 'Was just a childish thing that happen. A little thing. We caan' go on behavin' like children.'

Beatrice was taken aback.

'You could have two wives like Daddy,' she cajoled. 'I would be your first wife. Sylvana the second.'

'One man. One wife. You went to school. You know that. We got to behave like big people now,' he sneered as he pushed her away and walked out of the kitchen.

Standing there on her own, Beatrice's mouth went dry and

a high-pitched zinging noise sounded in her ears. The quiet of the empty kitchen protected her momentarily from the noise of the gaiety and excitement outside.

The children had been shouting a welcome as they rushed to accompany Father Napier up the sloping ground from the river. She could see his black-clad figure shimmering in the heat as the children vied to help him carry the familiar tin trunk that always caught the rays of the sun.

She stepped back into the dark wooden doorway, into the familiar smells of home. As she watched the priest walk towards the house, a tree of ice seemed to grow up inside her, up from her feet, through her own trunk, branching along her arms and up into her head. It grew and spread and settled. McKinnon went out to greet him and she saw the two men disappear up the steps, and then heard them going along the veranda over her head and into the house.

Outside, the wind tugged a few small clouds across the blue emptiness. The sun pushed its way into the centre of the sky as if manoeuvring into the best place to watch the wedding.

'Where is she?' whispered Mamai Maba to Zuna as they waited for the ceremony to begin upstairs.

'Must be she hidin' sheself,' replied Zuna.

And, indeed, Beatrice found herself unexpectedly shrinking back into the kitchen. She remembered that she had been supposed to fetch Sylvana some sorrel drink. She stared at the red sorrel juice lying motionless in several pans and gourds on the table. Nothing had prepared her for this. For the first time, she experienced an icy grief and sense of desolation. A plaintive Wapisiana chant went round and round in her head. She used to hear it as a child when somebody died, before Father Napier's zealous frenzy had converted so many villages to Catholicism.

The breeze from the open door cooled the damp patches

on the front of her blouse. The squeak-squeaking of the upstairs shutter twanged at her nerves. Everything had gone quiet. The ceremony must be underway.

She had missed the wedding. It was over. Someone wound up the phonograph. Music trailed out of the upstairs windows. She could hear the tump-tump of a dance line caterpillaring round the room. There was a yell as the phonographs packed in and the musicians took over. She could hear laughter as people helped themselves to rum, parakari, guarana and cashew liquor. The party started to liven up. A slim youth with bad teeth rushed into the kitchen looking for sorrel. He was laughing and smiling at Beatrice, assuming that she was in the same mood as himself. He went out, spilling some drink from the calabash in each hand.

Beatrice slipped off her shoes and walked away from the ranch.

KANAIMA

Leaving the settlement behind and putting as much distance as possible between herself and the sounds of the wedding party afforded Beatrice some relief. Beads of sweat broke out on her face and a dark patch of sweat, in the centre of her back, marked her blouse.

She walked northwards along a trail with a few stunted, scrubby bushes on either side. The scorching wind began to bluster, hissing and singing across the savannahs. After a while, it blew more steadily. A long-legged jabiru bird stalked along the dry bed of a stream beside her.

A prolonged, harsh rattle like a shak-shak brought her to an instinctive standstill. She waited, motionless, for about ten minutes until she saw the zigzag pattern of the rattlesnake's tubular body slide into the cool shade of a termite's nest.

She pulled at a strand of black hair as she walked, twisting it round her fingers. She had thought the ceremony would leave her unmoved. Not true. She had imagined she could survive it with no ill effects.

Walking numbed the grief. Some distance from the house, she stepped for a moment on to a large flat rock-stone that lay across the path. Standing in the sun, in the full light of day, Beatrice McKinnon underwent some kind of seizure. Her head snapped back. As she stared at the sun, her eyes rolled back in her head. Her arms were flung up in mid-air and remained there quite rigid for several seconds in some sort of fit or spasm.

During those few seconds, all the grief turned into violent fury. The hairs on her head bristled with rage. Her face turned dark, her mouth began to work, her features contorted. The wind blew strands of black hair across her mouth. At the same time, a noise erupted from her throat, a long, choking rattle that seemed to have its origins in the base of her spine and shook her whole body.

When she came back to her senses, she was throwing up at the side of the track and her eyes stung with the tears that come with vomiting. In a sort of stupor, she chose one of the many criss-crossing trails and made her way to Koko Lupi's house on the outermost reaches of the settlement.

Koko Lupi's house was a dismal, poky hut, reeking of smoke from the clay-brick stove. Chickens and ducks wandered about outside and by the door stood a hollowed log and a pounder. Some fresh fish lay on a bamboo table covered in palm fronds. Beatrice could not see as she first entered but she heard a shuffling flutter like a bird rising from its nest.

'Kaimen?' Koko Lupi greeted her in Wapisiana. As Beatrice's eyes adjusted to the darkness, she could see Koko Lupi's toothless face, sharp as a hawk. Two of her grand-children, with dirty faces, stared listlessly from where they sat on their sleeping mats. A debris of half-eaten corn-cobs, turtle-shells and bones lay on the earth floor. A colony of red ants attacked the shreds of fruit on a sucked mango seed.

'I want something to make the priest dead.' Beatrice spat her request right out. The voice came straight from her belly, much deeper than usual.

Koko Lupi shuffled around and poked through various piles of seeds, beans, dried plants, birds' eggs, dried cassava leaves, various powders in calabashes and two mounds of little wisdom stones. All these were arranged on blocks of tree trunks next to a pot of fish and cassava stew.

Eventually, she picked up some dark brown beans and wrapped them in a leaf.

'Grate them and put them in the food. It would take a very strong piaiman to recover from these. They don't work all at once. They work over a long, long time. I don't like him either. He tries to strike the sun out of the sky. Him with his dead god on a stick. He thinks he can stand between the sun and the moon. Give him this and leave the rest to the sun. The sun will finish him off.'

Beatrice took them.

'Don't use them near here. No. No.' She waved her arms in front of her face as if trying to shoo away a hornet.

Then she asked with an unpleasant leer: 'How is your brother?'

'He is all right,' said Beatrice calmly.

Koko Lupi picked up some leaves and swizzled them between her hands.

'Take some of these leaves. They won't make you fly but they'll make you walk fast. They will make it like your legs have been whittled down to the bone and you can run along on the points like the wind. You rub the leaves all over your body like this.' She rubbed Beatrice's arm vigorously with a few of the leaves. The arm tingled and went numb.

When Beatrice arrived back at Waronawa after nightfall, there were hammocks slung everywhere with an orchestra of drunken snores coming from them. About twenty bodies lay in the upstairs room. Silently, she collected tasso, farine and a hammock for her journey. One of the musicians lay sprawled across the kitchen table.

Her plan was to reach the village of Baidanau which Father Napier would have to pass through on his way to the Wai-Wai. She must get there before him. That was where Aro, Shibi-din's wife, now lived as the second wife of the touchau. Beatrice knew that if she told Aro that the priest was going to insist on a man having only one wife, Aro would worry about her position. She would almost certainly agree to doctor his food with the grated beans.

Before she left, Beatrice went and peeped in at Sonny. He was rocking in his small hammock and by the light of the moon she could see that his eyes were open and staring into a dark corner of the room. It was not possible to tell whether he was awake or asleep. She crept out again. There were plenty of people to look after him while she was away.

It was the same journey that she had once made with Danny. She took a boat and paddled for the first few miles, then made her way across the savannahs until she reached the edge of the forest. It was easier to travel across the savannahs before the sun rose.

As she was about to enter the forest, she remembered being taught by Uncle Shibi-din that she should explain to the maigok, the forest spirit, the nature and purpose of her journey. This she did and then set off, nervous but determined.

The trees towered in ghostly grey columns, lacking all foliage until the top. If she looked up, filigree tracery patches of colourless sky were just visible between the leaves.

She did not look up often. The danger was underfoot. Fallen trees had crashed across the trails and the forest was littered with great rocks. In some places, crevices covered with leaves and twigs gave a treacherous impression of a firm footing. Roots of trees where the earth had been washed away formed an eerie network, stretching over chasms some forty or fifty feet deep, at the bottom of which she could see water running. Sometimes, she had to balance along a tacouba, straddling a creek twenty feet below. Despite rubbing herself with the leaves, she seemed to go at a snail's pace. The boulders became bigger. She moved along in a humid grey gloom. She marked the trail as she went. Once or twice she lost it but soon found it again.

After two days, the nature of the landscape changed. The deep forest thinned out. The rarely used trail became ill-defined. There was no water to be had. Worst of all, there were pale thickets of giant thorns, some three to six feet high. Previously, Wapisiana had attempted to take cattle through on this route and to transport goods, but every journey became such an ordeal that it had fallen into disuse.

Beatrice felt almost weightless. Fuelled with cool rage, she continued through the arid wasteland.

It was outside the village of Baidanau that she caught sight of Aro on her way to bathe. Aro was astonished that Beatrice had made such a journey on her own. After Beatrice had spoken to her for a while, she nodded seriously and took the package of beans without hesitation.

Later that day, after Beatrice had gone, Aro heard a noise outside her house as if people were mumbling or talking in low voices. Anxiously, she peered through the window, but it was only the hens circling a rattlesnake, walking round it and saying: 'Coo. Coo. Coo.'

On his return journey to the Wai-Wai, Father Napier sat back in the corial and weighed up his achievements. He was happy. Plagued by the heat and insects, but happy. The men paddled the boat steadily. Titus, the Macusi with broad flat cheekbones, and his young son Linus were accompanying him as they had the first time. Father Napier cast his mind back over his achievements like a general reliving a successful military campaign.

Single-handed, he had converted most of the Macusi in the north. After an irritating delay, for which he mainly blamed McKinnon's resistance, he had made inroads into the Wapisiana in the south. His brow puckered as he thought of McKinnon for a moment and wondered how such a hospitable man could hold such despicable views. Father Napier had thought that McKinnon would return to the fold after the business with Beatrice and Danny, but McKinnon had just become more evasive, distracted and withdrawn. The priest was satisfied with the way he had handled the affair between Beatrice and Danny. He was especially gratified by Danny's marriage to Sylvana.

As soon as they arrived at Baidanau, Father Napier's party was provided with a pot of stewed peppers. There was no meat in the pot. Father Napier burned his tongue as he dipped his bread into the stew and ate it. A stout, friendly woman, one of the wives of the touchau, brought him some pieces of yam which were dry and a dingy brown colour. Linus, Titus's young son, polished off half the yams which Father Napier found too dry to eat.

The next morning, Linus complained of a sore mouth. Father Napier waited two more days but Linus became worse and the priest decided that he could no longer keep the people in the next village waiting. He had heard that some people, including several Wai-Wai, had already assembled there and he did not want to disappoint them. He set off, leaving Titus to nurse his son, telling them to catch up as soon as Linus recovered.

Shortly after leaving Baidanau, Father Napier felt unwell. He had a sharp pain under his tongue. They pitched camp for the night. After a day's walk, both his tongue and his gums started to swell. His throat felt in shreds. He had earache, headache and high fever. As they proceeded, it became increasingly difficult for him to open his mouth. To utter a whole sentence was impossible. Father Napier wrapped himself in his hammock against the cold night air and waited for the comfort of daylight. By nightfall of the next day they reached a village where there was water, but his tongue and gums were coated with white, foul-smelling pus. He could neither spit nor swallow. It was pointless trying to continue his journey. They turned round and headed back for Baidanau.

Back at Baidanau, Father Napier discovered a tin of condensed milk that someone had slipped into his bag after the wedding at Waronawa. Linus lay in his hammock, his mouth distended and full of white matter. The priest managed to give him the last rites. Barely able to speak himself, Father Napier indicated that they should bring milk for himself and the boy. They brought milk for him but refused to give it to the boy.

'He dead already,' they said.

For four days, Father Napier eked out the cow's milk with the condensed milk. High fever had him in a constant sweat. His soutane was streaked with yellowy-white mucus and pus. He craved milk, milk and only milk. Water was not able to relieve or satisfy him. Since the onset of the illness he had been unable to sleep. He was hardly aware when Linus had died. Titus buried him and came to tell the priest that he was leaving.

After a week, Father Napier became convinced that his only hope of survival was to beg for a horse and make his way back to Danny McKinnon's house at Wichabai.

The villagers agreed to let him have a horse. His guide had to sit on the horse behind him because he was not strong enough to stay upright on his own.

It was the worst ride imaginable. Once they left the forest, heat blasted the savannahs. The horse had to pick its way over huge clods of dried earth, some two feet across and one and a half feet high, before they struck a trail.

Father Napier longed to see Danny. He felt that Danny would be kind to him. Danny was under an obligation to him. He had saved Danny's soul.

But when they finally arrived, Danny and Sylvana were not there. They had gone to Ruruwau where he was helping to build a house for an Indian family. A message was sent. Some hours later, Danny arrived on horseback. Unable to speak, the priest wrote down what had happened. Danny immediately sent for his sisters to come from Waronawa and help.

Not more than two hours after Danny had helped Father Napier into his hammock, the sound of horses announced the arrival of Beatrice, Alice and Wifreda, who had not yet returned to Pirara after the wedding. All three of them were garlanded with smiles and proceeded straightaway to administer comfort.

They washed his face and hands, scrubbed the room with lemons to freshen the air and slipped spoonfuls of tapioca porridge into his mouth. He noticed Wifreda sprinkling brown nutmeg on to it, to make it more delicious, but each time a spoon touched his lips, he winced and wrenched his head away.

Every day, the McKinnon sisters rode over. After two weeks Father Napier began to feel better. He sat up in a chair. The McKinnons sat around him, smiling but not talking. He found the presence of Beatrice something of an embarrassment, but she seemed perfectly at ease and unruffled by the situation.

Danny swung in his hammock.

'Fancy,' he said to the priest, 'even after all your teaching, these Indians are still superstitious.'

When it pleased him, Danny spoke as if he were not one himself.

He went on casually: 'They've been telling me you've been poisoned.'

Father Napier laughed. Wifreda looked uncomfortable. Alice chipped in with what she had heard.

'Somebody told me there was a Macusi man who had two wives and you taught him to behave like a Christian and give one up. The Macusi wife was so vex with you that she follow you to where you were going and put poison in a yam you ate. They showed me the poison she used – a dark brown bean. It has effects that last for months. You must be careful.'

Beatrice listened, composed and thoughtful, her head to one side. Wifreda butted in.

'Macusis are like that. Untrustworthy. We Wapisiana wouldn't do that. Did you find the tin of milk I put in your bag?' she asked, quickly.

'Oh, that was you, was it? I swear that milk saved my life.'

A silence fell on the room. The guava tree next to the house was bearing fruit. Now and then, one tumbled on to the roof. Danny levered himself out of his hammock and wedged his vaqueiro hat on to his head.

'I have to be at Ruruwau before dark.'

Making sure the priest was comfortable, the McKinnons said their goodbyes and left. Wifreda was returning to Pirara. The others felt no need to come back now that Father Napier was so much better. His helpers would see to his needs.

Danny turned his horse to the left and headed for Ruruwau. The women headed straight on for Waronawa.

It was another full week before Father Napier felt well enough to travel to his base mission at St Ignatius. Still a little unsteady on his feet, he collected together his belongings, including the tin trunk, and set off.

FIRE-BURN

Father Napier only undertook light duties at St Ignatius until his strength returned. Then he decided it was time to retrace his missionary route through the whole savannah region and inspect the progress of each mission he had set up.

He travelled on horseback, but for some reason he could not keep his focus on the tracks. His mind kept wandering. The silver-blue sheen of the sandpaper leaves on the ground reminded him of the Scottish lakes of his boyhood and he thought with longing of the cool Highlands.

The sun tormented him more than it had done previously. After riding through Wapisiana territory in the south savannahs for a week, he began to dread the heat of the midday sun.

Not far from Aishalton was a tiny hut which served as the District Commissioner's office on his rare tours of duty. On one trip, Father Napier decided to shelter there.

All he wanted was a cool place to rest before continuing his journey. He forced open the wooden door. It had not been open for months. The imprisoned air from inside burst out to greet him in a blast of heat. His nostrils tingled with the sweet, dry dust from the palm roof which made him want to sneeze. If anything, it was hotter inside than out. He found it almost impossible to breathe. Father Napier choked back a sob. There was no furniture in the room apart from a small table and a chair. He sat on the chair and it collapsed. He became childishly tearful as he realised there was no escape from the scorching heat.

In a moment of petulance, he knew exactly what to do. Fight fire with fire. He wasted no time. He pulled out some grey palm stalks and dried brown leaves from the wall and laid them underneath the table. He set them alight and strode out of the hut, never looking back at the aery flames which flickered to and fro on the roof, barely visible, making the air above it ripple with heat.

Four weeks later, Father Napier turned up on foot at Pirara in the north savannahs. Wifreda and Sam Deershanks now had a sizeable ranch of their own with the usual settlement of Macusi houses around it. Wifreda had felt odd at first, living in Macusi territory, but after the first two of her sons were born there, she began to feel more relaxed.

Father Napier appeared to be very depressed when he arrived and asked if he could stay there for a while. Sam and Wifreda responded warmly and agreed that he could stay as long as he wanted.

The first night, Wifreda felt too shy to try and say grace at the table with the priest present. She asked him if he would say it. He started to say the familiar words and then found himself singing 'The Erl King' by Schubert.

Feeling confused and out of place, he went to his room.

Over the next few days, he seemed happier and spent the time playing a collection of records which Sam Deershanks had acquired for his wind-up gramophone. At mealtimes, Father Napier told them how he had spent the last few weeks visiting his missions in the south and how pleased he was with their progress. He related with some pride how, single-handed, he had secured most of the north savannahs, a good proportion of the south and had made a start with the Wai-Wai in the name of the Master.

But the vaqueiros and other Amerindians who passed through told a different story.

It seemed that Father Napier had been setting fire to mission churches wherever he went. In Shea, the villagers looked on in astonishment as he seized a mallet and smashed the skulls of three puppies on the altar of their little church before setting fire to the walls with a kerosene-soaked club. In Sand Creek, it was said that the palm thatch of the roof of the church began to blaze of its own accord as he approached. Others described the priest throwing kerosene in the doorway and using wax matches to light it.

The priest's progress through the savannahs had been marked by beacons, blazes, burning timbers, fires, flames and furnaces. Of the twenty-two missions he had founded in his fourteen-year ministry, he had burned sixteen to the ground.

Wifreda's face screwed up with the effort of understanding, as she sat at the table with Sam one evening, trying with her left hand to stop their youngest son wriggling off the bench. There were several barefoot vaqueiros standing around drinking coffee. The news came flying in like a swarm of marabunta hornets. Confirmations. Contradictions. Variations. Denials.

No one had seen Father Napier all day. Eventually, it was decided that Sam should investigate tactfully and ask Father Napier what had been happening. It was late the same night when Sam Deershanks broke into Father Napier's room which had been locked since morning. The room was empty. Father Napier had already gone.

It had been dark when Father Napier lowered himself out

of the window and on to the ground-level verandah. He managed to slide down the housepost without waking the occupants of two hammocks slung outside and he picked his way as silently as possible towards the track which led to the road. He was heading for St Ignatius. Moonlight flooded the savannahs. The squat shadows of sandpaper trees menaced him at intervals.

Lately, he had found difficulty in holding on to his train of thought and since the mention of the poison, he had lost some of his confidence in the McKinnons, with the exception of Danny.

As he walked through the night, his thoughts zoomed off unexpectedly in ways that excited him. They seemed headed for realms of revelation and glory. The rasp of his own breathing and the scrunching of his footsteps were the only sounds to be heard as he strode along. He felt inspired. The idea struck him that he must build a railway for the faithful from Georgetown to Roraima. The Pope would lead the procession on to the first train. He could see the Pontiff leaning out of the first-class compartment, waving and blessing the crowd.

Halfway to St Ignatius, Father Napier performed a short, wild and ecstatic dance in the middle of the savannah night. Two Macusi men who had come out to hunt deer froze for a moment, thinking that one of the termite nests had started to dance. Then, realising who it was, they waited in a hollow until he had passed.

Father Napier continued to walk until the moon shifted over to the north-east. Then, sweating but cool, he sat on the earth and gazed up at the brilliant stars. After a few minutes, ecstasy took hold of him again and filled him with enough energy to resume his journey at twice the pace.

By the time he reached St Ignatius, he was flying.

'Wake up, boys. Wake up. Hurry. We're going to Georgetown.'

The two boys, Salvador and Paul, scrabbled around sleepily in the dark and hurried down to the creek to bathe. Father Napier rushed around packing up his tin trunk, hammock and a few provisions. He decided that they would first go to Annai. Once there, he would send a message to Danny to come and take him to Georgetown. Sometimes he forgot why he needed to go there so urgently and then he would remember – of course, to build the Pope's railway.

They set off before dawn. On the way, they passed a smallholding belonging to a settler from Trinidad, a surly man who had failed twice at tobacco planting and was now involved in a disastrous scheme to freight turtle eggs to Port O'Spain.

Father Napier burst into his house and shook him awake. Within minutes there was an argument involving some gramophone records which the man accused Father Napier of stealing. The priest stormed out and soon the trio were headed once more for Annai. The stars began to pale and fade in the dawn light. Objects became clearer. Their three silhouettes stood out on the black line of the horizon, the priest striding jerkily behind Salvador and Paul who walked in single file ahead of him.

At mid-morning, they stopped at the Macusi village of Mora. The village was empty. Almost the entire population had gone to Annai early that morning to barter gun-caps, eggs, farine and fish for provisions. Only one woman stayed behind, sitting on the ground and lethargically spinning cotton. The priest's party did not stop at the village but pushed on. An hour later they had reached two lean-to sheds where the Mora villagers normally sheltered on their way to and from Annai. Still, Father Napier refused to stop and rest.

Six miles further on, Father Napier put his tin box down

and collapsed on the ground exhausted. Salvador and Paul waited in silence some twenty yards ahead. The sun lashed down on the priest. Mounting panic drove him to change his mind about their destination.

'I think we had better head back to Pirara,' he called to the two boys, trying to combat vertiginous rushes of giddiness. They all turned back.

They reached the same two sheds which now struck Father Napier as forlorn and desolate. He badly wanted to find Danny McKinnon. He split the boys up, sending Salvador to Pirara with a note for Danny who frequently passed through there. He instructed Paul to go back to the village of Mora and return with fresh cassava for them to cook.

When the boys had gone, he sat down on the ground under the palm-leaf shelter. He opened his tin trunk and took out some papers showing his register of baptisms for the Taruma Indians. A light breeze took them and scattered them so that he had to dive after them.

Experiencing a huge weariness in his bones and scarcely able to stand, he managed to blow up a fire so that when the cassava arrived he would be able to cook it. He trembled. His black habit was drenched with perspiration. He took it off and with it his shirt and hung them up. He stepped outside but his knees gave way and deposited him on the ground. He lay there with his cheek against the hot, gritty earth.

After a while, he could not resist pushing a big kokerite leaf, which lay nearby, into the flames. For a few seconds, he was enthralled by the beauty of the flames which looked like sacred, jagged leaves.

Almost immediately, the shed walls caught fire and then the roof which was lined with oily consit paper. The sheds were wholly ablaze within minutes. Father Napier rushed inside to rescue his tin trunk and papers. He snatched his cassock from the beam, shoved some books and diaries into the trunk and dragged it outside. Even ten feet away from the fire, he could not stand the heat. He left the trunk and ran further away. Gradually, the fire subsided but his hammock, shirt and camera had all gone. So had the two sheds.

Night came. There was no sign of Paul and the cassava. He lay on the ground, exhausted but unable to sleep. He prayed but there were unaccountable gaps in the prayers where he could not remember the words.

At daylight, he set off back to Mora to look for Paul. He thought he knew the way but the numerous forks of the trail confused him and before long he found himself in the middle of a treeless expanse of red, lumpy ground having lost sight of any trail at all.

He unbuttoned his soutane under which he wore nothing but his trousers and braces. He walked fifty yards in one direction and then changed his mind and stumbled fifty yards in another. Then, to his immense relief, he recognised a large rock and some shrubs that meant he was a matter of yards away from the village which was in a slight dip in the landscape.

He walked towards the houses. Some fowls scratched around. The place still seemed deserted. Then, through the window of one of the houses, he saw young Paul asleep in a hammock. The same woman who had been spinning cotton the day before was there again, still working. He asked her to bake some cassava for him. She refused. Annoyed, he set about baking it for himself in one of the outhouses. He found a small turtle which he told Paul to boil. Paul did as he was told but added so much salt made from vegetable ash that the meat was inedible. He excused himself by saying that the sun liked milk and salt. Father Napier shook his head in exasperation and flung the meat away.

The villagers ignored Father Napier, turning away from the voltage of his blue eyes. No one would give him anything to drink. He asked for cassiri. They told him it was finished. He begged for something to eat. One by one they all disappeared into their houses. In counterpoint to the ecstasy he had experienced during his night's walk, he now felt a groundswell of unease.

That night, he slept on open ground outside the village. When he opened his eyes in the morning, the first thing he saw was the small figure of Paul setting off with his hammock over his shoulder, along the trail which skirts the mountains. The boy walked steadily away beneath the blue sky, never once looking back.

A man was dogging his footsteps. One of the Mora villagers, a lame man of about forty, was following the priest's every move. Finally, he addressed Father Napier in Macusi.

'I wish you would go away. We don't want you here.'

Father Napier was now ravenously hungry. He appeased the man by preparing to depart. The task of packing his trunk should have been easy but he kept taking out as many of the papers as he put in. In the end, by dint of frantic efforts, he replaced all his effects in the tin trunk.

The man became even more insistent that he leave. Father Napier began to fear that the man might take his bow and arrow and shoot him. He lifted the trunk and staggered slightly. As he moved off, he realised that he had left his soutane on the other side of the village, but it seemed unwise to try and retrieve it.

For the first time ever, he walked in the savannahs without his black habit. He wended his way downhill, picking his path between rocks. Travelling on an empty stomach, his mouth felt parched but he was sustained by extraordinary rushes of gaiety.

It was the hottest day he could ever remember. Soon the feelings of gaiety wore off. His throat felt like a rough wooden board with tiny flints set in it. He sweated. He felt weak. He longed for milk even though it pained him to swallow. Dizzy and light-headed, he struck out in part of the savannah where there was not a single tree for shade.

The whole country had dried up. Some farmers had set fire to the land. There were charred clumps of grass on the blackened earth and some of the grasses had formed what looked like a web of grey hair. He looked for the presence of cattle, thinking they would be near water. Spotting a small group of cows some way off to his left, he took a detour over stony ground, but when he reached them they barely lifted their heads. Their hides and flanks were covered with sores. And there was no sign of water. He found his way back to the meandering trail and pushed on, supporting the tin trunk first on one hip and then the other.

He held on to the idea that Danny McKinnon was the one man who would help him and determined to head for Pirara in the hope of seeing him. But there was no map and there was no trail that he could see. He did have a compass which remained intact in his trunk. He consulted it and kept changing course. He managed to carry the trunk, although he had to stop and rest with increasing frequency. By now his skin was hanging off in strips like ribbons which fluttered in the breeze as he walked.

He was in a furnace. If only he could escape the roasting sun for a few minutes, he would be all right. Every so often a tremendous roaring engulfed him on all sides, as if the sun had turned into a jaguar on the attack. Each time this happened, he lifted his hand involuntarily as if to fend something off. However hard he tried to pray and keep the image of Christ before him, the stories told to him by the boys always surfaced in his mind: the sun dressing the jaguar in yellow to represent him on earth; the sun disguised as a red macaw; the sun selecting a brown wife from those offered by the water spirit because the white one and the black one both melted. The jaguar sun roared and slashed at his skin again.

Out of nowhere came a voice.

'It come like the sun trying to burn up the world.'

Startled, Father Napier looked up to see a man and a boy of about twelve facing him. It was the man who had spoken. He was smiling in a friendly way. They took him to their camp. There was only farine to eat. It felt like gravel in his throat. That night he lay by their fire tossing and turning.

When he awoke, they had already left. Under some trees, he spotted a small stagnant pool. He rinsed his mouth and bathed but did not dare drink. He was unable to put his trousers back on because they chafed him and so he continued his journey without them.

The sun hammered relentlessly down on the figure of the stark-naked priest picking his way slowly across the savannahs.

A Macusi farmer brought the note to Mr Herbert, an elderly, grizzled settler from the coast. The note was signed by a Brazilian rancher from Bom Success. It read:

I have just come across Father Napier wandering about the savannahs quite mad. He is headed for your place. Secure him and hold him until the police can come from Annai.

When he arrived, Father Napier was invited to lie down on the couch and rest. Suddenly, he felt he was being strangled. He opened his eyes to find the Macusi pulling a towel round his neck as hard as he could while Mr Herbert stood at the foot of the couch with ropes. He lost consciousness. When he came to, he was bound hand and foot. The two men took him to Annai.

Waiting there was Danny McKinnon.

They were all in a canoe travelling down the Essequibo River to Bartica. Father Napier lay trussed like a chicken in the bottom of the boat, his head jammed against a sack of woody-smelling cassava roots. He was wearing his soutane again, which Danny had somehow retrieved from Mora.

'Are you going to allow me to be seized like this?' he expostulated, as Danny manoeuvred the boat to catch the mid-stream current.

'I will do what I can,' came the reply.

From where he lay in the bottom of the boat, Father Napier could look up into Danny's burnished copper face, eyes narrowed into slits against the bright light. His face was surrounded by a halo of suns and for the first time Father Napier recognised Danny as an Indian. He twisted himself round as if trying to shade himself from the glare.

Later, he bit Danny in the leg.

Danny was in charge of bringing Father Napier to Georgetown. They camped for three days at Potaro Mouth. Danny told the priest that he was expecting some mail there and they must wait for it. In fact, he had just succumbed to an urge to go hunting round Tumatumari. He took two of the men with him and disappeared into the bush for two days.

When they finally pulled into the landing stage at Bartica, the town was full of people who had come to attend the annual fair. Few people witnessed the wild struggles of Father Napier as he was dragged out of the boat and on to the land.

Instead, all eyes were focused on the Ladies' Stepping Race.

Four well-dressed black women walked quietly round the three-quarter-mile course in the hot sun. They proceeded along the track in a dignified single file, smiling and thoroughly enjoying being the object of such attention.

There was no attempt at competition because there were four prizes for the event. With no need to hurry, the procession wound slowly along, the women acknowledging the sporadic applause and waves from spectators and friends with gracious nods and smiles.

Five hundred yards away, Father Napier was being man-handled on to the river steamer that would take him to Georgetown.

Once Danny McKinnon had seen him safely stowed on board in the hands of the authorities, he turned his boat round and headed back to the Rupununi, stopping off near Tumatumari once more to hunt the agouti which seemed to be in abundance in that area.

ASYLUM

Father Napier was driven in an open carriage to the Brickdam Presbytery in Georgetown between two policemen. A passer-by paused to see what was going on and witnessed a thin priest in a black soutane, resisting with agitated movements the restraining arm of his escort.

In the noon-day sun, the priest's hair glinted the same reddish gold as the edge of a bible. His pale blue eyes burned with indignation at the affront of being manhandled by the police. He glared at each one of them in turn. His beard and moustache were short, straggly and unkempt.

There was a scuffle as the police tried to persuade him to leave the carriage. Once they had manoeuvred him inside, another priest took him up the wooden stairs and gave him a cup of tea before driving him to the general hospital.

They left him in the seamen's ward that night. All night long he begged for food but was given none. Nor did he catch any sleep, although he had been carried upstairs and placed on a bed. As soon as they left him on the bed, he sat up and began shouting that he had been poisoned and they carried him downstairs again and put him in canvas restraints.

The next day, despite having been told that he was going

to Dutch Guiana and from there back to England, he was taken by ferry steamer to the asylum in Berbice.

The asylum at Canje was built on the site of the old Dutch barracks. It was set a good way back from the road, near some tall cabbage palms, in an isolated patch of ground near Canje Creek. Local people gave the place a wide berth because a miasma of unhappiness seemed to hang around it.

All the same, in those days, the asylum possessed some remarkable features. There were two vegetable gardens and an ancient cannon. There was a concert hall with a gallery where musicians from outside would sometimes entertain the inmates and which also served as a theatre where patients could mount their own shows. Those patients who were well enough had formed a band with ukelele, banjo and drum and sometimes boatmen on Canje Creek heard tentative melodies carried towards them on the breeze.

It was another hot day when Father Napier's carriage approached the asylum. The carriage had to swerve to avoid a black man standing, naked and immobile, in the middle of the road. His entire body was coated with grey dust that looked as if it had come from volcanic lava. He stood, rigid as a statue, one finger raised as if in remonstrance, pointing to where the Berbice River opened out into the Atlantic. He remained oblivious to the carriage and its occupants as they passed.

Near the entrance, a weary nurse with a full bosom was clapping her hands and calling: 'Jacka . . . Jacka,' to another man who could not be persuaded to come in but who stayed just outside the door, whipping a team of invisible horses, turning them to right and left, the obstacles, terrors and dangers in his path clearly visible from the changing expressions on his face.

As soon as they entered the main wooden building, a patient glided towards them, a graceful East Indian man who spent his time making a political speech which never halted and which had no end. Every day, this man could be heard as he left his own block, addressing his unseen audience quietly and persuasively.

When he saw Father Napier and his escort, he immediately came forward to include them in this intimate address, ornamenting his speech with charming gestures, every movement and every facial expression seeming to be in deadly earnest. It appeared to make no difference whether he faced a real audience or not. Sometimes he mounted the stage of the little theatre and, whenever people grew tired of the fluent speechifying, the warders would lead him gently from the platform and he continued talking as if nothing had happened, all the way back to the dormitory.

But Father Napier spoiled all this by becoming violent.

All patients wore the same coarse white blouse and trousers. A piece of coloured cloth on the right arm showed to which block they belonged. As soon as he had been relieved of his priest's garments and dressed in these, Father Napier smashed all the window shutters and jumped out on to the dry grass below. After that, he was put into what people called the 'Snake Pit'.

The cage was twelve foot by twelve foot and another twelve foot high. One wall was composed of strong bars, the other three made of jalousies. The lowest jalousie was ten inches from the floor. A cold sea breeze blew all night. During the day, he was a spectacle to be gazed on by passers-by. He longed to be able to speak with someone, but those who came to stare all went away when he tried to engage them in conversation.

He determined to escape. Once at Waronawa, he had read one of McKinnon's books describing an escape from the Bastille. He would do the same. The mattress in the cage had a hole in it. At night, Father Napier tugged and pulled at the coconut fibres inside until the watchman caught him.

At six-thirty in the morning, he was taken to the public bathroom where inmates washed under the pumps. There he was forced to take off his clothes and march through the crowd. When he had washed, he was taken out down some steps and thrust into the cage again. This time they had taken away the mattress and blanket. The same operation was conducted each day.

One of the effects of the poison was that he had no saliva in his mouth. He needed fluid desperately. The sago, green plantain, sweet potatoes and sloppy rice, he found himself unable to stomach. He implored them to give him milk. He burned with heat and he burned with cold. He burned until he believed he was the sun travelling on its journey to the north-east, seeking milk and salt, and finally giving in to the forces of darkness. He felt that he had been captured, like the sun, and was being held in a dark pot, waiting to hear the crack of Chico's gun that would shatter the clay and release him, pale from incarceration, to make his way back into the sky.

One night, during a violent storm, the thunder did, indeed, crack fiercely over Canje Creek and Father Napier crowed and skipped round the cage in glee, expecting imminent release.

After sunset, when the cold wind from the river plagued him, whipping at his legs and ankles, he did not allow himself to sleep. Imitating the sun's journey to Iken, he walked around the cage all night. The rain blew in, wetting the floor and making him slip and slide as he struggled on his journey. One night, he slipped eight times and knocked his head against the wall of bars.

Every night in the cage he got worse.

One night, exhausted, he fell. Looking up he seemed to see

the giant, sandstone, perpendicular cliffs of Mount Roraima in the savannahs. There it stood, outside the bars of his cage, never free of the clouds which shifted and evaporated and formed odd shapes as he watched. He found himself effortlessly climbing the slanting ledges and wooded gullies of the flat-topped mountain.

Everything became clear. He remembered that he was destined to build a railway from Georgetown to Roraima and on the top of Mount Roraima he would construct a great city and the Pope would come and live there with his entire court. The Pope would embrace him for his vision and inspiration. Flinging himself in exultation on the flat top of Mount Roraima, he fingered the rough, stony surface of the mountain. He lifted his head and noticed the yellow, rocky desert, littered with boulders.

Suddenly, he realised he had been tricked. He was not on a mountain at all. He was standing on the flat stump of what had been an enormous tree. It had been chopped down. He looked up. He was utterly exposed to his enemy. The sun was bent on destroying him. The pale, metallic sphere in the sky was a shield behind which . . . Father Napier began to scream. He felt his skin turn to sharp-edged crystals. He screamed to the sun for mercy.

The night watchman came and stood outside the cage and fingered his chin as he spoke.

'O Lor'. How the man punish,' he said kindly, shaking his head as the stark-naked priest crawled, weeping and pleading, slithering from one side of the wet wooden cage to the other desperately trying to escape from the mighty deluge that would, any minute, erupt from the severed trunk of the tree.

In July of that same year, Father Napier was sent back to England on the steamer *Orinoco* that travelled via Madeira and Le Havre to Plymouth.

At some point on the long journey home, the priest undertook the painful task of setting fire to his own memories, leaving behind only arched structures, charred ruins, smoking vaults and empty spaces in his head. Members of his family who came to meet him at the docks were shocked at the change in him. He was vague and unfocused and could hardly remember anything of his many years' ministry in the Rupununi.

He spent the last years of his life in the austere, but secure headquarters of the Jesuits in Edinburgh. Occasionally, he gave talks to the novitiates on his experiences amongst the Indians of Guiana. He had one photograph which always aroused interest, showing about thirty alligators resting on the rocks alongside the Ireng River. Mists hung about them and they all had their mouths open as though in ecstasy. Father Napier did not like to field questions after these talks. He would pack up speedily and return to his single room.

One lasting fear remained with him. He could not bear to hear the organ played. It was as if those swelling, vibrating chords unfastened the earth beneath his feet revealing a chasm. This meant, to his bitter disappointment, that he was unable to attend many of the services in church, a longed-for haven of peace and calm. He received special dispensation and attended mass only when he felt able.

Some months after he had arrived there, a novitiate knocked on the door of his room and said that a Mr Alexander McKinnon had called to see him. There was no reply from inside the room although the novitiate knew that Father Napier was in there. He knocked again but there was only silence and the visitor was told that Father Napier was unable to receive him.

STAR-FIELD

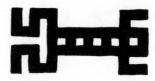

Beatrice was swimming in the lake at the back of the house. The water felt like satin. It was nearly the end of the afternoon and the sky was dull and cloudy. The next day she was due to leave the Rupununi for good.

Eventually, even she had agreed that she would have to go. Whereas people had tolerated, although not particularly liked, her relationship with Danny, when they began to suspect her of being a kanaima, they were appalled and attitudes towards her changed altogether. It was not unknown for a brother and sister to live together, usually just outside the village. Nobody approved of it, but nobody tried to stop it. But Kanaima was the spirit of revenge, either in the form of an assassin with practised methods, or in the form of any animal or object into which the assassin had sent his life-force. Vengeance attacks were more terrifying than incest.

When the rumours about Beatrice started to spread, she resigned herself with surprising patience to her fate. It became well known that she had visited Baidanau. She had been sighted making her way there across the savannahs. Then Aro, the woman to whom she had given the beans, became nervous about being blamed and reinforced the rumours by insisting that Beatrice was a kanaima, that she had turned herself into a rattlesnake and poisoned both the priest and the little boy, Linus.

Once that was being whispered around, it was impossible for her to stay. Even the people in the settlement at Waronawa looked at her askance.

Everything at Waronawa was changing. McKinnon had already left.

He had ostensibly gone to the Great Exposition in Wembley, England, for a month, taking four Wapisiana men with him to exhibit their crafts. The Wapisiana had returned without him. They said that he had gone to live in Scotland permanently. A short while later they heard that he had married 'officially'.

Maba and Zuna, when asked how they felt about this, laughed and shrugged.

'We had him when he was young. We had the best of him. Someone else can have what little there is left.'

Before leaving, he had arranged for Beatrice to stay with some acquaintances of his in Montreal. The authorities in Georgetown had been enquiring about certain irregularities in the savannahs. Some years before, McKinnon had been made travelling magistrate for the district – a post which he largely ignored, having always been impressed by the Indians' ability to keep order without government. The idea that he might now be expected to investigate his own daughter's actions disturbed him. He was not bothered about any poisoning. He was more worried that the incest would be revealed.

On his rare visits to Georgetown, one man had been hinting that he would like to buy him out. McKinnon grabbed the opportunity. He could not sell the land because he did not own it, but he sold the man nearly all his cattle. He left the family with the house he had built and a hundred head of cattle. Then he set sail for England.

Beatrice floated in the water. She was thinking about Sonny. It had been decided that Sonny should stay behind and be raised by Wifreda alongside her own sons. He had Beatrice's pale complexion and heart-shaped face. His black eyes were the shape of dolphins. Although he was now about five, he hardly ever spoke. Beatrice loved him but felt that he should never have been born – that she had expelled a beautiful secret out of her body that should have remained there. He was a secret made flesh. Sonny turned away from all embraces, even his mother's, and did not seem particularly attached to anybody. He showed no distress when she told him she was leaving.

She stood up in the water which reached up to her breasts and started to wade to the edge of the lake where the bamboo and reeds grew. Then she turned again, floating on her back and kicking her legs, hoping vaguely that the giant red macaw that was supposed to live under the waters would come up and drag her down, but nothing happened. It was difficult to believe that she was leaving all this. Maba had said things would quieten down in time and people would forget. Beatrice was not so sure. Even Auntie Bobo, whom she had known all her life, had turned away from her and walked off when she saw her coming.

Not that Beatrice felt that she had done anything wrong. Whatever had happened between Danny and herself still felt so natural that she could not believe there was anything bad about it. Perhaps in that underwater world that Maba had told her about as a child, she would be united with Danny again. She dipped under the water until she could breathe no longer and was forced to surface. She could not find the entry to it. She and Danny had been expelled into everyday life. Danny had accepted it more easily than she had. Nothing that she learned at the convent ever made as much sense to her as what she had learned at Waronawa.

Dusk descended as she floated there in the warm waters. Bats looped and flitted overhead. Her thoughts switched to Father Napier. About him she felt no guilt. When Danny had returned from Bartica and described his journey with the mad priest, Beatrice felt calm and peaceful as if some sort of natural justice had been executed and she had been the instrument of it.

It was now all but dark. As she was about to climb out through the reeds, a sudden fierce shower made her duck back under the water and wait till the rain stopped. The rain felt colder than the water in the lake so she kept as much of herself underwater as possible.

Night finally fell as the rain ceased. The rain clouds passed and the stars came out again. Danny came out of the house and shouted to her. He had left Sylvana and his two children at Wichabai and come to take her and her bags to Annai the next day.

'You have your bags packed and ready? I want us to leave before first light.'

Wifreda had ridden over from Pirara to say goodbye and to collect Sonny. She was in the house with the rest of the family, her face tight and anxious. She did not like goodbyes. The thought of ever having to leave the savannahs filled her with dread. It was impossible for her to understand how Beatrice was so calm about it. Besides, she felt some guilt about the whole business, having been the cause of Beatrice and Danny's elopement in the first place. And she experienced a sort of ache, in advance, knowing she would miss her sister.

Wifreda now had three sons of her own. She could not imagine leaving any of them. In fact, she had already decided not to have them educated in Georgetown but to bring in a teacher from outside for all the children at Pirara. But Beatrice had just frowned a little when she sorted out some things for Sonny and had handed them to Wifreda as if she were going away for no more than a weekend.

'Coming,' Beatrice shouted back to Danny. 'Where are you?'

'Here,' he said. 'Come and look over here.'

She pulled herself out of the water and felt for her towel on a bush. Wrapping it round her, she walked towards his voice. Then she saw what he meant.

A field of fireflies, caught by the sudden shower, had settled on the ground. They winked in the blackness, as brilliant in the dark underfoot as the stars in the sky above. It was as if the vast night sky had unfolded under their feet as well as over their heads and they were suspended in space. For a long time she stood there, feeling that she was where she was meant to be, standing in the sky with Danny.

Then Danny turned and she heard his padding footsteps as he walked back to the house. After a minute or two she followed him.

THE ICE COFFIN

It was not until her second winter in Canada that Beatrice came to understand that the devil has to do with cold, not heat as most people think. She stood on top of Mount Royal, wearing a fur muffler and hat, near to where the horse buggies waited to take tourists back down the mountain.

The few people who were about kept their heads down against the icy wind and flurries of fine snow, barely noticing the young woman in the grey Cossack hat who walked through the sleet over to the side of the concourse and looked out over the city. Although someone might just have noticed her remarkable eyes, black, wide-set and with a slight cast in the right one, that made her look involuntarily flirtatious.

Beatrice was contemplating whether or not to marry Horatio Sands.

She held on to the rail and looked out over the frosty city and the frozen river. Below her stood the huge grain elevators and the tiered, rectangular outlines of the white Sun Life building. Sparks from an electric trolley moved along the city streets like a firefly.

It was then that it occurred to her that what she had been taught at the convent was wrong. The nuns had told them that hell is one hot place, full of fires and conflagrations. She bit her lip and frowned as she surveyed the city spread out beneath her. It is not, she thought. It is a deep, dark coldness from which there is no recovery. There seemed to be no escape, in any direction, from the arctic blanket that covered Canada. The idea both frightened and comforted her. She snuggled down in the fur collar of her coat and waited for her friends.

Everything seemed to have brought her to a point where she was about to make a decision she had hoped to avoid. She could feel herself drifting towards marriage. And the odd thing was that she felt she would be marrying to spite the world in some way. As if she would be saying to the world: There. See. Look what you made me do. The way some people's suicide is an act of triumphant aggression. Although no one was forcing her to do it and nobody really cared whether she married or not.

Some children screamed and raced behind her towards the toboggan slide.

When she first arrived in Canada, Beatrice stayed with some acquaintances of her father. For a while, despite her initial shyness, she had sold silk stockings in their store. Then she found an office job with the Canadian Pacific Railway and moved into the YWCA. It was congenial enough there. Every night, the warden, a gentle, dreamy-eyed woman in her fifties, would come to their rooms and rap on the door saying: 'It's after eleven o'clock, ladies. Would you care to whisper?'

For the first six months or so Beatrice felt quite numb. Once, in a store window, she saw an assistant handling a mechanical doll that walked. The shop girl picked up the doll and put it down somewhere else where it continued walking. That's how I feel, thought Beatrice, as though someone had picked me up and put me down somewhere else and I'd just continued walking.

Now, as she blinked away the fine snow that stuck to her lashes and stung her face, she could hear the laughter of the other girls from the hostel as they walked up the hill to join her.

Often, on Saturdays, they met at the café on the mountain and then went into the museum nearby to see the shrunken Indian head preserved in spirits. Beatrice found it as fascinating as the others, the small wizened head.

The group of four girls waved and shouted their hellos as they approached, panting and laughing and grimacing, holding on to each other like a multi-legged animal as they scrunched up the snowy path, their dragon breath curling away behind them.

As they walked towards the museum entrance, Olive Ransome, a podgy, square-faced girl with a galaxy of spots, started to question Beatrice about Horatio Sands.

'What did he say when he came to tea?' The girls at the hostel were allowed to have visitors to tea on Sundays.

'He just said: "I wish I could see more of you,"' replied Beatrice, shrugging her shoulders with indifference.

They all shrieked and collapsed in giggles. For the next few weeks, 'I wish I could see more of you' became a catch phrase that could set any of them off into gales of laughter.

Olive Ransome was particularly envious that Beatrice had mysteriously found her way on to the magic escalator that led to marriage. When Beatrice looked into her eager, resentful face, she almost decided to go ahead with it just to annoy Olive.

They hurried into the warmth of the museum and stood in the usual place in front of the glass case. Beatrice studied the shrunken head. The colouration of the three-inch head was still vivid, almost like stage make-up, giving it an unusual sense of animation. The complexion retained its ruddy brown. The strong, prominent cheeks looked to her as if they had been rouged with annatto. The black hair shone. The familiar lips stayed open in a conspiratorial smile. The face reminded Beatrice of her grandmother.

How amazed these girls would be if they knew I had a son, thought Beatrice.

'Where does she come from?' asked one of the girls.

'I don't know. Down south, somewhere,' replied another.

Beatrice grew to like Horatio Sands. He worked on the third floor of the same building as her. She was on the first floor in the audit department of the Canadian Pacific Railway, adding figures in a ledger. Once, Horatio had stopped her in the foyer of the building in Dominion Square.

'I'm always standing behind you in the lift,' he said as he introduced himself. He had a long, raw-boned face that was slightly lopsided. The cheekbones seemed to slant one way and his jaw the other, making his face look as though it was always asking a question.

He offered to buy her a coffee in the Blue Counter, a cake department in one of the big stores in St Catherine Street. The first time Beatrice visited the luxurious pink Ladies' Toilets, she thought she was in a palace. The attendant spoke to her in a French patois that she did not understand. She stayed there for a while, breathing in the scent of essence of violets and admiring the mirrors and the pink-and-silver-frosted décor of the surroundings. When she returned, she found that Horatio had ordered pecan pie and ice-cream for her. She felt a certain warmth towards him. He repeated the same jokes often. People teased him about his name and he would put one hand over his eye and pretend to be Nelson.

Going to the Blue Counter became a regular event.

Sometimes she and Horatio visited other sights in the city. Once, when they went inside Notre-Dame Cathedral, Beatrice felt faint and had to sit down on one of the back seats. The fan vaulting of the high ceiling reminded her of the great arching cathedral of mora, greenheart and silk-cotton trees in the forests back home. Seeing over her head this icy forest petrified in stone made her feel that she too was dead and fossilised. She asked Horatio, without explaining why, if they could leave.

Sometimes a travelling theatre company arrived in town. Staff at the nearby theatre would brush the dust-covered seats and the place would be opened for a week. The girls from the hostel would rush to watch the play, usually a melodrama with someone dying on the scaffold. Then the theatre would shut down again for months. Other times they went to the picture-house.

Once, when spring had almost come and the ice in the St Lawrence River crushed and began to melt, a travelling circus came to town with a fun-fair.

They all bought tickets.

As soon as they entered the enclosure, the roaring of a beast and the dank, animal smells of the circus unsettled Beatrice. Jostling crowds also made her uneasy. The girls stood in front of a cramped cage. A sickly tiger, full of mange, cowered in a corner. Beatrice felt the faint warning signs of an approaching migraine.

'I don't think I'm going inside to watch the circus. I have a headache coming on. I'll stay outside around the fun-fair and meet you afterwards.' Horatio asked if she would like him to stay with her but she said no and he joined the others at the ticket queue.

To find a little peace, she paid some money and slipped through the flap of an adjacent blue-and-white-striped tent where she could be sheltered from the popping electric fairy lights and jangling music.

Inside the tent was quiet. There was a smell of sawdust and

a chill in the air. Beatrice was the only customer. She went and sat on one of the benches set out for the audience. Then she realised what was generating the chill in the air.

Two trestles had been placed on the ground with three planks resting on top. On the planks stood a hollow, coffin-shaped block of ice, large enough to contain a human body. The top and sides were about six inches thick and it was open at one end. Apart from patches of frostiness, the ice was mainly transparent, clear enough at any rate to see that it was empty.

Beatrice sat down on the front bench directly facing the coffin. A considerable amount of time passed before the tent flap opened and another woman came in. The bench creaked as the woman seated herself at the other end of it. It took another twenty minutes before the organisers decided there were enough people for the show to begin.

There was a moment or two of shuffling behind the tent flaps, which were then clumsily pulled aside to reveal two men in tailcoats escorting a short, fat, but muscular Native American Indian woman with shoulder-length black hair, wearing nothing but a beaded head-band and a yellow swimming costume. The woman stepped forward in a businesslike way, threw up her arms, circus fashion, and bowed to the smattering of people. The audience stared with the concentration of farmers at a cattle auction.

At this point, the show-masters invited everybody up to touch the ice coffin, to inspect it thoroughly in order to ensure that no hoax was being perpetrated. Beatrice stepped forward and touched the ice. Her fingers reddened. It was certainly real ice. She put her face down and gazed through the open end. In places, patches of frost caused a deeper opacity. The coffin breathed its chilly breath on her and she stepped back. The audience returned to their benches.

The performer spat on her hands and rubbed them

together before exposing her arms so that people could see there was no covering of any sort, just bare flesh. The yellow costume cut into her fat brown thighs. She kicked off her high-heels and allowed her two male escorts to lift her and slide her, feet first, into the icy coffin. The spectators watched intently as the two men sealed up the open end of the coffin with another square block of ice, packing handfuls of snow from a bucket into the cracks.

All eyes were fixed on the coffin. The woman lay motionless inside. The audience remained silent except for the occasional shuffle. After a while, Beatrice began to worry that the woman's air must be in short supply. In a minute or so, surely, she would be unable to breathe. Beatrice could almost feel the anguished burning of the flesh on ice. She tried to see whether the woman was still breathing. Astounded and horrified, she stared at the woman in the ice tomb. The circus artist must surely be released now or die, she thought, and then lapsed into a state that felt like eternity without passage of time.

She had no idea how long it was before the two men began to scoop the snow and ice from where they had packed it to seal the cracks. They took away the square block of ice from the end of the coffin. Beatrice took an enormous, involuntary gasp of air as the woman slid out and bowed to the audience. She felt as though she herself had been freed.

As she went out of the tent, she caught sight of the Indian woman standing near the entrance, laughing and drinking a glass of beer.

Beatrice looked over at the woman who raised her glass and smiled, her fat cheeks pushing her eyes into narrow ovals which nonetheless radiated warmth. The smile made Beatrice suddenly elated.

She hurried off to find her friends. Horatio was looking for her with two hot meat pies in his hand. Beatrice took hers and stamped her feet to get warm. Her headache had vanished. Everything looked bright. It was possible to survive the ice coffin and emerge unscathed. For the first time for months she felt lively. The feeling spilled over into a renewed affection for Horatio.

Beatrice married Horatio Sands in the Church of the Immaculate Conception in Waverly Street. To his family's distress, he became a Catholic in order to marry her.

Horatio knew little about Beatrice except what she had told him, that she came from the Rupununi district of the Guianas in South America. But Horatio could never remember where the Guianas were, even after she had shown him on a map. And she never spoke about it much. He found he could never keep the geography of the place in his head. It somehow slipped away from him.

For two years they worked hard to furnish their home. They had moved to an apartment in Hutchinson Street. It had three rooms and a thick, wooden verandah which she liked.

Helped by her friends from the hostel, she had chosen to decorate the place in rose and lavender. She kept the hardwood floors polished and protected by scatter rugs, but most of all she loved the electric bedside light which she had saved for and bought at Eaton's. There was plenty about her new life that she enjoyed. It felt easy and comfortable, if a little unreal.

Then one night as she and Horatio were returning, arm in arm, from the picture-house, Beatrice saw the Indian woman from the circus again. She was sprawled, drunk, in an illuminated shop doorway with abrasions and purple bruises all over her face. It was a freezing cold night but alcohol with its burning inner fire prevented her from feeling the cold. Her legs were splayed open and the coat she wore, which was made of some kind of animal hide, was unbuttoned and showed a thin cotton dress beneath. The woman appeared to recognise her.

'Hey,' she called out to Beatrice as they approached. 'Hey. Are you Iroquois? What people are you from?' She took a swig from a bottle and burbled a chant, the spilt liquor shining on her chin: 'A dillar a dollar, a ten o'clock scholar. Why did you come so soon? Help me, dear. Please help me.'

Horatio took a firm grip on Beatrice's arm and guided her quickly past to protect her from any unpleasantness.

The woman stared at Beatrice.

'OK. OK. I understand,' she mumbled, her head sinking on to her chest.

That night, after Horatio had made love to her in his usual way, like a little boy holding tight to a comforter, Beatrice found herself unable to sleep. The lightweight love-making sessions required no real involvement on her part. Normally, she liked lying there afterwards in those freshly laundered sheets, enjoying her home and planning a next purchase after he had fallen asleep. But she was appalled that she had ignored the Indian woman in the street. It was a betrayal. She sat up in bed. Horatio was asleep. Shadows and lights from the traffic outside moved across the window-blinds. She wanted to get up but was frightened of waking Horatio. The neon light from the diner across the road flashed a pale red arc on to the wall beside the bed. She lay down again wide awake.

Finally, she fell into a restless sleep. A distant train hooted slowly three times on its departure for the prairies and, in her dream, the sound somehow turned into the wail of the giant otters that she used to hear calling along the Rupununi River.

The dream turned into a night terror. She was awake but paralysed, a giantess, unable to move or speak. Her thighs had become immovably heavy and turned into the banks of the Potaro River, covered in vegetation in which herds of peccary scurried and swerved. She turned into her own sexual landscape. The silent silver stream of the river between her legs carried in it the reflections of clouds and a flight of macaws. The river flowed on through the steep escarpments. She felt tugging undercurrents beneath its surface. Still the smooth stream of silver gathered momentum, racing towards the great falls where it dropped, thundering into the ravine below.

Rainbows always hung in the mist at the top of the falls. She remembered her mother telling her that a rainbow was the spirit of a sickly boy. At intervals, the river was caught up as it flowed on out of sight, caught up once, twice and then less frequently, caught up by the bush-covered banks, glistening like a needle as it disappeared into the distance.

And there suddenly was her mother, standing on the bank, shaking her head and screwing up her eyes against the sun as she spoke.

'Boat run a falls. Caan' come back.'

Beatrice came to gradually. She was soaked in sweat. Her limbs felt like lead. She was still not sure that she could move. The refrigerator sighed and rattled in the kitchen. Eventually, she wiggled her toes. Relieved to find they worked, she tried cautiously to move her left leg. It obeyed her. Then she dared to turn and look at the outline of Horatio's head. How odd, she thought, to be lying here with my head two inches from his and for my head to be still full of forest and savannah while his is probably full of the Montreal of his youth with its electric trams and toboggan slides. How odd that these two worlds should be lying inches from each other.

She tried to look at him as he slept but it was too dark to see. Gently, she manoeuvred herself out of the bed. She tiptoed over to the door, wrapped herself in a dressing-gown and slipped silently into the parlour. The couch springs gave as she sat down and leaned back against the anti-macassar. She kept thinking about the woman. Perhaps, after all, the woman had been safer inside the ice coffin at the fun-fair than out of it. She wondered if it was better for her own people to preserve themselves within their own traditions or to allow change. For a long time she stared into the darkness. Life was easy the way she now lived. She had even learned to play tennis.

Oh Montreal, Montreal. What was she to do there?

As she fell into a doze with her head against the back of the sofa, she could hear Mamai Maba's voice again.

'Hot and bitter or cold and sweet. Everything in the world is divided up like that.'

SINGULARITY

From the time of his arrival at Pirara Sonny showed no signs of missing his mother or anyone else for that matter. In some ways, Wifreda felt closer to him than she did to her own sons – he was even more unsociable than she was. Occasionally she found herself a little in awe of him. He seemed to be marked out by some terrible innocence. A compelling purity.

Whereas her own boys ran wild, exploring and developing headlong into youth, Sonny remained absolute in his quietness and self-containment. He struck her as being like the seed of a kokerite tree which refuses to grow, as if growth was a weakness, a loss of integrity, as if everything was packed inside him and refusing to unfold lest it lose its perfection. There was always a feeling about Sonny that he walked around in his own moonlight. Wifreda was aware of a special responsibility in being his guardian.

She punished the others when they teased him. At first, she tried to get him to join in with them, but he became distressed and withdrew even further into himself and so she just let him be. Sonny would spend weeks making his arrows and bow and then take them away on his own. Instead of shooting fish with them, he would practise, for months on end, with endless, obsessive patience, always using the same spot on an ite-palm tree for a target.

As befitted someone conceived around the time of an eclipse, Sonny was a walking event-horizon. A singularity. No one knew what went on inside.

The ranch at Pirara grew and prospered under Sam Deershank's management. Both the Mamais now lived with Wifreda and Sam and spent most of their days, and some nights, fishing. The youngest of McKinnon's sons, Freddie, had just achieved his heart's desire and started work as a vaqueiro, chasing cattle under Sam's watchful eye.

Over the years, Danny spent more time at Pirara than at his own house at Wichabai. He had taken to drinking heavily and his wife frequently escaped with their children back to her parents in Brazil. Danny's figure was no longer lean. Physically, he had burgeoned into a much heavier man than the slim youth who had obsessed his sister. His eyes had more or less disappeared, sunk into fleshy cheeks. Parakari and rum drinking had filled him out and his weight emphasised an increasingly coarse cruelty. Once when he was digging a new latrine with one of the vaqueiros, they quarrelled. The hole was deep. The man couldn't scramble out.

'Stay there and christen it with your own shit,' yelled Danny as he walked away.

He roamed around the country, trading balata. Sometimes he took Sonny travelling with him. Sonny never spoke on those journeys or showed any interest in where he was going.

As Danny became increasingly unreliable, his Brazilian employers threatened to sack him. Sometimes he vanished for months at a time. There were rumours that he had other families in different forest villages. But he was too taciturn for people to challenge him about it.

When he disappeared, he would go into the forest on his own and erect a rough bush-house. There he relaxed and felt more alive. He could see and smell better. No one troubled him about clothes for the children, the failure of cassava crops or medicine for his wife.

Once there, he never gave his family a second thought. Nor did he think about Beatrice or the past. All he did was track a labba through the bush, or lie for hours on the damp ground trying to smoke an agouti out of its hole, or wait in the steaming heat at the edge of a creek for a fish to bite.

One year when Sonny had grown taller than she was, Wifreda made her annual visit to Georgetown for supplies.

While she was there, she hired a young woman to come back with her to the Rupununi and give the children some education. The new tutor was called Nancy Freeman. She was a young, lithe, light-skinned eighteen year old with a snub nose, two crinkly plaits and plenty of energy.

School began in the house at half-past eight for all the children living on the Pirara settlement. Nancy Freeman often despaired. She battled to control Wifreda's boys. Some mornings when classes were due to begin, she would see a horse pass the window with three of the boys astride it and she would not see them again for the rest of the day. When the boys got too unruly, she would call Sam Deershanks who had been midwife to all of them. Despite his threats, he turned out to be a big softie and would only use the strip of cowskin to lash the chair-leg that the culprit was sitting on.

Sonny sat at a desk apart from the others. When she asked the class to write their full names at the top of a page, he just wrote: 'Sonny'. Miss Freeman queried it with the others.

'Everyone should have a handle to his name,' said Miss Freeman, smiling.

But he had none. They called him Sonny. Other than that

he had no name. He didn't know who he was or where he came from. Sitting at his desk, he was a slender figure who, unlike the others, gave her no problems. Yet he was a rebel in an unusual and delicate sense. He was a rebel through absence. He managed to be there and not to be there at the same time. Sometimes he slept, eyes wide open.

He rarely spoke and when he did it was no more than a whisper. But he answered and was obedient, responding sometimes with a faint smile as if something was amusing him.

Gradually, Nancy Freeman discovered that what Sonny wanted more than anything else was to keep himself secret. In an era of discovery, revelation and the examination of every aspect of life, an era when every part of the world was being photographed, filmed, rediscovered, analysed, discussed and presented to a voracious public; when communications and networking were speeding up, when all previously inaccessible tribes were being brought out into the open, investigated and put on display, all Sonny wanted was concealment, secrecy and silence.

He seemed to be permanently in some inner state of lunar excess. It was no use pushing him. Mostly he tried to avoid people. On the rare occasions when he spoke, his observations were curious, detached and intelligent. Whenever an adult spoke emphatically to him, he seemed impressed and listened carefully. The way he listened unsettled people. He seemed to listen more to the stresses than the meaning of the words, as if trying to detect a subterranean rhythm, an ancient and recurring beat which would give him a clue as to what the speaker really meant. Sometimes he responded with delight, as if he had discovered the true meaning of what was being told to him. This disturbed the speaker who might have been saying something quite inconsequential or might even have been scolding him. People were disconcerted. It made the speaker feel as if he were not in control of what was being said.

Most people thought that Sonny wasn't all there.

At first, the new teacher tried to befriend him. Later, she came to understand that Sonny was alone by choice. Love, friendship, intimacy of any sort produced in him a sense of suffocation. He veered away from it. Any contact seemed like a violation. Solitude enraptured him. He had undertaken some inner, tremulous journey and he pursued his course with the joy and delicacy of a tracker. People made well-meaning attempts to get Sonny to participate in the world. But for him, nothing could equal the thrill of withdrawing from it.

One morning, as the sun streamed in through the windows, Miss Freeman was trying to teach multiplication tables and English grammar amidst tears and sulks and the sound of scraping chairs. The door opened and Wifreda came into the room, frowning so that her low hairline came even closer to her eyebrows. She seemed a little flustered.

'Nancy, a Mr Evelyn Waugh, or some such body, has arrived here. He wants a haircut. Leave the schooling for the moment. He'll probably stay a day or two and then beat it back down to wherever the hell he came from.'

Wifreda was usually anxious in the presence of strangers although she was always as hospitable as the savannahs required.

Nancy Freeman turned to the class and said, without much hope of being obeyed: 'There's a white man here and he will be very vex if you don't sit down quietly and learn your sums.'

Through the window, the children stared at the white man who had dismounted from his sweating bay horse in the yard. One of the Macusi vaqueiros, a stocky man with a limp, came and took the horse to be watered. The visitor with a compressed face and shrewd eyes waited, leaning on a snake-wood stick. Clearly, his feet hurt him. He was looking round with unmitigated horror at his surroundings.

Nancy, in her friendly, breezy way, brought out a chair and gave him a haircut there and then on the expanse of ground between the house and the green waters of the Pirara River.

Later that night, when the evening meal was finished, the whole family went outside and walked up and down in the moonlight, reciting Sorrowful Mysteries aloud, as they had been taught by the new priest. Mr Waugh asked if he could join them, explaining that he was a recent convert.

Wifreda slung up a hammock for the guest and hoped that Danny, who was staying at Pirara just then, would not get drunk and become obnoxious. But Danny, always unpredictable, listened to the visitor in an unusually polite and sociable way as the two men reclined in hammocks on the outside verandah with a bottle of rum on the ground between them.

Overhead, the stars hung in the sky, so brilliant that they seemed to have come deliberately close enough to watch the two men. The writer looked at Danny's slanting eyes which glinted in the moonlight. His cheeks were puffy through drinking too much. Evelyn Waugh was reminded, disconcertingly, of Josef Stalin.

'What brought you so far from home?' Danny asked.

Evelyn Waugh frowned a little waspishly.

'Domestic matters,' he replied, after a pause. And then added, rather peevishly: 'My marriage ended. I prefer not to talk about it.'

'Same here,' said Danny.

And for a moment, the overlapping desire not to talk

brought them into intimacy, the stoic silence of the Indian grasping hands with the natural reticence of the English upper middle classes.

As if he had already said too much, the writer added: 'However, I now can't wait to return to England. I find it excruciatingly dull in this part of the world. Nothing appears to happen here. What do you find to do?'

'Not much,' said Danny.

Sitting a few yards away was the ancient figure of Koko Lupi, watching them but not joining in. She had been summoned from the south savannahs by Wifreda because Sonny was having fits. Sonny had always been entranced by the moon. He liked to sleep, eyes open, bathed in moonlight. But from the onset of puberty, he had suffered fits when the moon was full.

'The moon come for he,' said Koko Lupi and prescribed that Wifreda burn fowl feathers under his nose and then make him drink water containing the ashes of the feathers.

When he asked her, Koko Lupi informed Mr Waugh that she had flown there.

'Pretends to fly,' wrote Waugh in his diary afterwards.

In the house later that night, Mr Waugh asked Danny if he would like to hear him read some Dickens. He had brought a copy of *Dombey and Son* with him. Although Danny could be cruel, there was something about the stranger that he liked. And so he fetched a light – a wick floating in beef fat – and some more rum and two glasses which he put down on the small table and listened patiently for as long as Mr Waugh cared to read. Mr Waugh sat with one leg up on the wooden arm of his Berbice chair, holding the book at an angle to catch the feeble light. After a while, Danny's attention faltered as he remembered the occasion, long ago in his childhood, when another white man had come and played Mozart sonatas on a violin.

'Shall I stop?' said Mr Waugh, noticing the loss of concentration.

'No. Please go on,' said Danny politely. 'Please to carry on.'

In the first light of morning, there was a creaking sound as the writer, clad in his pyjamas, turned heavily in his hammock, uncomfortable and chilled. He imagined having to stay in such a place for ever. He nearly fell out as he reached down to the floor to pick up his notebook and pen. 'The plight of a civilised man trapped amongst savages,' he wrote, and then added a series of question marks to remind him of the savages he had left in his own land.

As he prepared to leave, he stopped packing to write in his diary: 'Wrote bad article yesterday but have thought of plot for short story. Could call it "The Man Who Liked Dickens".'

Outside, Danny cranked up the truck with violent turns of the handle. He had promised to give Mr Waugh a lift over to St Ignatius to meet the new priest. After Father Napier's departure, there had been no Catholic priest in the Rupununi for many years. The new one, just appointed, had attended Stonyhurst College in England and knew several of Waugh's acquaintances.

The writer felt less bleak. Up until then the entire journey had been like an unendurable, self-inflicted penance. That shared moment of silence with Danny McKinnon had helped. Somehow he felt that he had turned the corner. The fact that he had conceived an idea for a piece of fiction was a good sign.

The morning that Mr Waugh left, all the children had waved him off and nobody had returned to the schoolroom. Nancy Freeman waited in the empty room for a bit and then reluctantly abandoned all idea of teaching that day and strolled down past the giant mango trees towards the river. There, through a secluded patch of trees, she saw the figure of Sonny. She approached quietly to within a few yards of him and watched him perform an amazing feat with his arrows and bow.

He had his back to her and did not know she was there. He shot one arrow high up into the trunk of the ite palm, almost out of sight at the top. Then he shot another into the butt of the first and then another into the butt of the second and so on until a fine arch of arrows formed from the trunk of the tree to the ground. He turned round, saw Nancy and smiled.

It was a radiant, dark, dazzling smile that she never forgot, as he stood there in his white shirt and brown shorts. Then he walked away downhill towards the creek.

She went forward to examine the arch of arrows but as she came up to it the whole structure collapsed with the arrows falling all awry.

Nobody knew exactly what happened to Sonny. He disappeared a year or so after that. Rumours sprang up about his vanishing but nobody seemed able to pinpoint the time or place where he had gone missing. There were reported sightings of him here and there, sometimes in a certain village, or someone would say they had seen him pulling cassava in the mountains. He ceased to exist gradually as the reports grew less.

Because of the rumours that his mother was a kanaima, nobody searched too hard for him. Some people said he had gone into the mountains to train as a kanaima himself. More than one person suspected he was a 'turn-tiger', that he was able to transform himself into a jaguar. Privately, Wifreda did not think so, but understanding his preference for solitude, she did think it possible that he had gone to live in one of the deserted jaguar caves beneath the great black boulders in the Kanaku Mountains.

Sonny's apotheosis came after several people swore they had seen him near Bottle Mountain, standing at the place where a number of trails all cross, the rising sun between two mountain peaks catching him in a prism of light so that he seemed to dazzle where he stood.

The sight had so surprised one Macusi man out hunting that he had returned and tried to trace the prints of the figure he had seen. The hunter was a meticulous and practical man who was irritated by matters that had no explanation.

As he examined the footprints, he saw that they were overlaid with splayed jaguar prints that appeared to go backwards. He assumed that someone was trying to play tricks with a severed tiger foot in order to put off pursuers. He followed the mish-mash of prints into the foothills of the mountains, losing them briefly where the grey stones bridged a rushing creek. He crossed the creek to the other side.

It was there that he stopped trying to follow the vanished prints and began to follow the alluring sound of laughter.

Following the sound of solitary merriment, he climbed up the steep narrow trail towards the waterfall, relishing the smell of dense wet vegetation. The sun slashed through tangled, broken leaves but he looked down, treading carefully over the rocks, shrubs and fallen tree branches that littered the ascent, and so he did not see a hammock slung over his head in the trees.

He had never heard such gaiety. Soon, his ears were assailed by different sounds in turn, each seeming to come from the same place as the laughter – a toucan with its yelp like a puppy; the whoop-whooping of a tree-frog; and then the mouse-like chirpings of bats in broad daylight, which disconcertingly dissolved into giggles. The only constant was the waterfall clamouring in the background. Between each sound came a peal of such infectious laughter that the man could do nothing but stand there with a big smile on his face, listening. He started to giggle himself and shook his head. It's either a parrot or some sort of ventriloquist, he thought.

When he reached the small waterfall from which all the sounds seemed to originate, there was nothing there except a pile of carelessly abandoned clothes on the flat boulders in front of the fall. There was no sign of the owner whom he presumed to be swimming somewhere nearby. He examined the clothes; an elegant cream suit, the trousers supported by a solid belt of carved leather; a pair of expensive dark glasses with gold frames and a set of car keys whose metal had grown hot in the sun.

He waited for a few hours until approaching darkness made him pick his way back down, profoundly disappointed not to have found the source of such numinous laughter.

Wifreda waited anxiously for a while and then wrote to Beatrice in Canada about the mystery, saying that Sonny had just left and wandered off somewhere. Maybe he went to town, she wrote, or was killed by an animal or moved across to Brazil. Nobody knows. A body was found sitting in the river, face in the water as if looking for something, hair streaming, thumb and leg part eaten away. But nobody knew for certain who it was.

Beatrice received the letter, concealed it from her husband and later tore it up.

She wrote to Wifreda saying that perhaps it was just as well and thanking her for all she had done. She now had four children with Horatio. They had moved to a house in Ville St Laurent on the outskirts of Montreal. The children attended the local school. What with the routine of seeing to the children and looking after Horatio she barely had time to remember that other love which had flowed always under the grind of daily life; a sweet underground river that sometimes broke through to the surface and made its own music, but mainly stayed hidden, so that she only carried the echoes of its song.

Occasionally, she did think of the boy she had left behind, strange, beautiful and isolate. Then, for a while, life with Horatio and her other children would seem quite unreal.

PART THREE

A TAPIR FOR A WIFE

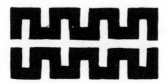

Auntie Wifreda thought she could tolerate being blind as long as Beatrice's face did not keep floating into the blackness. She tried to imagine how she would manage back at home in the Rupununi. Marietta and Bla-Bla would have to help her. It might be possible to use Bla-Bla as a sort of blind person's walking stick. Perhaps one of the dogs could be trained as a guide dog. Nothing to be done about fate. At least she had been able to see for most of her life.

When Chofy found out what had happened, he took her immediately to the hospital. The surgeon was puzzled.

'As far as I can see,' he said to Chofy privately, after examining both eyes, 'the operation on the right eye was a success. I can find no organic reason for her to lose her sight like this. It might be stress. There is such a thing as hysterical blindness. Let her rest for a week and then bring her back and we will see where to go from there.'

Chofy guided her up the steps to her room in Thomas Street. Auntie Wifreda felt her way around until she found the chair and sat in it.

'You seem so calm about it all,' said Chofy.

Staring sightlessly straight ahead of her, Wifreda told him

for the first time the whole story of his Uncle Danny's affair with Beatrice; Father Napier's madness; the existence and disappearance of Sonny; the eclipse and the threat that Beatrice had uttered to make her blind.

'Like a termite,' she said, as Chofy bathed her forehead and brushed her silver hair. Chofy finished and laid the hairbrush on the stool next to the bed. 'Now you know why I don' want to talk any more about eclipses or Sonny or Evelyn Waugh or any of it.'

Chofy heated some food up for her on the stove outside.

'Go,' she said, when he had given her a plate of cook-up rice. 'There's nothing you can do. Just roll me a cigarette before you leave.'

'How is your Auntie Wifreda?' asked Rosa anxiously, when he returned.

'Same way,' said Chofy. 'Do you believe in superstition?'

'Absolutely not.' Rosa sat up on the bed in mock outrage. 'Nor in religion. I'm a complete rationalist.'

He kept what he had been told to himself.

Over the next few nights, when Chofy and Rosa had finished making love, and with the heat pressing down on them so that even the weight of the sheet was too much to bear, they lay talking, face to face, jacked up on their elbows, legs and feet twisted round each other.

'But why were you living with your Auntie Wifreda anyway? Where were your own parents?'

The chance to talk about himself was such a delicious luxury that Chofy continued into the early hours of the morning while she listened with great attention, trying to fight off sleepiness. He twisted himself round in the bed.

'My father, Freddie, died in the Rupununi when I was seven. That was a disaster for me. Nothing felt the same after that. When he was buried at Sand Creek it was raining hard. The coffin rested in water and mud. All the village came. Apparently, it was only when I saw the earth being thrown on the coffin that I realised what was happening. I don' remember too much but they said I jumped into the grave and they had to carry me away kicking and struggling.'

'What did he die of?' asked Rosa, frowning in sympathy.

'Another Indian had accused him of stealing a horse. My father lost his temper and shouted at him to clear out. People said that the man came back and stole one of my father's footprints and put it in the creek. People believe things like that,' Chofy added hastily. 'Soon my father became breathless and his foot swelled up like a football. Great, deep holes appeared in his foot-bottom. He peed himself and it fell into puddles like creek water. His leg swelled and then his body. He began to bleed from his bottom like he have a period. That's one of the signs of kanaima. On the night he died, he said he wanted to sling his hammock outside to get more air. People said they saw a stranger, an Amerindian man nearby. Then he died. My mother was a Wapisiana from Sand Creek. She left after that and went over to Brazil and Auntie Wifreda raised me, with my cousin Tenga whose mother had died too.'

'But you said you were partly raised by a priest,' she said.

'Oh yes. Well, that was after my Uncle Danny attacked me one time. He was living with us and drinking heavily. He nearly killed me. I would never forget it. I was about twelve and I had just learned a story from one of the vaqueiros. We were all sitting round the table. I was excited and I was telling it to Auntie Wifreda, jumping up and down with all the gestures and so on. Uncle Danny was slouched at the table, surly as usual, gulping down bowls of parakari, the birthmark on his head standing out red – always a danger sign. The story I was telling was about a couple with one son. Shall I tell it to you?'

Rosa gave Chofy a sympathetic nuzzle of encouragement. Chofy was wide awake.

'I remember every word of it. There was a couple with a son. The wife was very cruel. The child cried and she beat him and dumped him in a pineapple field. A female bush-cow, that's a tapir, heard the child and moved over to see what it was. Moved by the child's crying, she took him home. In the forest, the child grew up under her loving care. When he was fully grown, they began to live together as man and wife. Several years passed happily and then one day she became pregnant.

'The man went hunting in the forest. Chasing a deer one night, he accidentally stumbled on the village where he was born. The people told him all about himself and how he had been left to die by his cruel mother. He felt very comfortable in the village and stayed on there to join the men in their fieldwork. As they sat eating their meal, the hunters began to talk about a certain bush-cow they had been seeing around the place. They decided to go hunting for it the next day.

'The man felt sad that his wife would be killed but he could not save her. He did not want the men to know she was his wife. So as not to arouse suspicion, he went with them on the hunting expedition. He even asked to be the watchman by the river where he would be the first to shoot at her. When the hunters found her, they chased after her. She could smell her husband and ran towards him. He shot an arrow which pierced her neck and she fell to the ground and died, the child still in her womb.

'The husband rushed forward, cut out a full human baby boy from her belly. He took the child home to care for him, but after only four days, the child turned into a poisonous plant. He made use of the plant for fishing. That's how we came to learn how to poison fish.

'That was the story, exactly as I told it. Something in it must have upset Uncle Danny because the next thing I knew, he had me by the throat and was dragging me to the window. He was pushing me backwards through the window, holding me down over the sill and throttling me, accusing me of lying and stealing and all sorts of things. Auntie Wifreda threw hot coffee on him to stop him. Well, Uncle Danny was a big man. He stood there, his chest heaving with these dry sobs. We were all terribly embarrassed. I was crying too. In the end, he staggered outside, still very drunk, picked up a spade leaning against the wall and smashed one of the outhouses to pieces.

'After that Auntie Wifreda took me over to the priest's house and I stayed there for a while. He was very good to me, even sent me to school in Georgetown for a year.'

'I thought you said you didn't know any mythology.'

'Oh I know plenty stories like that.'

Rosa's eyes were closing. He poked her in the ribs:

'I think I'm talking to myself here,' said Chofy, pretending to be offended and squeezing her till she responded with a fit of sleepy giggles. His own eyes were closing but he kept himself awake, not wanting to lose a minute of her lying next to him. He felt he was cradling something precious that would never be given to him again. He ran his hand down the curve of her hip.

'What sort of stories does Evelyn Waugh write?' Chofy asked suddenly.

'Not stories like that,' mumbled Rosa, turning in his arms. 'But there's room for all sorts of stories. How did you come by your name – Chofoye? It's a lovely name.'

In deference to Rosa's clear-headed rationalism, Chofy suppressed his own superstitious fear. He had been brought up either not to reveal his name or not to explain its meaning. He had felt uncomfortable even when he first told her.

'I told you. It's a Wai-Wai name meaning "rapids" or "fast-flowing waters". If you say it out loud, you can hear it makes the sound of water exploding over rocks. Uncle Danny suggested it when I was born and my father liked it.'

During those nights, Chofy told her everything he could remember about his life. Sometimes he spoke lying on his back with one arm round her. Sometimes he levered himself on to his elbow and talked while he felt her soft breath tickle his cheek like a duck feather.

The only thing he did not tell her was that he was married with a child of his own. He excised Marietta and Bla-Bla out of the story, hoping against hope that something would turn up to resolve the impossible. He did not think of the future and felt no guilt, just a terror that Rosa would find out and that everything would be finished between them.

He ran his finger over her upturned profile. The outline reminded him of something.

'Do you know how they cut keys?' he said, looking at her from the side. 'They run the key through a machine that cuts it out the opposite way – backwards.'

Rosa looked on her map for the road that contained the private residence of the Canadian High Commissioner. There were now two reasons for her increasing determination to visit the Rupununi. Despite Auntie Wifreda's discouraging noises, she was convinced that visiting the Rupununi would help her research and now her deepening involvement with Chofy had aroused a curiosity and she longed to see where he came from. She could not understand his reluctance to help her. He always seemed to find some excuse to prevent them from going there together which made her more committed than ever to finding a way of getting there somehow.

'I can't leave my job,' he said.

'I want to see where you come from,' she pleaded, to no avail.

It was in pursuit of this aim that Rosa climbed out of a cab and walked up the drive of the Canadian High Commission in Georgetown. William Bevan, the Canadian High Commissioner, frequently flew to the Rupununi by private plane for a sporting weekend's duck or deer-hunting. She had met his wife briefly at a cultural event and befriended her. It was an outside chance but she hoped to be able to accompany Monica Bevan's husband on one of his trips.

Monica Bevan invited Rosa into the front room of their official residence which was unpleasantly chilled from the cross-ventilated air-conditioning. She was a nervous beaver of a woman with neatly set grey hair, beset by fears of illness.

'I always boil any water for twenty minutes and never drink the milk. I'm near a nervous breakdown. Living here wears you down. The stress. It's counted as a hardship posting, you know.' She fidgeted with a soapstone Inuit carving she had brought with her from Canada and continued bleating with self-pity. Rosa listened patiently to the litany of complaints.

'You can't get anything done. Nothing works. The fax and the telex don't work. There are satellite phones but the government hasn't paid the cable charges. Poor Bill has had to go off early this morning to deal with some scam concerning forged visas.'

In the doorway, the new East Indian houseboy hovered, never knowing when to interrupt and serve the coffee, the tray balanced precariously on his forearm. Mrs Bevan did not notice him dancing backwards and forwards across the threshold of the room.

'There are a hundred and fifty people a day queuing

outside the High Commission and now they're asking us to provide shelter for them. They come to Canada. They have no skills. They live on welfare in better conditions than they've ever known in their lives. They get free education – the schools here have no pencils or equipment. Come outside and see the pool,' she said – suddenly aware that she might be depressing her visitor.

They went towards the automatic sliding doors that led on to the garden and the kidney-shaped blue swimming pool. The houseboy backed out and returned to the kitchen without serving the coffee.

'I was wondering if I might be able to fly into the Rupununi when your husband next goes in,' ventured Rosa tentatively.

'Of course, my dear. Come to dinner with us on Friday and you can fix it up with him. We are entertaining the American Ambassador and his wife and a few others.'

'Thank you. May I bring a partner?' Rosa asked shyly.

'Certainly.' She looked round in exasperation. 'You see – I ask the staff for coffee and they completely ignore me.' She showed Rosa to the door, shaking her head in disbelief.

RAINSTORM

Two days later, the air grew dark and a deluge fell on the city. Rosa sat on her bed. She had realised only lately that she was falling in love, vaguely recollecting the sensation from years before. It had dawned on her with gradual delight. Oberon juice, she called it, smiling to herself. I've been sprinkled with Oberon juice. She folded her clothes into piles of clean and dirty in a daze of thoughtful astonishment. Would her daughter mind? Probably not. Her ex-husband now lived in Amsterdam. He had remarried. What sort of future could she have with Chofy? Unimaginable. But she began to plan one all the same, wondering if she could find a job at the University of Guyana.

As she got up to put her research papers on the table, spiky rain began to lance at angles through the jalousie slats wetting the reddish wooden floor and making it shine. She went over to look out and then shut the windows. As she switched on the light, pipefuls of water began to gurgle out over the zinc roof that protected the verandah. Indira, the assistant cook, came up the stairs bearing an avocado salad and some rice and peas which she placed on the dressing-table.

'The rain does not want you to go to university today,'

she announced sombrely, before disappearing down the stairs again.

Rosa and Chofy had arranged to go to the university to hear Wormoal's lecture on Amerindian mythology. They had argued about it. Chofy did not want to go. He suspected her motives for wanting to go. He was plainly jealous of Wormoal. She explained that she did not even like the anthropologist but that she had promised to give him some support in his lecture. Besides, his paper was intriguing and included material about Wapisiana Indians, even if he did seem to be a bit of a fascist in some of his views.

'You should be interested,' she told a sulking Chofy. Finally, Chofy agreed to accompany her rather than risk her meeting up with Wormoal on her own.

Later in the afternoon when the rain stopped, Rosa walked from Brickdam over to the library. Glittering necklaces of water circled the corner cafés and rum shops as she threaded her way round the gleaming puddles that filled gaping holes in the road.

By the time Chofy hurried out of the building, the rain was sheeting down once more. He tried to protect his head with his hands. Rosa was drenched, her clothes clinging to her. They ran for the mini-bus.

When they reached the university, the rain had reduced to a steady drizzle and a mist still hung in the air. The shoddily built university had a deserted feel to it. A lone cow cropped the campus grass. Instead of the revolutionary slogans that usually deck a university campus, the graffiti on the wall pleaded: 'TEXTS NOW'. 'SANITATION NOW'. 'WHERE ARE THE FACILITIES???'.

Inside the faculty, water dripped through the ceilings and hallways. They climbed the open stairs. Rosa skidded and nearly fell on the wet plank floor. The seminar room where the lecture was to be held was empty. There were no chairs.

Rainwater dripped on to the desks. This was Chofy's first ever visit to the university. It depressed him. He felt uncomfortable and out of place there.

'Greetings. You braved the storm.' Carmella de Pereira, Chofy's boss who had organised the lecture together with the university librarian, bustled in. Noticing the way they stood close together, she shot a curious, slightly disapproving look in their direction.

'Mr Wormoal not here yet, I see,' she said and breezed out again. Two black students and one East Indian girl ambled in, wiped down the desks and sat on them. Gradually, they were joined by some others.

Wormoal finally arrived shaking an umbrella, rain dripping down his glasses which he took off to wipe, making his eyes look vulnerable, like creatures when a stone is lifted from over them.

He saw Rosa and Chofy and came over to them. Rosa introduced Chofy.

'Ah. I've been wanting to meet you.' He blinked. 'The Wapisiana with the Wai-Wai name. It means "explosion of waters", doesn't it?' He touched Chofy lightly on the arm. The touch reminded Chofy of the light fingering of the pickpockets in Stabroek market. He nodded warily. Wormoal put his glasses on again and peered at Chofy.

'Very good to meet you. You know I spent time with the south savannah Indians. The McKinnons are a well-known family. I met several of them. Now which one are you?'

Chofy tensed, dreading that Wormoal would know about Marietta. He wished he had obeyed the feeling of foreboding about Wormoal that had warned him against coming.

'Freddie's son. Sand Creek,' He mumbled.

Wormoal glanced at his watch.

'But perhaps we could talk afterwards – please excuse me for the moment, I have to sort out my lecture.'

He turned away to unpack his notes and write some headings on the blackboard. Rosa and Chofy found two dryish chairs and sat down. The piece of chalk Wormoal held slid across the wet surface of the blackboard as he tried to write the words 'Eclipse – a Rational Analysis of Myth'. Water leaked from the ceiling directly above his head. Chofy watched the words disintegrate. Wormoal shook his head in annoyance. He tried again and the chalk skidded off the board. By now, rain was penetrating at other points of the ceiling. A student, used to the situation, slipped out and returned with two buckets. No sooner had he done this than the plaster burst overhead and a waterfall descended into the room.

Carmella de Pereira burst through the door at the same time.

'I'm sorry, everybody.' She laughed gamely. 'We shall have to cancel. The whole department is flooding. I advise you to take off your shoes and make your way out. There is a torrent outside. Come with me, Mr Wormoal. I will take you for tea with Mr Smiley, the librarian, where it is DRY.' Her tinkling laugh echoed as she swept him off down corridors awash with flood water.

'I told you it would be a waste of time,' said Chofy, moodily, but relieved all the same that he would not have to speak to Wormoal.

'Well, he was talking about Wapisiana Indians and their mythology. I thought you would be interested.'

'We could have been in bed,' said Chofy.

After leaving the university, Chofy went to check on Auntie Wifreda and found no change in her condition. He walked back to the Lodge. The deluge had passed. It was a beautiful evening. The air was clear and the sky streaked with green and pink. Ragged wisps of grey cloud hung noticeably low over the red roofs of Georgetown.

He crept up the stairs to surprise Rosa. As he passed the veranda of the floor below the attic, he saw the American executives from Hawk Oil relaxing in easy chairs, drinking beer and gazing out over the city as if it belonged to them. Wormoal had come back and was drinking with them. To Chofy's concern, he heard his name mentioned.

Wormoal was saying in the confident tone of an expert: 'Chofoye is a Wai-Wai name, you see, meaning "explosion of waters".'

One of the Americans replied: 'Well, we're leaving tomorrow morning and we sure need to know the Amerindian word for explosion where we're going.' There was laughter. 'What did you say it was . . . Chofoye?' The American went on to explain about the seismic surveys for oil that they were conducting in the Rupununi.

'We explode dynamite every few hundred yards at or near the ground surface. The sound waves are recorded on geophones and show us potential oil or gas-trapping structures underground.' The American pulled down his sock to rub at a mosquito bite.

It disturbed Chofy to hear his name discussed by strangers. He slipped past, making sure that Wormoal did not catch sight of him.

Rosa was curled up barefoot on the sofa, wearing a pale-pink crêpe dress that exposed her neck and her breasts. She was busy scribbling messages on postcards.

'I forgot to tell you.' She stretched her legs and smiled up at him as he came in. 'We've been invited to dinner at the Canadian High Commission.'

Chofy stopped in his tracks.

'Well, I wouldn't be going. I hate that sort of thing. I didn't even like going to the university. I don' have the right clothes. I feel out of place. I don' know what to say to those people.'

'Oh come with me,' Rosa pleaded. 'I don't much like those people either, but it might help me get to the Rupununi.'

'Why are you always so keen to go there?' He slumped into a chair, scowling, knowing that if she visited the Rupununi she would be bound to discover about Marietta and Bla-Bla. She opened her eyes wide and looked at him with concern.

'No. I can't bear it. I don' like those sort of snooty-head people.' He made a stand at stubbornness.

'Please.' She bit her lip and looked anxiously at him.

He felt himself melting at her plea. It was difficult to refuse her anything. Besides, he suddenly remembered his uncle Danny telling him: 'To refuse an invitation to the feast is to declare war.' He hesitated.

'All right. Why do I do everything for you? And always give in to you? Because you give me a permanent erection, that's why.' He came over to the sofa and put his arms round her and laid his head on her shoulder, breathing in the smell that always aroused him.

'I think about you all the time. I want to build a house. I want to build a house for you and till the land and put up a fence. I want to spend the rest of my life with you. I want to paint the house I build . . . I don't want to live without you,' he sighed.

He had almost called her Marietta. He had spoken just those words to Marietta twenty years earlier.

'I'm so weak for you,' he said, resting his head on her shoulder and nuzzling at her neck.

BABOONS
MAKING COFFEE

That year in the Rupununi, rodeo took place later than
usual on the Easter Sunday and Monday because Easter
itself was late.

Marietta had begun the long walk from Moco-moco to
Lethem at dawn while it was still cool. She carried about
twenty empty woven baskets to sell, some cylindrical, some in
the shape of a howler monkey's voice-box. Strung together,
they weighed little and bobbed on either side of her like
water wings. Bla-Bla had gone ahead the night before and
slung his hammock in trees outside the stockade. He was
competing in one of the children's events and wanted to
be there at dawn to take the horse he was riding down to
the river and bathe him.

It was halfway through the morning when Marietta arrived.
Reggae music boomed out from the entrance. Ducking under
the barrier in order not to pay, Marietta made her way over to
the stalls. A large tent twenty yards away housed the bar where
people already stood or sat drinking. An influx of Brazilians
had arrived and some coastlanders sprawled at the tables.

Events had already started. Marietta had missed the wild-
cow milking competition and the children riding a greased

pig. The stockade where the events took place was a huge area fenced off and consisting of nothing but arid clods of dry, dusty, pale-brown earth. Motor bikes stuttered as people came and went from the fair. Cheers and jeers erupted from the onlookers in the stand as the vaqueiros rode wild bulls or broncos like sailors trying to keep upright in a storm-tossed sea. Onlookers leaned against the fence blinking away the dust and sweat from their eyes.

It was the first rodeo Marietta had ever attended without Chofy and she missed him. In some ways, she had found life easier in the Rupununi when Chofy was not there. After the long stretches of silence punctuated with quarrels that had been the recent pattern of their marriage, it was initially a relief to be without him. But now she could have done with some company. Her father and grandfather had stayed at home to help with the cassava farm.

A Macusi man she vaguely recognised from Shulinab staggered up to her drunk as a snake, black hair shining, his breath smelling hot and sour, and put his burning hand on her arm. He must know Chofy isn't here, she thought. That's why he's behaving like this. She shook him off and left her baskets to be sold on one of the stalls. More than half the people at the rodeo were strangers to her these days.

A loudspeaker announced the under-elevens' horse race. Marietta made her way over the lumpy ground at the back of the stockade to where Bla-Bla's race would take place. He was riding a neighbour's horse. The young riders were out of sight a mile away down the strip of land that formed the course. A steward ushered the spectators back so that they would not be trampled. Marietta felt a flutter of excitement. The first sign of the juvenile riders was a small puff of white dust in the distance. Then after a few moments, the ground beneath their feet began to vibrate and Marietta tried to push forward to see. Three minutes later, the horses were in sight thundering towards them. Craning forward through the flying dust, Marietta caught a momentary glimpse of Bla-Bla's furiously eager little face, his eyes slitted against the dust, his bare feet thumping the sides of his horse. He was biting his bottom lip and lashing the horse wildly with a piece of snake-whip bush. They went by too fast for her to see who had won.

'I brought third,' a panting Bla-Bla announced to his mother, proudly, his hair spiking up, his face red.

'Why you din' come first? You too fat, that's why. Horse can't carry you. You eat too much. I don't want to hear about no third,' said Marietta and Bla-Bla went off to cool his horse in the river, pleased with himself all the same.

The sky was colourless overhead. The grinding thump of the reggae music irritated Marietta. Rodeo felt empty and pointless without Chofy there to discuss the events. She collected the money from her basket sales and waited for Bla-Bla to return. Then they went close up to the fence to watch the tug-of-war, last event of the day. One team consisted of twenty-four coastlanders or settlers and some Brazilians. The other consisted of twenty-four Wapisiana vaqueiros from the south savannahs. The Indians were half the height and weight of the coastlanders. They did not seem to have a chance.

As soon as the tugging began, Marietta found herself yelling for the south-savannah team even though it seemed hopeless. First one group and then the other was pulled past the central marker. After about five minutes the coastlanders began to quarrel and shout conflicting instructions to each other, sometimes letting the rope go with one hand in order to gesticulate. The Indians at the other end of the rope never said a word but every time the coastlanders gave an inch or let up for a second, they dug their heels in and pulled together. Ten minutes later, the impossible had occurred and the tiny south-savannah vaqueiros, used to handling wild cattle, had pulled the other team in disarray towards them until they collapsed in a heap.

Marietta and Bla-Bla stood on the trail with three other Wapisiana women just outside the rodeo, all of them smiling. Marietta had a slight headache. Although pleased by the victory, she felt dispirited somehow and wanted to get away from the music, the crowds, the booming loudspeakers and the scree scree of the referees' whistles. It was as if she no longer belonged in her own landscape. The small group of women chatted happily, feeling good to know that they could talk quietly in Wapisiana and that passing outsiders would not be able to understand them. The wind was getting up. Marietta looked up at the sky.

'When it start properly, it go be rain for months,' she said. The others nodded. They said their goodbyes. The further away she was from the rodeo, the more peaceful Marietta felt. They left Lethem behind and started the long walk over the savannahs. A goat was eating from a bush by the side of the track. When they were nearly home, Marietta and Bla-Bla stopped to wait for an alligator which was stepping across the road towards the creek. Then they went on until they reached the gateposts and walked down the slope to the house.

Just before daybreak the next day, Marietta called Bla-Bla to get up while she started to make bakes. It was the beginning of the new school term. To her surprise, Bla-Bla had settled down and attended school regularly after his father left. His father's absence seemed to have made him more responsible. One of his jobs was to grind corn and feed the fowls in the morning before school. While it was still dark, they went to fetch water from the creek. Bla-Bla led the way, yawning, a bucket in each hand. Daylight grew stronger and on the way back, trying not to spill water, Marietta pointed out the morning mists hanging in the Kanaku Mountains.

'Look,' she said, nodding in the direction of the mountains and laughing. 'Baboons making coffee.'

Bla-Bla grinned. She looked at the sky and began to hurry.

'Come. Come quick. Rain,' she said.

As she spoke, the air seemed to boil and turn grey. Heavy drops of rain started to plummet down and the two of them rushed into the house as fast as possible without spilling the water. Bla-Bla shot out again and made a dash for the latrine. He dived inside, pulled down his pants and sat naked and shivering on the warm wooden board with a hole that formed the seat. A lizard scuttled into the wattle sides of the latrine. Lightning flashed. Rain pelted down on the roof. Thunder rumbled, reverberated and then crashed overhead. Bla-Bla ducked at the sound. Frightened by the violence of the storm, he put his hands together and decided to pray. All he could remember was something he had learned the previous term at school that felt to him like a prayer. As the air grew darker and took on a bruised, greenish hue, he rattled off what he had learned out loud:

'Always speak quietly and courteously,
A quiet voice is a mark of refinement,
If you have to interrupt anyone speaking
Always say excuse me, please.
Cover your mouth with your hand when you yawn.
Cover your mouth with your hand
And turn your head aside when you cough.

'Amen,' he added. His hymn to manners finished, Bla-Bla cleaned himself with a piece of stick and waited for the storm to abate. Torrential waters hammered on the leaf roof over his

315

head. When he was unable any longer to withstand the terror of the storm, Bla-Bla scampered, heart thumping, through the lashing spears of rain for the house. Inside, he took off his shorts, wrung them out and sat on the floor.

'I tremblin',' he said. 'When is Daddy coming back?'

The school Bla-Bla attended was more than a mile away. It consisted of one long room on stilts under a palm thatch. The room was divided into three sections by two blackboards on easels – so it was always possible to hear a low hum from one of the other classes.

Bla-Bla set off carrying a shuttlecock made from a corn-cob with feathers stuck in one end. In his pocket, he kept a kokerite seed with the perfectly bored circular hole that means it contains a little white grub. On the way, he snapped off a twig from the wet sucubera tree to squeeze the white paste from it that can be used for glue and stuck some seeds on to his shuttlecock for decoration.

Bla-Bla had discovered that it was possible to enjoy school. After mid-morning break every day, his class had a reading lesson when they took it in turns to stand up and read out loud. The book was passed to him. He had just stood up to do his best when the sound of bare feet thumping up the wooden steps to the schoolroom distracted everybody. The whole class looked towards the door. To his astonishment, Marietta came marching right in. She saw Bla-Bla standing up in the class. Because she was a little embarrassed, she ignored the schoolteacher and spoke straight to him in Wapisiana. It was forbidden to speak Wapisiana or Macusi at school.

'Bla-Bla. You know where is the parrot?'

She was frowning with worry and sweating from the walk. The parrot was her favourite. It had gone missing and she'd searched the house, the nearby fruit trees and down by the creek before walking all the way to the school.

Everyone giggled except the dapper black teacher from the coast, who did not understand the language and who, anyway, was eaten up with rage because his wife had left him. Unable to withstand the hardships of savannah life, she had returned to Georgetown and left him to work out his contract while she spent the money.

Bla-Bla smiled at his mother. It made him feel proud and shy to see her familiar figure in the school. Some children had no parents, but everybody would know that he belonged to someone. He answered her in Wapisiana.

'I haven't seen the parrot, Mamai. Sometimes, he sits in the small mango tree at the back.'

Marietta grunted and pounded back down the stairs.

The blow took Bla-Bla utterly by surprise. It stunned and cut. The strap caught him on the side of the head but the blow seemed to coil round the root of his tongue. The teacher was asking him something angrily and telling him to speak English. But his English deserted him and he was unable to answer: the strap whistled and landed on the other side of his head and the top of his left shoulder. Instinctively, he held on to the desk but nearly lost his balance.

Tiny electric shocks ran from his cheek to the fingertips of his left hand. He stared down at the wooden desk, speechless with misery. Since his father left, he had especially wanted to do well. He had done everything he could to please the teacher. The ugliness of the blows shocked him. The teacher told him to sit down and he did. The little girl who sat next to him was looking at him, her eyes full of worry.

During the morning break, Bla-Bla stayed apart from the others and refused to speak, as if the blows had driven him back to some period before speech, as old as silence. It was not until he was walking home on his own at the end of the afternoon that he allowed himself to sob.

Halfway home, on a hillside, he passed an elderly Macusi

woman sitting outside her house which was open on one side like a shed. She had her back to the sun to save her eyes from the glare as she wove tibisiri baskets. Her husband plodded wearily up the hill with a gourd of water on his shoulder. Despite being Wapisiana, Bla-Bla felt oddly linked to them, as if they all shared the same hardships, as if some sort of fate bound them together. Nobody spoke. There was a sense of defeat in the air as the sun slid towards the west.

He walked on towards home. From an early age, Bla-Bla had puzzled over how he could make things better for his own people. He sensed injustice in the way they were treated and it troubled him. Sometimes, in his hammock at nights, he imagined building defences around the village to keep intruders away. He planned battles and attacks.

Suddenly, Bla-Bla missed his father badly and also Auntie Wifreda's comforting presence in the house. At night, he used to accompany Auntie Wifreda to the latrine, carrying the big pole used for knocking down mangoes. He walked ahead with the pole and the kerosene lamp and she followed, sometimes singing a hymn and sometimes a Wapisiana song in her wavery voice.

He came to the creek. There, he jumped and slid down to crouch at the water's edge. A houri fish lay at the bottom but the water was clear and the fish too alert for him to be able to 'hold' it as his father had taught him. He went a little way upstream and muddied the water so that, as the sediment moved down, it clouded over the fish in the same way that the clouds obliterate the moon at night. Then he walked silently back to the fish. Very gently, as the muddied water drifted over it, he cupped his hand and held the fish, docile now that it could no longer see, clasping it in a delicate, firm grip and lifting it from the water.

When he reached home, he gave the fish to Marietta to cook and said nothing about what had happened at school.

As soon as he came in the house, Marietta took the fish and sent Bla-Bla straight out again on the fourteen-mile walk to the post office to see if any money had arrived from Georgetown. He set off on the journey, collecting two friends on the way.

They had walked for about five miles when a truck came flying towards them along the red road that was still drying out after the storm earlier in the day. The truck was heading towards their village, grit and red clay spitting up from the wheels. An East Indian with a cigarette in his mouth drove at speed. He was bringing the Americans from Hawk Oil to set up their seismic oil surveys. There was only one road. The boys were hot, tired and thirsty. They thought that if they could catch a lift – even if it meant going back to the village – they could come out again with the truck and get a ride all the way to the post office.

They tried to flag the truck down as it passed. The driver laughed.

'Walk, buck boys,' he yelled as they roared past, the Americans grinning out from the back of the truck which splashed the boys as it roared by on the rutted track.

The sun burned down in the silence left behind by the truck as it disappeared in the distance. It was Bla-Bla's idea to make a trap for the men.

A mile further down the road, there were shrubs on either side of the road where it narrowed. The boys looked for stones, flat and sharp enough for digging. They worked like demons until their hair shone with sweat. Overhead, a tiny but persistent washi bird attacked a much bigger chicken hawk on the wing to try and get feathers for its nest. After about two hours, and covered in dust, they had scooped out two deep holes in the parallel ruts of the track.

A shower sent the boys scurrying to the side of the road for shelter. They stood under the glittering bush. Milky orange puddles filled the dips, holes and ruts in the road. Bla-Bla inspected their handiwork. The holes were about two feet deep. They covered them with branches and twigs and laid broad leaves on top. Then they scattered sandy earth on the whole lot.

As they stood back to survey their work, Bla-Bla realised the truck was a four-wheel drive and would be able to dig itself out with the back wheels. So they dug a third hole. Waist deep. They covered it in the same way with leaves, sticks, bush and bits of rock.

When the job was done, they walked the rest of the way to the post office, bought sweets for the return journey, hung around watching the men outside the abattoir for a while and sky-larked around, forgetting completely about the men in the truck.

When they came home from school the next day, they heard the trap had worked. The truck had crashed. The men, livid with fury, had had to walk back to the village for help and stay the night there. The East Indian driver had arrived at Marietta's the next day while Bla-Bla was still at school.

'Bla-Bla, they'll kill you.' Marietta was frightened. 'They said if they find you they will kill you.'

But Bla-Bla denied knowing anything about it. All the boys stuck to their story whether they were questioned separately or together. The men never came back to the house.

DINNER AT THE
HIGH COMMISSION

It was an hour before her dinner party at the High
Commission was due to begin and Mrs Monica Bevan
looked anxiously through the glass doors on to the lawn
at the back. A downpour had left mirror patches in the
waterlogged brown grass. She would not be able to serve
brandy outside after dinner as she had planned.

She checked the table. Each guest had a small crystal
finger-bowl, the water scented with one or two petals of
sweet-smelling orchids. Then she ran her eye over the
condiments, a variety of pepper-sauces and small bowls
of local salted peanuts. A silver epergne filled with fresh
hibiscus and frangipani graced the centre of the table.

It seemed to her that the staff, including Anita and Indira,
whom she had borrowed from Mynheer Nicklaus Lodge for
the evening, did not appreciate the urgency of the situation.
They had hardly bothered to peel the sweet potatoes before
tossing them into the pot in a lackadaisical, crosspatch sort
of way. One of the three extra helpers employed for the
occasion had put out fresh toilet rolls and then had to lie
down in the spare room with a headache.

Monica Bevan fussed over the placements. The guests

were the American Ambassador, Richard Evergreen, and his elegant wife June; Olly Sampson, Minister of Finance, and his wife Suzette; Eric Chang, the Chinese restaurateur, an oddball joker whom she suspected wore rouge, but on whom she could rely for lighthearted banter should conversation dry up; three Hawk Oil executives who had recently arrived, one of whom was bringing his wife – the others she had matched up with her bridge-playing lady friends; two of the other Hawk Oil men had had to cancel, having already left for the Rupununi; Rosa Mendelson and her escort and finally, of course, her own husband, Bill.

Half an hour later all the guests were seated.

To his alarm, Chofy found himself separated from Rosa and placed next to an enormous woman, denizen of bridge-playing haunts. She was dressed in stiff shot-silk that rustled like dry savannah grasses in the wind. He found that he could not stop sneaking looks over at Rosa. She had never seemed more beautiful. A low-necked, short-sleeved black dress showed off her creamy breasts and rounded arms. Her eyes sparkled with pleasure. She appeared completely relaxed with a radiance and animation that came from feeling no need to impress. It took his breath away to think that he was involved with her, that he had seen her naked, made love to her. With some trepidation he looked across at the burly figure of the Canadian High Commissioner, Bill Bevan. The man spent time in the Rupununi. He might know some of the McKinnons. Chofy was as haunted as ever by the fear that somehow his marriage would be revealed.

Rosa, for her part, was listening courteously to her neighbour, Mr Eric Chang, and passing him a plate of bread rolls. She caught Chofy's eye and smiled. He struck her as being by far the most handsome man at the table. Then and there she made up her mind to tell him, at the first reasonable opportunity, that she had fallen head over heels in love with him.

Chofy remained alert and on tenterhooks, watching and copying the other guests. Nothing escaped his notice. He observed carefully which knives, forks or spoons were used for which course and immediately, almost simultaneously, followed suit. He observed how the other guests placed their napkins on their knees and ingeniously did the same. He skilfully anticipated the needs of those around him and passed the salt, pepper-sauce or water jug to anyone who required it. He made small talk to his neighbour as he saw the others doing. But all the time, he felt like a mysterious servant who, for some reason or other, had been allowed to sit amongst the guests. He was astounded at being there. Suddenly, he reminded himself of how he was used to spending his days, up to his waist in water, scraping deer-hides in the creek. If he and Rosa were to share a future together, his nerves would not be able to tolerate this sort of occasion too often. It was an ordeal, as taxing as his first hunt, to be endured as seldom as possible and overcome.

As far as the nervous equilibrium of the hostess was concerned, the dinner got off to a bad start. The same East Indian houseboy who had skipped so nimbly back and forth across the threshold on Rosa's first visit now appeared in his evening manifestation. He shouldered his way through the door with a plate of crab soup in each hand, his arms bent and raised, the top half of his body wavering to and fro in contradistinction to his head, as if performing an exquisite traditional Hindu dance.

Mrs Bevan held her breath. Not until all the guests were served with the bright pink soup did she turn her attention to the conversation. Eric Chang was holding forth on the subject of elections.

'At the last election, I spotted my dead father on the electoral roll and two people had already cast their vote in his name.' He dabbed his mouth with a napkin and gave a high-pitched laugh.

The American Ambassador, a dark rather hunched man full of professional resentment at having ended up with his last diplomatic posting in such a politically insignificant place, turned to Olly Sampson, the finance minister.

'I think the IMF will probably refuse you any loan unless elections are supervised and a certain level of productivity guaranteed.'

In his own way, gentle Olly Sampson loved his country. Every day he went to his office at the Ministry of Finance and despaired. The figures for the foreign debt made him feel ill. It was like struggling in a quicksand. He always sat through these dinners in smiling misery, hoping against all the odds that someone would say, 'Look old chap, or buddy, or mein Freund, we think we'll just cancel the debt.'

'How did the colonists manage to build roads and courts and churches and even railway systems?' he once groaned to a colleague.

'Slavery,' his colleague had replied tartly.

'Oh yes.' No good thinking of reintroducing that. Once, although he had never mentioned it to a soul, Olly had the idea of turning the whole country into an enormous theme park for tourists. They would re-create their history as a spectacle. People could act being slaves. Ships full of indentured labourers would arrive in the docks. Visitors would stare at Amerindian villages where the villagers would be obliged to return to traditional dress and customs. Hollywood films could be made and package dramas created for the American and European education industries.

Recently, however, an irrepressible fantasy kept surfacing in his mind. It had first occurred to him when he was fretting, late at night, over budget figures. He imagined himself getting to his feet at the United Nations in New York or Geneva and making a solemn announcement that went something like this:

Ladies and Gentlemen, I should like to inform you, on behalf of the nation state of Guyana, that we are going to resign from being a country. We can't make it work. We have tried. We have done our best. It is not possible. The problems are insoluble. From midnight tonight, we shall cease trading. The country is now disbanded. We will voluntarily liquidate ourselves. The nation will disperse quietly, a little shamefaced but so what. We had a go.

Different people have suggested different solutions. Do it this way. Try that. Let me have a go. Nothing works. We are at the mercy of the rich countries. A team of management consultants from the United States could not find the answer, and for not finding the answer, we had to pay them an amount that substantially increased our national debt. We give in, gracefully, but we give in.

And then he imagined himself, quietly and with dignity, putting his papers in his briefcase, bowing to the hushed assembly, returning to clear out his office and going for a walk with his wife along the sea wall.

At that moment, Olly Sampson's wife was nudging him and he came to with a start, realising that conversation had ceased and the American Ambassador was expecting an answer.

'Oh, the IMF is designed to keep the rich rich and make the poor even poorer. Last time they insisted we cut the sugar workers' wages. There were massive strikes. The whole economy deteriorated. What to do?'

'I've been helping out in a soup kitchen since I arrived,' drawled the born-again Christian wife of one of the oil men. She had a face as round as a radar dish and despairing blue eyes.

'Ah. The poor are another country,' giggled Mr Chang. He turned to Rosa. 'Are you staying at the Pegasus?'

'No,' said Rosa. 'At Mynheer Nicklaus.'

'Just as well,' sniggered Eric Chang, 'we call the Pegasus the Pigasus. The rooms are damp with humidity and mildew. A different insect occupies each room and when the business-men open the windows to let in some air, mosquitoes as big as helicopters fly in.'

At that moment, Anita the cook marched through the door as though she were at a mass drill, bearing a dish of baked butter-fish in white creamed sauce. Indira followed with the cassava cakes and the East Indian boy, Rodney Singh, brought up the rear with the steamed callaloo.

Bill Bevan, the host, became aware of the most silent of the guests. He turned to Chofy.

'I must say I like your part of the world. I like to go to the Rupununi for a little sport at weekends. Have you been hunting recently?'

There was a slight hush as if everyone at the table was worried that Chofy would not be able to rise to the challenge. Chofy clenched his stomach muscles, cleared his throat and despite the stiffness of his borrowed shirt and the sweatiness of his palms, managed to speak.

'Not for a while. The last thing I missed catching was a sloth. We weren't fast enough. My cousin spotted one at the top of a kokerite tree. He raced to climb up. As he climbed, the sloth moved very slowly, edging its way along a branch to the very tip. As my cousin neared the top, the branch with the sloth on it bowed gradually under the animal's weight and the sloth, very, very slowly, reached out and transferred itself to the branch of the neighbouring tree. My cousin scrambled down and began to climb up the next tree. Exactly the same thing happened. The sloth barely seemed to move. Yet somehow, without hurrying, it always just escaped his grasp as he shinned frantically up one tree after another. They are creatures with great timing.'

Everybody had stopped eating and turned to listen to him, smiling at the story. It went down well. They all laughed and an immediate buzz of conversation started up round the table as he finished. A warmth had been generated amongst the guests. Rosa smiled affectionately at him. Chofy smoothed back his black hair and realised that the story had been some sort of social triumph. He relaxed and laughed with the others.

The staff trio marched in again, this time bringing the dishes of salad with avocado, cucumber, tomato and shallot and the breadfruit chips.

'These Hawk Oil boys aren't giving you any problems?' asked the Canadian High Commissioner jovially. Hawk Oil, having been granted a two-million-acre concession to look for oil in the Rupununi, had recently started their explorations.

'No, not as far as I . . .'

A wild cry interrupted Chofy.

No one saw Eric Chang slide his hand down the inside of Rodney Singh's left thigh. Everyone saw the avocado salad fly in the air and slide down the front of the American Ambassador's wife.

Monica Bevan's face turned scarlet. Her husband rose clumsily to see if he could help.

'No that's OK, really. It's all right.' Mrs Evergreen dabbed at the front of her dress with her napkin and inspected her lap for damage. Her smile remained unchipped. Her stomach knotted with fury.

Mrs Bevan left the room ostensibly to deal with the service problem. In fact, she went upstairs to her bedroom and opened her mouth in a wide and silent scream for two whole minutes. When she found the strength to return to the kitchen, she found that Rodney Singh had run home and the others were looking at her with reproach, talking about aunty-men. Or were they saying anti-men? She really could not tell.

Quickly she organised for the chicken fricassee and the rice with black-eye peas to be served and went back into the dining-room with a damp cloth.

Eric Chang remained unperturbed. He beamed around the table.

'Only a minor disaster,' he said. 'In this country, a change of disaster is always refreshing. In Guyana it is always disaster that comes up trumps. What has happened to the young man? Perhaps I should go and see.'

'He's gone home,' said Mrs Bevan. Which news put Eric Chang in a sulk for the rest of the evening.

Anita walked in grimly, this time as though she were leading a murder hunt. She presented the cheese board and the fingers of fudge and little peppermints. Indira served coffee wearing an expression like Cassandra's after another of her forecasts had been disbelieved.

Rosa caught Chofy's eye and had to look away quickly. They were both hardly able to contain their giggles.

At the end of the evening, Mrs Bevan was saying fulsomely to them: 'You must come again,' while directing a frosty shoulder at Mr Chang.

When they were safely inside the taxi, Rosa and Chofy clung on to each other and screamed with laughter.

'And what about you?' said Rosa, bursting with excited delight. 'If you're not careful you'll have to spend the rest of your life relating bush stories at dinner parties.'

LOVE GONE A FISH

Through the half-open door of the bathroom, he watched Rosa sponge herself down.

He liked to look at her without her knowing. Sometimes he watched secretly while she brushed her hair in front of the oval mirror of the rosewood dressing-table. Sometimes he came across her by chance on the telephone, stretching out her long legs on the sofa. He would stand gazing at her until she spotted him and smiled. It gave him the same feeling of alert excitement as when he had tracked a labba or a deer in the bush and the animal just continued foraging for food without realising he was there. It put him at an advantage in the hunt.

Rosa switched on the shower and nothing happened.

'Oh shit. The water's off again. It must have gone off just this second.'

She filled a calabash with water from the bucket and sluiced herself down with it. Chofy watched the almond curves of her breast, waist and hip. Then she sat on the wooden toilet seat, her face cupped thoughtfully in her hands. From where he was, in the dark, he heard the sound come and go as if she were pouring slow, obstinate, hesitant, golden syrup.

She wiped herself and came and stood naked by the window.

'Don't stand there. I don't want anyone else to see you.' He felt oddly jealous of anyone else seeing her like that.

'It's dark. No one can see me,' she said and went on standing there. 'What will we do when I have to return to England? It's soon.'

'We must discuss it. Come away from the window.'

He came up behind her and she pushed his hands away. He went over to the bed, undressed and lay down.

'Come and lie down with me.'

Rosa was half trying to overhear what the Americans were saying on the verandah below. They were having a final nightcap and, seemingly, still chuckling over Chofy's story about the sloth. Then they started to talk about the Rupununi and when they were due to join their colleagues there and she realised that she had not managed to ask Bill Bevan if she could accompany him. Her failure to do so seemed somehow typical of what happened in this country – a demonstration of the second law of thermodynamics. Everything tending towards inertia. She tried to remember the relevant laws. Something to do with entropy and disorder increasing with time. From below came the sound of ice clinking against glass tumblers and she strained her ears again to hear what was going on.

'Wait a minute. I'm trying to hear something,' she said to Chofy.

Bats flitted round the sapodilla tree and a glittering moth dipped in and out of the headlights of a car parked in the yard.

'Come and lie with me.'

She leaned her elbows lazily on the windowsill.

'Shhh. I can hear what they're saying,' she whispered.

Before she knew what had happened, Chofy was on his

feet, stumbling in the semi-darkness to pull on his green Y-fronts and pants.

'What's happening?' she asked.

'You don't want me. I'm going. I shall leave you in peace and stop harassing you. I'm off.' He left the smart shirt he had borrowed on a chair and began to button on his own bright shirt. In the half-light, she could see his face like stone.

'Oh don't be silly,' she said.

'I'm not being silly. I can see you don' want me physically. I should not like to impose myself on you,' he said formally. Now she could sense the fullness of his rage, as he laced up his boots.

'I do want you. Of course I do.' She danced over to the bed and rolled on it, kicking her legs in a sort of protest.

Chofy walked, in one of his controlled tempers, through the long attic, past the stiff settle and the table on which stood a vase of dried grasses. She heard his boots clattering down the wooden stairs.

After a few minutes, when it was clear he was not coming back, she fixed the mosquito net, pulled the sheet over her shoulder and tried to sleep. She had missed the chance to tell him how she felt. Even a sloth has better timing, she thought ruefully as she drifted off.

Two hours later, Rosa woke with a raging fever. The onset was rapid. She sat up in bed and recalled how she had been soaked by the rain when they went to the university. Now, her eyes and nose were streaming. Soon her nightshirt and sheets were soaked with sweat. For a moment, in the moonlight, a sort of delirium affected her and the patterns on the sheets looked like moving insects, butterflies, dragonflies and cockroaches.

She slid from underneath the ghostly cocoon of her mosquito net and went to look for something to quell the fever. Feeling her way further down the attic, she switched on the light which hung, a small yellow bulb, almost doused by the vastness of the tropical night. Her nose streamed with ammonia. On the draining-board stood a coffee cup. She rinsed it and poured herself out some rum. There was something exciting about the fever, despite the discomfort of her streaming eyes and nose. It infected her with a powerful restlessness.

Outside, it was windy. The open window framed a portrait of dark, chaotic night. Across the road, she could just make out the branches of an awara tree, tossing slowly like the plumes of a circus horse. The house teemed with air. Breezes entered through the open Demerara shutters in starts and sallies like jazz riffs.

'I've come back to say I'm sorry.' Chofy stood, contrite, at the far end of the attic. His boots squeaked as he came over and hugged her.

All the time she slept, he had stayed downstairs, just walking around in the large rooms where patches of moonlight shimmered on the polished floors of greenheart wood. He found a bow and arrows hung on the wall for ornamental purposes, and let fly an arrow across the room into the side of a giant armchair. Then, for a while, he had lain down on the sofa in the gallery which had once been used for dances, looking up at the slender columns and the painted cupola in the ceiling, staring into the shadows by the oak sideboard laden with dusty silver platters, wondering what to do.

He stepped back from the hug. 'I'm married,' he said, unhappily. 'And I have a son.'

She was only momentarily taken aback.

'I thought someone as nice as you wouldn't be on their own.'

To keep at bay the feeling that elements beyond her control had shifted in some subtle way to do with mistiming and that a whole unravelling process had been set in motion, she teased him while absorbing the implications of what he had just said.

'See how much you upset me by storming off like that. I've got fever because of it.'

'Of course I stormed off. Wouldn't you? Love gone a fish, I thought. Come, let me put you to bed.'

He took her to bed, loosed the mosquito net and helped her back in. Then he sat on the side of the bed under the net with her.

'When I was downstairs, I nearly cried because I thought I'd lost you.'

'And whose fault would that be, may I ask? Who stomped off?'

He bunched up the cotton pillow behind her head, still holding her in his arms.

'I'm so frightened of losing you. Once, when I was about fourteen, I was playing football. It was one of those matches when I was playing really well. Everything was set up for me to score. I was given a beautiful short pass. The goal was more or less open in front of me. The goalie was way over to one side. It should have been easy and I slipped. I wanted so much to please everybody and I knew how important it was.

'And it seems to me that my life has always been like that. Just when everything is waiting there for me, I fail. I don't seem to have the killer instinct. Either my confidence fails me or, in my nervousness, I try too hard. I think that's it. I try too hard.'

He kissed her mouth.

'You'll get my cold.'

'I want everything you've got. I want to make love to you now.'

'But I've got fever.'

'Don't you get randy when you have fever? I do.'

He undressed and slipped into the hot bed.

The temperature let loose an extravagant energy in her body. The fever was like another lover making love to her at the same time as Chofy. The illness was exhilarating. Every time Chofy kissed her for too long, she was unable to breathe and snatched her head away to open her mouth for air. His body became as hot as hers until they both lay there, slippery, drenched with sweat and exhausted.

Chofy slid out of the bed. He went and heated some water and made her a hot drink with rum, limes and Demerara sugar. He came back with it. The misty gauze of the mosquito net softened the outlines of her body's curves as she lay there. He thought it was like looking at her through a waterfall.

'You lookin' rosy. You look like a mermaid,' he whispered.

He lifted up the net and gave her the drink. She sniffed and reached for a handkerchief.

'I still want to be with you, you know,' he said. 'Whatever happens. You have opened my life up for me. Nothing could make me go back to where I was before.'

He stroked her hot head as she sipped the drink.

'Look. I found some sandalwood oil on a shelf. Let me rub you with it.' He started to rub the oil into her neck and shoulders and over her breasts.

'What is your wife like?' she asked, putting the drink down.

'I think the marriage is over. It's been dead for a while. She is younger than me. That's unusual for us Indians. We usually marry older women.'

'Why is that?' snuffled Rosa, resting her head in his groin and holding on to his bent knee as he worked the oil down into the front of her body.

'I don' know. They say that young girls are more interested in status than sex. They use sex to set themselves up for life, to hook a partner, not so much because they like it. It's the older women who really enjoy it. We don't have mirrors much, or magazines or pictures or images. We like the real thing. I don' know why. It's just our custom.

'Loving time done, I suppose,' he said, sadly, as he finished and put the stopper on the bottle.

She groaned and then lifted her head up.

'Who says so?' she croaked.

Eventually, they fell into an exhausted sleep.

THE AMERINDIAN
HOSTEL

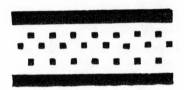

The gate of the Amerindian hostel in Princess Street remained locked at night. Amerindians coming to town from the bush for one reason or other could obtain a few nights' lodging there for a small fee.

The hospital had rung the warden earlier, telling him to expect three new arrivals. The Lokono Arawak warden, a short, anxious man, was new to the job and determined to make a success of it. He waited up late for the new arrivals. The office was small and stuffy. He took a Bristol cigarette from the pack in his top shirt pocket, paused and then lit it. Cigarettes were precious. He allowed himself one cigarette a day. There were four left. He would not be able to afford more until the end of the week.

Long after midnight, when Rosa and Chofy were both fast asleep on the other side of town, the warden heard the sound of voices and the squeaking of the front gate. He made his way along the dingy corridor and stepped out into the night.

The black woman employed as a guard opened the tall metal gate. Two or three of the wives in residence, babies in their arms, came out on to the verandah to see who had turned up so late.

A woman in her thirties and two men stepped through into the forecourt. There was an unmistakable expression of gravity on their faces.

The oldest member of the party was a skinny shrimp of a man in faded pink shorts that were held up by a belt tied with a bit of string. He was barefoot. On his head he wore a frayed straw hat with its wide brim turned up. Under the brim, the warden noticed a pair of bright eyes in a shrivelled face with healthily clear skin. At his side, the warden was more concerned to notice, he carried a shotgun, the barrel of which reached up to his shoulder.

The warden ushered them into his office where the old man leaned his gun against the wall and they all sat down wearily to face him across the desk.

'I'm sorry we can't offer you refreshment. The kitchen is closed now. But we have a water tank in the courtyard if you need to drink.'

They all shook their heads in refusal.

'How is the boy?' the warden asked, screwing up his face and leaning forward across the table as if he were a deaf man listening for an answer.

'How is your son? Tell me what happened,' he asked the woman with concern.

'Bad.' Her voice was tremulous. 'The doctors don't know if he can live. He has very terrible injuries and his spine is shattered in two places. They tell me he will be paralyse if he lives.'

'Oh my. Oh dear. Oh I'm sorry to hear that.' The warden shook his head sympathetically. He paused for a second and then offered them each a cigarette which they accepted gratefully. 'But what happened exactly?'

The woman sat with her hands in her lap and continued without lighting her cigarette.

'The Hawk Oil men are prospecting in our area. They have

337

divided the land up into grids. Every hundred yards or so they drill and explode dynamite twenty yards under the earth. It is not supposed to break the surface. But sometimes it does and then again some of the oil men does use dynamite to blow up fish in the rivers.

'I don't know what exactly happen but my son had set a maswali fish-trap in a sidestream and built a little dam further down. In the morning he went to check it. We heard the explosion. The next thing we knew, one of our neighbours was running along the trail, running in the hot sun, shouting shouting shouting for us to come. And we found Bla-Bla by the river. Two fish still in the trap. Blood everywhere. The bones of his legs laid bare. Kaboura flies, sandflies and mosquitoes swarming all over him.'

The warden glanced over at the old man with concern. A transparent tear was wriggling from the outer edge of his eye down his cheek and his lower jaw worked in a fierce, grinding motion to maintain control of his emotions. The warden looked back to the other man who showed no feeling as the woman pushed back her dark hair with one hand and continued the story.

'We managed to get him on to a Hawk Oil plane that was flying down. They let us come on it. This is my grandfather. My father has stayed at home to look after the farm. And this is my husband's cousin who came to find us at the hospital when he heard the news. My husband is not at his lodgings and we can't find him, so he doesn't know yet.'

The old man wiped his cheek with the back of his fist.

Tenga acknowledged the old man's distress calmly.

'Grandfather is very close to the boy. He's getting old. That's why he finds it difficult to control himself. He can speak English but he prefers Wapisiana or Portuguese.'

The warden took out his register from the drawer.

'I must enter your details in this book, then I will show

338

you where you can sleep. You want to rest now? What will you do? Go back to the hospital in the morning?'

The woman looked uncertain.

'Yes,' she said doubtfully.

The warden wrote down the day's date in one column and the time in another.

'What is your name?'

'I am Marietta McKinnon. My grandfather here is called Joseph Correia.'

'Village?'

'Moco-moco.'

'Region?'

'They call it Region Nine. We call it Rupununi.'

'Tribe?'

'Wapisiana. But we livin' in a Macusi village.'

'My name is Tenga McKinnon,' said the younger of the two men. 'I live in Pakuri but I'm Wapisiana too and I think I had better stay here tonight to look after these folk.'

'You're meant to stay only for three days, but I'm sure we can stretch that if you need to be here for longer.' He turned to the old man. 'Why did you bring your gun along, Grandfather?'

The old man looked blank.

'He'd been shooting bush-hog,' answered Marietta. 'A whole herd of wild hog wandered into the village. In the morning mists one of the children looked out of the window and thought they were jumbies and woke up the whole village. The hogs had come down from the Kanaku Mountains. My son wanted to go hunting with the men but he went to check his fish-trap first. Grandad still had his gun with him when we lifted Bla-Bla on to the plane.'

'Well. They won't let you walk round the streets of Georgetown with that. Leave it in your room when you go out. It will be safe. There's not much theft in here.'

'You're Arawak?' enquired Tenga cautiously.

'Yes. From the north-west originally. I don't speak Macusi or Wapisiana. I don't even speak much Arawak.'

'That guard on the gate,' asked Tenga, 'is to protect us from the coastlanders or to protect the coastlanders from us?'

The warden laughed.

'Both, I think. I only just got this job lately. I want to nice up the place, you know. Make it somewhere special where our people can come. I been cleaning out the toilets and bath-house. One of the fellows staying here helped me. You should have seen the place. Disgusting. We were on our hands and knees for three weeks scrubbing the bathrooms. Come. I'll show you your rooms. Tread carefully now. There are no lights out here. As it's so late, and you're family, I goin' put you in one room for tonight and then you can move into the women's quarters tomorrow,' he told Marietta. 'Do you have your hammocks?'

'Yes,' replied Marietta, almost overcome with exhaustion.

A boy of about eleven with his arm in a plaster cast was slinking shyly along the corridor, his back to the wall.

'How are you, Harold? That arm mending? You should be in bed.'

The boy remained silent. They walked past him and up some stairs. The warden opened the door of a hot, concrete cell with disintegrating plaster on the walls. He flashed his torch around the room to let them see what was there. The torchlight sent some cockroaches scurrying for the dark and illuminated two iron-frame beds, a geography of stains on the old mattresses. Under the window stood a table with a faded red plastic jug on it. Apart from that the room was bare. He directed the beam to where there were hooks for their hammocks on the wall.

'This is it. I wish you good-night. And I will be hoping and praying that the boy is all right.'

'Where do you think Chofy can be?' Marietta asked Tenga. They had gone from the hospital to his lodgings. The people there said Chofy only came back there now and then. Tenga shook his head. Then he told Marietta that Chofy might be in a certain big house in town.

'You must take me there,' she insisted.

'We'll go there tomorrow before we go to the hospital.'

'No. We'll go there now,' insisted Marietta.

Tenga looked at her anguished face and agreed to take her.

'Why do you think he is there?' she asked.

'I'm not sure that he is there,' Tenga prevaricated. 'He made friends with someone there.'

Marietta was too distressed and tired to take in what he was saying. Her grandfather had already slung his hammock and was asleep.

The guard let them out of the gate. Tenga and Marietta set off across town. The night was warm and quiet except for a steady, muted chorus of frogs. When they reached the house, they asked the watchman if Chofy McKinnon was there and explained that his son had been badly injured. Tenga waited outside. The gateman showed Marietta the stairs which led to the attic, an expression of malicious satisfaction on his face.

She walked up the two flights of stairs, feeling her way in the dark, and tentatively pushed open the door to the attic. Some light from the moon spilled in through the windows on to the floors of polished greenheart wood. She stood where she was and called his name. Her voice sounded nervous and a little cracked.

'Chofy. Chofy.' She tried to overcome her embarrassment and called a little louder. 'Chofy.' Perhaps she would wake other people up. She waited for a few minutes. The house felt enormous and strange to her. She began to sweat with nervousness.

'It's me. Marietta. Where are you?'

She walked on further through the attic.

'Chofy?'

There was a thump and a scuffling noise from just ahead of her. Chofy came towards her, out of the shadows, naked, from the other end of the attic.

'What's happened? What are you doing here?' He had his pants in his hand.

Marietta stood still. He switched on the light and blinked at her. The sight of her square figure standing there made his heart pound. He looked at the solid reddish-brown arms hanging at her sides, the gleaming black hair and the rough red triangle where the sun had caught the V-shape neck of her brown cotton T-shirt. She looked to him like a figure moulded entirely from red Rupununi clay, utterly out of place in these surroundings.

'What is happening?' she asked. 'What are you doing here? There has been a terrible accident. Bla-Bla is in hospital. They say he might die.' Tears began to roll out of her eyes.

She looked past him and saw a movement behind where he stood.

'Who is that? What is happening?'

Chofy was too shocked to answer. Marietta moved past him to the place where the bedroom was divided off. She saw Rosa sitting up in the bed, the sheet pulled up to her neck.

'Oh. I am sorry,' said Marietta, confused. She stepped back to where Chofy stood pulling on his pants.

'Well, I can see now what you have been doing. You don' care no more about Bla-Bla and me.' She turned to go away.

Chofy was standing there shaking his head.

'Tell me what has happened to Bla-Bla,' he begged.

'The Hawk Oil people blew him up. He has head injuries. He is not conscious. His spine . . .'

Marietta sat down on a wooden chair and wept silently, wiping the tears away with the heel of her fist.

Chofy came and knelt by her.

'Come. Are you staying at the hostel? We will go back there. Or should we go straight to the hospital now?'

'They won't let us in now. It is too late. They said they would ring the hostel if he got worse, but I had to leave and find you.'

'Well, let us hurry back there now.' Chofy felt for the keys to his bicycle padlock. 'How did you find me here?'

'Tenga brought me.'

Chofy went back briefly into the bedroom and said a few words to Rosa. Then he walked with Marietta to the stairs.

The sight of Bla-Bla festooned with tubes, his hair still sticking up like a manicole leaf although his head had been split open and shaved behind his right ear, left Chofy feeling cold and numb. Marietta and her grandfather stayed behind in the hospital while Chofy and Tenga went to find them some food.

Outside the hospital, on the dried-grass verge by a stinking ditch, he and Tenga had a furious row in the blazing heat of midday.

Tenga blamed Chofy for deserting his own people.

'But it wouldn't have made any difference if I had been in the Rupununi or in Georgetown. It was an accident. It would have happened anyway,' said Chofy.

'You don't understand. You know what they are saying? One of the Americans saw a little boy in the area and he pointed to the danger spot and shouted: "Chofoye. Chofoye." He said he was trying to warn him. He thought it was an Amerindian word for explosion. Bla-Bla must have misunderstood and run towards the spot because he thought his father had come home. The stupid Americans didn't even realise he

343

spoke English – let alone that we all have different languages anyway. And you come to town and mix with these people. You find some fancy piece to sleep with while everybody at home struggling to keep things going. You make me sick.'

Chofy became silent. He felt so guilty.

They collected up some food and went back to the hospital. Marietta and her grandfather came out to eat and Chofy and Tenga took their turn at the bedside.

Bla-Bla drifted in and out of consciousness. He did not recognise his father or mother. When he was conscious, he burbled in Portuguese and Wapisiana and asked for water and he talked to a man he could see in the corner of the room, who had a parrot sitting on his shoulder.

The next day, Chofy and Marietta climbed the open wrought-iron steps of the public hospital up to the intensive care unit.

A sickly breeze of ill-health seemed to waft over them as the nurse, a few paces ahead, let herself through some plastic swing doors. Neither of them had mentioned Rosa since the night Marietta arrived in the house. An iron silence crushed the subject out of existence. Both parents focused entirely on Bla-Bla.

The Cuban doctor stood at the top of the stairs. He looked tired. His white coat was grubby and creased. He breathed in and raised his shoulders trying to find a way of saying what it was necessary to say. The couple stood three steps below him.

'Mr and Mrs McKinnon. I am very sorry. There was nothing more we could do for your son.'

The East Indian nurse who had come out with him, her large, liquid eyes swimming with sympathy, took them each by the arm and led them into a spacious storage cupboard stacked with shining aluminium pans and kidney dishes.

'Would you like to wait here a minute. It's not so public. We are just getting him ready.'

'Ready?' Marietta queried.

'There are just one or two things we have to do, dismantle the tubes and equipment, and then you can come and see him.'

She left Chofy and Marietta standing in the storage cupboard in silence. Chofy held Marietta awkwardly around her broad shoulders. He could feel her entire body shaking.

When they entered the room, Bla-Bla looked tiny in the bed. The nurse had tried to smooth down his jet-black hair but it still stuck up in front like two crossed fingers. His top lip was curled back in a sort of snarl.

'It's not right for him to be so still,' whispered Marietta. 'He ran everywhere.'

As Chofy stared at the stern and exhausted little face, he felt a crushing pain in his chest and his arms seemed to lose their life. The expression on Bla-Bla's face was a sneer of accusation. It seemed to accuse him of many things: of abandoning his family, deserting his son, of not being able to keep the land safe for his children. With shock, he felt that he had lost not only a child but a whole continent.

In the corner of the room by the window stood Bla-Bla's small bow and four arrows which had accompanied him from the time of the accident. Marietta went and picked them up. Bla-Bla had made the arrows himself. The dark flight feathers belonged to a powis bird. Stuck in the cotton binding at one end of the bow was the two-inch-long red feather of a scarlet macaw. She pulled it out and fixed it in Bla-Bla's hair, just behind his ear. Then she reached under the sheet and felt for his hand.

'He's so cold. If only I could warm him.'

The nurse was waiting tactfully in the doorway. Eventually, she asked if they needed help with the burial arrangements.

Marietta turned and drew herself up to face the nurse directly.

'We could not leave him to bury here. This town has nothing to do with us. We do not belong here. He will come home with us.'

The nurse looked enquiringly at Chofy.

'But you know we have to do things fast because of the heat.'

'Go to that house where your friend lives.' Marietta turned to Chofy and spoke with determination. 'And see if she will help make the Hawk Oil people fly us out.'

Chofy tore through the streets. He heard his own breath whistle as he ran. Some vindictive force seemed to have deliberately employed people to act out scenes of everyday happiness and relaxation around him. Shopkeepers chatted in doorways. Street vendors smiled. A cyclist whistled as he glided past. Children in brown school uniform skipped along the dried-grass verges. The whole town felt to be on holiday.

Chofy bounded up the stairs of the house two at a time. When he found Rosa at the top, he could not bring himself immediately to say his son was dead.

'We have to ask the Americans if they will carry us back to the Rupununi,' he said quickly, out of breath. 'You must help.'

His tongue felt like a pebble in his mouth as it twisted round the unfamiliar words.

'My son is dead.'

He gasped with the effort of saying it. Rosa tried to put her arms around him but he was rigid and unresponsive, his face impassive. She tried to kiss him. His face was as stiff as leather. At that moment she knew that it was too late to reveal her own love in the way she had been planning to do when the time was right. Nothing keeps in the tropics, someone

346

had warned her. Bad timing. Events had foreclosed on the possibility. The doors had shut in her face. Love trumped by disaster.

'I love you,' she said anyway, rather tamely, as they ran downstairs. It fell on deaf ears. A few phone calls later a Land Rover pulled into the yard of the house. The plane was leaving at four o'clock. If the legal niceties could be tied up, they would collect up Auntie Wifreda and fly the whole family back.

Rosa kissed him goodbye at the gate. Chofy seemed embarrassed.

'I'll let you know what happens. I love you,' said Chofy perfunctorily. 'I must see that Marietta is all right.'

'But I'm going back to England in three weeks. You don't even have my address.'

'Write to me care of the Amerindian hostel,' he said, dully. 'The warden there is trustworthy.'

He scrambled on board the vehicle. An American with a scrubbed pink face and tufted eyebrows was driving. He pushed back his baseball cap as they waited for the iron gates to be opened.

'Jeez. I'm real sorry to hear about your son. Jeez, that's a tragedy. We've fixed for the boys at the other end to meet the plane with a Range Rover and take you wherever you need to go. Was the little guy insured? If he was insured you can bet Hawk Oil will give you a whole heap of compensation. They're a good company like that.'

Chofy made no reply.

Marietta and Tenga had fetched Auntie Wifreda who stood with her face towards the sun in order to feel the heat. They were all waiting outside the hospital. The American helped them to collect Bla-Bla's body which was small enough to lie in the aisle of the fourteen-seater plane.

During the journey, Auntie Wifreda began to notice a dim

fuzzy light replacing the blackness. By the time they reached the Rupununi, she had difficulty focusing, but she could see. She said nothing, not wishing to express any pleasure in the circumstances. The first thing she saw was Marietta's broad flat cheekbones and expressionless face as she stared out of the plane window at the Rupununi River winding below. When the plane landed on the airstrip, another of the Americans' sparkling new vehicles was waiting to transport the family to Moco-moco.

Bla-Bla was buried at the back of the house. The priest was in the south savannahs, too far away to get there in time, and so they wrapped Bla-Bla in his hammock and put his bow and arrows in with him and put him in the earth.

Afterwards, the whole place felt evil as if poison dripped from the thatch. Even the parrots stayed quiet. The dogs moped around the house. Auntie Wifreda rested in her hammock for the first few days and then got up and went fishing as usual. The eye which had been operated on was completely clear and functioned normally. The other eye retained its waterfall but she was able to manage better than before.

Marietta did the chores and tended the cassava farm, but Chofy could tell that the life had gone out of her.

Even in the short while she had been away, her parents had not been able to cope with the cassava farm and weeds had sprung up.

When Chofy and Marietta were clearing these weeds one morning, Marietta turned and said to him: 'If you want to we will split.' Her voice sounded flat, disinterested.

'I don' think I want that,' he said, thoughtfully.

Once he was out in the open again, the sight of the vast plains, the grasses leaning with the wind and the familiar ridges of the Kanaku Mountains soothed Chofy and steadied him somewhat. The great, unchanging open spaces gave him time and a frame in which to think. Despite the grief and guilt, in the savannahs his son's death seemed contained within a certain order of things and not just an extra, random confusion, as everything was in the city. From a distance, the affair with Rosa began to seem like a sort of bewitchment, something unreal.

There was a lot of work to be done on the house. He threw himself into it. The roof needed re-thatching. Two of the bloodwood beams had split and parts of the structure needed to be fixed. He decided to use parakaran wood for houseposts. That was the hardest sort of wood.

Auntie Wifreda seemed to draw strength from having her feet back on the rust-red earth of the savannahs. She undertook chores with an astonishing vigour for one of her age. Three weeks after the burial, she took the tin trunk that served for her dressing-table and opened it. Inside were Father Napier's diaries, mouldy but protected from wood-ants by the metal container. The trunk also contained a copy of *Dombey and Son* that Evelyn Waugh had left with her at Pirara.

Without opening the diaries, she lugged all six volumes of them outside, made a bonfire and threw them on. The growing pile of ashes reminded her of the days when she used to burn fowl feathers for Sonny during his moon-fits. She picked up the copy of *Dombey and Son* and was about to throw it on the flames when she changed her mind. Perhaps the school could use it.

'What are you doing?' complained Marietta as she saw the diaries go up in flames. 'We could have used that paper to wrap things.'

'We should have done this a long time ago,' replied Auntie Wifreda, grimly.

It was planting time. In the cool of the dawn, Marietta dug a fresh bed for the cucumber seedlings. All round, tender tips of green sprouted and buds uncurled tiny clenched fists. In the afternoon, she and Chofy borrowed two horses and rode over to Marietta's parents' place to see about starting up again with one or two cattle. The rains were beginning. The savannahs had turned green. The air was sweet, the breeze fresh.

On the way, they stopped by a fast-flowing creek. In the middle stood two smooth boulders, rounded like turtle backs.

'Turtles. Keepers of the secret,' said Marietta, out of habit.

They rode the horses down into a wide creek that reached up to mid-flank on the animals. The creek water was pearly grey. The leaves of the trees did not quite meet overhead, leaving a tracery of blank sky visible above them. Without warning, Chofy's head was reeling, his ears full of water, and he was spluttering upside down in the creek. His horse clambered up the bank and bolted for home.

Marietta doubled up with laughter.

'You been away too long. Don' you remember that horse? You have to do his girth up tight because he pushes his belly out when you saddle him and then draws it in when he's crossing a creek and throws you off so he can get home early.'

Chofy, soaking wet, stood on the bank and dabbed at his bleeding head with a leaf while Marietta sat on the ground and cried with laughter.

The wing of Rosa's plane dipped sideways almost immediately after take-off, just as the sun rose over the three counties of Berbice, Essequibo and Demerara. Rosa stared out of the window. The forest below looked like a bed of parsley. One or two clouds dotted beneath the plane made the pinky-brown Demerara River look as though it were flowing through the sky.

Dazzling white light glinted along the side of the silver wing, turning it momentarily into the flaming sword of the cherubim protecting the Garden of Eden.

Wormoal was on the same plane. He leaned across the aisle.

'I've had a very successful trip,' he said, beaming through his glasses. I've got most of the information I needed. I think I know as much as it's possible to know about the eclipse mythology in these parts.' He patted his briefcase triumphantly and returned to reading some papers.

Rosa turned to gaze out of the window, half expecting to be able to see Chofy weeding or planting below. She had been made desolate by his departure. It was not until he had left Georgetown that she realised what she had lost. She went and left her name and address at the Amerindian hostel as Chofy suggested but she hardly expected to hear from him. The rest of her time at the Mynheer Nicklaus Lodge she felt restless and miserable.

When she arrived in England she would have to try and keep herself occupied. There would be endless distractions there: films, friends, concerts, lectures, work, a hundred ways of passing the time. Her stomach churned at the thought of lost possibilities. In an effort to recover her composure, she turned back to the hermetically sealed existence inside the plane, pulling out a folder of work from her bag.

'Evelyn Waugh – a Post-colonial Perspective,' she wrote on the front of her notebook as the plane flew on towards Trinidad.

As the plane drew gradually further away from the coast of Guyana, Marietta bathed vigorously in the creek, creaming the water with soapy froth as she washed her hair. She climbed out on to the red scree, rubbed herself with a towel, dressed and went to feed the chickens before coming to where Auntie Wifreda lay in her hammock. She recounted her dreams as usual.

'This time I dreamt about eggs. Eggs everywhere. Chickens laying in the bushes. In the trees. On the ground.'

'That is life coming back after all your problems,' said Auntie Wifreda. 'Fertility and growth. Food too. It means hope and coming back to life.'

'Yes,' said Marietta, and then, practical as ever, added: 'Or maybe I was just thinking about eggs.'

EPILOGUE

I am busy lying in my hammock, warming my behind over the embers of silverballi wood – the smoke of which is supposed to make people quarrelsome, but makes me amorous – waiting for some high-octane chiquita, some little Miss Hotbody to pass my way and spot my bronze, barrel thigh hanging enticingly over the side. Although it's no use any woman winding her arse in front of me unless she fulfils three conditions: she has a good job, a Porsche and can make love swinging through the trees on a rope of liana.

The moral of the story? Listen, before I even began, I stowed my conscience under a bush so that it could not hamper me in any way whatsoever.

I will say one thing, however. There are three strands of insanity in this world: love, religion and politics, each one so dangerous that it has to be kept in an institution; religion in a church or a temple like a mad dog; love confined to marriage, escaping at society's peril; politics chained to parliaments because of the genocides and wars that take place when it gets loose.

There is something obnoxious about modern politicians, don't you think? Not far to the south of where I come from there is a tribe of people for whom physical beauty is the main criterion for access to political power. Travellers come across them lying in their hammocks preening themselves, decked with feathers from humming-birds and macaws. The men wear their hair long. No one in that community would dream of taking notice of someone as ugly as most current Heads of State. Not only do we Indians know how to make ourselves attractive. We are also brilliant at divining what you would like to hear and saying it, so you can never be really sure what we think. Another art suited to politics. Ventriloquism at its zenith. My grandmother taught me to rely daily on the pleasures of artifice and, more importantly, the tactics of warfare – surprise, deception and disguise, that art of mixing the visible with the invisible.

Armed with her advice, I travelled through Europe in search of the parrot who was supposed to be my heart. I got into all sorts of trouble. (Where I'm known, they think well of me. Where I'm not, who gives a shit?) I would have gone to university but I could find no courses where they studied the resemblances of animals in human faces; the effects of electro-magnetic fields on human behaviour or the relationship between banquets and death.

Let me take a minute here to extol the inventiveness of death. What could be more creative? Each death unique like a fingerprint. At home we regularly have a rendezvous of carcasses of the dead so they don't feel left out. All those who have died since the last feast are regularly dug up, disinterred and brought along. Some are dried and withered, others have what looks like a sort of parchment on their bones. Some seem to have been baked or smoked. Some are turning to putrefaction, others swarming with worms. They are all diligently carried to the clearing and seated round the fire. In this jolly company, I always relate stories of a certain rapscallion, a character born from silence, who is driven mainly by trickery and the desire to eat meat, a character whose antics would be enough to make a corpse laugh.

You see, for us it is the sort of death you die that determines your afterlife, not the sort of life you have lived. You have your ideas of reincarnation upside down. We progress through life towards the perfect state of being an animal – the nirvana of responding only to desires. Animals that behave badly – a jaguar, for instance, that hesitates before the kill – would slide down the scale to become human.

People get things the wrong way round. Take phobias. Psychologists look in the past for the explanations instead of the future. Phobias are warnings. If you are frightened to go to the top of a high building, it is probably because you are destined to fall off one.

Where was I? Yes. In Europe. It was while I was in Europe that I nearly became fatally infected by the epidemic of separatism that was raging there. The virus transmutes. Sometimes it appears as nationalism, sometimes as racism, sometimes as religious orthodoxy. My experience in the rain forests of South America provided me with no immunity to it.

It was very infectious. I felt my mouth twitching with unaccustomed fervour. Chameleon-like I marched amongst them. The Serbs, the Scots, the English, the Basques, the Muslims, the Chechens – everybody was at it. I crammed my mouth full of Belgian hand-made chocolates to avoid speaking out and giving myself away. I saw that the desire to be with your own kind exerts a powerful attraction.

In an effort to rid myself of the affliction, I used my ventriloquial gifts to reproduce the voice of a dissenting heckler (for safety's sake always making it sound as if it came from a considerable distance away from where I stood).

I succumbed. Suddenly, I longed for the golden savannahs and the streaming sunshine. I reminded myself that I come from a people who enjoy gentle loving, slow fucking and good company. We stroll about, swim, hunt, drink parakari, joke, fuck slowly in a hammock, saunter off into the bush for a good shit and then fuck some more. Aw, what a fucking life!

I decided to give up my quest for the parrot, temporarily, and head for home – sweet irony – to my own people. Back in my village I debated seriously with myself the appeal of staying with your own kind rather than mixing on equal terms; the virtues of untrammelled nature; the split between magic and science. I was getting nowhere happily when the ear-blasting sound of a helicopter landing brought me from my hammock. Lo and behold! I was confronted by the notorious Cosmetics Queen, the tycoon who frequently drops in on my village searching for recipes from indigenous people. I told her immediately of the wonderful face cream we make from ants' balls.

She swallowed it. Eyeing my grandmother's spectacular black hair, she asked her what traditional recipe she used to keep it so shiny.

Before I could slap my hand over her mouth, my grand-mother replied shyly: 'Brylcreem – when I can get it.'

Despite this, the tycoon set about organising a Brazil-nut plantation. The pay was good as she had promised. But it turned out that no one had time to mend their huts or plant their farms. Then it turned out that those who planted the nuts were paid less than those who harvested the nuts and those who harvested them were paid less than those who pounded them for hair-oil. Fights broke out as the wives of the harvesters left their husbands for the pounders. Turmoil ensued. Cries of 'I goin' break she blasted leg' resounded through the forest. Heads bounced off rocks. Teeth sank into buttocks. Arrows thwacked into arms and legs. The village collapsed. We all headed for another part of the forest.

I confided in my grandmother and told her that I had not found the parrot despite trekking all through Europe. She said that the parrot had returned home to South America, but that in large areas the forest was cut down or the trees were poisoned and denuded and looked like a regatta of ships' masts. She told me that the parrot had been seen fluttering from pole to pole but that it had no feathers and a big tumour on its neck.

For a long time I sobbed.

And then I thought: Well, you know you can't trust grandmothers – they're full of all that crap. Mine can't tell the past from the future – they're both woven together on her wonky loom. Unable to decide whether we should stick to ourselves or throw ourselves on the mercy of the wide world, and sick to death of ants, jiggers, mosquitoes, tics, flies, bugs and cyanide in the rivers, I decided to return and take up residence once more in the stars.

Now that I'm leaving I will let you into the secret of my name. It is Macun . . . No. I've changed my mind. But yes. I will tell you the story of the parrot. Another time.

ACKNOWLEDGEMENTS

Thanks to:

George Simon.

Chofoye Melville who gave permission for the loan of his name to a character quite unlike himself.

Wayland Gordon who, similarly, loaned his nickname.

Elaine Radzik for advice on a formal dinner menu.

The Royal Astronomical Society.

The London Arts Board.